## The yellowbacks... classics of popular fiction

The yellowjackets or yellowbacks were a great series of bestselling adventure and crime thrillers that had its origins in the mid to late 19th century following on from the 'penny dreadfuls'. They virtually began the mass market revolution of the early 20th century with a clear standard format and imprint/series livery (what would today be called branding). Hodder & Stoughton published the yellow jackets in two main series with series run dates of: 1923-1939 and later 1949-1957.

As the tagline ('where thrillers really began') on the back cover implies, the imprint and series focused on thrillers that were the bestsellers of their time. This current reissue or retro revival if you will, brings back many of these masterpieces, now classics in their own way and extends it further by including key titles from that period that were either great crime or thriller or even general commercial fiction (including sub-genres of noir, horror, gothic, romance, westerns etc) influences of their time. There are some perennial favourites and many rarities either lost or not easily available being revived in the current series. Writers and characters ranged from adventure heroes like Bulldog Drummond, Allan Quatermain, Richard Hannay or the Saint through thriller grandmasters Edgar Wallace and E. Phillips Oppenheim, crime and mystery maestros like Patricia Wentworth, GK Chesterton, Agatha Christie and the Detection club, to western and swashbucklers like Zane Grey, Max Brand, Captain Blood and even romance or general fiction classics like Hermina Black, Denise Robins, Marie Corelli or Stella Morton. These were books that had storytelling at their heart and always entertained.

The yellowbacks had both hardback (with varying design elements) and paperback (which built the series look) versions with the latter still carrying the imprint 'yellowjacket'. The current reissues pay tribute to both and use an amalgam of elements from both editions while retaining the complete yellow (or 'mustard-plaster') livery with the author's name in blue beveled type with a 'simulated emboss' effect and a white outer 'outline', and the book title in black. These reissues retain the distinctive size of the original mass market paperback and follow the three main category variations—the thrillers (crime, westerns, mystery, adventure) had blue lettering for the author's name, while Romance and 'softer general fiction had red; and other categories like humour had green.

For more detail and a full list of titles visit https://www.hachetteindia.com/home/yellowbacks

# THE ROULETABILLE OMNIBUS

THE ROULETABILLE OMNIBUS

**Gaston Leroux** (1868-1927) was a French journalist and author of detective fiction. He was born in Paris in 1868. He grew up on the Normandy coast, where he developed a passion for fishing and sailing. Upon reaching adulthood, he qualified as a lawyer, but, upon his father's death, his received a large inheritance, and left the law to become a writer. He first found fame as an investigative reporter on L'Echo de Paris, and travelled the world in a variety of disguises, reporting on a wide range of topics from volcanic eruptions to palace revolutions. In 1907, he changed career once again, and started work as a novelist, finding critical and commercial success with works such as *The Mystery of the Yellow Room* (1907) and *The Phantom of the Opera* (1911). Leroux continued to be a prolific writer until his death in 1927 – the result of complications following an operation.

# THE ROULETABILLE OMNIBUS

Gaston Leroux

The Mystery of the Yellow Room

The Perfume of the Lady in Black

hachette

*The Rouletabille Omnibus*
*The Mystery of the Yellow Room* (in French *Le mystère de la chambre jaune*) published serially in France in the periodical *L'Illustration* from September 1907 to November 1907, then in book form in 1908 by Editions Pierre Lafitte. *La Parfum de la Dame en Noir* (*The Perfume of the Lady in Black*) was first published in 1909.



1



The texts in these editions in most cases have been reprinted as is, with minimal editorial changes and by and large no bowdlerizing for political correctness; though in some editions, a few words and phrases considered archaic, or those considered offensive now, along with archaic punctuation may have been modified in places to make the text more accessible to today's readers. The narratives, language, beliefs, social mores and/or cultural depictions, in these volumes are a reflection of their times and must be viewed as such. They may also contain certain cultural, racial and gender prejudices and stereotypes that may be outdated or clearly wrong then and wrong today; but their removal would be tantamount to claiming these prejudices never existed. The Publisher does not endorse or support those depictions or stereotypes; and these books have been made available for a discerning audience that will read it for entertainment value and a chronicle/record of popular fiction of past times.

Cover design by Priya Singh adapted from the original classic yellowjacket by Hodder & Stoughton.

Cover illustration by Ishan Trivedi.

Series note: Some of the books in the series (unless otherwise credited) may have cover or inside illustrations from the original yellowbacks or early editions, and while full restoration has been attempted, some images may be grainy or faded due to the condition of the original material. The end notes or bonus material or blurb details may have been sourced from the public domain or free use publications such as Wikipedia and attribution is hereby made also allowing similar free use reproduction from here. Sources requiring further specific attribution may write in and further detailing and/or corrections shall be made in subsequent printings/editions.

Reprint specifications may be subject to change including but not limited to finishes, paper, colour sections.

ISBN: 978-93-5731-236-3

Hachette Book Publishing India Pvt. Ltd.
4th & 5th Floors, Corporate Centre,
Plot No. 94, Sector 44, Gurugram - 122 003, India

Typeset in Electra LT STD 10/12.5 pt by Manipal Technologies Limited, Manipal

Printed and bound in India by Manipal Technologies Limited, Manipal

MIX
Paper from responsible sources
FSC™ C043100

# CONTENTS


1. The Mystery of the Yellow Room 1

2. The Perfume of the Lady in Black 249

# The Mystery of the Yellow Room

# CONTENTS


I. In Which We Begin Not to Understand 5
II. In Which Joseph Rouletabille Appears for the First Time 15
III. "A Man Has Passed Like a Shadow Through the Blinds" 22
IV. "In the Bosom of Wild Nature" 32
V. In Which Joseph Rouletabille Makes a Remark to Monsieur Robert Darzac Which Produces Its Little Effect 37
VI. In the Heart of the Oak Grove 42
VII. In Which Rouletabille Sets Out on an Expedition Under the Bed 55
VIII. The Examining Magistrate Questions Mademoiselle Stangerson 64
IX. Reporter and Detective 71
X. "We Shall Have to Eat Red Meat—Now" 80
XI. In Which Frederic Larsan Explains How the Murderer Was Able to Get Out of "The Yellow Room" 88
XII. Frederic Larsan's Cane 109
XIII. "The Presbytery Has Lost Nothing of Its Charm, Nor the Garden Its Brightness" 115
XIV. "I Expect the Assassin This Evening" 128

XV. The Trap 135
XVI. Strange Phenomenon of the Dissociation of Matter 146
XVII. The Inexplicable Gallery 149
XVIII. Rouletabille Has Drawn a Circle Between the Two Bumps on His Forehead 157
XIX. Rouletabille Invites Me to Breakfast at the Donjon Inn 160
XX. An Act of Mademoiselle Stangerson 173
XXI. On the Watch 178
XXII. The Incredible Body 187
XXIII. The Double Scent 191
XXIV. Rouletabille Knows the Two Halves of the Murderer 195
XXV. Rouletabille Goes on a Journey 203
XXVI. In Which Joseph Rouletabille is Awaited with Impatience 205
XXVII. In Which Joseph Rouletabille Appears in All His Glory 212
XXVIII. In Which It is Proved That One Does Not Always Think of Everything 239
XXIX. The Mystery of Mademoiselle Stangerson 243

# I

## IN WHICH WE BEGIN NOT TO UNDERSTAND

It is not without a certain emotion that I begin to recount here the extraordinary adventures of Joseph Rouletabille. Down to the present time he had so firmly opposed my doing it that I had come to despair of ever publishing the most curious of police stories of the past fifteen years. I had even imagined that the public would never know the whole truth of the prodigious case known as that of "The Yellow Room", out of which grew so many mysterious, cruel, and sensational dramas, with which my friend was so closely mixed up, if, propos of a recent nomination of the illustrious Stangerson to the grade of grandcross of the Legion of Honour, an evening journal—in an article, miserable for its ignorance, or audacious for its perfidy—had not resuscitated a terrible adventure of which Joseph Rouletabille had told me he wished to be forever forgotten.

"The Yellow Room"! Who now remembers this affair which caused so much ink to flow fifteen years ago? Events are so quickly forgotten in Paris. Has not the very name of the Nayves trial and the tragic history of the death of little Menaldo passed out of mind? And yet the public attention was so deeply interested in the details of the trial that the occurrence of a ministerial crisis was completely unnoticed at the time. Now The "Yellow Room" trial, which, preceded that of the Nayves by some years, made far more noise. The entire world hung for months over this obscure problem—the most obscure, it seems to me, that has ever challenged the perspicacity of our police or taxed the conscience of our judges. The solution of the problem baffled everybody who tried to find it. It was like a dramatic rebus with which old Europe and new America alike became fascinated. That is, in truth—I am permitted to say, because there cannot be any author's vanity in all this, since I do nothing more than transcribe facts on which an exceptional documentation enables me to throw a new light—that is because, in truth, I do not know that, in the domain of reality or imagination, one can discover or recall to mind anything comparable, in its mystery, with the natural mystery of "The Yellow Room".

That which nobody could find out, Joseph Rouletabille, aged eighteen, then a reporter engaged on a leading journal, succeeded in discovering. But when, at the Assize Court, he brought in the key to the whole case, he did not tell the whole truth. He only allowed so much of it to appear as sufficed to ensure the acquittal of an innocent man. The reasons which he had for his reticence no longer exist. Better still, the time has come for my friend to speak out fully. You are going to know all; and, without further preamble, I am going to place before your eyes the problem of "The Yellow Room" as it was placed before the eyes of the entire world on the day following the enactment of the drama at the Château du Glandier.

On the 25th of October, 1892, the following note appeared in the latest edition of the "Temps":

"A frightful crime has been committed at the Glandier, on the border of the forest of Sainte-Genevieve, above Epinay-sur-Orge, at the house of Professor Stangerson. On that night, while the master was working in his laboratory, an attempt was made to assassinate Mademoiselle Stangerson, who was sleeping in a chamber adjoining this laboratory. The doctors do not answer for the life of Mdlle. Stangerson."

The impression made on Paris by this news may be easily imagined. Already, at that time, the learned world was deeply interested in the labours of Professor Stangerson and his daughter. These labours—the first that were attempted in radiography—served to open the way for Monsieur and Madame Curie to the discovery of radium. It was expected the Professor would shortly read to the Academy of Sciences a sensational paper on his new theory,—the Dissociation of Matter,—a theory destined to overthrow from its base the whole of official science, which based itself on the principle of the Conservation of Energy. On the following day, the newspapers were full of the tragedy. The "Matin," among others, published the following article, entitled: "A Supernatural Crime":

"These are the only details," wrote the anonymous writer in the "Matin"—"we have been able to obtain concerning the crime of the Château du Glandier. The state of despair in which Professor Stangerson is plunged, and the impossibility of getting any information from the lips of the victim, have rendered our investigations and those of justice so difficult that, at present, we cannot form the least idea of what has passed in "The Yellow Room" in which Mdlle. Stangerson, in her night-dress, was found lying on the floor in the agonies of death. We have, at least, been able to interview Daddy Jacques—as he is called in the country—a old servant in the Stangerson family. Daddy Jacques entered "The Yellow Room" at the same time as the Professor. This chamber adjoins the laboratory. Laboratory and "Yellow Room" are in a pavilion at the end of the park, about three hundred metres (a thousand feet) from the château.

"'It was half-past twelve at night,' this honest old man told us, 'and I was in the laboratory, where Monsieur Stangerson was still working, when the thing happened. I had been cleaning and putting instruments in order all the evening and was waiting for Monsieur Stangerson to go to bed. Mademoiselle Stangerson had worked with her father up to midnight; when the twelve strokes of midnight had sounded by the cuckoo-clock in the laboratory, she rose, kissed Monsieur Stangerson and bade him good-night. To me she said "bon soir, Daddy Jacques" as she passed into "The Yellow Room". We heard her lock the door and shoot the bolt, so that I could not help laughing, and said to Monsieur: "There's Mademoiselle double-locking herself in,—she must be afraid of the 'Bete du bon Dieu!'" Monsieur did not even hear me, he was so deeply absorbed in what he was doing. Just then we heard the distant miawing of a cat. "Is that going to keep us awake all night?" I said to myself; for I must tell you, Monsieur, that, to the end of October, I live in an attic of the pavilion over "The Yellow Room", so that Mademoiselle should not be left alone through the night in the lonely park. It was the fancy of Mademoiselle to spend the fine weather in the pavilion; no doubt, she found it more cheerful than the château and, for the four years it had been built, she had never failed to take up her lodging there in the spring. With the return of winter, Mademoiselle returns to the château, for there is no fireplace in "The Yellow Room".

"'We were staying in the pavilion, then—Monsieur Stangerson and me. We made no noise. He was seated at his desk. As for me, I was sitting on a chair, having finished my work and, looking at him, I said to myself: "What a man!—what intelligence!—what knowledge!" I attach importance to the fact that we made no noise; for, because of that, the assassin certainly thought that we had left the place. And, suddenly, while the cuckoo was sounding the half after midnight, a desperate clamour broke out in "The Yellow Room". It was the voice of Mademoiselle, crying "Murder!—murder!—help!" Immediately afterwards revolver shots rang out and there was a great noise of tables and furniture being thrown to the ground, as if in the course of a struggle, and again the voice of Mademoiselle calling, "Murder!—help!—Papa!—Papa!—"

"'You may be sure that we quickly sprang up and that Monsieur Stangerson and I threw ourselves upon the door. But alas! it was locked, fast locked, on the inside, by the care of Mademoiselle, as I have told you, with key and bolt. We tried to force it open, but it remained firm. Monsieur Stangerson was like a madman, and truly, it was enough to make him one, for we heard Mademoiselle still calling "Help!—help!" Monsieur Stangerson showered terrible blows on the door, and wept with rage and sobbed with despair and helplessness.

"'It was then that I had an inspiration. "The assassin must have entered by the window!" I cried;—"I will go to the window!" and I rushed from the pavilion and ran like one out of his mind.

"'The inspiration was that the window of "The Yellow Room" looks out in such a way that the park wall, which abuts on the pavilion, prevented my at once reaching the window. To get up to it one has first to go out of the park. I ran towards the gate and, on my way, met Bernier and his wife, the gate-keepers, who had been attracted by the pistol reports and by our cries. In a few words I told them what had happened, and directed the concierge to join Monsieur Stangerson with all speed, while his wife came with me to open the park gate. Five minutes later she and I were before the window of "The Yellow Room".

"'The moon was shining brightly and I saw clearly that no one had touched the window. Not only were the bars that protect it intact, but the blinds inside of them were drawn, as I had myself drawn them early in the evening, as I did every day, though Mademoiselle, knowing that I was tired from the heavy work I had been doing, had begged me not to trouble myself, but leave her to do it; and they were just as I had left them, fastened with an iron catch on the inside. The assassin, therefore, could not have passed either in or out that way; but neither could I get in.

"'It was unfortunate,—enough to turn one's brain! The door of the room locked on the inside and the blinds on the only window also fastened on the inside; and Mademoiselle still calling for help!—No! she had ceased to call. She was dead, perhaps. But I still heard her father, in the pavilion, trying to break down the door.

"'With the concierge I hurried back to the pavilion. The door, in spite of the furious attempts of Monsieur Stangerson and Bernier to burst it open, was still holding firm; but at length, it gave way before our united efforts,—and then what a sight met our eyes! I should tell you that, behind us, the concierge held the laboratory lamp—a powerful lamp, that lit the whole chamber.

"'I must also tell you, monsieur, that 'The Yellow Room' is a very small room. Mademoiselle had furnished it with a fairly large iron bedstead, a small table, a night-commode; a dressing-table, and two chairs. By the light of the big lamp we saw all at a glance. Mademoiselle, in her night-dress, was lying on the floor in the midst of the greatest disorder. Tables and chairs had been overthrown, showing that there had been a violent struggle. Mademoiselle had certainly been dragged from her bed. She was covered with blood and had terrible marks of fingernails on her throat,—the flesh of her neck having been almost torn by the nails. From a wound on the right temple a stream of blood had run down and made a little pool on the floor. When Monsieur Stangerson saw his daughter in that state, he threw himself on his knees beside her, uttering a cry of despair. He ascertained that she still breathed. As to us, we searched for the wretch who had tried to kill our mistress, and I swear to you, monsieur, that, if we had found him, it would have gone hard with him!

"'But how to explain that he was not there, that he had already escaped? It passes all imagination!—Nobody under the bed, nobody behind the furniture!—All that we discovered were traces, bloodstained marks of a man's large hand on the walls and on the door; a big handkerchief red with blood, without any initials, an old cap, and many fresh footmarks of a man on the floor,—footmarks of a man with large feet whose boot-soles had left a sort of sooty impression. How had this man got away? How had he vanished? Don't forget, monsieur, that there is no chimney in "The Yellow Room". He could not have escaped by the door, which is narrow, and on the threshold of which the concierge stood with the lamp, while her husband and I searched for him in every corner of the little room, where it is impossible for anyone to hide himself. The door, which had been forced open against the wall, could not conceal anything behind it, as we assured ourselves. By the window, still in every way secured, no flight had been possible. What then?—I began to believe in the Devil.

"'But we discovered my revolver on the floor!—Yes, my revolver! Oh! that brought me back to the reality! The Devil would not have needed to steal my revolver to kill Mademoiselle. The man who had been there had first gone up to my attic and taken my revolver from the drawer where I kept it. We then ascertained, by counting the cartridges, that the assassin had fired two shots. Ah! it was fortunate for me that Monsieur Stangerson was in the laboratory when the affair took place and had seen with his own eyes that I was there with him; for otherwise, with this business of my revolver, I don't know where we should have been,—I should now be under lock and bar. Justice wants no more to send a man to the scaffold!'"

The editor of the "Matin" added to this interview the following lines:

"We have, without interrupting him, allowed Daddy Jacques to recount to us roughly all he knows about the crime of 'The Yellow Room'. We have reproduced it in his own words, only sparing the reader the continual lamentations with which he garnished his narrative. It is quite understood, Daddy Jacques, quite understood, that you are very fond of your masters; and you want them to know it, and never cease repeating it—especially since the discovery of your revolver. It is your right, and we see no harm in it. We should have liked to put some further questions to Daddy Jacques—Jacques—Louis Moustier—but the inquiry of the examining magistrate, which is being carried on at the château, makes it impossible for us to gain admission at the Glandier; and, as to the oak wood, it is guarded by a wide circle of policemen, who are jealously watching all traces that can lead to the pavilion, and that may perhaps lead to the discovery of the assassin. "We have also wished to question the concierges, but they are invisible. Finally, we have waited in a roadside inn, not far from the gate of the château, for the departure of Monsieur de Marquet, the magistrate of Corbeil. At half-past five we saw him and his clerk and, before he was able to enter his carriage, had an opportunity to ask him the following question:

"'Can you, Monsieur de Marquet, give us any information as to this affair, without inconvenience to the course of your inquiry?'

"'It is impossible for us to do it,' replied Monsieur de Marquet. 'I can only say that it is the strangest affair I have ever known. The more we think we know something, the further we are from knowing anything!'

"We asked Monsieur de Marquet to be good enough to explain his last words; and this is what he said,—the importance of which no one will fail to recognise:

"'If nothing is added to the material facts so far established, I fear that the mystery which surrounds the abominable crime of which Mademoiselle Stangerson has been the victim will never be brought to light; but it is to be hoped, for the sake of our human reason, that the examination of the walls, and of the ceiling of "The Yellow Room"—an examination which I shall tomorrow intrust to the builder who constructed the pavilion four years ago—will afford us the proof that may not discourage us. For the problem is this: we know by what way the assassin gained admission,—he entered by the door and hid himself under the bed, awaiting Mademoiselle Stangerson. But how did he leave? How did he escape? If no trap, no secret door, no hiding place, no opening of any sort is found; if the examination of the walls—even to the demolition of the pavilion—does not reveal any passage practicable—not only for a human being, but for any being whatsoever—if the ceiling shows no crack, if the floor hides no underground passage, one must really believe in the Devil, as Daddy Jacques says!'"

And the anonymous writer in the "Matin" added in this article—which I have selected as the most interesting of all those that were published on the subject of this affair—that the examining magistrate appeared to place a peculiar significance to the last sentence: "One must really believe in the Devil, as Jacques says."

The article concluded with these lines: "We wanted to know what Daddy Jacques meant by the cry of the Bete Du Bon Dieu." The landlord of the Donjon Inn explained to us that it is the particularly sinister cry which is uttered sometimes at night by the cat of an old woman,—Mother Angenoux, as she is called in the country. Mother Angenoux is a sort of saint, who lives in a hut in the heart of the forest, not far from the grotto of Sainte-Genevieve.

"'The Yellow Room', the Bete Du Bon Dieu, Mother Angenoux, the Devil, Sainte-Genevieve, Daddy Jacques,—here is a well entangled crime which the stroke of a pickaxe in the wall may disentangle for us tomorrow. Let us at least hope that, for the sake of our human reason, as the examining magistrate says. Meanwhile, it is expected that Mademoiselle Stangerson—who has not ceased to be delirious and only pronounces one word distinctly, 'Murderer! Murderer!'—will not live through the night."

In conclusion, and at a late hour, the same journal announced that the Chief of the Surete had telegraphed to the famous detective, Frederic Larsan, who had been sent to London for an affair of stolen securities, to return immediately to Paris.

# II

## IN WHICH JOSEPH ROULETABILLE APPEARS FOR THE FIRST TIME

I remember as well as if it had occurred yesterday, the entry of young Rouletabille into my bedroom that morning. It was about eight o'clock and I was still in bed reading the article in the "Matin" relative to the Glandier crime.

But, before going further, it is time that I present my friend to the reader.

I first knew Joseph Rouletabille when he was a young reporter. At that time I was a beginner at the Bar and often met him in the corridors of examining magistrates, when I had gone to get a "permit to communicate" for the prison of Mazas, or for Saint-Lazare. He had, as they say, "a good nut." He seemed to have taken his head—round as a bullet—out of a box of marbles, and it is from that, I think, that his comrades of the press—all determined billiard-players—had given him that nickname, which was to stick to him and be made illustrious by him. He was always as red as a tomato, now gay as a lark, now grave as a judge. How, while still so young—he was only sixteen and a half years old when I saw him for the first time—had he already won his way on the press? That was what everybody who came into contact with him might have asked, if they had not known his history. At the time of the affair of the woman cut in pieces in the Rue Oberskampf—another forgotten story—he had taken to one of the editors of the "Epoque,"—a paper then rivalling the "Matin" for information,—the left foot, which was missing from the basket in which the gruesome remains were discovered. For this left foot the police had been vainly searching for a week, and young Rouletabille had found it in a drain where nobody had thought of looking for it. To do that he had dressed himself as an extra sewer-man, one of a number engaged by the administration of the city of Paris, owing to an overflow of the Seine.

When the editor-in-chief was in possession of the precious foot and informed as to the train of intelligent deductions the boy had been led to make, he was divided between the admiration he felt for such detective cunning in a brain of a lad of sixteen years, and delight at being able to exhibit, in the "morgue window" of his paper, the left foot of the Rue Oberskampf.

"This foot," he cried, "will make a great headline."

Then, when he had confided the gruesome packet to the medical lawyer attached to the journal, he asked the lad, who was shortly to become famous as Rouletabille, what he would expect to earn as a general reporter on the "Epoque"?

"Two hundred francs a month," the youngster replied modestly, hardly able to breathe from surprise at the proposal.

"You shall have two hundred and fifty," said the editor-in-chief; "only you must tell everybody that you have been engaged on the paper for a month. Let it be quite understood that it was not you but the 'Epoque' that discovered the left foot of the Rue Oberskampf. Here, my young friend, the man is nothing, the paper everything."

Having said this, he begged the new reporter to retire, but before the youth had reached the door he called him back to ask his name. The other replied:

"Joseph Josephine."

"That's not a name," said the editor-in-chief, "but since you will not be required to sign what you write it is of no consequence."

The boy-faced reporter speedily made himself many friends, for he was serviceable and gifted with a good humour that enchanted the most severe-tempered and disarmed the most zealous of his companions. At the Bar cafe, where the reporters assembled before going to any of the courts, or to the Prefecture, in search of their news of crime, he began to win a reputation as an unraveller of intricate and obscure affairs which found its way to the office of the Chief of the Surete. When a case was worth the trouble and Rouletabille—he had already been given his nickname—had been started on the scent by his editor-in-chief, he often got the better of the most famous detective.

It was at the Bar cafe that I became intimately acquainted with him. Criminal lawyers and journalists are not enemies, the former need advertisement, the latter information. We chatted together, and I soon warmed towards him. His intelligence was so keen, and so original!—and he had a quality of thought such as I have never found in any other person.

Some time after this I was put in charge of the law news of the "Cri du Boulevard." My entry into journalism could not but strengthen the ties which united me to Rouletabille. After a while, my new friend being allowed to carry out an idea of a judicial correspondence column, which he was allowed to sign "Business," in the "Epoque," I was often able to furnish him with the legal information of which he stood in need.

Nearly two years passed in this way, and the better I knew him, the more I learned to love him; for, in spite of his careless extravagance, I had discovered in him what was, considering his age, an extraordinary seriousness of mind. Accustomed as I was to seeing him gay and, indeed, often too gay, I would many times find him plunged in the deepest melancholy. I tried then to question him as to the cause of this change of humour, but each time he laughed and made me no answer. One day, having questioned him about his parents, of whom he never spoke, he left me, pretending not to have heard what I said.

While things were in this state between us, the famous case of The "Yellow Room" took place. It was this case which was to rank him as the leading newspaper reporter, and to obtain for him the reputation of being the greatest detective in the world. It should not surprise us to find in the one man the perfection of two such lines of activity if we remember that the daily press was already beginning to transform itself and to become what it is today—the gazette of crime.

Morose-minded people may complain of this; for myself I regard it a matter for congratulation. We can never have too many arms, public or private, against the criminal. To this some people may answer that, by continually publishing the details of crimes, the press ends by encouraging their commission. But then, with some people we can never do right. Rouletabille, as I have said, entered my room that morning of the 26th of October, 1892. He was looking redder than usual, and his eyes were bulging out of his head, as the phrase is, and altogether he appeared to be in a state of extreme excitement. He waved the "Matin" with a trembling hand, and cried:

"Well, my dear Sainclair,—have you read it?"

"The Glandier crime?"

"Yes; 'The Yellow Room'!—What do you think of it?"

"I think that it must have been the Devil or the Bete du Bon Dieu that committed the crime."

"Be serious!"

"Well, I don't much believe in murderers who make their escape through walls of solid brick. I think Daddy Jacques did wrong to leave behind him the weapon with which the crime was committed and, as he occupied the attic immediately above Mademoiselle Stangerson's room, the builder's job ordered by the examining magistrate will give us the key of the enigma and it will not be long before we learn by what natural trap, or by what secret door, the old fellow was able to slip in and out, and return immediately to the laboratory to Monsieur Stangerson, without his absence being noticed. That, of course, is only an hypothesis."

Rouletabille sat down in an armchair, lit his pipe, which he was never without, smoked for a few minutes in silence—no doubt to calm the excitement which, visibly, dominated him—and then replied:

"Young man," he said, in a tone the sad irony of which I will not attempt to render, "young man, you are a lawyer and I doubt not your ability to save the guilty from conviction; but if you were a magistrate on the bench, how easy it would be for you to condemn innocent persons!—You are really gifted, young man!"

He continued to smoke energetically, and then went on:

"No trap will be found, and the mystery of 'The Yellow Room' will become more and more mysterious. That's why it interests me. The examining magistrate is right; nothing stranger than this crime has ever been known."

"Have you any idea of the way by which the murderer escaped?" I asked.

"None," replied Rouletabille—"none, for the present. But I have an idea as to the revolver; the murderer did not use it."

"Good Heavens! By whom, then, was it used?"

"Why—by Mademoiselle Stangerson."

"I don't understand,—or rather, I have never understood," I said.

Rouletabille shrugged his shoulders.

"Is there nothing in this article in the 'Matin' by which you were particularly struck?"

"Nothing,—I have found the whole of the story it tells equally strange."

"Well, but—the locked door—with the key on the inside?"

"That's the only perfectly natural thing in the whole article."

"Really!—And the bolt?"

"The bolt?"

"Yes, the bolt—also inside the room—a still further protection against entry? Mademoiselle Stangerson took quite extraordinary precautions! It is clear to me that she feared someone. That was why she took such precautions—even Daddy Jacques's revolver—without telling him of it. No doubt she didn't wish to alarm anybody, and least of all, her father. What she dreaded took place, and she defended herself. There was a struggle, and she used the revolver skilfully enough to wound the assassin in the hand—which explains the impression on the wall and on the door of the large, blood-stained hand of the man who was searching for a means of exit from the chamber. But she didn't fire soon enough to avoid the terrible blow on the right temple."

"Then the wound on the temple was not done with the revolver?"

"The paper doesn't say it was, and I don't think it was; because logically it appears to me that the revolver was used by Mademoiselle Stangerson against the assassin. Now, what weapon did the murderer use? The blow on the temple seems to show that the murderer wished to stun Mademoiselle Stangerson,—after he had unsuccessfully tried to strangle her. He must have known that the attic was inhabited by Daddy Jacques, and that was one of the reasons, I think, why he must have used a quiet weapon,—a life-preserver, or a hammer."

"All that doesn't explain how the murderer got out of 'The Yellow Room'," I observed.

"Evidently," replied Rouletabille, rising, "and that is what has to be explained. I am going to the Château du Glandier, and have come to see whether you will go with me."

"I?—"

"Yes, my boy. I want you. The 'Epoque' has definitely entrusted this case to me, and I must clear it up as quickly as possible."

"But in what way can I be of any use to you?"

"Monsieur Robert Darzac is at the Château du Glandier."

"That's true. His despair must be boundless."

"I must have a talk with him."

Rouletabille said it in a tone that surprised me. "Is it because—you think there is something to be got out of him?" I asked.

"Yes."

That was all he would say. He retired to my sitting-room, begging me to dress quickly.

I knew Monsieur Robert Darzac from having been of great service to him in a civil action, while I was acting as secretary to Maitre Barbet Delatour. Monsieur Robert Darzac, who was at that time about forty years of age, was a professor of physics at the Sorbonne. He was intimately acquainted with the Stangersons, and, after an assiduous seven years' courtship of the daughter, had been on the point of marrying her. In spite of the fact that she has become, as the phrase goes, "a person of a certain age," she was still remarkably good-looking. While I was dressing I called out to Rouletabille, who was impatiently moving about my sitting-room:

"Have you any idea as to the murderer's station in life?"

"Yes," he replied; "I think if he isn't a man in society, he is, at least, a man belonging to the upper class. But that, again, is only an impression."

"What has led you to form it?"

"Well,—the greasy cap, the common handkerchief, and the marks of the rough boots on the floor," he replied.

"I understand," I said; "murderers don't leave traces behind them which tell the truth."

"We shall make something out of you yet, my dear Sainclair," concluded Rouletabille.

# III

## "A MAN HAS PASSED LIKE A SHADOW THROUGH THE BLINDS"

Half an hour later Rouletabille and I were on the platform of the Orleans station, awaiting the departure of the train which was to take us to Epinay-sur-Orge.

On the platform we found Monsieur de Marquet and his Registrar, who represented the Judicial Court of Corbeil. Monsieur Marquet had spent the night in Paris, attending the final rehearsal, at the Scala, of a little play of which he was the unknown author, signing himself simply "Castigat Ridendo."

Monsieur de Marquet was beginning to be a "noble old gentleman." Generally he was extremely polite and full of gay humour, and in all his life had had but one passion,—that of dramatic art. Throughout his magisterial career he was interested solely in cases capable of furnishing him with something in the nature of a drama. Though he might very well have aspired to the highest judicial positions, he had never really worked for anything but to win a success at the romantic Porte-Saint-Martin, or at the sombre Odeon.

Because of the mystery which shrouded it, the case of "The Yellow Room" was certain to fascinate so theatrical a mind. It interested him enormously, and he threw himself into it, less as a magistrate eager to know the truth, than as an amateur of dramatic embroglios, tending wholly to mystery and intrigue, who dreads nothing so much as the explanatory final act.

So that, at the moment of meeting him, I heard Monsieur de Marquet say to the Registrar with a sigh:

"I hope, my dear Monsieur Maleine, this builder with his pickaxe will not destroy so fine a mystery."

"Have no fear," replied Monsieur Maleine, "his pickaxe may demolish the pavilion, perhaps, but it will leave our case intact. I have sounded the walls and examined the ceiling and floor and I know all about it. I am not to be deceived."

Having thus reassured his chief, Monsieur Maleine, with a discreet movement of the head, drew Monsieur de Marquet's attention to us. The face of that gentleman clouded, and, as he saw Rouletabille approaching, hat in hand, he sprang into one of the empty carriages saying, half aloud to his Registrar, as he did so, "Above all, no journalists!"

Monsieur Maleine replied in the same tone, "I understand!" and then tried to prevent Rouletabille from entering the same compartment with the examining magistrate.

"Excuse me, gentlemen,—this compartment is reserved."

"I am a journalist, Monsieur, engaged on the 'Epoque,'" said my young friend with a great show of gesture and politeness, "and I have a word or two to say to Monsieur de Marquet."

"Monsieur is very much engaged with the inquiry he has in hand."

"Ah! his inquiry, pray believe me, is absolutely a matter of indifference to me. I am no scavenger of odds and ends," he went on, with infinite contempt in his lower lip, "I am a theatrical reporter; and this evening I shall have to give a little account of the play at the Scala."

"Get in, sir, please," said the Registrar.

Rouletabille was already in the compartment. I went in after him and seated myself by his side. The Registrar followed and closed the carriage door.

Monsieur de Marquet looked at him.

"Ah, sir," Rouletabille began, "You must not be angry with Monsieur de Maleine. It is not with Monsieur de Marquet that I desire to have the honour of speaking, but with Monsieur 'Castigat Ridendo.' Permit me to congratulate you—personally, as well as the writer for the 'Epoque.'" And Rouletabille, having first introduced me, introduced himself.

Monsieur de Marquet, with a nervous gesture, caressed his beard into a point, and explained to Rouletabille, in a few words, that he was too modest an author to desire that the veil of his pseudonym should be publicly raised, and that he hoped the enthusiasm of the journalist for the dramatist's work would not lead him to tell the public that Monsieur "Castigat Ridendo" and the examining magistrate of Corbeil were one and the same person.

"The work of the dramatic author may interfere," he said, after a slight hesitation, "with that of the magistrate, especially in a province where one's labours are little more than routine."

"Oh, you may rely on my discretion!" cried Rouletabille.

The train was in motion.

"We have started!" said the examining magistrate, surprised at seeing us still in the carriage.

"Yes, Monsieur,—truth has started," said Rouletabile, smiling amiably,—"on its way to the Château du Glandier. A fine case, Monsieur de Marquet,—a fine case!"

"An obscure—incredible, unfathomable, inexplicable affair—and there is only one thing I fear, Monsieur Rouletabille,—that the journalists will be trying to explain it."

My friend felt this a rap on his knuckles.

"Yes," he said simply, "that is to be feared. They meddle in everything. As for my interest, monsieur, I only referred to it by mere chance,—the mere chance of finding myself in the same train with you, and in the same compartment of the same carriage."

"Where are you going, then?" asked Monsieur de Marquet.

"To the Château du Glandier," replied Rouletabille, without turning.

"You'll not get in, Monsieur Rouletabille!"

"Will you prevent me?" said my friend, already prepared to fight.

"Not I!—I like the press and journalists too well to be in any way disagreeable to them; but Monsieur Stangerson has given orders for his door to be closed against everybody, and it is well guarded. Not a journalist was able to pass through the gate of the Glandier yesterday."

Monsieur de Marquet compressed his lips and seemed ready to relapse into obstinate silence. He only relaxed a little when Rouletabille no longer left him in ignorance of the fact that we were going to the Glandier for the purpose of shaking hands with an "old and intimate friend," Monsieur Robert Darzac—a man whom Rouletabille had perhaps seen once in his life.

"Poor Robert!" continued the young reporter, "This dreadful affair may be his death,—he is so deeply in love with Mademoiselle Stangerson."

"His sufferings are truly painful to witness," escaped like a regret from the lips of Monsieur de Marquet.

"But it is to be hoped that Mademoiselle Stangerson's life will be saved."

"Let us hope so. Her father told me yesterday that, if she does not recover, it will not be long before he joins her in the grave. What an incalculable loss to science his death would be!"

"The wound on her temple is serious, is it not?"

"Evidently; but, by a wonderful chance, it has not proved mortal. The blow was given with great force."

"Then it was not with the revolver she was wounded," said Rouletabille, glancing at me in triumph.

Monsieur de Marquet appeared greatly embarrassed.

"I didn't say anything—I don't want to say anything—I will not say anything," he said. And he turned towards his Registrar as if he no longer knew us.

But Rouletabille was not to be so easily shaken off. He moved nearer to the examining magistrate and, drawing a copy of the "Matin" from his pocket, he showed it to him and said:

"There is one thing, Monsieur, which I may enquire of you without committing an indiscretion. You have, of course, seen the account given in the 'Matin'? It is absurd, is it not?"

"Not in the slightest, Monsieur."

"What! 'The Yellow Room' has but one barred window—the bars of which have not been moved—and only one door, which had to be broken open—and the assassin was not found!"

"That's so, monsieur,—that's so. That's how the matter stands."

Rouletabille said no more but plunged into thought. A quarter of an hour thus passed.

Coming back to himself again he said, addressing the magistrate:

"How did Mademoiselle Stangerson wear her hair on that evening?"

"I don't know," replied Monsieur de Marquet.

"That's a very important point," said Rouletabille. "Her hair was done up in bands, wasn't it? I feel sure that on that evening, the evening of the crime, she had her hair arranged in bands."

"Then you are mistaken, Monsieur Rouletabille," replied the magistrate; "Mademoiselle Stangerson that evening had her hair drawn up in a knot on the top of her head,—her usual way of arranging it—her forehead completely uncovered. I can assure you, for we have carefully examined the wound. There was no blood on the hair, and the arrangement of it has not been disturbed since the crime was committed."

"You are sure! You are sure that, on the night of the crime, she had not her hair in bands?"

"Quite sure," the magistrate continued, smiling, "because I remember the Doctor saying to me, while he was examining the wound, 'It is a great pity Mademoiselle Stangerson was in the habit of drawing her hair back from her forehead. If she had worn it in bands, the blow she received on the temple would have been weakened.' It seems strange to me that you should attach so much importance to this point."

"Oh! if she had not her hair in bands, I give it up," said Rouletabille, with a despairing gesture.

"And was the wound on her temple a bad one?" he asked presently.

"Terrible."

"With what weapon was it made?"

"That is a secret of the investigation."

"Have you found the weapon—whatever it was?"

The magistrate did not answer.

"And the wound in the throat?"

Here the examining magistrate readily confirmed the decision of the doctor that, if the murderer had pressed her throat a few seconds longer, Mademoiselle Stangerson would have died of strangulation.

"The affair as reported in the 'Matin,'" said Rouletabille eagerly, "seems to me more and more inexplicable. Can you tell me, Monsieur, how many openings there are in the pavilion? I mean doors and windows."

"There are five," replied Monsieur de Marquet, after having coughed once or twice, but no longer resisting the desire he felt to talk of the whole of the incredible mystery of the affair he was investigating. "There are five, of which the door of the vestibule is the only entrance to the pavilion,—a door always automatically closed, which cannot be opened, either from the outer or inside, except with the two special keys which are never out of the possession of either Daddy Jacques or Monsieur Stangerson. Mademoiselle Stangerson had no need for one, since Daddy Jacques lodged in the pavilion and because, during the daytime, she never left her father. When they, all four, rushed into "The Yellow Room", after breaking open the door of the laboratory, the door in the vestibule remained closed as usual and, of the two keys for opening it, Daddy Jacques had one in his pocket, and Monsieur Stangerson the other. As to the windows of the pavilion, there are four; the one window of 'The Yellow Room' and those of the laboratory looking out on to the country; the window in the vestibule looking into the park."

"It is by that window that he escaped from the pavilion!" cried Rouletabille.

"How do you know that?" demanded Monsieur de Marquet, fixing a strange look on my young friend.

"We'll see later how he got away from 'The Yellow Room'," replied Rouletabille, "but he must have left the pavilion by the vestibule window."

"Once more,—how do you know that?"

"How? Oh, the thing is simple enough! As soon as he found he could not escape by the door of the pavilion his only way out was by the window in the vestibule, unless he could pass through a grated window. The window of 'The Yellow Room' is secured by iron bars, because it looks out upon the open country; the two windows of the laboratory have to be protected in like manner for the same reason. As the murderer got away, I conceive that he found a window that was not barred,—that of the vestibule, which opens on to the park,—that is to say, into the interior of the estate. There's not much magic in all that."

"Yes," said Monsieur de Marquet, "but what you have not guessed is that this single window in the vestibule, though it has no iron bars, has solid iron blinds. Now these iron blinds have remained fastened by their iron latch; and yet we have proof that the murderer made his escape from the pavilion by that window! Traces of blood on the inside wall and on the blinds as well as on the floor, and footmarks, of which I have taken the measurements, attest the fact that the murderer made his escape that way. But then, how did he do it, seeing that the blinds remained fastened on the inside? He passed through them like a shadow. But what is more bewildering than all is that it is impossible to form any idea as to how the murderer got out of 'The Yellow Room', or how he got across the laboratory to reach the vestibule! Ah, yes, Monsieur Rouletabille, it is altogether as you said, a fine case, the key to which will not be discovered for a long time, I hope."

"You hope, Monsieur?"

Monsieur de Marquet corrected himself.

"I do not hope so,—I think so."

"Could that window have been closed and refastened after the flight of the assassin?" asked Rouletabille.

"That is what occurred to me for a moment; but it would imply an accomplice or accomplices,—and I don't see—"

After a short silence he added:

"Ah—if Mademoiselle Stangerson were only well enough today to be questioned!"

Rouletabille following up his thought, asked:

"And the attic?—There must be some opening to that?"

"Yes; there is a window, or rather skylight, in it, which, as it looks out towards the country, Monsieur Stangerson has had barred, like the rest of the windows. These bars, as in the other windows, have remained intact, and the blinds, which naturally open inwards, have not been unfastened. For the rest, we have not discovered anything to lead us to suspect that the murderer had passed through the attic."

"It seems clear to you, then, Monsieur, that the murderer escaped—nobody knows how—by the window in the vestibule?"

"Everything goes to prove it."

"I think so, too," confessed Rouletabille gravely.

After a brief silence, he continued:

"If you have not found any traces of the murderer in the attic, such as the dirty footmarks similar to those on the floor of 'The Yellow Room', you must come to the conclusion that it was not he who stole Daddy Jacques's revolver."

"There are no footmarks in the attic other than those of Daddy Jacques himself," said the magistrate with a significant turn of his head. Then, after an apparent decision, he added: "Daddy Jacques was with Monsieur Stangerson in the laboratory—and it was lucky for him he was."

"Then what part did his revolver play in the tragedy?—It seems very clear that this weapon did less harm to Mademoiselle Stangerson than it did to the murderer."

The magistrate made no reply to this question, which doubtless embarrassed him. "Monsieur Stangerson," he said, "tells us that the two bullets have been found in 'The Yellow Room', one embedded in the wall stained with the impression of a red hand—a man's large hand—and the other in the ceiling."

"Oh! Oh! in the ceiling!" muttered Rouletabille. "In the ceiling! That's very curious!—In the ceiling!"

He puffed awhile in silence at his pipe, enveloping himself in the smoke. When we reached Savigny-sur-Orge, I had to tap him on the shoulder to arouse him from his dream and come out on to the platform of the station.

There, the magistrate and his Registrar bowed to us, and by rapidly getting into a cab that was awaiting them, made us understand that they had seen enough of us.

"How long will it take to walk to the Château du Glandier?" Rouletabille asked one of the railway porters.

"An hour and a half or an hour and three quarters—easy walking," the man replied.

Rouletabille looked up at the sky and, no doubt, finding its appearance satisfactory, took my arm and said:

"Come on!—I need a walk."

"Are things getting less entangled?" I asked.

"Not a bit of it!" he said, "More entangled than ever! It's true, I have an idea—"

"What's that?" I asked.

"I can't tell you what it is just at present—it's an idea involving the life or death of two persons at least."

"Do you think there were accomplices?"

"I don't think it—"

We fell into silence. Presently he went on:

"It was a bit of luck, our falling in with that examining magistrate and his Registrar, eh? What did I tell you about that revolver?" His head was bent down, he had his hands in his pockets, and he was whistling. After a while I heard him murmur:

"Poor woman!"

"Is it Mademoiselle Stangerson you are pitying?"

"Yes; she's a noble woman and worthy of being pitied!—a woman of a great, a very great character—I imagine—I imagine."

"You know her then?"

"Not at all. I have never seen her."

"Why, then, do you say that she is a woman of great character?"

"Because she bravely faced the murderer; because she courageously defended herself—and, above all, because of the bullet in the ceiling."

I looked at Rouletabille and inwardly wondered whether he was not mocking me, or whether he had not suddenly gone out of his senses. But I saw that he had never been less inclined to laugh, and the brightness of his keenly intelligent eyes assured me that he retained all his reason. Then, too, I was used to his broken way of talking, which only left me puzzled as to his meaning, till, with a very few clear, rapidly uttered words, he would make the drift of his ideas clear to me, and I saw that what he had previously said, and which had appeared to me void of meaning, was so thoroughly logical that I could not understand how it was I had not understood him sooner.

# IV

## "IN THE BOSOM OF WILD NATURE"

The Château du Glandier is one of the oldest châteaux in the Ile de France, where so many building remains of the feudal period are still standing. Built originally in the heart of the forest, in the reign of Philip le Bel, it now could be seen a few hundred yards from the road leading from the village of Sainte-Genevieve to Monthery. A mass of inharmonious structures, it is dominated by a donjon. When the visitor has mounted the crumbling steps of this ancient donjon, he reaches a little plateau where, in the seventeenth century, Georges Philibert de Sequigny, Lord of the Glandier, Maisons-Neuves and other places, built the existing town in an abominably rococo style of architecture.

It was in this place, seemingly belonging entirely to the past, that Professor Stangerson and his daughter installed themselves to lay the foundations for the science of the future. Its solitude, in the depths of woods, was what, more than all, had pleased them. They would have none to witness their labours and intrude on their hopes, but the aged stones and grand old oaks. The Glandier—ancient Glandierum—was so called from the quantity of glands (acorns) which, in all times, had been gathered in that neighbourhood. This land, of present mournful interest, had fallen back, owing to the negligence or abandonment of its owners, into the wild character of primitive nature. The buildings alone, which were hidden there, had preserved traces of their strange metamorphoses. Every age had left on them its imprint; a bit of architecture with which was bound up the remembrance of some terrible event, some bloody adventure. Such was the château in which science had taken refuge—a place seemingly designed to be the theatre of mysteries, terror, and death.

Having explained so far, I cannot refrain from making one further reflection. If I have lingered a little over this description of the Glandier, it is not because I have reached the right moment for creating the necessary atmosphere for the unfolding of the tragedy before the eyes of the reader. Indeed, in all this matter, my first care will be to be as simple as is possible. I have no ambition to be an author. An author is always something of a romancer, and God knows, the mystery of "The Yellow Room" is quite full enough of real tragic horror to require no aid from literary effects. I am, and only desire to be, a faithful "reporter." My duty is to report the event; and I place the event in its frame—that is all. It is only natural that you should know where the things happened.

I return to Monsieur Stangerson. When he bought the estate, fifteen years before the tragedy with which we are engaged occurred, the Château du Glandier had for a long time been unoccupied. Another old château in the neighbourhood, built in the fourteenth century by Jean de Belmont, was also abandoned, so that that part of the country was very little inhabited. Some small houses on the side of the road leading to Corbeil, an Inn, called the "Auberge du Donjon," which offered passing hospitality to waggoners; these were about all to represent civilisation in this out-of-the-way part of the country, but a few leagues from the capital.

But this deserted condition of the place had been the determining reason for the choice made by Monsieur

Stangerson and his daughter. Monsieur Stangerson was already celebrated. He had returned from America, where his works had made a great stir. The book which he had published at Philadelphia, on the "Dissociation of Matter by Electric Action," had aroused opposition throughout the whole scientific world. Monsieur Stangerson was a Frenchman, but of American origin. Important matters relating to a legacy had kept him for several years in the United States, where he had continued the work begun by him in France, whither he had returned in possession of a large fortune. This fortune was a great boon to him; for, though he might have made millions of dollars by exploiting two or three of his chemical discoveries relative to new processes of dyeing, it was always repugnant to him to use for his own private gain the wonderful gift of invention he had received from nature. He considered he owed it to mankind, and all that his genius brought into the world went, by this philosophical view of his duty, into the public lap.

If he did not try to conceal his satisfaction at coming into possession of this fortune, which enabled him to give himself up to his passion for pure science, he had equally to rejoice, it seemed to him, for another cause. Mademoiselle Stangerson was, at the time when her father returned from America and bought the Glandier estate, twenty years of age. She was exceedingly pretty, having at once the Parisian grace of her mother, who had died in giving her birth, and all the splendour, all the riches of the young American blood of her parental grandfather, William Stangerson. A citizen of Philadelphia, William Stangerson had been obliged to become naturalised in obedience to family exigencies at the time of his marriage with a French lady, she who was to be the mother of the illustrious Stangerson. In that way the professor's French nationality is accounted for.

Twenty years of age, a charming blonde, with blue eyes, milk-white complexion, and radiant with divine health, Mathilde

Stangerson was one of the most beautiful marriageable girls in either the old or the new world. It was her father's duty, in spite of the inevitable pain which a separation from her would cause him, to think of her marriage; and he was fully prepared for it. Nevertheless, he buried himself and his child at the Glandier at the moment when his friends were expecting him to bring her out into society. Some of them expressed their astonishment, and to their questions he answered: "It is my daughter's wish. I can refuse her nothing. She has chosen the Glandier."

Interrogated in her turn, the young girl replied calmly: "Where could we work better than in this solitude?" For Mademoiselle Stangerson had already begun to collaborate with her father in his work. It could not at the time be imagined that her passion for science would lead her so far as to refuse all the suitors who presented themselves to her for over fifteen years. So secluded was the life led by the two, father and daughter, that they showed themselves only at a few official receptions and, at certain times in the year, in two or three friendly drawing-rooms, where the fame of the professor and the beauty of Mathilde made a sensation. The young girl's extreme reserve did not at first discourage suitors; but at the end of a few years, they tired of their quest.

One alone persisted with tender tenacity and deserved the name of "eternal fiance," a name he accepted with melancholy resignation; that was Monsieur Robert Darzac. Mademoiselle Stangerson was now no longer young, and it seemed that, having found no reason for marrying at five-and-thirty, she would never find one. But such an argument evidently found no acceptance with Monsieur Robert Darzac. He continued to pay his court—if the delicate and tender attention with which he ceaselessly surrounded this woman of five-and-thirty could be called courtship—in face of her declared intention never to marry.

Suddenly, some weeks before the events with which we are occupied, a report—to which nobody attached any importance, so incredible did it sound—was spread about Paris, that Mademoiselle Stangerson had at last consented to "crown" the inextinguishable flame of Monsieur Robert Darzac! It needed that Monsieur Robert Darzac himself should not deny this matrimonial rumour to give it an appearance of truth, so unlikely did it seem to be well founded. One day, however, Monsieur Stangerson, as he was leaving the Academy of Science, announced that the marriage of his daughter and Monsieur Robert Darzac would be celebrated in the privacy of the Château du Glandier, as soon as he and his daughter had put the finishing touches to their report summing up their labours on the "Dissociation of Matter." The new household would install itself in the Glandier, and the son-in-law would lend his assistance in the work to which the father and daughter had dedicated their lives.

The scientific world had barely had time to recover from the effect of this news, when it learned of the attempted assassination of Mademoiselle under the extraordinary conditions which we have detailed and which our visit to the chateau was to enable us to ascertain with yet greater precision. I have not hesitated to furnish the reader with all these retrospective details, known to me through my business relations with Monsieur Robert Darzac. On crossing the threshold of The "Yellow Room" he was as well posted as I was.

# V

## IN WHICH JOSEPH ROULETABILLE MAKES A REMARK TO MONSIEUR ROBERT DARZAC WHICH PRODUCES ITS LITTLE EFFECT

Rouletabille and I had been walking for several minutes, by the side of a long wall bounding the vast property of Monsieur Stangerson and had already come within sight of the entrance gate, when our attention was drawn to an individual who, half bent to the ground, seemed to be so completely absorbed in what he was doing as not to have seen us coming towards him. At one time he stooped so low as almost to touch the ground; at another he drew himself up and attentively examined the wall; then he looked into the palm of one of his hands, and walked away with rapid strides. Finally he set off running, still looking into the palm of his hand. Rouletabille had brought me to a standstill by a gesture.

"Hush! Frederic Larsan is at work! Don't let us disturb him!"

Rouletabille had a great admiration for the celebrated detective. I had never before seen him, but I knew him well by reputation. At that time, before Rouletabille had given proof of his unique talent, Larsan was reputed as the most skilful unraveller of the most mysterious and complicated crimes. His reputation was worldwide, and the police of London, and even of America, often called him in to their aid when their own national inspectors and detectives found themselves at the end of their wits and resources.

No one was astonished, then, that the head of the Surete had, at the outset of the mystery of "The Yellow Room", telegraphed his precious subordinate to London, where he had been sent on a big case of stolen securities, to return with all haste. Frederic who, at the Surete, was called the "great Frederic," had made all speed, doubtless knowing by experience that, if he was interrupted in what he was doing, it was because his services were urgently needed in another direction; so, as Rouletabille said, he was that morning already "at work." We soon found out in what it consisted.

What he was continually looking at in the palm of his right hand was nothing but his watch, the minute hand of which he appeared to be noting intently. Then he turned back still running, stopping only when he reached the park gate, where he again consulted his watch and then put it away in his pocket, shrugging his shoulders with a gesture of discouragement. He pushed open the park gate, reclosed and locked it, raised his head and, through the bars, perceived us. Rouletabille rushed after him, and I followed. Frederic Larsan waited for us.

"Monsieur Fred," said Rouletabille, raising his hat and showing the profound respect, based on admiration, which the young reporter felt for the celebrated detective, "can you tell me whether Monsieur Robert Darzac is at the château at this moment? Here is one of his friends, of the Paris Bar, who desires to speak with him."

"I really don't know, Monsieur Rouletabille," replied Fred, shaking hands with my friend, whom he had several times met in the course of his difficult investigations. "I have not seen him."

"The concierges will be able to inform us no doubt?" said Rouletabille, pointing to the lodge the door and windows of which were close shut.

"The concierges will not be able to give you any information, Monsieur Rouletabille."

"Why not?"

"Because they were arrested half an hour ago."

"Arrested!" cried Rouletabille; "Then they are the murderers!"

Frederic Larsan shrugged his shoulders.

"When you can't arrest the real murderer," he said with an air of supreme irony, "you can always indulge in the luxury of discovering accomplices."

"Did you have them arrested, Monsieur Fred?"

"Not I!—I haven't had them arrested. In the first place, I am pretty sure that they have not had anything to do with the affair, and then because—"

"Because of what?" asked Rouletabille eagerly.

"Because of nothing," said Larsan, shaking his head.

"Because there were no accomplices!" said Rouletabille.

"Aha!—you have an idea, then, about this matter?" said Larsan, looking at Rouletabille intently, "Yet you have seen nothing, young man—you have not yet gained admission here!"

"I shall get admission."

"I doubt it. The orders are strict."

"I shall gain admission, if you let me see Monsieur Robert Darzac. Do that for me. You know we are old friends. I beg of you, Monsieur Fred. Do you remember the article I wrote about you on the gold bar case?"

The face of Rouletabille at the moment was really funny to look at. It showed such an irresistible desire to cross the threshold beyond which some prodigious mystery had occurred; it appealed with so much eloquence, not only of the mouth and eyes, but with all its features, that I could not refrain from bursting into laughter. Frederic Larsan, no more than myself, could retain his gravity. Meanwhile, standing on the other side of the gate, he calmly put the key in his pocket. I closely scrutinised him.

He might be about fifty years of age. He had a fine head, his hair turning grey; a colourless complexion, and a firm profile. His forehead was prominent, his chin and cheeks clean shaven. His upper lip, without moustache, was finely chiselled. His eyes were rather small and round, with a look in them that was at once searching and disquieting. He was of middle height and well built, with a general bearing elegant and gentlemanly. There was nothing about him of the vulgar policeman. In his way, he was an artist, and one felt that he had a high opinion of himself. The sceptical tone of his conversation was that of a man who had been taught by experience. His strange profession had brought him into contact with so many crimes and villanies that it would have been remarkable if his nature had not been a little hardened.

Larsan turned his head at the sound of a vehicle which had come from the chateau and reached the gate behind him. We recognised the cab which had conveyed the examining magistrate and his Registrar from the station at Epinay.

"Ah!" said Frederic Larsan, "if you want to speak with Monsieur Robert Darzac, he is here."

The cab was already at the park gate and Robert Darzac was begging Frederic Larsan to open it for him, explaining that he was pressed for time to catch the next train leaving Epinay for Paris. Then he recognised me. While Larsan was unlocking the gate, Monsieur Darzac inquired what had brought me to the Glandier at such a tragic moment. I noticed that he was frightfully pale, and that his face was lined as if from the effects of some terrible suffering.

"Is Mademoiselle getting better?" I immediately asked.

"Yes," he said. "She will be saved perhaps. She must be saved!"

He did not add "or it will be my death"; but I felt that the phrase trembled on his pale lips.

Rouletabille intervened:

"You are in a hurry, Monsieur; but I must speak with you. I have something of the greatest importance to tell you."

Frederic Larsan interrupted:

"May I leave you?" he asked of Robert Darzac. "Have you a key, or do you wish me to give you this one."

"Thank you. I have a key and will lock the gate."

Larsan hurried off in the direction of the château, the imposing pile of which could be perceived a few hundred yards away.

Robert Darzac, with knit brow, was beginning to show impatience. I presented Rouletabille as a good friend of mine, but, as soon as he learnt that the young man was a journalist, he looked at me very reproachfully, excused himself, under the necessity of having to reach Epinay in twenty minutes, bowed, and whipped up his horse. But Rouletabille had seized the bridle and, to my utter astonishment, stopped the carriage with a vigorous hand. Then he gave utterance to a sentence which was utterly meaningless to me.

"The presbytery has lost nothing of its charm, nor the garden its brightness."

The words had no sooner left the lips of Rouletabille than I saw Robert Darzac quail. Pale as he was, he became paler. His eyes were fixed on the young man in terror, and he immediately descended from the vehicle in an inexpressible state of agitation.

"Come!—come in!" he stammered.

Then, suddenly, and with a sort of fury, he repeated:

"Let us go, monsieur."

He turned up by the road he had come from the château, Rouletabille still retaining his hold on the horse's bridle. I addressed a few words to Monsieur Darzac, but he made no answer. My looks questioned Rouletabille, but his gaze was elsewhere.

# VI

## IN THE HEART OF THE OAK GROVE

We reached the château, and, as we approached it, saw four gendarmes pacing in front of a little door in the ground floor of the donjon. We soon learned that in this ground floor, which had formerly served as a prison, Monsieur and Madame Bernier, the concierges, were confined. Monsieur Robert Darzac led us into the modern part of the château by a large door, protected by a projecting awning—a "marquise" as it is called. Rouletabille, who had resigned the horse and the cab to the care of a servant, never took his eyes off Monsieur Darzac. I followed his look and perceived that it was directed solely towards the gloved hands of the Sorbonne professor. When we were in a tiny sitting-room fitted with old furniture, Monsieur Darzac turned to Rouletabille and said sharply:

"What do you want?"

The reporter answered in an equally sharp tone:

"To shake you by the hand."

Darzac shrank back.

"What does that mean?"

Evidently he understood, what I also understood, that my friend suspected him of the abominable attempt on the life of Mademoiselle Stangerson. The impression of the bloodstained hand on the walls of The "Yellow Room" was in his mind. I looked at the man closely. His haughty face with its expression ordinarily so straightforward was at this moment strangely troubled. He held out his right hand and, referring to me, said:

"As you are a friend of Monsieur Sainclair who has rendered me invaluable services in a just cause, monsieur, I see no reason for refusing you my hand—"

Rouletabille did not take the extended hand. Lying with the utmost audacity, he said: "Monsieur, I have lived several years in Russia, where I have acquired the habit of never taking any but an ungloved hand."

I thought that the Sorbonne professor would express his anger openly, but, on the contrary, by a visibly violent effort, he calmed himself, took off his gloves, and showed his hands; they were unmarked by any cicatrix.

"Are you satisfied?"

"No!" replied Rouletabille. "My dear friend," he said, turning to me, "I am obliged to ask you to leave us alone for a moment."

I bowed and retired; stupefied by what I had seen and heard. I could not understand why Monsieur Robert Darzac had not already shown the door to my impertinent, insulting, and stupid friend. I was angry myself with Rouletabille at that moment, for his suspicions, which had led to this scene of the gloves.

For some twenty minutes I walked about in front of the château, trying vainly to link together the different events of the day. What was in Rouletabille's mind? Was it possible that he thought Monsieur Robert Darzac to be the murderer? How could it be thought that this man, who was to have married Mademoiselle Stangerson in the course of a few days, had introduced himself into "The Yellow Room" to assassinate his fiancee? I could find no explanation as to how the murderer had been able to leave "The Yellow Room"; and so long as that mystery, which appeared to me so inexplicable, remained unexplained, I thought it was the duty of all of us to refrain from suspecting anybody. But, then, that seemingly senseless phrase—"The presbytery has lost nothing of its charm, nor the garden its brightness"—still rang in my ears. What did it mean? I was eager to rejoin Rouletabille and question him.

At that moment the young man came out of the château in the company of Monsieur Robert Darzac, and, extraordinary to relate, I saw, at a glance, that they were the best of friends. "We are going to 'The Yellow Room". Come with us,' Rouletabille said to me. "You know, my dear boy, I am going to keep you with me all day. We'll breakfast together somewhere about here—"

"You'll breakfast with me, here, gentlemen—"

"No, thanks," replied the young man. "We shall breakfast at the Donjon Inn."

"You'll fare very badly there; you'll not find anything—"

"Do you think so? Well, I hope to find something there," replied Rouletabille. "After breakfast, we'll set to work again. I'll write my article and if you'll be so good as to take it to the office for me—"

"Won't you come back with me to Paris?"

"No; I shall remain here."

I turned towards Rouletabille. He spoke quite seriously, and Monsieur Robert Darzac did not appear to be in the least degree surprised.

We were passing by the donjon and heard wailing voices. Rouletabille asked:

"Why have these people been arrested?"

"It is a little my fault," said Monsieur Darzac. "I happened to remark to the examining magistrate yesterday that it was inexplicable that the concierges had had time to hear the revolver shots, to dress themselves, and to cover so great a distance as that which lies between their lodge and the pavilion, in the space of two minutes; for not more than that interval of time had elapsed after the firing of the shots when they were met by Daddy Jacques."

"That was suspicious evidently," acquiesced Rouletabille. "And were they dressed?"

"That is what is so incredible—they were dressed—completely—not one part of their costume wanting. The woman wore sabots, but the man had on laced boots. Now they assert that they went to bed at half-past nine. On arriving this morning, the examining magistrate brought with him from Paris a revolver of the same calibre as that found in the room (for he couldn't use the one held for evidence), and made his Registrar fire two shots in 'The Yellow Room' while the doors and windows were closed. We were with him in the lodge of the concierges, and yet we heard nothing, not a sound. The concierges have lied, of that there can be no doubt. They must have been already waiting, not far from the pavilion, waiting for something! Certainly they are not to be accused of being the authors of the crime, but their complicity is not improbable. That was why Monsieur de Marquet had them arrested at once."

"If they had been accomplices," said Rouletabille, "they would not have been there at all. When people throw themselves into the arms of justice with the proofs of complicity on them, you can be sure they are not accomplices. I don't believe there are any accomplices in this affair."

"Then, why were they abroad at midnight? Why don't they say?"

"They have certainly some reason for their silence. What that reason is, has to be found out; for, even if they are not accomplices, it may be of importance. Everything that took place on such a night is important."

We had crossed an old bridge thrown over the Douve and were entering the part of the park called the Oak Grove. The oaks here were centuries old. Autumn had already shrivelled their tawny leaves, and their high branches, black and contorted, looked like horrid heads of hair, mingled with quaint reptiles such as the ancient sculptors have made on the head of Medusa. This place, which Mademoiselle found cheerful and in which she lived in the summer season, appeared to us as sad and funereal now. The soil was black and muddy from the recent rains and the rotting of the fallen leaves; the trunks of the trees were black and the sky above us was now, as if in mourning, charged with great, heavy clouds.

And it was in this sombre and desolate retreat that we saw the white walls of the pavilion as we approached. A queer-looking building without a window visible on the side by which we neared it. A little door alone marked the entrance to it. It might have passed for a tomb, a vast mausoleum in the midst of a thick forest. As we came nearer, we were able to make out its disposition. The building obtained all the light it needed from the south, that is to say, from the open country. The little door closed on the park. Monsieur and Mademoiselle Stangerson must have found it an ideal seclusion for their work and their dreams.

```
 ______________________________________________________________
                       ditch                                   |
 ___________________________________________________________   |
 enclosing wall         ||          ||                   |     |
                        ||          ||                   |     |
                        ||___   1                        |d    |
                        ||bed|      ||                   |i    |
       PARK             ||___|_______||                  |t    |
                        ||:::::|  4  ||                  |c    |
                        ||::5::|     ||       2          |h    |
 oo  oo                 ||:::::|___  _||                 |     |
 Traces      oo         ||          ||                   |     |
             of   oo oo oo                               |     |
                 Footsteps||        ||                   |     |
                        ||          ||                   |     |
                        ||   3      ||________________|  |_______________
                        ||          ||       6         |       ditch
                        ||_____  _____||________________|_________________
                             door                         enclosing wall
```

Here is the ground plan of the pavilion. It had a ground-floor which was reached by a few steps, and above it was an attic, with which we need not concern ourselves. The plan of the ground-floor only, sketched roughly, is what I here submit to the reader.

1. *"The Yellow Room", with its one window and its one door opening into the laboratory.*
2. *Laboratory, with its two large, barred windows and its doors, one serving for the vestibule, the other for "The Yellow Room".*
3. *Vestibule, with its unbarred window and door opening into the park.*
4. *Lavatory.*
5. *Stairs leading to the attic.*
6. *Large and the only chimney in the pavilion, serving for the experiments of the laboratory.*

The plan was drawn by Rouletabille, and I assured myself that there was not a line in it that was wanting to help to the solution of the problem then set before the police. With the lines of this plan and the description of its parts before them, my readers will know as much as Rouletabille knew when he entered the pavilion for the first time. With him they may now ask: How did the murderer escape from "The Yellow Room"? Before mounting the three steps leading up to the door of the pavilion, Rouletabille stopped and asked Monsieur Darzac point blank:

"What was the motive for the crime?"

"Speaking for myself, Monsieur, there can be no doubt on the matter," said Mademoiselle Stangerson's fiance, greatly distressed. "The nails of the fingers, the deep scratches on the chest and throat of Mademoiselle Stangerson show that the wretch who attacked her attempted to commit a frightful crime. The medical experts who examined these traces yesterday affirm that they were made by the same hand as that which left its red imprint on the wall; an enormous hand, Monsieur, much too large to go into my gloves," he added with an indefinable smile.

"Could not that bloodstained hand," I interrupted, "have been the hand of Mademoiselle Stangerson who, in the moment of falling, had pressed it against the wall, and, in slipping, enlarged the impression?"

"There was not a drop of blood on either of her hands when she was lifted up," replied Monsieur Darzac.

"We are now sure," said I, "that it was Mademoiselle Stangerson who was armed with Daddy Jacques's revolver, since she wounded the hand of the murderer. She was in fear, then, of somebody or something."

"Probably."

"Do you suspect anybody?"

"No," replied Monsieur Darzac, looking at Rouletabille. Rouletabille then said to me:

"You must know, my friend, that the inquiry is a little more advanced than Monsieur de Marquet has chosen to tell us. He not only knows that Mademoiselle Stangerson defended herself with the revolver, but he knows what the weapon was that was used to attack her. Monsieur Darzac tells me it was a mutton-bone. Why is Monsieur de Marquet surrounding this mutton-bone with so much mystery? No doubt for the purpose of facilitating the inquiries of the agents of the Surete? He imagines, perhaps, that the owner of this instrument of crime, the most terrible invented, is going to be found amongst those who are well-known in the slums of Paris who use it. But who can ever say what passes through the brain of an examining magistrate?" Rouletabille added with contemptuous irony.

"Has a mutton-bone been found in 'The Yellow Room'?" I asked him.

"Yes, Monsieur," said Robert Darzac, "at the foot of the bed; but I beg of you not to say anything about it." (I made a gesture of assent.) "It was an enormous mutton-bone, the top of which, or rather the joint, was still red with the blood of the frightful wound. It was an old bone, which may, according to appearances, have served in other crimes. That's what Monsieur de Marquet thinks. He has had it sent to the municipal laboratory at Paris to be analysed. In fact, he thinks he has detected on it, not only the blood of the last victim, but other stains of dried blood, evidences of previous crimes."

"A mutton-bone in the hand of a skilled assassin is a frightful weapon," said Rouletabille, "a more certain weapon than a heavy hammer."

"The scoundrel has proved it to be so," said Monsieur Robert Darzac, sadly. "The joint of the bone found exactly fits the wound inflicted.

"My belief is that the wound would have been mortal, if the murderer's blow had not been arrested in the act by Mademoiselle Stangerson's revolver. Wounded in the hand, he dropped the mutton-bone and fled. Unfortunately, the blow had been already given, and Mademoiselle was stunned after having been nearly strangled. If she had succeeded in wounding the man with the first shot of the revolver, she would, doubtless, have escaped the blow with the bone. But she had certainly employed her revolver too late; the first shot deviated and lodged in the ceiling; it was the second only that took effect."

Having said this, Monsieur Darzac knocked at the door of the pavilion. I must confess to feeling a strong impatience to reach the spot where the crime had been committed. It was some time before the door was opened by a man whom I at once recognised as Daddy Jacques.

He appeared to be well over sixty years of age. He had a long white beard and white hair, on which he wore a flat Basque cap. He was dressed in a complete suit of chestnut-coloured velveteen, worn at the sides; sabots were on his feet. He had rather a waspish-looking face, the expression of which lightened, however, as soon as he saw Monsieur Darzac.

"Friends," said our guide. "Nobody in the pavilion, Daddy Jacques?"

"I ought not to allow anybody to enter, Monsieur Robert, but of course the order does not apply to you. These gentlemen of justice have seen everything there is to be seen, and made enough drawings, and drawn up enough reports —"

"Excuse me, Monsieur Jacques, one question before anything else," said Rouletabille.

"What is it, young man? If I can answer it—"

"Did your mistress wear her hair in bands, that evening? You know what I mean—over her forehead?"

"No, young man. My mistress never wore her hair in the way you suggest, neither on that day nor on any other. She had her hair drawn up, as usual, so that her beautiful forehead could be seen, pure as that of an unborn child!"

Rouletabille grunted and set to work examining the door, finding that it fastened itself automatically. He satisfied himself that it could never remain open and needed a key to open it. Then we entered the vestibule, a small, well-lit room paved with square red tiles.

"Ah! This is the window by which the murderer escaped!" said Rouletabille.

"So they keep on saying, monsieur, so they keep on saying! But if he had gone off that way, we should have been sure to have seen him. We are not blind, neither Monsieur Stangerson nor me, nor the concierges who are in prison. Why have they not put me in prison, too, on account of my revolver?"

Rouletabille had already opened the window and was examining the shutters.

"Were these closed at the time of the crime?"

"And fastened with the iron catch inside," said Daddy Jacques, "and I am quite sure that the murderer did not get out that way."

"Are there any bloodstains?"

"Yes, on the stones outside; but blood of what?"

"Ah!" said Rouletabille, "There are footmarks visible on the path—the ground was very moist. I will look into that presently."

"Nonsense!" interrupted Daddy Jacques; "The murderer did not go that way."

"Which way did he go, then?"

"How do I know?"

Rouletabille looked at everything, smelled everything. He went down on his knees and rapidly examined every one of the paving tiles. Daddy Jacques went on:

"Ah!—you can't find anything, monsieur. Nothing has been found. And now it is all dirty; too many persons have tramped over it. They wouldn't let me wash it, but on the day of the crime I had washed the floor thoroughly, and if the murderer had crossed it with his hobnailed boots, I should not have failed to see where he had been; he has left marks enough in Mademoiselle's chamber."

Rouletabille rose.

"When was the last time you washed these tiles?" he asked, and he fixed on Daddy Jacques a most searching look.

"Why—as I told you—on the day of the crime, towards half-past five—while Mademoiselle and her father were taking a little walk before dinner, here in this room: they had dined in the laboratory. The next day, the examining magistrate came and saw all the marks there were on the floor as plainly as if they had been made with ink on white paper. Well, neither in the laboratory nor in the vestibule, which were both as clean as a new pin, were there any traces of a man's footmarks. Since they have been found near this window outside, he must have made his way through the ceiling of 'The Yellow Room' into the attic, then cut his way through the roof and dropped to the ground outside the vestibule window. But—there's no hole, neither in the ceiling of 'The Yellow Room' nor in the roof of my attic—that's absolutely certain! So you see we know nothing—nothing! And nothing will ever be known! It's a mystery of the Devil's own making."

Rouletabille went down upon his knees again almost in front of a small lavatory at the back of the vestibule. In that position he remained for about a minute.

"Well?" I asked him when he got up.

"Oh! nothing very important,—a drop of blood," he replied, turning towards Daddy Jacques as he spoke. "While you were washing the laboratory and this vestibule, was the vestibule window open?" he asked.

"No, Monsieur, it was closed; but after I had done washing the floor, I lit some charcoal for Monsieur in the laboratory furnace, and, as I lit it with old newspapers, it smoked, so I opened both the windows in the laboratory and this one, to make a current of air; then I shut those in the laboratory and left this one open when I went out. When I returned to the pavilion, this window had been closed and Monsieur and Mademoiselle were already at work in the laboratory."

"Monsieur or Mademoiselle Stangerson had, no doubt, shut it?"

"No doubt."

"You did not ask them?"

After a close scrutiny of the little lavatory and of the staircase leading up to the attic, Rouletabille—to whom we seemed no longer to exist—entered the laboratory. I followed him. It was, I confess, in a state of great excitement. Robert Darzac lost none of my friend's movements. As for me, my eyes were drawn at once to the door of "The Yellow Room". It was closed and, as I immediately saw, partially shattered and out of commission.

My friend, who went about his work methodically, silently studied the room in which we were. It was large and well-lighted. Two big windows—almost bays—were protected by strong iron bars and looked out upon a wide extent of country. Through an opening in the forest, they commanded a wonderful view through the length of the valley and across the plain to the large town which could be clearly seen in fair weather. Today, however, a mist hung over the ground—and blood in that room!

The whole of one side of the laboratory was taken up with a large chimney, crucibles, ovens, and such implements as are needed for chemical experiments; tables, loaded with phials, papers, reports, an electrical machine,—an apparatus, as Monsieur Darzac informed me, employed by Professor Stangerson to demonstrate the Dissociation of Matter under the action of solar light—and other scientific implements.

Along the walls were cabinets, plain or glass-fronted, through which were visible microscopes, special photographic apparatus, and a large quantity of crystals.

Rouletabille, who was ferreting in the chimney, put his fingers into one of the crucibles. Suddenly he drew himself up, and held up a piece of half-consumed paper in his hand. He stepped up to where we were talking by one of the windows.

"Keep that for us, Monsieur Darzac," he said.

I bent over the piece of scorched paper which Monsieur Darzac took from the hand of Rouletabille, and read distinctly the only words that remained legible:

"Presbytery—lost nothing—charm, nor the gar—its brightness."

Twice since the morning these same meaningless words had struck me, and, for the second time, I saw that they produced on the Sorbonne professor the same paralysing effect. Monsieur Darzac's first anxiety showed itself when he turned his eyes in the direction of Daddy Jacques. But, occupied as he was at another window, he had seen nothing. Then tremblingly opening his pocket-book he put the piece of paper into it, sighing: "My God!"

During this time, Rouletabille had mounted into the opening of the fire-grate—that is to say, he had got upon the bricks of a furnace—and was attentively examining the chimney, which grew narrower towards the top, the outlet from it being closed with sheets of iron, fastened into the brickwork, through which passed three small chimneys.

"Impossible to get out that way," he said, jumping back into the laboratory. "Besides, even if he had tried to do it, he would have brought all that ironwork down to the ground. No, no; it is not on that side we have to search."

Rouletabille next examined the furniture and opened the doors of the cabinet. Then he came to the windows, through which he declared no one could possibly have passed. At the second window he found Daddy Jacques in contemplation.

"Well, Daddy Jacques," he said, "what are you looking at?"

"That policeman who is always going round and round the lake. Another of those fellows who think they can see better than anybody else!"

"You don't know Frederic Larsan, Daddy Jacques, or you wouldn't speak of him in that way," said Rouletabille in a melancholy tone. "If there is anyone who will find the murderer, it will be he." And Rouletabille heaved a deep sigh.

"Before they find him, they will have to learn how they lost him," said Daddy Jacques, stolidly.

At length we reached the door of "The Yellow Room" itself.

"There is the door behind which some terrible scene took place," said Rouletabille, with a solemnity which, under any other circumstances, would have been comical.

# VII

## IN WHICH ROULETABILLE SETS OUT ON AN EXPEDITION UNDER THE BED

Rouletabille having pushed open the door of "The Yellow Room" paused on the threshold saying, with an emotion which I only later understood, "Ah, the perfume of the lady in black!"

The chamber was dark. Daddy Jacques was about to open the blinds when Rouletabille stopped him.

"Did not the tragedy take place in complete darkness?" he asked.

"No, young man, I don't think so. Mademoiselle always had a nightlight on her table, and I lit it every evening before she went to bed. I was a sort of chambermaid, you must understand, when the evening came. The real chambermaid did not come here much before the morning. Mademoiselle worked late—far into the night."

"Where did the table with the night-light stand,—far from the bed?"

"Some way from the bed."

"Can you light the burner now?"

"The lamp is broken and the oil that was in it was spilled when the table was upset. All the rest of the things in the room remain just as they were. I have only to open the blinds for you to see."

"Wait."

Rouletabille went back into the laboratory, closed the shutters of the two windows and the door of the vestibule.

When we were in complete darkness, he lit a wax vesta, and asked Daddy Jacques to move to the middle of the chamber with it to the place where the night-light was burning that night.

Daddy Jacques who was in his stockings—he usually left his sabots in the vestibule—entered "The Yellow Room" with his bit of a vesta. We vaguely distinguished objects overthrown on the floor, a bed in one corner, and, in front of us, to the left, the gleam of a looking-glass hanging on the wall, near to the bed.

"That will do!—you may now open the blinds," said Rouletabille.

"Don't come any further," Daddy Jacques begged, "you may make marks with your boots, and nothing must be deranged; it's an idea of the magistrate's—though he has nothing more to do here."

And he pushed open the shutter. The pale daylight entered from without, throwing a sinister light on the saffron-coloured walls. The floor—for though the laboratory and the vestibule were tiled, "The Yellow Room" had a flooring of wood—was covered with a single yellow mat which was large enough to cover nearly the whole room, under the bed and under the dressing-table—the only piece of furniture that remained upright. The centre round table, the night-table and two chairs had been overturned. These did not prevent a large stain of blood being visible on the mat, made, as Daddy Jacques informed us, by the blood which had flowed from the wound on Mademoiselle Stangerson's forehead. Besides these stains, drops of blood had fallen in all directions, in line with the visible traces of the footsteps—large and black—of the murderer. Everything led to the presumption that these drops of blood had fallen from the wound of the man who had, for a moment, placed his red hand on the wall. There were other traces of the same hand on the wall, but much less distinct.

"See!—see this blood on the wall!" I could not help exclaiming. "The man who pressed his hand so heavily upon it in the darkness must certainly have thought that he was pushing at a door! That's why he pressed on it so hard, leaving on the yellow paper the terrible evidence. I don't think there are many hands in the world of that sort. It is big and strong and the fingers are nearly all one as long as the other! The thumb is wanting and we have only the mark of the palm; but if we follow the trace of the hand," I continued, "we see that, after leaving its imprint on the wall, the touch sought the door, found it, and then felt for the lock—"

"No doubt," interrupted Rouletabille, chuckling,—"only there is no blood, either on the lock or on the bolt!"

"What does that prove?" I rejoined with a good sense of which I was proud; "He might have opened the lock with his left hand, which would have been quite natural, his right hand being wounded."

"He didn't open it at all!" Daddy Jacques again exclaimed. "We are not fools; and there were four of us when we burst open the door!"

"What a queer hand!—Look what a queer hand it is!" I said.

"It is a very natural hand," said Rouletabille, "of which the shape has been deformed by its having slipped on the wall. The man dried his hand on the wall. He must be a man about five feet eight in height."

"How do you come at that?"

"By the height of the marks on the wall."

My friend next occupied himself with the mark of the bullet in the wall. It was a round hole.

"This ball was fired straight, not from above, and consequently, not from below."

Rouletabille went back to the door and carefully examined the lock and the bolt, satisfying himself that the door had certainly been burst open from the outside, and, further, that the key had been found in the lock on the inside of the chamber. He finally satisfied himself that with the key in the lock, the door could not possibly be opened from without with another key. Having made sure of all these details, he let fall these words: "That's better!"—Then sitting down on the ground, he hastily took off his boots and, in his socks, went into the room.

The first thing he did was to examine minutely the overturned furniture. We watched him in silence.

"Young fellow, you are giving yourself a great deal of trouble," said Daddy Jacques ironically.

Rouletabille raised his head and said:

"You have spoken the simple truth, Daddy Jacques; your mistress did not have her hair in bands that evening. I was a donkey to have believed she did."

Then, with the suppleness of a serpent, he slipped under the bed. Presently we heard him ask:

"At what time, Monsieur Jacques, did Monsieur and Mademoiselle Stangerson arrive at the laboratory?"

"At six o'clock."

The voice of Rouletabille continued:

"Yes,—he's been under here,—that's certain; in fact, there was no where else where he could have hidden himself. Here, too, are the marks of his hobnails. When you entered—all four of you—did you look under the bed?"

"At once,—we drew it right out of its place—"

"And between the mattresses?"

"There was only one on the bed, and on that Mademoiselle was placed; and Monsieur Stangerson and the concierge immediately carried it into the laboratory. Under the mattress there was nothing but the metal netting, which could not conceal anything or anybody. Remember, monsieur, that there were four of us and we couldn't fail to see everything—the chamber is so small and scantily furnished, and all was locked behind in the pavilion."

I ventured on a hypothesis:

"Perhaps he got away with the mattress—in the mattress!—Anything is possible, in the face of such a mystery! In their distress of mind Monsieur Stangerson and the concierge may not have noticed they were bearing a double weight; especially if the concierge were an accomplice! I throw out this hypothesis for what it is worth, but it explains many things,—and particularly the fact that neither the laboratory nor the vestibule bear any traces of the footmarks found in the room. If, in carrying Mademoiselle on the mattress from the laboratory of the chateau, they rested for a moment, there might have been an opportunity for the man in it to escape.

"And then?" asked Rouletabille, deliberately laughing under the bed.

I felt rather vexed and replied:

"I don't know,—but anything appears possible—"

"The examining magistrate had the same idea, monsieur," said Daddy Jacques, "and he carefully examined the mattress. He was obliged to laugh at the idea, monsieur, as your friend is doing now,—for whoever heard of a mattress having a double bottom?"

I was myself obliged to laugh, on seeing that what I had said was absurd; but in an affair like this one hardly knows where an absurdity begins or ends.

My friend alone seemed able to talk intelligently. He called out from under the bed.

"The mat here has been moved out of place,—who did it?"

"We did, monsieur," explained Daddy Jacques. "When we could not find the assassin, we asked ourselves whether there was not some hole in the floor—"

"There is not," replied Rouletabille. "Is there a cellar?"

"No, there's no cellar. But that has not stopped our searching, and has not prevented the examining magistrate and his Registrar from studying the floor plank by plank, as if there had been a cellar under it."

The reporter then reappeared. His eyes were sparkling and his nostrils quivered. He remained on his hands and knees. He could not be better likened than to an admirable sporting dog on the scent of some unusual game. And, indeed, he was scenting the steps of a man,—the man whom he has sworn to report to his master, the manager of the "Epoque." It must not be forgotten that Rouletabille was first and last a journalist.

Thus, on his hands and knees, he made his way to the four corners of the room, so to speak, sniffing and going round everything—everything that we could see, which was not much, and everything that we could not see, which must have been infinite.

The toilette table was a simple table standing on four legs; there was nothing about it by which it could possibly be changed into a temporary hiding-place. There was not a closet or cupboard. Mademoiselle Stangerson kept her wardrobe at the château.

Rouletabille literally passed his nose and hands along the walls, constructed of solid brickwork. When he had finished with the walls, and passed his agile fingers over every portion of the yellow paper covering them, he reached to the ceiling, which he was able to touch by mounting on a chair placed on the toilette table, and by moving this ingeniously constructed stage from place to place he examined every foot of it. When he had finished his scrutiny of the ceiling, where he carefully examined the hole made by the second bullet, he approached the window, and, once more, examined the iron bars and blinds, all of which were solid and intact. At last, he gave a grunt of satisfaction and declared "Now I am at ease!"

"Well,—do you believe that the poor dear young lady was shut up when she was being murdered—when she cried out for help?" wailed Daddy Jacques.

"Yes," said the young reporter, drying his forehead, "'The Yellow Room' was as tightly shut as an iron safe."

"That," I said, "is why this mystery is the most surprising I know. Edgar Allan Poe, in 'The Murders in the Rue Morgue,' invented nothing like it. The place of that crime was sufficiently closed to prevent the escape of a man; but there was that window through which the monkey, the perpetrator of the murder, could slip away! But here, there can be no question of an opening of any sort. The door was fastened, and through the window blinds, secure as they were, not even a fly could enter or get out."

"True, true," assented Rouletabille as he kept on drying his forehead, which seemed to be perspiring less from his recent bodily exertion than from his mental agitation. "Indeed, it's a great, a beautiful, and a very curious mystery."

"The Bete du bon Dieu," muttered Daddy Jacques, "the Bete du bon Dieu herself, if she had committed the crime, could not have escaped. Listen! Do you hear it? Hush!"

Daddy Jacques made us a sign to keep quiet and, stretching his arm towards the wall nearest the forest, listened to something which we could not hear.

"It's answering," he said at length. "I must kill it. It is too wicked, but it's the Bete du bon Dieu, and, every night, it goes to pray on the tomb of Sainte-Genevieve and nobody dares to touch her, for fear that Mother Angenoux should cast an evil spell on them."

"How big is the Bete du bon Dieu?"

"Nearly as big as a small retriever,—a monster, I tell you. Ah!—I have asked myself more than once whether it was not her that took our poor Mademoiselle by the throat with her claws. But the Bete du bon Dieu does not wear hobnailed boots, nor fire revolvers, nor has she a hand like that!" exclaimed Daddy Jacques, again pointing out to us the red mark on the wall. "Besides, we should have seen her as well as we would have seen a man—"

"Evidently," I said. "Before we had seen this 'Yellow Room', I had also asked myself whether the cat of Mother Angenoux—"

"You also!" cried Rouletabille.

"Didn't you?" I asked.

"Not for a moment. After reading the article in the 'Matin,' I knew that a cat had nothing to do with the matter. But I swear now that a frightful tragedy has been enacted here. You say nothing about the Basque cap, or the handkerchief, found here, Daddy Jacques?"

"Of course, the magistrate has taken them," the old man answered, hesitatingly.

"I haven't seen either the handkerchief or the cap, yet I can tell you how they are made," the reporter said to him gravely.

"Oh, you are very clever," said Daddy Jacques, coughing and embarrassed.

"The handkerchief is a large one, blue with red stripes and the cap is an old Basque cap, like the one you are wearing now."

"You are a wizard!" said Daddy Jacques, trying to laugh and not quite succeeding. "How do you know that the handkerchief is blue with red stripes?"

"Because, if it had not been blue with red stripes, it would not have been found at all."

Without giving any further attention to Daddy Jacques, my friend took a piece of paper from his pocket, and taking out a pair of scissors, bent over the footprints. Placing the paper over one of them he began to cut. In a short time he had made a perfect pattern which he handed to me, begging me not to lose it.

He then returned to the window and, pointing to the figure of Frederic Larsan, who had not quitted the side of the lake, asked Daddy Jacques whether the detective had, like himself, been working in "The Yellow Room"?

"No," replied Robert Darzac, who, since Rouletabille had handed him the piece of scorched paper, had not uttered a word, "He pretends that he does not need to examine 'The Yellow Room'. He says that the murderer made his escape from it in quite a natural way, and that he will, this evening, explain how he did it."

As he listened to what Monsieur Darzac had to say, Rouletabille turned pale.

"Has Frederic Larsan found out the truth, which I can only guess at?" he murmured. "He is very clever—very clever—and I admire him. But what we have to do today is something more than the work of a policeman, something quite different from the teachings of experience. We have to take hold of our reason by the right end."

The reporter rushed into the open air, agitated by the thought that the great and famous Fred might anticipate him in the solution of the problem of "The Yellow Room".

I managed to reach him on the threshold of the pavilion. "Calm yourself, my dear fellow," I said. "Aren't you satisfied?"

"Yes," he confessed to me, with a deep sigh. "I am quite satisfied. I have discovered many things."

"Moral or material?"

"Several moral,—one material. This, for example."

And rapidly he drew from his waistcoat pocket a piece of paper in which he had placed a light-coloured hair from a woman's head.

# VIII

## THE EXAMINING MAGISTRATE QUESTIONS MADEMOISELLE STANGERSON

Two minutes later, as Rouletabille was bending over the footprints discovered in the park, under the window of the vestibule, a man, evidently a servant at the château, came towards us rapidly and called out to Monsieur Darzac then coming out of the pavilion:

"Monsieur Robert, the magistrate, you know, is questioning Mademoiselle."

Monsieur Darzac uttered a muttered excuse to us and set off running towards the château, the man running after him.

"If the corpse can speak," I said, "it would be interesting to be there."

"We must know," said my friend. "Let's go to the château." And he drew me with him. But, at the château, a gendarme placed in the vestibule denied us admission up the staircase of the first floor. We were obliged to wait downstairs.

This is what passed in the chamber of the victim while we were waiting below.

The family doctor, finding that Mademoiselle Stangerson was much better, but fearing a relapse which would no longer permit of her being questioned, had thought it his duty to inform the examining magistrate of this, who decided to proceed immediately with a brief examination. At this examination, the Registrar, Monsieur Stangerson, and the doctor were present. Later, I obtained the text of the report of the examination, and I give it here, in all its legal dryness:

"Question. Are you able, mademoiselle, without too much fatiguing yourself, to give some necessary details of the frightful attack of which you have been the victim?

"Answer. I feel much better, monsieur, and I will tell you all I know. When I entered my chamber I did not notice anything unusual there.

"Q. Excuse me, mademoiselle,—if you will allow me, I will ask you some questions and you will answer them. That will fatigue you less than making a long recital.

"A. Do so, monsieur.

"Q. What did you do on that day?—I want you to be as minute and precise as possible. I wish to know all you did that day, if it is not asking too much of you.

"A. I rose late, at ten o'clock, for my father and I had returned home late on the night previously, having been to dinner at the reception given by the President of the Republic, in honour of the Academy of Science of Philadelphia. When I left my chamber, at half-past ten, my father was already at work in the laboratory. We worked together till midday. We then took half-an-hour's walk in the park, as we were accustomed to do, before breakfasting at the château. After breakfast, we took another walk for half an hour, and then returned to the laboratory. There we found my chambermaid, who had come to set my room in order. I went into 'The Yellow Room' to give her some slight orders and she directly afterwards left the pavilion, and I resumed my work with my father. At five o'clock, we again went for a walk in the park and afterward had tea.

"Q. Before leaving the pavilion at five o'clock, did you go into your chamber?

"A. No, monsieur, my father went into it, at my request to bring me my hat.

"Q. And he found nothing suspicious there?

"A. Evidently no, monsieur.

"Q. It is, then, almost certain that the murderer was not yet concealed under the bed. When you went out, was the door of the room locked?

"A. No, there was no reason for locking it.

"Q. You were absent from the pavilion some length of time, Monsieur Stangerson and you?

"A. About an hour.

"Q. It was during that hour, no doubt, that the murderer got into the pavilion. But how? Nobody knows. Footmarks have been found in the park, leading away from the window of the vestibule, but none has been found going towards it. Did you notice whether the vestibule window was open when you went out?

"A. I don't remember.

"Monsieur Stangerson. It was closed.

"Q. And when you returned?

"Mademoiselle Stangerson. I did not notice.

"M. Stangerson. It was still closed. I remember remarking aloud: 'Daddy Jacques must surely have opened it while we were away.'

"Q. Strange!—Do you recollect, Monsieur Stangerson, if during your absence, and before going out, he had opened it? You returned to the laboratory at six o'clock and resumed work?

"Mademoiselle Stangerson. Yes, monsieur.

"Q. And you did not leave the laboratory from that hour up to the moment when you entered your chamber?

"M. Stangerson. Neither my daughter nor I, monsieur. We were engaged on work that was pressing, and we lost not a moment,—neglecting everything else on that account.

"Q. Did you dine in the laboratory?

"A. For that reason.

"Q. Are you accustomed to dine in the laboratory?

"A. We rarely dine there.

"Q. Could the murderer have known that you would dine there that evening?

"M. Stangerson. Good Heavens!—I think not. It was only when we returned to the pavilion at six o'clock, that we decided, my daughter and I, to dine there. At that moment I was spoken to by my gamekeeper, who detained me a moment, to ask me to accompany him on an urgent tour of inspection in a part of the woods which I had decided to thin. I put this off until the next day, and begged him, as he was going by the château, to tell the steward that we should dine in the laboratory. He left me, to execute the errand and I rejoined my daughter, who was already at work.

"Q. At what hour, mademoiselle, did you go to your chamber while your father continued to work there?

"A. At midnight.

"Q. Did Daddy Jacques enter 'The Yellow Room' in the course of the evening?

"A. To shut the blinds and light the night-light.

"Q. He saw nothing suspicious?

"A. He would have told us if he had seen. Daddy Jacques is an honest man and very attached to me.

"Q. You affirm, Monsieur Stangerson, that Daddy Jacques remained with you all the time you were in the laboratory?

"M. Stangerson. I am sure of it. I have no doubt of that.

"Q. When you entered your chamber, mademoiselle, you immediately shut the door and locked and bolted it? That was taking unusual precautions, knowing that your father and your servant were there? Were you in fear of something, then?

"A. My father would be returning to the château and Daddy Jacques would be going to his bed. And, in fact, I did fear something.

"Q. You were so much in fear of something that you borrowed Daddy Jacques's revolver without telling him you had done so?

"A. That is true. I did not wish to alarm anybody,—the more, because my fears might have proved to have been foolish.

"Q. What was it you feared?

"A. I hardly know how to tell you. For several nights, I seemed to hear, both in the park and out of the park, round the pavilion, unusual sounds, sometimes footsteps, at other times the cracking of branches. The night before the attack on me, when I did not get to bed before three o'clock in the morning, on our return from the Elysee, I stood for a moment before my window, and I felt sure I saw shadows.

"Q. How many?

"A. Two. They moved round the lake,—then the moon became clouded and I lost sight of them. At this time of the season, every year, I have generally returned to my apartment in the château for the winter; but this year I said to myself that I would not quit the pavilion before my father had finished the resume of his works on the 'Dissociation of Matter' for the Academy. I did not wish that that important work, which was to have been finished in the course of a few days, should be delayed by a change in our daily habit. You can well understand that I did not wish to speak of my childish fears to my father, nor did I say anything to Daddy Jacques who, I knew, would not have been able to hold his tongue. Knowing that he had a revolver in his room, I took advantage of his absence and borrowed it, placing it in the drawer of my night-table.

"Q. You know of no enemies you have?

"A. None.

"Q. You understand, mademoiselle, that these precautions are calculated to cause surprise?

"M. Stangerson. Evidently, my child, such precautions are very surprising.

"A. No;—because I have told you that I had been uneasy for two nights.

"M. Stangerson. You ought to have told me of that! This misfortune would have been avoided.

"Q. The door of 'The Yellow Room' locked, did you go to bed?

"A. Yes, and, being very tired, I at once went to sleep.

"Q. The night-light was still burning?

"A. Yes, but it gave a very feeble light.

"Q. Then, mademoiselle, tell us what happened.

"A. I do not know whether I had been long asleep, but suddenly I awoke—and uttered a loud cry.

"M. Stangerson. Yes—a horrible cry—'Murder!'—It still rings in my ears.

"Q. You uttered a loud cry?

"A. A man was in my chamber. He sprang at me and tried to strangle me. I was nearly stifled when suddenly I was able to reach the drawer of my night-table and grasp the revolver which I had placed in it. At that moment the man had forced me to the foot of my bed and brandished in over my head a sort of mace. But I had fired. He immediately struck a terrible blow at my head. All that, monsieur, passed more rapidly than I can tell it, and I know nothing more.

"Q. Nothing?—Have you no idea as to how the assassin could escape from your chamber?

"A. None whatever—I know nothing more. One does not know what is passing around one, when one is unconscious.

"Q. Was the man you saw tall or short, little or big?

"A. I only saw a shadow which appeared to me formidable.

"Q. You cannot give us any indication?

"A. I know nothing more, monsieur, than that a man threw himself upon me and that I fired at him. I know nothing more."

Here the interrogation of Mademoiselle Stangerson concluded.

Rouletabille waited patiently for Monsieur Robert Darzac, who soon appeared.

From a room near the chamber of Mademoiselle Stangerson, he had heard the interrogatory and now came to recount it to my friend with great exactitude, aided by an excellent memory. His docility still surprised me. Thanks to hasty pencil-notes, he was able to reproduce, almost textually, the questions and the answers given.

It looked as if Monsieur Darzac were being employed as the secretary of my young friend and acted as if he could refuse him nothing; nay, more, as if under a compulsion to do so.

The fact of the closed window struck the reporter as it had struck the magistrate. Rouletabille asked Darzac to repeat once more Mademoiselle Stangerson's account of how she and her father had spent their time on the day of the tragedy, as she had stated it to the magistrate. The circumstance of the dinner in the laboratory seemed to interest him in the highest degree; and he had it repeated to him three times. He also wanted to be sure that the forest-keeper knew that the professor and his daughter were going to dine in the laboratory, and how he had come to know it.

When Monsieur Darzac had finished, I said: "The examination has not advanced the problem much."

"It has put it back," said Monsieur Darzac.

"It has thrown light upon it," said Rouletabille, thoughtfully.

# IX

## REPORTER AND DETECTIVE

The three of us went back towards the pavilion. At some distance from the building the reporter made us stop and, pointing to a small clump of trees to the right of us, said:

"That's where the murderer came from to get into the pavilion."

As there were other patches of trees of the same sort between the great oaks, I asked why the murderer had chosen that one, rather than any of the others. Rouletabille answered me by pointing to the path which ran quite close to the thicket to the door of the pavilion.

"That path is as you see, topped with gravel," he said; "the man must have passed along it going to the pavilion, since no traces of his steps have been found on the soft ground. The man didn't have wings; he walked; but he walked on the gravel which left no impression of his tread. The gravel has, in fact, been trodden by many other feet, since the path is the most direct way between the pavilion and the chateau. As to the thicket, made of the sort of shrubs that don't flourish in the rough season—laurels and fuchsias—it offered the murderer a sufficient hiding-place until it was time for him to make his way to the pavilion. It was while hiding in that clump of trees that he saw Monsieur and Mademoiselle Stangerson, and then Daddy Jacques, leave the pavilion. Gravel has been spread nearly, very nearly, up to the windows of the pavilion. The footprints of a man, parallel with the wall—marks which we will examine presently, and which I have already seen—prove that he only needed to make one stride to find himself in front of the vestibule window, left open by Daddy Jacques. The man drew himself up by his hands and entered the vestibule."

"After all it is very possible," I said.

"After all what? After all what?" cried Rouletabille.

I begged of him not to be angry; but he was too much irritated to listen to me and declared, ironically, that he admired the prudent doubt with which certain people approached the most simple problems, risking nothing by saying "that is so, or that is not so." Their intelligence would have produced about the same result if nature had forgotten to furnish their brain-pan with a little grey matter. As I appeared vexed, my young friend took me by the arm and admitted that he had not meant that for me; he thought more of me than that.

"If I did not reason as I do in regard to this gravel," he went on, "I should have to assume a balloon!—My dear fellow, the science of the aerostation of dirigible balloons is not yet developed enough for me to consider it and suppose that a murderer would drop from the clouds! So don't say a thing is possible, when it could not be otherwise. We know now how the man entered by the window, and we also know the moment at which he entered,—during the five o'clock walk of the professor and his daughter. The fact of the presence of the chambermaid—who had come to clean up 'The Yellow Room'—in the laboratory, when Monsieur Stangerson and his daughter returned from their walk, at half-past one, permits us to affirm that at half-past one the murderer was not in the chamber under the bed, unless he was in collusion with the chambermaid. What do you say, Monsieur Darzac?"

Monsieur Darzac shook his head and said he was sure of the chambermaid's fidelity, and that she was a thoroughly honest and devoted servant.

"Besides," he added, "at five o'clock Monsieur Stangerson went into the room to fetch his daughter's hat."

"There is that also," said Rouletabille.

"That the man entered by the window at the time you say, I admit," I said; "but why did he shut the window? It was an act which would necessarily draw the attention of those who had left it open."

"It may be the window was not shut at once," replied the young reporter. "But if he did shut the window, it was because of the bend in the gravel path, a dozen yards from the pavilion, and on account of the three oaks that are growing at that spot."

"What do you mean by that?" asked Monsieur Darzac, who had followed us and listened with almost breathless attention to all that Rouletabille had said.

"I'll explain all to you later on, Monsieur, when I think the moment to be ripe for doing so; but I don't think I have anything of more importance to say on this affair, if my hypothesis is justified."

"And what is your hypothesis?"

"You will never know if it does not turn out to be the truth. It is of much too grave a nature to speak of it, so long as it continues to be only a hypothesis."

"Have you, at least, some idea as to who the murderer is?"

"No, monsieur, I don't know who the murderer is; but don't be afraid, Monsieur Robert Darzac—I shall know."

I could not but observe that Monsieur Darzac was deeply moved; and I suspected that Rouletabille's confident assertion was not pleasing to him. Why, I asked myself, if he was really afraid that the murderer should be discovered, was he helping the reporter to find him? My young friend seemed to have received the same impression, for he said, bluntly:

"Monsieur Darzac, don't you want me to find out who the murderer was?"

"Oh!—I should like to kill him with my own hand!" cried Mademoiselle Stangerson's fiance, with a vehemence that amazed me.

"I believe you," said Rouletabille gravely; "but you have not answered my question."

We were passing by the thicket, of which the young reporter had spoken to us a minute before. I entered it and pointed out evident traces of a man who had been hidden there. Rouletabille, once more, was right.

"Yes, yes!" he said. "We have to do with a thing of flesh and blood, who uses the same means that we do. It'll all come out on those lines."

Having said this, he asked me for the paper pattern of the footprint which he had given me to take care of, and applied it to a very clear footmark behind the thicket. "Aha!" he said, rising.

I thought he was now going to trace back the track of the murderer's footmarks to the vestibule window; but he led us instead, far to the left, saying that it was useless ferreting in the mud, and that he was sure, now, of the road taken by the murderer.

"He went along the wall to the hedge and dry ditch, over which he jumped. See, just in front of the little path leading to the lake, that was his nearest way to get out."

"How do you know he went to the lake?"—

"Because Frederic Larsan has not quitted the borders of it since this morning. There must be some important marks there."

A few minutes later we reached the lake.

It was a little sheet of marshy water, surrounded by reeds, on which floated some dead water-lily leaves. The great Fred may have seen us approaching, but we probably interested him very little, for he took hardly any notice of us and continued to be stirring with his cane something which we could not see.

"Look!" said Rouletabille, "Here again are the footmarks of the escaping man; they skirt the lake here and finally disappear just before this path, which leads to the high road to Epinay. The man continued his flight to Paris."

"What makes you think that?" I asked, "Since these footmarks are not continued on the path?"

"What makes me think that?—Why these footprints, which I expected to find!" he cried, pointing to the sharply outlined imprint of a neat boot. "See!"—and he called to Frederic Larsan.

"Monsieur Fred, these neat footprints seem to have been made since the discovery of the crime."

"Yes, young man, yes, they have been carefully made," replied Fred without raising his head. "You see, there are steps that come, and steps that go back."

"And the man had a bicycle!" cried the reporter.

Here, after looking at the marks of the bicycle, which followed, going and coming, the neat footprints, I thought I might intervene.

"The bicycle explains the disappearance of the murderer's big footprints," I said. "The murderer, with his rough boots, mounted a bicycle. His accomplice, the wearer of the neat boots, had come to wait for him on the edge of the lake with the bicycle. It might be supposed that the murderer was working for the other."

"No, no!" replied Rouletabille with a strange smile. "I have expected to find these footmarks from the very beginning. These are not the footmarks of the murderer!"

"Then there were two?"

"No—there was but one, and he had no accomplice."

"Very good!—Very good!" cried Frederic Larsan.

"Look!" continued the young reporter, showing us the ground where it had been disturbed by big and heavy heels; "The man seated himself there, and took off his hobnailed boots, which he had worn only for the purpose of misleading detection, and then no doubt, taking them away with him, he stood up in his own boots, and quietly and slowly regained the high road, holding his bicycle in his hand, for he could not venture to ride it on this rough path. That accounts for the lightness of the impression made by the wheels along it, in spite of the softness of the ground. If there had been a man on the bicycle, the wheels would have sunk deeply into the soil. No, no; there was but one man there, the murderer on foot."

"Bravo!—bravo!" cried Fred again, and coming suddenly towards us and, planting himself in front of Monsieur Robert Darzac, he said to him:

"If we had a bicycle here, we might demonstrate the correctness of the young man's reasoning, Monsieur Robert Darzac. Do you know whether there is one at the château?"

"No!" replied Monsieur Darzac. "There is not. I took mine, four days ago, to Paris, the last time I came to the château before the crime."

"That's a pity!" replied Fred, very coldly. Then, turning to Rouletabille, he said: "If we go on at this rate, we'll both come to the same conclusion. Have you any idea, as to how the murderer got away from 'The Yellow Room'?"

"Yes," said my young friend; "I have an idea."

"So have I," said Fred, "and it must be the same as yours. There are no two ways of reasoning in this affair. I am waiting for the arrival of my chief before offering any explanation to the examining magistrate."

"Ah! Is the Chief of the Surete coming?"

"Yes, this afternoon. He is going to summon, before the magistrate, in the laboratory, all those who have played any part in this tragedy. It will be very interesting. It is a pity you won't be able to be present."

"I shall be present," said Rouletabille confidently.

"Really—you are an extraordinary fellow—for your age!" replied the detective in a tone not wholly free from irony. "You'd make a wonderful detective—if you had a little more method—if you didn't follow your instincts and that bump on your forehead. As I have already several times observed, Monsieur Rouletabille, you reason too much; you do not allow yourself to be guided by what you have seen. What do you say to the handkerchief full of blood, and the red mark of the hand on the wall? You have seen the stain on the wall, but I have only seen the handkerchief."

"Bah!" cried Rouletabille, "The murderer was wounded in the hand by Mademoiselle Stangerson's revolver!"

"Ah!—a simply instinctive observation! Take care!—You are becoming too strictly logical, Monsieur Rouletabille; logic will upset you if you use it indiscriminately. You are right, when you say that Mademoiselle Stangerson fired her revolver, but you are wrong when you say that she wounded the murderer in the hand."

"I am sure of it," cried Rouletabille.

Fred, imperturbable, interrupted him:

"Defective observation—defective observation!—the examination of the handkerchief, the numberless little round scarlet stains, the impression of drops which I found in the tracks of the footprints, at the moment when they were made on the floor, prove to me that the murderer was not wounded at all. Monsieur Rouletabille, the murderer bled at the nose!"

The great Fred spoke quite seriously. However, I could not refrain from uttering an exclamation.

The reporter looked gravely at Fred, who looked gravely at him. And Fred immediately concluded:

"The man allowed the blood to flow into his hand and handkerchief, and dried his hand on the wall. The fact is highly important," he added, "because there is no need of his being wounded in the hand for him to be the murderer."

Rouletabille seemed to be thinking deeply. After a moment he said:

"There is something—a something, Monsieur Frederic Larsan, much graver than the misuse of logic the disposition of mind in some detectives which makes them, in perfect good faith, twist logic to the necessities of their preconceived ideas. You, already, have your idea about the murderer, Monsieur Fred. Don't deny it; and your theory demands that the murderer should not have been wounded in the hand, otherwise it comes to nothing. And you have searched, and have found something else. It's dangerous, very dangerous, Monsieur Fred, to go from a preconceived idea to find the proofs to fit it. That method may lead you far astray. Beware of judicial error, Monsieur Fred, it will trip you up!"

And laughing a little, in a slightly bantering tone, his hands in his pockets, Rouletabille fixed his cunning eyes on the great Fred.

Frederic Larsan silently contemplated the young reporter who pretended to be as wise as himself. Shrugging his shoulders, he bowed to us and moved quickly away, hitting the stones on his path with his stout cane.

Rouletabille watched his retreat, and then turned toward us, his face joyous and triumphant.

"I shall beat him!" he cried. "I shall beat the great Fred, clever as he is; I shall beat them all!"

And he danced a double shuffle. Suddenly he stopped. My eyes followed his gaze; they were fixed on Monsieur Robert Darzac, who was looking anxiously at the impression left by his feet side by side with the elegant footmarks. There was not a particle of difference between them!

We thought he was about to faint. His eyes, bulging with terror, avoided us, while his right hand, with a spasmodic movement, twitched at the beard that covered his honest, gentle, and now despairing face. At length regaining his self-possession, he bowed to us, and remarking, in a changed voice, that he was obliged to return to the château, left us.

"The deuce!" exclaimed Rouletabille.

He, also, appeared to be deeply concerned. From his pocket-book he took a piece of white paper as I had seen him do before, and with his scissors, cut out the shape of the neat bootmarks that were on the ground. Then he fitted the new paper pattern with the one he had previously made—the two were exactly alike. Rising, Rouletabille exclaimed again: "The deuce!" Presently he added: "Yet I believe Monsieur Robert Darzac to be an honest man." He then led me on the road to the Donjon Inn, which we could see on the highway, by the side of a small clump of trees.

# X

## "WE SHALL HAVE TO EAT RED MEAT—NOW"

The Donjon Inn was of no imposing appearance; but I like these buildings with their rafters blackened with age and the smoke of their hearths—these inns of the coaching-days, crumbling erections that will soon exist in the memory only. They belong to the bygone days, they are linked with history. They make us think of the Road, of those days when highwaymen rode.

I saw at once that the Donjon Inn was at least two centuries old—perhaps older. Under its sign-board, over the threshold, a man with a crabbed-looking face was standing, seemingly plunged in unpleasant thought, if the wrinkles on his forehead and the knitting of his brows were any indication.

When we were close to him, he deigned to see us and asked us, in a tone anything but engaging, whether we wanted anything. He was, no doubt, the not very amiable landlord of this charming dwelling-place. As we expressed a hope that he would be good enough to furnish us with a breakfast, he assured us that he had no provisions, regarding us, as he said this, with a look that was unmistakably suspicious.

"You may take us in," Rouletabille said to him, "we are not policemen."

"I'm not afraid of the police—I'm not afraid of anyone!" replied the man.

I had made my friend understand by a sign that we should do better not to insist; but, being determined to enter the inn, he slipped by the man on the doorstep and was in the common room.

"Come on," he said, "it is very comfortable here."

A good fire was blazing in the chimney, and we held our hands to the warmth it sent out; it was a morning in which the approach of winter was unmistakable. The room was a tolerably large one, furnished with two heavy tables, some stools, a counter decorated with rows of bottles of syrup and alcohol. Three windows looked out on to the road. A coloured advertisement lauded the many merits of a new vermouth. On the mantelpiece was arrayed the innkeeper's collection of figured earthenware pots and stone jugs.

"That's a fine fire for roasting a chicken," said Rouletabille.

"We have no chicken—not even a wretched rabbit," said the landlord.

"I know," said my friend slowly; "I know—We shall have to eat red meat—now."

I confess I did not in the least understand what Rouletabille meant by what he had said; but the landlord, as soon as he heard the words, uttered an oath, which he at once stifled, and placed himself at our orders as obediently as Monsieur Robert Darzac had done, when he heard Rouletabille's prophetic sentence—"The presbytery has lost nothing of its charm, nor the garden its brightness." Certainly my friend knew how to make people understand him by the use of wholly incomprehensible phrases. I observed as much to him, but he merely smiled. I should have proposed that he give me some explanation; but he put a finger to his lips, which evidently signified that he had not only determined not to speak, but also enjoined silence on my part.

Meantime the man had pushed open a little side door and called to somebody to bring him half a dozen eggs and a piece of beefsteak. The commission was quickly executed by a strongly-built young woman with beautiful blonde hair and large, handsome eyes, who regarded us with curiosity.

The innkeeper said to her roughly:

"Get out!—and if the Green Man comes, don't let me see him."

She disappeared. Rouletabille took the eggs, which had been brought to him in a bowl, and the meat which was on a dish, placed all carefully beside him in the chimney, unhooked a frying-pan and a gridiron, and began to beat up our omelette before proceeding to grill our beefsteak. He then ordered two bottles of cider, and seemed to take as little notice of our host as our host did of him. The landlord let us do our own cooking and set our table near one of the windows.

Suddenly I heard him mutter:

"Ah!—there he is."

His face had changed, expressing fierce hatred. He went and glued himself to one of the windows, watching the road. There was no need for me to draw Rouletabille's attention; he had already left our omelette and had joined the landlord at the window. I went with him.

A man dressed entirely in green velvet, his head covered with a huntsman's cap of the same colour, was advancing leisurely, lighting a pipe as he walked. He carried a fowling-piece slung at his back. His movements displayed an almost aristocratic ease. He wore eyeglasses and appeared to be about five and forty years of age. His hair as well as his moustache were salt grey. He was remarkably handsome. As he passed near the inn, he hesitated, as if asking himself whether or no he should enter it; gave a glance towards us, took a few whiffs at his pipe, and then resumed his walk at the same nonchalant pace.

Rouletabille and I looked at our host. His flashing eyes, his clenched hands, his trembling lips, told us of the tumultuous feelings by which he was being agitated.

"He has done well not to come in here today!" he hissed.

"Who is that man?" asked Rouletabille, returning to his omelette.

"The Green Man," growled the innkeeper. "Don't you know him? Then all the better for you. He is not an acquaintance to make.—Well, he is Monsieur Stangerson's forest-keeper."

"You don't appear to like him very much?" asked the reporter, pouring his omelette into the frying-pan.

"Nobody likes him, monsieur. He's an upstart who must once have had a fortune of his own; and he forgives nobody because, in order to live, he has been compelled to become a servant. A keeper is as much a servant as any other, isn't he? Upon my word, one would say that he is the master of the Glandier, and that all the land and woods belong to him. He'll not let a poor creature eat a morsel of bread on the grass—his grass!"

"Does he often come here?"

"Too often. But I've made him understand that his face doesn't please me, and, for a month past, he hasn't been here. The Donjon Inn has never existed for him!—he hasn't had time!—been too much engaged in paying court to the landlady of the Three Lilies at Saint-Michel. A bad fellow!—There isn't an honest man who can bear him. Why, the concierges of the chateau would turn their eyes away from a picture of him!"

"The concierges of the chateau are honest people, then?"

"Yes, they are, as true as my name's Mathieu, monsieur. I believe them to be honest."

"Yet they've been arrested?"

"What does that prove?—But I don't want to mix myself up in other people's affairs."

"And what do you think of the murder?"

"Of the murder of poor Mademoiselle Stangerson?—A good girl much loved everywhere in the country. That's what I think of it—and many things besides; but that's nobody's business."

"Not even mine?" insisted Rouletabille.

The innkeeper looked at him sideways and said gruffly:

"Not even yours."

The omelette ready, we sat down at table and were silently eating, when the door was pushed open and an old woman, dressed in rags, leaning on a stick, her head doddering, her white hair hanging loosely over her wrinkled forehead, appeared on the threshold.

"Ah!—there you are, Mother Angenoux!—It's long since we saw you last," said our host.

"I have been very ill, very nearly dying," said the old woman. "If ever you should have any scraps for the Bete du Bon Dieu—?"

And she entered, followed by a cat, larger than any I had ever believed could exist. The beast looked at us and gave so hopeless a miau that I shuddered. I had never heard so lugubrious a cry.

As if drawn by the cat's cry a man followed the old woman in. It was the Green Man. He saluted by raising his hand to his cap and seated himself at a table near to ours.

"A glass of cider, Daddy Mathieu," he said.

As the Green Man entered, Daddy Mathieu had started violently; but visibly mastering himself he said:

"I've no more cider; I served the last bottles to these gentlemen."

"Then give me a glass of white wine," said the Green Man, without showing the least surprise.

"I've no more white wine—no more anything," said Daddy Mathieu, surlily.

"How is Madame Mathieu?"

"Quite well, thank you."

So the young woman with the large, tender eyes, whom we had just seen, was the wife of this repugnant and brutal rustic, whose jealousy seemed to emphasise his physical ugliness.

Slamming the door behind him, the innkeeper left the room. Mother Angenoux was still standing, leaning on her stick, the cat at her feet.

"You've been ill, Mother Angenoux?—Is that why we have not seen you for the last week?" asked the Green Man.

"Yes, Monsieur keeper. I have been able to get up but three times, to go to pray to Sainte-Genevieve, our good patroness, and the rest of the time I have been lying on my bed. There was no one to care for me but the Bete du bon Dieu!"

"Did she not leave you?"

"Neither by day nor by night."

"Are you sure of that?"

"As I am of Paradise."

"Then how was it, Madame Angenoux, that all through the night of the murder nothing but the cry of the Bete du bon Dieu was heard?"

Mother Angenoux planted herself in front of the forest-keeper and struck the floor with her stick.

"I don't know anything about it," she said. "But shall I tell you something? There are no two cats in the world that cry like that. Well, on the night of the murder I also heard the cry of the Bete du bon Dieu outside; and yet she was on my knees, and did not mew once, I swear. I crossed myself when I heard that, as if I had heard the devil."

I looked at the keeper when he put the last question, and I am much mistaken if I did not detect an evil smile on his lips. At that moment, the noise of loud quarrelling reached us. We even thought we heard a dull sound of blows, as if someone was being beaten. The Green Man quickly rose and hurried to the door by the side of the fireplace; but it was opened by the landlord who appeared, and said to the keeper:

"Don't alarm yourself, Monsieur—it is my wife; she has the toothache." And he laughed. "Here, Mother Angenoux, here are some scraps for your cat."

He held out a packet to the old woman, who took it eagerly and went out by the door, closely followed by her cat.

"Then you won't serve me?" asked the Green Man.

Daddy Mathieu's face was placid and no longer retained its expression of hatred.

"I've nothing for you—nothing for you. Take yourself off."

The Green Man quietly refilled his pipe, lit it, bowed to us, and went out. No sooner was he over the threshold than Daddy Mathieu slammed the door after him and, turning towards us, with eyes bloodshot, and frothing at the mouth, he hissed to us, shaking his clenched fist at the door he had just shut on the man he evidently hated:

"I don't know who you are who tell me 'We shall have to eat red meat—now'; but if it will interest you to know it—that man is the murderer!"

With which words Daddy Mathieu immediately left us. Rouletabille returned towards the fireplace and said:

"Now we'll grill our steak. How do you like the cider?—It's a little tart, but I like it."

We saw no more of Daddy Mathieu that day, and absolute silence reigned in the inn when we left it, after placing five francs on the table in payment for our feast.

Rouletabille at once set off on a three mile walk round Professor Stangerson's estate. He halted for some ten minutes at the corner of a narrow road black with soot, near to some charcoal-burners' huts in the forest of Sainte-Genevieve, which touches on the road from Epinay to Corbeil, to tell me that the murderer had certainly passed that way, before entering the grounds and concealing himself in the little clump of trees.

"You don't think, then, that the keeper knows anything of it?" I asked.

"We shall see that, later," he replied. "For the present I'm not interested in what the landlord said about the man. The landlord hates him. I didn't take you to breakfast at the Donjon Inn for the sake of the Green Man."

Then Rouletabille, with great precaution glided, followed by me, towards the little building which, standing near the park gate, served for the home of the concierges, who had been arrested that morning. With the skill of an acrobat, he got into the lodge by an upper window which had been left open, and returned ten minutes later. He said only, "Ah!"—a word which, in his mouth, signified many things.

We were about to take the road leading to the château, when a considerable stir at the park gate attracted our attention. A carriage had arrived and some people had come from the château to meet it. Rouletabille pointed out to me a gentleman who descended from it.

"That's the Chief of the Surete" he said. "Now we shall see what Frederic Larsan has up his sleeve, and whether he is so much cleverer than anybody else."

The carriage of the Chief of the Surete was followed by three other vehicles containing reporters, who were also desirous of entering the park. But two gendarmes stationed at the gate had evidently received orders to refuse admission to anybody. The Chief of the Surete calmed their impatience by undertaking to furnish to the press, that evening, all the information he could give that would not interfere with the judicial inquiry.

# XI

## IN WHICH FREDERIC LARSAN EXPLAINS HOW THE MURDERER WAS ABLE TO GET OUT OF "THE YELLOW ROOM"

Among the mass of papers, legal documents, memoirs, and extracts from newspapers, which I have collected, relating to the mystery of "The Yellow Room", there is one very interesting piece; it is a detail of the famous examination which took place that afternoon, in the laboratory of Professor Stangerson, before the Chief of the Surete. This narrative is from the pen of Monsieur Maleine, the Registrar, who, like the examining magistrate, had spent some of his leisure time in the pursuit of literature. The piece was to have made part of a book which, however, has never been published, and which was to have been entitled: "My Examinations." It was given to me by the Registrar himself, some time after the astonishing denouement to this case, and is unique in judicial chronicles.

Here it is. It is not a mere dry transcription of questions and answers, because the Registrar often intersperses his story with his own personal comments.

*THE REGISTRAR'S NARRATIVE*

The examining magistrate and I (the writer relates) found

ourselves in "The Yellow Room" in the company of the builder who had constructed the pavilion after Professor Stangerson's designs. He had a workman with him. Monsieur de Marquet had had the walls laid entirely bare; that is to say, he had had them stripped of the paper which had decorated them. Blows with a pick, here and there, satisfied us of the absence of any sort of opening. The floor and the ceiling were thoroughly sounded. We found nothing. There was nothing to be found. Monsieur de Marquet appeared to be delighted and never ceased repeating:

"What a case! What a case! We shall never know, you'll see, how the murderer was able to get out of this room!"

Then suddenly, with a radiant face, he called to the officer in charge of the gendarmes.

"Go to the château," he said, "and request Monsieur Stangerson and Monsieur Robert Darzac to come to me in the laboratory, also Daddy Jacques; and let your men bring here the two concierges."

Five minutes later all were assembled in the laboratory. The Chief of the Surete, who had arrived at the Glandier, joined us at that moment. I was seated at Monsieur Stangerson's desk ready for work, when Monsieur de Marquet made us the following little speech—as original as it was unexpected:

"With your permission, gentlemen—as examinations lead to nothing—we will, for once, abandon the old system of interrogation. I will not have you brought before me one by one, but we will all remain here as we are,—Monsieur Stangerson, Monsieur Robert Darzac, Daddy Jacques and the two concierges, the Chief of the Surete, the Registrar, and myself. We shall all be on the same footing. The concierges may, for the moment, forget that they have been arrested. We are going to confer together. We are on the spot where the crime was committed. We have nothing else to discuss but the crime. So let us discuss it freely—intelligently or otherwise, so long as we speak just what is in our minds. There need be no formality or method since this won't help us in any way."

Then, passing before me, he said in a low voice:

"What do you think of that, eh? What a scene! Could you have thought of that? I'll make a little piece out of it for the Vaudeville." And he rubbed his hands with glee.

I turned my eyes on Monsieur Stangerson. The hope he had received from the doctor's latest reports, which stated that Mademoiselle Stangerson might recover from her wounds, had not been able to efface from his noble features the marks of the great sorrow that was upon him. He had believed his daughter to be dead, and he was still broken by that belief. His clear, soft, blue eyes expressed infinite sorrow. I had had occasion, many times, to see Monsieur Stangerson at public ceremonies, and from the first had been struck by his countenance, which seemed as pure as that of a child—the dreamy gaze with the sublime and mystical expression of the inventor and thinker.

On those occasions his daughter was always to be seen either following him or by his side; for they never quitted each other, it was said, and had shared the same labours for many years. The young lady, who was then five and thirty, though she looked no more than thirty, had devoted herself entirely to science. She still won admiration for her imperial beauty which had remained intact, without a wrinkle, withstanding time and love. Who would have dreamed that I should one day be seated by her pillow with my papers, and that I should see her, on the point of death, painfully recounting to us the most monstrous and most mysterious crime I have heard of in my career? Who would have thought that I should be, that afternoon, listening to the despairing father vainly trying to explain how his daughter's assailant had been able to escape from him? Why bury ourselves with our work in obscure retreats in the depths of woods, if it may not protect us against those dangerous threats to life which meet us in the busy cities?

"Now, Monsieur Stangerson," said Monsieur de Marquet, with somewhat of an important air, "place yourself exactly where you were when Mademoiselle Stangerson left you to go to her chamber."

Monsieur Stangerson rose and, standing at a certain distance from the door of "The Yellow Room", said, in an even voice and without the least trace of emphasis—a voice which I can only describe as a dead voice:

"I was here. About eleven o'clock, after I had made a brief chemical experiment at the furnaces of the laboratory, needing all the space behind me, I had my desk moved here by Daddy Jacques, who spent the evening in cleaning some of my apparatus. My daughter had been working at the same desk with me. When it was her time to leave she rose, kissed me, and bade Daddy Jacques good-night. She had to pass behind my desk and the door to enter her chamber, and she could do this only with some difficulty. That is to say, I was very near the place where the crime occurred later."

"And the desk?" I asked, obeying, in thus mixing myself in the conversation, the express orders of my chief, "as soon as you heard the cry of 'murder' followed by the revolver shots, what became of the desk?"

Daddy Jacques answered.

"We pushed it back against the wall, here—close to where it is at the present moment—so as to be able to get at the door at once."

I followed up my reasoning, to which, however, I attached but little importance, regarding it as only a weak hypothesis, with another question.

"Might not a man in the room, the desk being so near to the door, by stooping and slipping under the desk, have left it unobserved?"

"You are forgetting," interrupted Monsieur Stangerson wearily, "that my daughter had locked and bolted her door, that the door had remained fastened, that we vainly tried to force it open when we heard the noise, and that we were at the door while the struggle between the murderer and my poor child was going on—immediately after we heard her stifled cries as she was being held by the fingers that have left their red mark upon her throat. Rapid as the attack was, we were no less rapid in our endeavours to get into the room where the tragedy was taking place."

I rose from my seat and once more examined the door with the greatest care. Then I returned to my place with a despairing gesture.

"If the lower panel of the door," I said, "could be removed without the whole door being necessarily opened, the problem would be solved. But, unfortunately, that last hypothesis is untenable after an examination of the door—it's of oak, solid and massive. You can see that quite plainly, in spite of the injury done in the attempt to burst it open."

"Ah!" cried Daddy Jacques, "It is an old and solid door that was brought from the château—they don't make such doors now. We had to use this bar of iron to get it open, all four of us—for the concierge, brave woman she is, helped us. It pains me to find them both in prison now."

Daddy Jacques had no sooner uttered these words of pity and protestation than tears and lamentations broke out from the concierges. I never saw two accused people crying more bitterly. I was extremely disgusted. Even if they were innocent, I could not understand how they could behave like that in the face of misfortune. A dignified bearing at such times is better than tears and groans, which, most often, are feigned.

"Now then, enough of that snivelling," cried Monsieur de Marquet; "and, in your interest, tell us what you were doing under the windows of the pavilion at the time your mistress was being attacked; for you were close to the pavilion when Daddy Jacques met you."

"We were coming to help!" they whined.

"If we could only lay hands on the murderer, he'd never taste bread again!" the woman gurgled between her sobs.

As before we were unable to get two connecting thoughts out of them. They persisted in their denials and swore, by heaven and all the saints, that they were in bed when they heard the sound of the revolver shot.

"It was not one, but two shots that were fired!—You see, you are lying. If you had heard one, you would have heard the other."

"Mon Dieu! Monsieur—it was the second shot we heard. We were asleep when the first shot was fired."

"Two shots were fired," said Daddy Jacques. "I am certain that all the cartridges were in my revolver. We found afterward that two had been exploded, and we heard two shots behind the door. Was not that so, Monsieur Stangerson?"

"Yes," replied the Professor, "there were two shots, one dull, and the other sharp and ringing."

"Why do you persist in lying?" cried Monsieur de Marquet, turning to the concierges. "Do you think the police are the fools you are? Everything points to the fact that you were out of doors and near the pavilion at the time of the tragedy. What were you doing there? So far as I am concerned," he said, turning to Monsieur Stangerson, "I can only explain the escape of the murderer on the assumption of help from these two accomplices. As soon as the door was forced open, and while you, Monsieur Stangerson, were occupied with your unfortunate child, the concierge and his wife facilitated the flight of the murderer, who, screening himself behind them, reached the window in the vestibule, and sprang out of it into the park. The concierge closed the window after him and fastened the blinds, which certainly could not have closed and fastened of themselves. That is the conclusion I have arrived at. If anyone here has any other idea, let him state it."

Monsieur Stangerson intervened:

"What you say was impossible. I do not believe either in the guilt or in the connivance of my concierges, though I cannot understand what they were doing in the park at that late hour of the night. I say it was impossible, because Madame Bernier held the lamp and did not move from the threshold of the room; because I, as soon as the door was forced open, threw myself on my knees beside my daughter, and no one could have left or entered the room by the door, without passing over her body and forcing his way by me! Daddy Jacques and the concierge had but to cast a glance round the chamber and under the bed, as I had done on entering, to see that there was nobody in it but my daughter lying on the floor."

"What do you think, Monsieur Darzac?" asked the magistrate.

Monsieur Darzac replied that he had no opinion to express. Monsieur Dax, the Chief of the Surete who, so far, had been listening and examining the room, at length deigned to open his lips:

"While search is being made for the criminal, we had better try to find out the motive for the crime; that will advance us a little," he said. Turning towards Monsieur Stangerson, he continued, in the even, intelligent tone indicative of a strong character, "I understand that Mademoiselle was shortly to have been married?"

The professor looked sadly at Monsieur Robert Darzac.

"To my friend here, whom I should have been happy to call my son—to Monsieur Robert Darzac."

"Mademoiselle Stangerson is much better and is rapidly recovering from her wounds. The marriage is simply delayed, is it not, Monsieur?" insisted the Chief of the Surete.

"I hope so.

"What! Is there any doubt about that?"

Monsieur Stangerson did not answer. Monsieur Robert Darzac seemed agitated. I saw that his hand trembled as it fingered his watch-chain. Monsieur Dax coughed, as did Monsieur de Marquet. Both were evidently embarrassed.

"You understand, Monsieur Stangerson," he said, "that in an affair so perplexing as this, we cannot neglect anything; we must know all, even the smallest and seemingly most futile thing concerning the victim—information apparently the most insignificant. Why do you doubt that this marriage will take place? You expressed a hope; but the hope implies a doubt. Why do you doubt?"

Monsieur Stangerson made a visible effort to recover himself.

"Yes, Monsieur," he said at length, "you are right. It will be best that you should know something which, if I concealed it, might appear to be of importance; Monsieur Darzac agrees with me in this."

Monsieur Darzac, whose pallor at that moment seemed to me to be altogether abnormal, made a sign of assent. I gathered he was unable to speak.

"I want you to know then," continued Monsieur Stangerson, "that my daughter has sworn never to leave me, and adheres firmly to her oath, in spite of all my prayers and all that I have argued to induce her to marry. We have known Monsieur Robert Darzac many years. He loves my child; and I believed that she loved him; because she only recently consented to this marriage which I desire with all my heart. I am an old man, Monsieur, and it was a happy hour to me when I knew that, after I had gone, she would have at her side, one who loved her and who would help her in continuing our common labours. I love and esteem Monsieur Darzac both for his greatness of heart and for his devotion to science. But, two days before the tragedy, for I know not what reason, my daughter declared to me that she would never marry Monsieur Darzac."

A dead silence followed Monsieur Stangerson's words. It was a moment fraught with suspense.

"Did Mademoiselle give you any explanation,—did she tell you what her motive was?" asked Monsieur Dax.

"She told me she was too old to marry—that she had waited too long. She said she had given much thought to the matter and while she had a great esteem, even affection, for Monsieur Darzac, she felt it would be better if things remained as they were. She would be happy, she said, to see the relations between ourselves and Monsieur Darzac become closer, but only on the understanding that there would be no more talk of marriage."

"That is very strange!" muttered Monsieur Dax.

"Strange!" repeated Monsieur de Marquet.

"You'll certainly not find the motive there, Monsieur Dax," Monsieur Stangerson said with a cold smile.

"In any case, the motive was not theft!" said the Chief impatiently.

"Oh! we are quite convinced of that!" cried the examining magistrate.

At that moment the door of the laboratory opened and the officer in charge of the gendarmes entered and handed a card to the examining magistrate. Monsieur de Marquet read it and uttered a half angry exclamation:

"This is really too much!" he cried.

"What is it?" asked the Chief.

"It's the card of a young reporter engaged on the 'Epoque,' a Monsieur Joseph Rouletabille. It has these words written on it: 'One of the motives of the crime was robbery.'"

The Chief smiled.

"Ah,—young Rouletabille—I've heard of him he is considered rather clever. Let him come in."

Monsieur Joseph Rouletabille was allowed to enter. I had made his acquaintance in the train that morning on the way to Epinay-sur-Orge. He had introduced himself almost against my wish into our compartment. I had better say at once that his manners, and the arrogance with which he assumed to know what was incomprehensible even to us, impressed him unfavourably on my mind. I do not like journalists. They are a class of writers to be avoided as the pest. They think that everything is permissible and they respect nothing. Grant them the least favour, allow them even to approach you, and you never can tell what annoyance they may give you. This one appears to be scarcely twenty years old, and the effrontery with which he dared to question us and discuss the matter with us made him particularly obnoxious to me. Besides, he had a way of expressing himself that left us guessing as to whether he was mocking us or not. I know quite well that the 'Epoque' is an influential paper with which it is well to be on good terms, but the paper ought not to allow itself to be represented by sneaking reporters.

Monsieur Joseph Rouletabille entered the laboratory, bowed to us, and waited for Monsieur de Marquet to ask him to explain his presence.

"You pretend, Monsieur, that you know the motive for the crime, and that that motive—in the face of all the evidence that has been forthcoming—was robbery?"

"No, Monsieur, I do not pretend that. I do not say that robbery was the motive for the crime, and I don't believe it was."

"Then, what is the meaning of this card?"

"It means that robbery was one of the motives for the crime."

"What leads you to think that?"

"If you will be good enough to accompany me, I will show you."

The young man asked us to follow him into the vestibule, and we did. He led us towards the lavatory and begged Monsieur de Marquet to kneel beside him. This lavatory is lit by the glass door, and, when the door was open, the light which penetrated was sufficient to light it perfectly. Monsieur de Marquet and

Monsieur Joseph Rouletabille knelt down on the threshold, and the young man pointed to a spot on the pavement.

"The stones of the lavatory have not been washed by Daddy Jacques for some time," he said; "that can be seen by the layer of dust that covers them. Now, notice here, the marks of two large footprints and the black ash they left where they have been. That ash is nothing else than the charcoal dust that covers the path along which you must pass through the forest, in order to get directly from Epinay to the Glandier. You know there is a little village of charcoal-burners at that place, who make large quantities of charcoal. What the murderer did was to come here at midday, when there was nobody at the pavilion, and attempt his robbery."

"But what robbery?—Where do you see any signs of robbery? What proves to you that a robbery has been committed?" we all cried at once. "What put me on the trace of it," continued the journalist...

"Was this?" interrupted Monsieur de Marquet, still on his knees.

"Evidently," said Rouletabille.

And Monsieur de Marquet explained that there were on the dust of the pavement marks of two footsteps, as well as the impression, freshly-made, of a heavy rectangular parcel, the marks of the cord with which it had been fastened being easily distinguished.

"You have been here, then, Monsieur Rouletabille? I thought I had given orders to Daddy Jacques, who was left in charge of the pavilion, not to allow anybody to enter."

"Don't scold Daddy Jacques, I came here with Monsieur Robert Darzac."

"Ah,—Indeed!" exclaimed Monsieur de Marquet, disagreeably, casting a side-glance at Monsieur Darzac, who remained perfectly silent.

"When I saw the mark of the parcel by the side of the footprints, I had no doubt as to the robbery," replied Monsieur Rouletabille. "The thief had not brought a parcel with him; he had made one here—a parcel with the stolen objects, no doubt; and he put it in this corner intending to take it away when the moment came for him to make his escape. He had also placed his heavy boots beside the parcel,—for, see—there are no marks of steps leading to the marks left by the boots, which were placed side by side. That accounts for the fact that the murderer left no trace of his steps when he fled from 'The Yellow Room', nor any in the laboratory, nor in the vestibule. After entering 'The Yellow Room' in his boots, he took them off, finding them troublesome, or because he wished to make as little noise as possible. The marks made by him in going through the vestibule and the laboratory were subsequently washed out by Daddy Jacques. Having, for some reason or other, taken off his boots, the murderer carried them in his hand and placed them by the side of the parcel he had made,—by that time the robbery had been accomplished. The man then returned to 'The Yellow Room' and slipped under the bed, where the mark of his body is perfectly visible on the floor and even on the mat, which has been slightly moved from its place and creased. Fragments of straw also, recently torn, bear witness to the murderer's movements under the bed."

"Yes, yes,—we know all about that," said Monsieur de Marquet.

"The robber had another motive for returning to hide under the bed," continued the astonishing boy-journalist. "You might think that he was trying to hide himself quickly on seeing, through the vestibule window, Monsieur and Mademoiselle Stangerson about to enter the pavilion. It would have been much easier for him to have climbed up to the attic and hidden there, waiting for an opportunity to get away, if his purpose had been only flight.—No! No!—he had to be in 'The Yellow Room'."

Here the Chief intervened.

"That's not at all bad, young man. I compliment you. If we do not know yet how the murderer succeeded in getting away, we can at any rate see how he came in and committed the robbery. But what did he steal?"

"Something very valuable," replied the young reporter.

At that moment we heard a cry from the laboratory. We rushed in and found Monsieur Stangerson, his eyes haggard, his limbs trembling, pointing to a sort of bookcase which he had opened, and which, we saw, was empty. At the same instant he sank into the large armchair that was placed before the desk and groaned, the tears rolling down his cheeks, "I have been robbed again! For God's sake, do not say a word of this to my daughter. She would be more pained than I am." He heaved a deep sigh and added, in a tone I shall never forget: "After all, what does it matter,—so long as she lives!"

"She will live!" said Monsieur Darzac, in a voice strangely touching.

"And we will find the stolen articles," said Monsieur Dax. "But what was in the cabinet?"

"Twenty years of my life," replied the illustrious professor sadly, "or rather of our lives—the lives of myself and my daughter! Yes, our most precious documents, the records of our secret experiments and our labours of twenty years were in that cabinet. It is an irreparable loss to us and, I venture to say, to science. All the processes by which I had been able to arrive at the precious proof of the destructibility of matter were there—all. The man who came wished to take all from me,—my daughter and my work—my heart and my soul."

And the great scientist wept like a child.

We stood around him in silence, deeply affected by his great distress. Monsieur Darzac pressed closely to his side, and tried in vain to restrain his tears—a sight which, for the moment, almost made me like him, in spite of an instinctive repulsion which his strange demeanour and his inexplicable anxiety had inspired me.

Monsieur Rouletabille alone,—as if his precious time and mission on earth did not permit him to dwell in the contemplation on human suffering—had, very calmly, stepped up to the empty cabinet and, pointing at it, broke the almost solemn silence. He entered into explanations, for which there was no need, as to why he had been led , which included the simultaneous discovery he had made in the lavatory, and the empty precious cabinet in the laboratory. The first thing that had struck him, he said, was the unusual form of that piece of furniture. It was very strongly built of fire-proof iron, clearly showing that it was intended for the keeping of most valuable objects. Then he noticed that the key had been left in the lock. "One does not ordinarily have a safe and leave it open!" he had said to himself. This little key, with its brass head and complicated wards, had strongly attracted him,—its presence had suggested robbery.

Monsieur de Marquet appeared to be greatly perplexed, as if he did not know whether he ought to be glad of the new direction given to the inquiry by the young reporter, or sorry that it had not been done by himself. In our profession and for the general welfare, we have to put up with such mortifications and bury selfish feelings. That was why Monsieur de Marquet controlled himself and joined his compliments with those of Monsieur Dax. As for Monsieur Rouletabille, he simply shrugged his shoulders and said: "There's nothing at all in that!" I should have liked to box his ears, especially when he added: "You will do well, Monsieur, to ask Monsieur Stangerson who usually kept that key?"

"My daughter," replied Monsieur Stangerson, "she was never without it.

"Ah! then that changes the aspect of things which no longer corresponds with Monsieur Rouletabille's ideas!" cried Monsieur de Marquet. "If that key never left Mademoiselle Stangerson, the murderer must have waited for her in her room for the purpose of stealing it; and the robbery could not have been committed until after the attack had been made on her. But after the attack four persons were in the laboratory! I can't make it out!"

"The robbery," said the reporter, "could only have been committed before the attack upon Mademoiselle Stangerson in her room. When the murderer entered the pavilion he already possessed the brass-headed key."

"That is impossible," said Monsieur Stangerson in a low voice.

"It is quite possible, Monsieur, as this proves."

And the young rascal drew a copy of the "Epoque" from his pocket, dated the 21st of October (I recall the fact that the crime was committed on the night between the 24th and 25th), and showing us an advertisement, he read:

"'Yesterday a black satin reticule was lost in the Grands Magasins de la Louvre. It contained, amongst other things, a small key with a brass head. A handsome reward will be given to the person who has found it. This person must write, poste restante, bureau 40, to this address: M. A. T. H. S. N.' Do not these letters suggest Mademoiselle Stangerson?" continued the reporter. "The 'key with a brass head'—is not this the key? I always read advertisements. In my business, as in yours, Monsieur, one should always read the personals.' They are often the keys to intrigues, that are not always brass-headed, but which are none the less interesting. This advertisement interested me specially; the woman of the key surrounded it with a kind of mystery. Evidently she valued the key, since she promised a big reward for its restoration! And I thought on these six letters: M. A. T. H. S. N. The first four at once pointed to a

Christian name; evidently I said Math is Mathilde. But I could make nothing of the two last letters. So I threw the journal aside and occupied myself with other matters. Four days later, when the evening paper appeared with enormous headlines announcing the murder of Mademoiselle Stangerson, the letters in the advertisement mechanically recurred to me. I had forgotten the two last letters, S. N. When I saw them again I could not help exclaiming, 'Stangerson!' I jumped into a cab and rushed into the bureau No. 40, asking: 'Have you a letter addressed to M. A. T. H. S. N.?' The clerk replied that he had not. I insisted, begged and entreated him to search. He wanted to know if I were playing a joke on him, and then told me that he had had a letter with the initials M. A. T. H. S. N, but he had given it up three days ago, to a lady who came for it. 'You come today to claim the letter, and the day before yesterday another gentleman claimed it! I've had enough of this,' he concluded angrily. I tried to question him as to the two persons who had already claimed the letter; but whether he wished to entrench himself behind professional secrecy,—he may have thought that he had already said too much,—or whether he was disgusted at the joke that had been played on him—he would not answer any of my questions."

Rouletabille paused. We all remained silent. Each drew his own conclusions from the strange story of the poste restante letter. It seemed, indeed, that we now had a thread by means of which we should be able to follow up this extraordinary mystery.

"Then it is almost certain," said Monsieur Stangerson, "that my daughter did lose the key, and that she did not tell me of it, wishing to spare any anxiety, and that she begged whoever had found it to write to the poste restante. She evidently feared that, by giving our address, inquiries would have resulted that would have apprised me of the loss of the key. It was quite logical, quite natural for her to have taken that course—for I have been robbed once before."

"Where was that, and when?" asked the Chief of the Surete.

"Oh! many years ago, in America, in Philadelphia. There were stolen from my laboratory the drawings of two inventions that might have made the fortune of a man. Not only have I never learnt who the thief was, but I have never heard even a word of the object of the robbery, doubtless because, in order to defeat the plans of the person who had robbed me, I myself brought these two inventions before the public, and so rendered the robbery of no avail. From that time on I have been very careful to shut myself in when I am at work. The bars to these windows, the lonely situation of this pavilion, this cabinet, which I had specially constructed, this special lock, this unique key, all are precautions against fears inspired by a sad experience."

"Most interesting!" remarked Monsieur Dax.

Monsieur Rouletabille asked about the reticule. Neither Monsieur Stangerson nor Daddy Jacques had seen it for several days, but a few hours later we learned from Mademoiselle Stangerson herself that the reticule had either been stolen from her, or she had lost it. She further corroborated all that had passed just as her father had stated. She had gone to the poste restante and, on the 23rd of October, had received a letter which, she affirmed, contained nothing but a vulgar pleasantry, which she had immediately burned.

To return to our examination, or rather to our conversation. I must state that the Chief of the Surete having inquired of Monsieur Stangerson under what conditions his daughter had gone to Paris on the 20th of October, we learned that Monsieur Robert Darzac had accompanied her, and Darzac had not been again seen at the château from that time to the day after the crime had been committed. The fact that Monsieur Darzac was with her in the Grands Magasins de la Louvre when the reticule disappeared could not pass unnoticed, and, it must be said, strongly awakened our interest.

This conversation between magistrates, accused, victim, witnesses and journalist, was coming to a close when quite a theatrical sensation—an incident of a kind displeasing to Monsieur de Marquet—was produced. The officer of the gendarmes came to announce that Frederic Larsan requested to be admitted,—a request that was at once complied with. He held in his hand a heavy pair of muddy boots, which he threw on the pavement of the laboratory.

"Here," he said, "are the boots worn by the murderer. Do you recognise them, Daddy Jacques?"

Daddy Jacques bent over them and, stupefied, recognised a pair of old boots which he had, some time back, thrown into a corner of his attic. He was so taken aback that he could not hide his agitation.

Then pointing to the handkerchief in the old man's hand, Frederic Larsan said:

"That's a handkerchief astonishingly like the one found in 'The Yellow Room'."

"I know," said Daddy Jacques, trembling, "they are almost alike."

"And then," continued Frederic Larsan, "the old Basque cap also found in 'The Yellow Room' might at one time have been worn by Daddy Jacques himself. All this, gentlemen, proves, I think, that the murderer wished to disguise his real personality. He did it in a very clumsy way—or, at least, so it appears to us. Don't be alarmed, Daddy Jacques; we are quite sure that you were not the murderer; you never left the side of Monsieur Stangerson. But if Monsieur Stangerson had not been working that night and had gone back to the château after parting with his daughter, and Daddy Jacques had gone to sleep in his attic, no one would have doubted that he was the murderer. He owes his safety, therefore, to the tragedy having been enacted too soon,—the murderer, no doubt, from the silence in the laboratory, imagined that it was empty, and that the moment for action had come. The man who had been able to introduce himself here so mysteriously and to leave so many evidences against Daddy Jacques, was, there can be no doubt, familiar with the house. At what hour exactly he entered, whether in the afternoon or in the evening, I cannot say. One familiar with the proceedings and persons of this pavilion could choose his own time for entering 'The Yellow Room'."

"He could not have entered it if anybody had been in the laboratory," said Monsieur de Marquet.

"How do we know that?" replied Larsan. "There was the dinner in the laboratory, the coming and going of the servants in attendance. There was a chemical experiment being carried on between ten and eleven o'clock, with Monsieur Stangerson, his daughter, and Daddy Jacques engaged at the furnace in a corner of the high chimney. Who can say that the murderer—an intimate!—a friend!—did not take advantage of that moment to slip into 'The Yellow Room', after having taken off his boots in the lavatory?"

"It is very improbable," said Monsieur Stangerson.

"Doubtless—but it is not impossible. I assert nothing. As to the escape from the pavilion—that's another thing, the most natural thing in the world."

For a moment Frederic Larsan paused,—a moment that appeared to us a very long time. The eagerness with which we awaited what he was going to tell us may be imagined.

"I have not been in 'The Yellow Room'," he continued, "but I take it for granted that you have satisfied yourselves that he could have left the room only by way of the door; it is by the door, then, that the murderer made his way out. At what time? At the moment when it was most easy for him to do so; at the moment when it became most explainable—so completely explainable that there can be no other explanation. Let us go over the moments which followed after the crime had been committed. There was the first moment, when Monsieur Stangerson and Daddy Jacques were close to the door, ready to bar the way. There was the second moment, during which Daddy Jacques was absent and Monsieur Stangerson was left alone before the door. There was a third moment, when Monsieur Stangerson was joined by the concierge. There was a fourth moment, during which Monsieur Stangerson, the concierge and his wife and Daddy Jacques were before the door. There was a fifth moment, during which the door was burst open and 'The Yellow Room' entered. The moment at which the flight is explainable is the very moment when there was the least number of persons before the door. There was one moment when there was but one person,—Monsieur Stangerson. Unless a complicity of silence on the part of Daddy Jacques is admitted—in which I do not believe—the door was opened in the presence of Monsieur Stangerson alone and the man escaped.

"Here we must admit that Monsieur Stangerson had powerful reasons for not arresting, or not causing the arrest of the murderer, since he allowed him to reach the window in the vestibule and closed it after him!—That done, Mademoiselle Stangerson, though horribly wounded, had still strength enough, and no doubt in obedience to the entreaties of her father, to refasten the door of her chamber, with both the bolt and the lock, before sinking on the floor. We do not know who committed the crime; we do not know of what wretch Monsieur and Mademoiselle Stangerson are the victims, but there is no doubt that they both know! The secret must be a terrible one, for the father had not hesitated to leave his daughter to die behind a door which she had shut upon herself,—terrible for him to have allowed the assassin to escape. For there is no other way in the world to explain the murderer's flight from 'The Yellow Room'!"

The silence which followed this dramatic and lucid explanation was appalling. We all of us felt grieved for the illustrious professor, driven into a corner by the pitiless logic of Frederic Larsan, forced to confess the whole truth of his martyrdom or to keep silent, and thus make a yet more terrible admission. The man himself, a veritable statue of sorrow, raised his hand with a gesture so solemn that we bowed our heads to it as before something sacred. He then pronounced these words, in a voice so loud that it seemed to exhaust him:

"I swear by the head of my suffering child that I never for an instant left the door of her chamber after hearing her cries for help; that that door was not opened while I was alone in the laboratory; and that, finally, when we entered 'The Yellow Room', my three domestics and I, the murderer was no longer there! I swear I do not know the murderer!"

Must I say it,—in spite of the solemnity of Monsieur Stangerson's words, we did not believe in his denial. Frederic Larsan had shown us the truth and it was not so easily given up.

Monsieur de Marquet announced that the conversation was at an end, and as we were about to leave the laboratory, Joseph Rouletabille approached Monsieur Stangerson, took him by the hand with the greatest respect, and I heard him say:

"I believe you, Monsieur."

I here close the citation which I have thought it my duty to make from Monsieur Maleine's narrative. I need not tell the reader that all that passed in the laboratory was immediately and faithfully reported to me by Rouletabille.

# XII

## FREDERIC LARSAN'S CANE

It was not till six o'clock that I left the château, taking with me the article hastily written by my friend in the little sitting-room which Monsieur Robert Darzac had placed at our disposal. The reporter was to sleep at the château, taking advantage of the to me inexplicable hospitality offered him by Monsieur Robert Darzac, to whom Monsieur Stangerson, in that sad time, left the care of all his domestic affairs. Nevertheless he insisted on accompanying me to the station at Epinay. In crossing the park, he said to me:

"Frederic is really very clever and has not belied his reputation. Do you know how he came to find Daddy Jacques's boots?—Near the spot where we noticed the traces of the neat boots and the disappearance of the rough ones, there was a square hole, freshly made in the moist ground, where a stone had evidently been removed. Larsan searched for that stone without finding it, and at once imagined that it had been used by the murderer with which to sink the boots in the lake. Fred's calculation was an excellent one, as the success of his search proves. That escaped me; but my mind was turned in another direction by the large number of false indications of his track which the murderer left, and by the measure of the black foot-marks corresponding with that of Daddy Jacques's boots, which

I had established without his suspecting it, on the floor of 'The Yellow Room'. All which was a proof, in my eyes, that the murderer had sought to turn suspicion on to the old servant. Up to that point, Larsan and I are in accord; but no further. It is going to be a terrible matter; for I tell you he is working on wrong lines, and I—I, must fight him with nothing!"

I was surprised at the profoundly grave accent with which my young friend pronounced the last words.

He repeated:

"Yes—terrible!—terrible! For it is fighting with nothing, when you have only an idea to fight with."

At that moment we passed by the back of the château. Night had come. A window on the first floor was partly open. A feeble light came from it as well as some sounds which drew our attention. We approached until we had reached the side of a door that was situated just under the window. Rouletabille, in a low tone, made me understand, that this was the window of Mademoiselle Stangerson's chamber. The sounds which had attracted our attention ceased, then were renewed for a moment, and then we heard stifled sobs. We were only able to catch these words, which reached us distinctly: "My poor Robert!"—Rouletabille whispered in my ear:

"If we only knew what was being said in that chamber, my inquiry would soon be finished."

He looked about him. The darkness of the evening enveloped us; we could not see much beyond the narrow path bordered by trees, which ran behind the chateau. The sobs had ceased.

"If we can't hear we may at least try to see," said Rouletabille.

And, making a sign to me to deaden the sound of my steps, he led me across the path to the trunk of a tall beech tree, the white bole of which was visible in the darkness. This tree grew exactly in front of the window in which we were so much interested, its lower branches being on a level with the first floor of the chateau. From the height of those branches one might certainly see what was passing in Mademoiselle Stangerson's chamber. Evidently that was what Rouletabille thought, for, enjoining me to remain hidden, he clasped the trunk with his vigorous arms and climbed up. I soon lost sight of him amid the branches, and then followed a deep silence. In front of me, the open window remained lighted, and I saw no shadow move across it. I listened, and presently from above me these words reached my ears:

"After you!"

"After you, pray!"

Somebody was overhead, speaking,—exchanging courtesies. What was my astonishment to see on the slippery column of the tree two human forms appear and quietly slip down to the ground. Rouletabille had mounted alone, and had returned with another.

"Good evening, Monsieur Sainclair!"

It was Frederic Larsan. The detective had already occupied the post of observation when my young friend had thought to reach it alone. Neither noticed my astonishment. I explained that to myself by the fact that they must have been witnesses of some tender and despairing scene between Mademoiselle Stangerson, lying in her bed, and Monsieur Darzac on his knees by her pillow. I guessed that each had drawn different conclusions from what they had seen. It was easy to see that the scene had strongly impressed Rouletabille in favour of Monsieur Robert Darzac; while, to Larsan, it showed nothing but consummate hypocrisy, acted with finished art by Mademoiselle Stangerson's fiance.

As we reached the park gate, Larsan stopped us.

"My cane!" he cried. "I left it near the tree."

He left us, saying he would rejoin us presently.

"Have you noticed Frederic Larsan's cane?" asked the young reporter, as soon as we were alone. "It is quite a new one, which I have never seen him use before. He seems to take great care of it—it never leaves him. One would think he was afraid it might fall into the hands of strangers. I never saw it before today. Where did he find it? It isn't natural that a man who had never before used a walking-stick should, the day after the Glandier crime, never move a step without one. On the day of our arrival at the château, as soon as he saw us, he put his watch in his pocket and picked up his cane from the ground—a proceeding to which I was perhaps wrong not to attach some importance."

We were now out of the park. Rouletabille had dropped into silence. His thoughts were certainly still occupied with Frederic Larsan's new cane. I had proof of that when, as we came near to Epinay, he said:

"Frederic Larsan arrived at the Glandier before me; he began his inquiry before me; he has had time to find out things about which I know nothing. Where did he find that cane?" Then he added: "It is probable that his suspicion—more than that, his reasoning—has led him to lay his hand on something tangible. Has this cane anything to do with it? Where the deuce could he have found it?"

As I had to wait twenty minutes for the train at Epinay, we entered a wine shop. Almost immediately the door opened and Frederic Larsan made his appearance, brandishing his famous cane.

"I found it!" he said laughingly.

The three of us seated ourselves at a table. Rouletabille never took his eyes off the cane; he was so absorbed that he did not notice a sign Larsan made to a railway employee, a young man with a chin decorated by a tiny blond and ill-kept beard. On the sign he rose, paid for his drink, bowed, and went out. I should not myself have attached any importance to the circumstance, if it had not been recalled to my mind, some months later, by the reappearance of the man with the beard at one of the most tragic moments of this case. I then learned that the youth was one of Larsan's assistants and had been charged by him to watch the going and coming of travellers at the station of Epinay-sur-Orge. Larsan neglected nothing in any case on which he was engaged.

I turned my eyes again on Rouletabille.

"Ah,—Monsieur Fred!" he said, "When did you begin to use a walking-stick? I have always seen you walking with your hands in your pockets!"

"It is a present," replied the detective.

"Recent?" insisted Rouletabille.

"No, it was given to me in London."

"Ah, yes, I remember—you have just come from London. May I look at it?"

"Oh!—certainly!"

Fred passed the cane to Rouletabille. It was a large yellow bamboo with a crutch handle and ornamented with a gold ring. Rouletabille, after examining it minutely, returned it to Larsan, with a bantering expression on his face, saying:

"You were given a French cane in London!"

"Possibly," said Fred, imperturbably.

"Read the mark there, in tiny letters: Cassette, 6a, Opera."

"Cannot English people buy canes in Paris?"

When Rouletabille had seen me into the train, he said:

"You'll remember the address?"

"Yes,—Cassette, 6a, Opera. Rely on me; you shall have word tomorrow morning."

That evening, on reaching Paris, I saw Monsieur Cassette, dealer in walking-sticks and umbrellas, and wrote to my friend:

"A man unmistakably answering to the description of Monsieur Robert Darzac—same height, slightly stooping, putty-coloured overcoat, bowler hat—purchased a cane similar to the one in which we are interested, on the evening of the crime, about eight o'clock. Monsieur Cassette had not sold another such cane during the last two years. Fred's cane is new. It is quite clear that it's the same cane. Fred did not buy it, since he was in London. Like you, I think that he found it somewhere near Monsieur Robert Darzac. But if, as you suppose, the murderer was in The 'Yellow Room' for five, or even six hours, and the crime was not committed until towards midnight, the purchase of this cane proves an incontestable alibi for Darzac."

# XIII

## "THE PRESBYTERY HAS LOST NOTHING OF ITS CHARM, NOR THE GARDEN ITS BRIGHTNESS"

A week after the occurrence of the events I have just recounted—on the 2nd of November, to be exact—I received at my home in Paris the following telegraphic message: "Come to the Glandier by the earliest train. Bring revolvers. Friendly greetings. Rouletabille."

I have already said, I think, that at that period, being a young barrister with but few briefs, I frequented the Palais de Justice rather for the purpose of familiarising myself with my professional duties than for the defence of the widow and orphan. I could, therefore, feel no surprise at Rouletabille disposing of my time. Moreover, he knew how keenly interested I was in his journalistic adventures in general and, above all, in the murder at the Glandier. I had not heard from him for a week, nor of the progress made with that mysterious case, except by the innumerable paragraphs in the newspapers and by the very brief notes of Rouletabille in the "Epoque." Those notes had divulged the fact that traces of human blood had been found on the mutton-bone, as well as fresh traces of the blood of Mademoiselle Stangerson—the old stains belonged to other crimes, probably dating years back.

It may be easily imagined that the crime engaged the attention of the press throughout the world. No crime known had more absorbed the minds of people. It appeared to me, however, that the judicial inquiry was making but very little progress; and I should have been very glad, if, on the receipt of my friend's invitation to rejoin him at the Glandier, the despatch had not contained the words, "Bring revolvers."

That puzzled me greatly. Rouletabille telegraphing for revolvers meant that there might be occasion to use them. Now, I confess it without shame, I am not a hero. But here was a friend, evidently in danger, calling on me to go to his aid. I did not hesitate long; and after assuring myself that the only revolver I possessed was properly loaded, I hurried towards the Orleans station. On the way I remembered that Rouletabille had asked for two revolvers; I therefore entered a gunsmith's shop and bought an excellent weapon for my friend.

I had hoped to find him at the station at Epinay; but he was not there. However, a cab was waiting for me and I was soon at the Glandier. Nobody was at the gate, and it was only on the threshold of the château that I met the young man. He saluted me with a friendly gesture and threw his arms about me, inquiring warmly as to the state of my health.

When we were in the little sitting-room of which I have spoken, Rouletabille made me sit down.

"It's going badly," he said.

"What's going badly?" I asked.

"Everything."

He came nearer to me and whispered:

"Frederic Larsan is working with might and main against Darzac."

This did not astonish me. I had seen the poor show Mademoiselle Stangerson's fiance had made at the time of the examination of the footprints. However, I immediately asked:

"What about that cane?"

"It is still in the hands of Frederic Larsan. He never lets go of it."

"But doesn't it prove the alibi for Monsieur Darzac?"

"Not at all. Gently questioned by me, Darzac denied having, on that evening, or on any other, purchased a cane at Cassette's. However," said Rouletabille, "I'll not swear to anything; Monsieur Darzac has such strange fits of silence that one does not know exactly what to think of what he says."

"To Frederic Larsan this cane must mean a piece of very damaging evidence. But in what way? The time when it was bought shows it could not have been in the murderer's possession."

"The time doesn't worry Larsan. He is not obliged to adopt my theory which assumes that the murderer got into 'The Yellow Room' between five and six o'clock. But there's nothing to prevent him assuming that the murderer got in between ten and eleven o'clock at night. At that hour Monsieur and Mademoiselle Stangerson, assisted by Daddy Jacques, were engaged in making an interesting chemical experiment in the part of the laboratory taken up by the furnaces. Larsan says, unlikely as that may seem, that the murderer may have slipped behind them. He has already got the examining magistrate to listen to him. When one looks closely into it, the reasoning is absurd, seeing that the 'intimate'—if there is one—must have known that the professor would shortly leave the pavilion, and that the 'friend' had only to put off operating till after the professor's departure. Why should he have risked crossing the laboratory while the professor was in it? And then, when he had got into 'The Yellow Room'?

"There are many points to be cleared up before Larsan's theory can be admitted. I sha'n't waste my time over it, for my theory won't allow me to occupy myself with mere imagination. Only, as I am obliged for the moment to keep silent, and Larsan sometimes talks, he may finish by coming out openly against Monsieur

Darzac,—if I'm not there," added the young reporter proudly. "For there are surface evidences against Darzac, much more convincing than that cane, which remains incomprehensible to me, all the more so as Larsan does not in the least hesitate to let Darzac see him with it!—I understand many things in Larsan's theory, but I can't make anything of that cane.

"Is he still at the château?"

"Yes; he hardly ever leaves it!—He sleeps there, as I do, at the request of Monsieur Stangerson, who has done for him what Monsieur Robert Darzac has done for me. In spite of the accusation made by Larsan that Monsieur Stangerson knows who the murderer is he yet affords him every facility for arriving at the truth,—just as Darzac is doing for me."

"But you are convinced of Darzac's innocence?"

"At one time I did believe in the possibility of his guilt. That was when we arrived here for the first time. The time has come for me to tell you what has passed between Monsieur Darzac and myself."

Here Rouletabille interrupted himself and asked me if I had brought the revolvers. I showed him them. Having examined both, he pronounced them excellent, and handed them back to me.

"Shall we have any use for them?" I asked.

"No doubt; this evening. We shall pass the night here—if that won't tire you?"

"On the contrary," I said with an expression that made Rouletabille laugh.

"No, no," he said, "this is no time for laughing. You remember the phrase which was the 'open sesame' of this château full of mystery?"

"Yes," I said, "perfectly,—'The presbytery has lost nothing of its charm, nor the garden its brightness.' It was the phrase which you found on the half-burned piece of paper amongst the ashes in the laboratory."

"Yes; at the bottom of the paper, where the flame had not reached, was this date: 23rd of October. Remember this date, it is highly important. I am now going to tell you about that curious phrase. On the evening before the crime, that is to say, on the 23rd, Monsieur and Mademoiselle Stangerson were at a reception at the Elysee. I know that, because I was there on duty, having to interview one of the savants of the Academy of Philadelphia, who was being feted there. I had never before seen either Monsieur or Mademoiselle Stangerson. I was seated in the room which precedes the Salon des Ambassadeurs, and, tired of being jostled by so many noble personages, I had fallen into a vague reverie, when I scented near me the perfume of the lady in black.

"Do you ask me what is the 'perfume of the lady in black'? It must suffice for you to know that it is a perfume of which I am very fond, because it was that of a lady who had been very kind to me in my childhood,—a lady whom I had always seen dressed in black. The lady who, that evening, was scented with the perfume of the lady in black, was dressed in white. She was wonderfully beautiful. I could not help rising and following her. An old man gave her his arm and, as they passed, I heard voices say: 'Professor Stangerson and his daughter.' It was in that way I learned who it was I was following.

"They met Monsieur Robert Darzac, whom I knew by sight. Professor Stangerson, accosted by Mr. Arthur William Rance, one of the American savants, seated himself in the great gallery, and Monsieur Robert Darzac led Mademoiselle Stangerson into the conservatory. I followed. The weather was very mild that evening; the garden doors were open. Mademoiselle Stangerson threw a fichu shawl over her shoulders and I plainly saw that it was she who was begging Monsieur Darzac to go with her into the garden. I continued to follow, interested by the agitation plainly exhibited by the bearing of Monsieur Darzac. They slowly passed along the wall abutting on the

Avenue Marigny. I took the central alley, walking parallel with them, and then crossed over for the purpose of getting nearer to them. The night was dark, and the grass deadened the sound of my steps. They had stopped under the vacillating light of a gas jet and appeared to be both bending over a paper held by Mademoiselle Stangerson, reading something which deeply interested them. I stopped in the darkness and silence.

"Neither of them saw me, and I distinctly heard Mademoiselle Stangerson repeat, as she was refolding the paper: 'The presbytery has lost nothing of its charm, nor the garden its brightness!'—It was said in a tone at once mocking and despairing, and was followed by a burst of such nervous laughter that I think her words will never cease to sound in my ears. But another phrase was uttered by Monsieur Robert Darzac: 'Must I commit a crime, then, to win you?' He was in an extraordinarily agitated state. He took the hand of Mademoiselle Stangerson and held it for a long time to his lips, and I thought, from the movement of his shoulders, that he was crying. Then they went away.

"When I returned to the great gallery," continued Rouletabille, "I saw no more of Monsieur Robert Darzac, and I was not to see him again until after the tragedy at the Glandier. Mademoiselle was near Mr. Rance, who was talking with much animation, his eyes, during the conversation, glowing with a singular brightness. Mademoiselle Stangerson, I thought, was not even listening to what he was saying, her face expressing perfect indifference. His face was the red face of a drunkard. When Monsieur and Mademoiselle Stangerson left, he went to the bar and remained there. I joined him, and rendered him some little service in the midst of the pressing crowd. He thanked me and told me he was returning to America three days later, that is to say, on the 26th (the day after the crime). I talked with him about Philadelphia; he told me he had lived there for five-and-twenty years, and that it was there he had met the illustrious Professor Stangerson and his daughter. He drank a great deal of champagne, and when I left him he was very nearly drunk.

"Such were my experiences on that evening, and I leave you to imagine what effect the news of the attempted murder of Mademoiselle Stangerson produced on me,—with what force those words pronounced by Monsieur Robert Darzac, 'Must I commit a crime, then, to win you?' recurred to me. It was not this phrase, however, that I repeated to him, when we met here at Glandier. The sentence of the presbytery and the bright garden sufficed to open the gate of the château. If you ask me if I believe now that Monsieur Darzac is the murderer, I must say I do not. I do not think I ever quite thought that. At the time I could not really think seriously of anything. I had so little evidence to go on. But I needed to have at once the proof that he had not been wounded in the hand.

"When we were alone together, I told him how I had chanced to overhear a part of his conversation with Mademoiselle Stangerson in the garden of the Elysee; and when I repeated to him the words, 'Must I commit a crime, then, to win you?' he was greatly troubled, though much less so than he had been by hearing me repeat the phrase about the presbytery. What threw him into a state of real consternation was to learn from me that the day on which he had gone to meet Mademoiselle Stangerson at the Elysee, was the very day on which she had gone to the Post Office for the letter. It was that letter, perhaps, which ended with the words: 'The presbytery has lost nothing of its charm, nor the garden its brightness.' My surmise was confirmed by my finding, if you remember, in the ashes of the laboratory, the fragment of paper dated October the 23rd. The letter had been written and withdrawn from the Post Office on the same day.

"There can be no doubt that, on returning from the Elysee that night, Mademoiselle Stangerson had tried to destroy that compromising paper. It was in vain that Monsieur Darzac denied that that letter had anything whatever to do with the crime. I told him that in an affair so filled with mystery as this, he had no right to hide this letter; that I was persuaded it was of considerable importance; that the desperate tone in which Mademoiselle Stangerson had pronounced the prophetic phrase,—that his own tears, and the threat of a crime which he had professed after the letter was read—all these facts tended to leave no room for me to doubt. Monsieur Darzac became more and more agitated, and I determined to take advantage of the effect I had produced on him. 'You were on the point of being married, Monsieur,' I said negligently and without looking at him, 'and suddenly your marriage becomes impossible because of the writer of that letter; because as soon as his letter was read, you spoke of the necessity for a crime to win Mademoiselle Stangerson. Therefore there is someone between you and her—someone who is preventing your marriage with her—someone who has attempted to kill her, so that she should not be able to marry!' And I concluded with these words: 'Now, monsieur, you have only to tell me in confidence the name of the murderer!'—The words I had uttered must have struck him ominously, for when I turned my eyes on him, I saw that his face was haggard, the perspiration standing on his forehead, and terror showing in his eyes.

"'Monsieur,' he said to me, 'I am going to ask of you something which may appear insane, but in exchange for which I place my life in your hands. You must not tell the magistrates of what you saw and heard in the garden of the Elysee,—neither to them nor to anybody. I swear to you, that I am innocent, and I know, I feel, that you believe me; but I would rather be taken for the guilty man than see justice go astray on that phrase, "The presbytery has lost nothing of its charm, nor the garden its brightness." The judges must know nothing about that phrase. All this matter is in your hands. Monsieur, I leave it there; but forget the evening at the Elysee. A hundred other roads are open to you in your search for the criminal. I will open them for you myself. I will help you. Will you take up your quarters here?—You may remain here to do as you please.—Eat—sleep here—watch my actions—the actions of all here. You shall be master of the Glandier, Monsieur; but forget the evening at the Elysee.'"

Rouletabille here paused to take breath. I now understood what had appeared so unexplainable in the demeanour of Monsieur Robert Darzac towards my friend, and the facility with which the young reporter had been able to install himself on the scene of the crime. My curiosity could not fail to be excited by all I had heard. I asked Rouletabille to satisfy it still further. What had happened at the Glandier during the past week?—Had he not told me that there were surface indications against Monsieur Darzac much more terrible than that of the cane found by Larsan?

"Everything seems to be pointing against him," replied my friend, "and the situation is becoming exceedingly grave. Monsieur Darzac appears not to mind it much; but in that he is wrong. I was interested only in the health of Mademoiselle Stangerson, which was daily improving, when something occurred that is even more mysterious than—than the mystery of 'The Yellow Room'!"

"Impossible!" I cried, "What could be more mysterious than that?"

"Let us first go back to Monsieur Robert Darzac," said Rouletabille, calming me. "I have said that everything seems to be pointing against him. The marks of the neat boots found by Frederic Larsan appear to be really the footprints of Mademoiselle Stangerson's fiance. The marks made by the bicycle may have been made by his bicycle. He had usually left it at the château; why did he take it to Paris on that particular occasion? Was it because he was not going to return again to the château? Was it because, owing to the breaking off of his marriage, his relations with the Stangersons were to cease? All who are interested in the matter affirm that those relations were to continue unchanged.

"Frederic Larsan, however, believes that all relations were at an end. From the day when Monsieur Darzac accompanied Mademoiselle Stangerson to the Grands Magasins de la Louvre until the day after the crime, he had not been at the Glandier. Remember that Mademoiselle Stangerson lost her reticule containing the key with the brass head while she was in his company. From that day to the evening at the Elysee, the Sorbonne professor and Mademoiselle Stangerson did not see one another; but they may have written to each other. Mademoiselle Stangerson went to the Post Office to get a letter, which Larsan says was written by Robert Darzac; for knowing nothing of what had passed at the Elysee, Larsan believes that it was Monsieur Darzac himself who stole the reticule with the key, with the design of forcing her consent, by getting possession of the precious papers of her father—papers which he would have restored to him on condition that the marriage engagement was to be fulfilled.

"All that would have been a very doubtful and almost absurd hypothesis, as Larsan admitted to me, but for another and much graver circumstance. In the first place here is something which I have not been able to explain—Monsieur Darzac had himself, on the 24th, gone to the Post Office to ask for the letter which Mademoiselle had called for and received on the previous evening. The description of the man who made application tallies in every respect with the appearance of Monsieur Darzac, who, in answer to the questions put to him by the examining magistrate, denies that he went to the Post Office. Now even admitting that the letter was written by him—which I do not believe—he knew that Mademoiselle Stangerson had received it, since he had seen it in her hands in the garden at the Elysee. It could not have been he, then, who had gone to the Post Office, the day after the 24th, to ask for a letter which he knew was no longer there.

"To me it appears clear that somebody, strongly resembling him, stole Mademoiselle Stangerson's reticule and in that letter, had demanded of her something which she had not sent him. He must have been surprised at the failure of his demand, hence his application at the Post Office, to learn whether his letter had been delivered to the person to whom it had been addressed. Finding that it had been claimed, he had become furious. What had he demanded? Nobody but Mademoiselle Stangerson knows. Then, on the day following, it is reported that she had been attacked during the night, and, the next day, I discovered that the Professor had, at the same time, been robbed by means of the key referred to in the poste restante letter. It would seem, then, that the man who went to the Post Office to inquire for the letter must have been the murderer. All these arguments Larsan applies as against Monsieur Darzac. You may be sure that the examining magistrate, Larsan, and myself, have done our best to get from the Post Office precise details relative to the singular personage who applied there on the 24th of October. But nothing has been learned. We don't know where he came from—or where he went. Beyond the description which makes him resemble Monsieur Darzac, we know nothing.

"I have announced in the leading journals that a handsome reward will be given to a driver of any public conveyance who drove a fare to No. 40, Post Office, about ten o'clock on the morning of the 24th of October. Information to be addressed to 'M. R.,' at the office of the 'Epoque'; but no answer has resulted. The man may have walked; but, as he was most likely in a hurry, there was a chance that he might have gone in a cab. Who, I keep asking myself night and day, is the man who so strongly resembles Monsieur Robert Darzac, and who is also known to have bought the cane which has fallen into Larsan's hands?

"The most serious fact is that Monsieur Darzac was, at the very same time that his double presented himself at the Post Office, scheduled for a lecture at the Sorbonne. He had not delivered that lecture, and one of his friends took his place. When I questioned him as to how he had employed the time, he told me that he had gone for a stroll in the Bois de Boulogne. What do you think of a professor who, instead of giving his lecture, obtains a substitute to go for a stroll in the Bois de Boulogne? When Frederic Larsan asked him for information on this point, he quietly replied that it was no business of his how he spent his time in Paris. On which Fred swore aloud that he would find out, without anybody's help.

"All this seems to fit in with Fred's hypothesis, namely, that Monsieur Stangerson allowed the murderer to escape in order to avoid a scandal. The hypothesis is further substantiated by the fact that Darzac was in 'The Yellow Room' and was permitted to get away. That hypothesis I believe to be a false one.—Larsan is being misled by it, though that would not displease me, did it not affect an innocent person. Now does that hypothesis really mislead Frederic Larsan? That is the question—that is the question."

"Perhaps he is right," I cried, interrupting Rouletabille. "Are you sure that Monsieur Darzac is innocent?—It seems to me that these are extraordinary coincidences—"

"Coincidences," replied my friend, "are the worst enemies to truth."

"What does the examining magistrate think now of the matter?"

"Monsieur de Marquet hesitates to accuse Monsieur Darzac, in the absence of absolute proofs. Not only would he have public opinion wholly against him, to say nothing of the Sorbonne, but Monsieur and Mademoiselle Stangerson. She adores Monsieur Robert Darzac. Indistinctly as she saw the murderer, it would be hard to make the public believe that she could not have recognised him, if Darzac had been the criminal. No doubt 'The Yellow Room' was very dimly lit; but a night-light, however small, gives some light. Here, my boy, is how things stood when, three days, or rather three nights ago, an extraordinarily strange incident occurred."

# XIV

## "I EXPECT THE ASSASSIN THIS EVENING"

"I must take you," said Rouletabille, "so as to enable you to understand, to the various scenes. I myself believe that I have discovered what everybody else is searching for, namely, how the murderer escaped from "The Yellow Room", without any accomplice, and without Mademoiselle Stangerson having had anything to do with it. But so long as I am not sure of the real murderer, I cannot state the theory on which I am working. I can only say that I believe it to be correct and, in any case, a quite natural and simple one. As to what happened in this place three nights ago, I must say it kept me wondering for a whole day and a night. It passes all belief. The theory I have formed from the incident is so absurd that I would rather matters remained as yet unexplained."

Saying which the young reporter invited me to go and make the tour of the château with him. The only sound to be heard was the crunching of the dead leaves beneath our feet. The silence was so intense that one might have thought the château had been abandoned. The old stones, the stagnant water of the ditch surrounding the donjon, the bleak ground strewn with the dead leaves, the dark, skeleton-like outlines of the trees, all contributed to give to the desolate place, now filled with its awful mystery, a most funereal aspect. As we passed round the donjon, we met the Green Man, the forest-keeper, who did not greet us, but walked by as if we had not existed. He was looking just as I had formerly seen him through the window of the Donjon Inn. He had still his fowling-piece slung at his back, his pipe was in his mouth, and his eyeglasses on his nose.

"An odd kind of fish!" Rouletabille said to me, in a low tone.

"Have you spoken to him?" I asked.

"Yes, but I could get nothing out of him. His only answers are grunts and shrugs of the shoulders. He generally lives on the first floor of the donjon, a big room that once served for an oratory. He lives like a bear, never goes out without his gun, and is only pleasant with the girls. The women, for twelve miles round, are all setting their caps for him. For the present, he is paying attention to Madame Mathieu, whose husband is keeping a lynx eye upon her in consequence."

After passing the donjon, which is situated at the extreme end of the left wing, we went to the back of the château. Rouletabille, pointing to a window which I recognised as the only one belonging to Mademoiselle Stangerson's apartment, said to me:

"If you had been here, two nights ago, you would have seen your humble servant at the top of a ladder, about to enter the château by that window."

As I expressed some surprise at this piece of nocturnal gymnastics, he begged me to notice carefully the exterior disposition of the château. We then went back into the building.

"I must now show you the first floor of the château, where I am living," said my friend.

To enable the reader the better to understand the disposition of these parts of the dwelling, I annex a plan of the first floor of the right wing, drawn by Rouletabille the day after the extraordinary phenomenon occurred, the details of which I am about to relate.

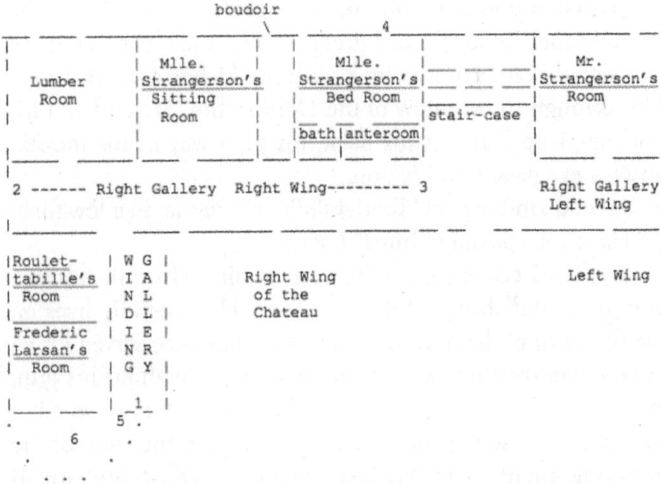


Rouletabille motioned me to follow him up a magnificent flight of stairs ending in a landing on the first floor. From this landing one could pass to the right or left wing of the château by a gallery opening from it. This gallery, high and wide, extended along the whole length of the building and was lit from the front of the château facing the north. The rooms, the windows of which looked to the south, opened out of the gallery. Professor Stangerson inhabited the left wing of the building. Mademoiselle Stangerson had her apartment in the right wing.

We entered the gallery to the right. A narrow carpet, laid on the waxed oaken floor, which shone like glass, deadened the sound of our footsteps. Rouletabille asked me, in a low tone, to walk carefully, as we were passing the door of Mademoiselle Stangerson's apartment. This consisted of a bedroom, an anteroom, a small bathroom, a boudoir, and a drawing-room. One could pass from one to another of these rooms without having to go by way of the gallery. The gallery continued straight to the western end of the building, where it was lit by a high window (window 2 on the plan). At about two-thirds of its length this gallery, at a right angle, joined another gallery following the course of the right wing.

The better to follow this narrative, we shall call the gallery leading from the stairs to the eastern window, the "right" gallery and the gallery quitting it at a right angle, the "off-turning" gallery (winding gallery in the plan). It was at the meeting point of the two galleries that Rouletabille had his chamber, adjoining that of Frederic Larsan, the door of each opening on to the "off-turning" gallery, while the doors of Mademoiselle Stangerson's apartment opened into the "right" gallery. (See the plan.)

Rouletabille opened the door of his room and after we had passed in, carefully drew the bolt. I had not had time to glance round the place in which he had been installed, when he uttered a cry of surprise and pointed to a pair of eyeglasses on a side-table.

"What are these doing here?" he asked.

I should have been puzzled to answer him.

"I wonder," he said, "I wonder if this is what I have been searching for. I wonder if these are the eyeglasses from the presbytery!"

He seized them eagerly, his fingers caressing the glass. Then looking at me, with an expression of terror on his face, he murmured, "Oh!—Oh!"

He repeated the exclamation again and again, as if his thoughts had suddenly turned his brain.

He rose and, putting his hand on my shoulder, laughed like one demented as he said:

"Those glasses will drive me silly! Mathematically speaking the thing is possible; but humanly speaking it is impossible—or afterwards—or afterwards—"

Two light knocks struck the door. Rouletabille opened it. A figure entered. I recognised the concierge, whom I had seen when she was being taken to the pavilion for examination. I was surprised, thinking she was still under lock and key. This woman said in a very low tone:

"In the grove of the parquet."

Rouletabille replied: "Thanks."—The woman then left. He again turned to me, his look haggard, after having carefully refastened the door, muttering some incomprehensible phrases.

"If the thing is mathematically possible, why should it not be humanly!—And if it is humanly possible, the matter is simply awful." I interrupted him in his soliloquy:

"Have they set the concierges at liberty, then?" I asked.

"Yes," he replied, "I had them liberated, I needed people I could trust. The woman is thoroughly devoted to me, and her husband would lay down his life for me."

"Oho!" I said, "When will he have occasion to do it?"

"This evening,—for this evening I expect the murderer."

"You expect the murderer this evening? Then you know him?"

"I shall know him; but I should be mad to affirm, categorically, at this moment that I do know him. The mathematical idea I have of the murderer gives results so frightful, so monstrous, that I hope it is still possible that I am mistaken. I hope so, with all my heart!"

"Five minutes ago, you did not know the murderer; how can you say that you expect him this evening?"

"Because I know that he must come."

Rouletabille very slowly filled his pipe and lit it. That meant an interesting story. At that moment we heard someone walking in the gallery and passing before our door. Rouletabille listened. The sound of the footstep died away in the distance.

"Is Frederic Larsan in his room?" I asked, pointing to the partition.

"No," my friend answered. "He went to Paris this morning,—still on the scent of Darzac, who also left for Paris. That matter will turn out badly. I expect that Monsieur Darzac will be arrested in the course of the next week. The worst of it is that everything seems to be in league against him,—circumstances, things, people. Not an hour passes without bringing some new evidence against him. The examining magistrate is overwhelmed by it—and blind."

"Frederic Larsan, however, is not a novice," I said.

"I thought so," said Rouletabille, with a slightly contemptuous turn of his lips, "I fancied he was a much abler man. I had, indeed, a great admiration for him, before I got to know his method of working. It's deplorable. He owes his reputation solely to his ability; but he lacks reasoning power,—the mathematics of his ideas are very poor."

I looked closely at Rouletabille and could not help smiling, on hearing this boy of eighteen talking of a man who had proved to the world that he was the finest police sleuth in Europe.

"You smile?" he said. "You are wrong! I swear I will outwit him—and in a striking way! But I must make haste about it, for he has an enormous start on me—given him by Monsieur Robert Darzac, who is this evening going to increase it still more. Think of it!—every time the murderer comes to the château, Monsieur Darzac, by a strange fatality, absents himself and refuses to give any account of how he employs his time."

"Every time the assassin comes to the château!" I cried. "Has he returned then—?"

"Yes, during that famous night when the strange phenomenon occurred."

I was now going to learn about the astonishing phenomenon to which Rouletabille had made allusion half an hour earlier without giving me any explanation of it. But I had learned never to press Rouletabille in his narratives. He spoke when the fancy took him and when he judged it to be right. He was less concerned about my curiosity than he was for making a complete summing up for himself of any important matter in which he was interested.

At last, in short rapid phrases, he acquainted me with things which plunged me into a state bordering on complete bewilderment. Indeed, the results of that still unknown science known as hypnotism, for example, were not more inexplicable than the disappearance of the "matter" of the murderer at the moment when four persons were within touch of him. I speak of hypnotism as I would of electricity, for of the nature of both we are ignorant and we know little of their laws. I cite these examples because, at the time, the case appeared to me to be only explicable by the inexplicable,—that is to say, by an event outside of known natural laws. And yet, if I had had Rouletabille's brain, I should, like him, have had a presentiment of the natural explanation; for the most curious thing about all the mysteries of the Glandier case was the natural manner in which he explained them.

I have among the papers that were sent me by the young man, after the affair was over, a notebook of his, in which a complete account is given of the phenomenon of the disappearance of the "matter" of the assassin, and the thoughts to which it gave rise in the mind of my young friend. It is preferable, I think, to give the reader this account, rather than continue to reproduce my conversation with Rouletabille; for I should be afraid, in a history of this nature, to add a word that was not in accordance with the strictest truth.

# XV

## THE TRAP

(EXTRACT FROM THE NOTEBOOK OF JOSEPH ROULETABILLE)

"Last night—the night between the 29th and 30th of October—" wrote Joseph Rouletabille, "I woke up towards one o'clock in the morning. Was it sleeplessness, or noise without?—The cry of the Bete du Bon Dieu rang out with sinister loudness from the end of the park. I rose and opened the window. Cold wind and rain; opaque darkness; silence. I reclosed my window. Again the sound of the cat's weird cry in the distance. I partly dressed in haste. The weather was too bad for even a cat to be turned out in it. What did it mean, then—that imitating of the mewing of Mother Angenoux' cat so near the château? I seized a good-sized stick, the only weapon I had, and, without making any noise, opened the door.

"The gallery into which I went was well lit by a lamp with a reflector. I felt a keen current of air and, on turning, found the window open, at the extreme end of the gallery, which I call the 'off-turning' gallery, to distinguish it from the 'right' gallery, on to which the apartment of Mademoiselle Stangerson opened. These two galleries cross each other at right angles. Who had left that window open? Or, who had come to open it? I went to the window and leaned out. Five feet below me there was a sort of terrace over the semi-circular projection of a room on the ground-floor. One could, if one wanted, jump from the window on to the terrace, and allow oneself to drop from it into the court of the chateau. Whoever had entered by this road had, evidently, not had a key to the vestibule door. But why should I be thinking of my previous night's attempt with the ladder?—Because of the open window—left open, perhaps, by the negligence of a servant? I reclosed it, smiling at the ease with which I built a drama on the mere suggestion of an open window.

"Again the cry of the Bete du Bon Dieu!—and then silence. The rain ceased to beat on the window. All in the château slept. I walked with infinite precaution on the carpet of the gallery. On reaching the corner of the 'right' gallery, I peered round it cautiously. There was another lamp there with a reflector which quite lit up the several objects in it,—three chairs and some pictures hanging on the wall. What was I doing there? Perfect silence reigned throughout. Everything was sunk in repose. What was the instinct that urged me towards Mademoiselle Stangerson's chamber? Why did a voice within me cry: 'Go on, to the chamber of Mademoiselle Stangerson!' I cast my eyes down upon the carpet on which I was treading and saw that my steps were being directed towards Mademoiselle Stangerson's chamber by the marks of steps that had already been made there. Yes, on the carpet were traces of footsteps stained with mud leading to the chamber of Mademoiselle Stangerson. Horror! Horror!—I recognised in those footprints the impression of the neat boots of the murderer! He had come, then, from without in this wretched night. If you could descend from the gallery by way of the window, by means of the terrace, then you could get into the château by the same means.

"The murderer was still in the château, for here were marks as of returning footsteps. He had entered by the open window at the extremity of the 'off-turning' gallery; he had passed Frederic Larsan's door and mine, had turned to the right, and had entered Mademoiselle Stangerson's room. I am before the door of her ante-room—it is open. I push it, without making the least noise. Under the door of the room itself I see a streak of light. I listen—no sound—not even of breathing! Ah!—if I only knew what was passing in the silence that is behind that door! I find the door locked and the key turned on the inner side. And the murderer is there, perhaps. He must be there! Will he escape this time?—All depends on me!—I must be calm, and above all, I must make no false steps. I must see into that room. I can enter it by Mademoiselle Stangerson's drawing-room; but, to do that I should have to cross her boudoir; and while I am there, the murderer may escape by the gallery door—the door in front of which I am now standing.

"I am sure that no other crime is being committed, on this night; for there is complete silence in the boudoir, where two nurses are taking care of Mademoiselle Stangerson until she is restored to health.

"As I am almost sure that the murderer is there, why do I not at once give the alarm? The murderer may, perhaps, escape; but, perhaps, I may be able to save Mademoiselle Stangerson's life. Suppose the murderer on this occasion is not here to murder? The door has been opened to allow him to enter; by whom?—And it has been refastened—by whom?—Mademoiselle Stangerson shuts herself up in her apartment with her nurses every night. Who turned the key of that chamber to allow the murderer to enter?—The nurses,—two faithful domestics? The old chambermaid, Sylvia? It is very improbable. Besides, they slept in the boudoir, and Mademoiselle Stangerson, very nervous and careful, Monsieur Robert Darzac told me, sees to her own safety since she has been well enough to move about in her room, which I have not yet seen her leave. This nervousness and sudden care on her part, which had struck

Monsieur Darzac, had given me, also, food for thought. At the time of the crime in 'The Yellow Room', there can be no doubt that she expected the murderer. Was he expected this night?—Was it she herself who had opened her door to him? Had she some reason for doing so? Was she obliged to do it?—Was it a meeting for purposes of crime?—Certainly it was not a lover's meeting, for I believe Mademoiselle Stangerson adores Monsieur Darzac.

"All these reflections ran through my brain like a flash of lightning. What would I not give to know!

"It is possible that there was some reason for the awful silence. My intervention might do more harm than good. How could I tell? How could I know I might not any moment cause another crime? If I could only see and know, without breaking that silence!

"I left the ante-room and descended the central stairs to the vestibule and, as silently as possible, made my way to the little room on the ground-floor where Daddy Jacques had been sleeping since the attack made at the pavilion.

"I found him dressed, his eyes wide open, almost haggard. He did not seem surprised to see me. He told me that he had got up because he had heard the cry of the Bete du bon Dieu, and because he had heard footsteps in the park, close to his window, out of which he had looked and, just then, had seen a black shadow pass by. I asked him whether he had a firearm of any kind. No, he no longer kept one, since the examining magistrate had taken his revolver from him. We went out together, by a little back door, into the park, and stole along the château to the point which is just below Mademoiselle Stangerson's window.

"I placed Daddy Jacques against the wall, ordering him not to stir from the spot, while I, taking advantage of a moment when the moon was hidden by a cloud, moved to the front of the window, out of the patch of light which came from it,—

for the window was half-open! If I could only know what was passing in that silent chamber! I returned to Daddy Jacques and whispered the word 'ladder' in his ear. At first I had thought of the tree which, a week ago, served me for an observatory; but I immediately saw that, from the way the window was half-opened, I should not be able to see from that point of view anything that was passing in the room; and I wanted, not only to see, but to hear, and—to act.

"Greatly agitated, almost trembling, Daddy Jacques disappeared for a moment and returned without the ladder, but making signs to me with his arms, as signals to me to come quickly to him. When I got near him he gasped: 'Come!'

"He led me round the château, past the donjon. Arrived there, he said:

"'I went to the donjon in search of my ladder, and in the lower part of the donjon which serves me and the gardener for a lumber room, I found the door open and the ladder gone. On coming out, that's what I caught sight of by the light of the moon.

"And he pointed to the further end of the château, where a ladder stood resting against the stone brackets supporting the terrace, under the window which I had found open. The projection of the terrace had prevented my seeing it. Thanks to that ladder, it was quite easy to get into the 'off-turning' gallery of the first floor, and I had no doubt of it having been the road taken by the unknown.

"We ran to the ladder, but at the moment of reaching it, Daddy Jacques drew my attention to the half-open door of the little semi-circular room, situated under the terrace, at the extremity of the right wing of the château, having the terrace for its roof. Daddy Jacques pushed the door open a little further and looked in.

"'He's not there!" he whispered.

"Who is not there?"

"The forest-keeper."

With his lips once more to my ear, he added:

"'Do you know that he has slept in the upper room of the donjon ever since it was restored?' And with the same gesture he pointed to the half-open door, the ladder, the terrace, and the windows in the 'off-turning' gallery which, a little while before, I had re-closed.

"What were my thoughts then? I had no time to think. I felt more than I thought.

"Evidently, I felt, if the forest-keeper is up there in the chamber (I say, if, because at this moment, apart from the presence of the ladder and his vacant room, there are no evidences which permit me even to suspect him)—if he is there, he has been obliged to pass by the ladder, and the rooms which lie behind his, in his new lodging, are occupied by the family of the steward and by the cook, and by the kitchens, which bar the way by the vestibule to the interior of the château. And if he had been there during the evening on any pretext, it would have been easy for him to go into the gallery and see that the window could be simply pushed open from the outside. This question of the unfastened window easily narrowed the field of search for the murderer. He must belong to the house, unless he had an accomplice, which I do not believe he had; unless—unless Mademoiselle Stangerson herself had seen that that window was not fastened from the inside. But, then,—what could be the frightful secret which put her under the necessity of doing away with obstacles that separated her from the murderer?

"I seized hold of the ladder, and we returned to the back of the château to see if the window of the chamber was still half-open. The blind was drawn but did not join and allowed a bright stream of light to escape and fall upon the path at our feet. I planted the ladder under the window. I am almost sure that I made no noise; and while Daddy Jacques remained at the foot of the ladder, I mounted it, very quietly, my stout stick in my hand. I held my breath and lifted my feet with the greatest care. Suddenly a heavy cloud discharged itself at that moment in a fresh downpour of rain.

"At the same instant the sinister cry of the Bete du bon Dieu arrested me in my ascent. It seemed to me to have come from close by me—only a few yards away. Was the cry a signal?—Had some accomplice of the man seen me on the ladder!—Would the cry bring the man to the window?—Perhaps! Ah, there he was at the window! I felt his head above me. I heard the sound of his breath! I could not look up towards him; the least movement of my head, and—I might be lost. Would he see me?—Would he peer into the darkness? No; he went away. He had seen nothing. I felt, rather than heard, him moving on tip-toe in the room; and I mounted a few steps higher. My head reached to the level of the window-sill; my forehead rose above it; my eyes looked between the opening in the blinds—and I saw—A man seated at Mademoiselle Stangerson's little desk, writing. His back was turned toward me. A candle was lit before him, and he bent over the flame, the light from it projecting shapeless shadows. I saw nothing but a monstrous, stooping back.

"Mademoiselle Stangerson herself was not there!—Her bed had not been lain on! Where, then, was she sleeping that night? Doubtless in the side-room with her women. Perhaps this was but a guess. I must content myself with the joy of finding the man alone. I must be calm to prepare my trap.

"But who, then, is this man writing there before my eyes, seated at the desk, as if he were in his own home? If there had not been that ladder under the window; if there had not been those footprints on the carpet in the gallery; if there had not been that open window, I might have been led to think that this man had a right to be there, and that he was there as a matter of course and for reasons about which as yet I knew nothing. But there was no doubt that this mysterious unknown was the man of 'The Yellow Room',—the man to whose murderous assault Mademoiselle Stangerson—without denouncing him—had had to submit. If I could but see his face! Surprise and capture him!

"If I spring into the room at this moment, he will escape by the right-hand door opening into the boudoir,—or crossing the drawing-room, he will reach the gallery and I shall lose him. I have him now and in five minutes more he'll be safer than if I had him in a cage.—What is he doing there, alone in Mademoiselle Stangerson's room?—What is he writing? I descend and place the ladder on the ground. Daddy Jacques follows me. We re-enter the château. I send Daddy Jacques to wake Monsieur Stangerson, and instruct him to await my coming in Mademoiselle Stangerson's room and to say nothing definite to him before my arrival. I will go and awaken Frederic Larsan. It's a bore to have to do it, for I should have liked to work alone and to have carried off all the honours of this affair myself, right under the very nose of the sleeping detective. But Daddy Jacques and Monsieur Stangerson are old men, and I am not yet fully developed. I might not be strong enough. Larsan is used to wrestling and putting on the handcuffs. He opened his eyes swollen with sleep, ready to send me flying, without in the least believing in my reporter's fancies. I had to assure him that the man was there!

"'That's strange!' he said; 'I thought I left him this afternoon in Paris.'

"He dressed himself in haste and armed himself with a revolver. We stole quietly into the gallery.

"'Where is he?' Larsan asked.

"'In Mademoiselle Stangerson's room.

"'And—Mademoiselle Stangerson?'

"'She is not in there.'

"'Let's go in.'

"'Don't go there! On the least alarm the man will escape. He has four ways by which to do it—the door, the window, the boudoir, or the room in which the women are sleeping.'

"'I'll draw him from below.'

"'And if you fail?—If you only succeed in wounding him—he'll escape again, without reckoning that he is certainly armed. No, let me direct the expedition, and I'll answer for everything.'

"'As you like,' he replied, with fairly good grace.

"Then, after satisfying myself that all the windows of the two galleries were thoroughly secure, I placed Frederic Larsan at the end of the 'off-turning' gallery, before the window which I had found open and had reclosed.

"'Under no consideration,' I said to him, 'must you stir from this post till I call you. The chances are even that the man, when he is pursued, will return to this window and try to save himself that way; for it is by that way he came in and made a way ready for his flight. You have a dangerous post.'

"'What will be yours?' asked Fred.

"'I shall spring into the room and knock him over for you.'

"'Take my revolver,' said Fred, 'and I'll take your stick.'

"'Thanks,' I said; 'You are a brave man.'

"I accepted his offer. I was going to be alone with the man in the room writing and was really thankful to have the weapon.

"I left Fred, having posted him at the window (No. 5 on the plan), and, with the greatest precaution, went towards Monsieur Stangerson's apartment in the left wing of the château. I found him with Daddy Jacques, who had faithfully obeyed my directions, confining himself to asking his master to dress as quickly as possible. In a few words I explained to Monsieur Stangerson what was passing. He armed himself with a revolver, followed me, and we were all three speedily in the gallery. Since I had seen the murderer seated at the desk ten minutes had elapsed. Monsieur Stangerson wished to spring upon the assassin at once and kill him. I made him understand that, above all, he must not, in his desire to kill him, miss him.

"When I had sworn to him that his daughter was not in the room, and in no danger, he conquered his impatience and left me to direct the operations. I told them that they must come to me the moment I called to them, or when I fired my revolver. I then sent Daddy Jacques to place himself before the window at the end of the 'right' gallery. (No. 2 on my plan.) I chose that position for Daddy Jacques because I believed that the murderer, tracked, on leaving the room, would run through the gallery towards the window which he had left open, and, instantly seeing that it was guarded by Larsan, would pursue his course along the 'right' gallery. There he would encounter Daddy Jacques, who would prevent his springing out of the window into the park. Under that window there was a sort of buttress, while all the other windows in the galleries were at such a height from the ground that it was almost impossible to jump from them without breaking one's neck. All the doors and windows, including those of the lumber-room at the end of the 'right' gallery—as I had rapidly assured myself—were strongly secured.

"Having indicated to Daddy Jacques the post he was to occupy, and having seen him take up his position, I placed Monsieur Stangerson on the landing at the head of the stairs not far from the door of his daughter's ante-room, rather than the boudoir, where the women were, and the door of which must have been locked by Mademoiselle Stangerson herself if, as I thought, she had taken refuge in the boudoir for the purpose of avoiding the murderer who was coming to see her. In any case, he must return to the gallery where my people were awaiting him at every possible exit.

"On coming there, he would see on his left, Monsieur Stangerson; he would turn to the right, towards the 'off-turning' gallery—the way he had pre-arranged for flight, where, at the intersection of the two galleries, he would see at once, as I have explained, on his left, Frederic Larsan at the end of the 'off-turning' gallery, and in front, Daddy Jacques, at the end of the 'right' gallery. Monsieur Stangerson and myself would arrive by way of the back of the château.—He is ours!—He can no longer escape us! I was sure of that.

"The plan I had formed seemed to me the best, the surest, and the most simple. It would, no doubt, have been simpler still, if we had been able to place someone directly behind the door of Mademoiselle's boudoir, which opened out of her bedchamber, and, in that way, had been in a position to besiege the two doors of the room in which the man was. But we could not penetrate the boudoir except by way of the drawing-room, the door of which had been locked on the inside by Mademoiselle Stangerson. But even if I had had the free disposition of the boudoir, I should have held to the plan I had formed; because any other plan of attack would have separated us at the moment of the struggle with the man, while my plan united us all for the attack, at a spot which I had selected with almost mathematical precision, the intersection of the two galleries.

"Having so placed my people, I again left the château, hurried to my ladder, and, replacing it, climbed up, revolver in hand.

"If there be any inclined to smile at my taking so many precautionary measures, I refer them to the mystery of 'The Yellow Room', and to all the proofs we have of the weird cunning of the murderer. Further, if there be some who think my observations needlessly minute at a moment when they ought to be completely held by rapidity of movement and decision of action, I reply that I have wished to report here, at length and completely, all the details of a plan of attack conceived so rapidly that it is only the slowness of my pen that gives an appearance of slowness to the execution. I have wished, by this slowness and precision, to be certain that nothing should be omitted from the conditions under which the strange phenomenon was produced, which, until some natural explanation of it is forthcoming, seems to me to prove, even better than the theories of Professor Stangerson, the Dissociation of Matter—I will even say, the instantaneous Dissociation of Matter."

# XVI

## STRANGE PHENOMENON OF THE DISSOCIATION OF MATTER

(EXTRACT FROM THE NOTEBOOK OF JOSEPH ROULETABILLE, continued)

"I am again at the window-sill," continues Rouletabille, "and once more I raise my head above it. Through an opening in the curtains, the arrangement of which has not been changed, I am ready to look, anxious to note the position in which I am going to find the murderer,—whether his back will still be turned towards me!—whether he is still seated at the desk writing! But perhaps—perhaps—he is no longer there!—Yet how could he have fled?—Was I not in possession of his ladder? I force myself to be cool. I raise my head yet higher. I look—he is still there. I see his monstrous back, deformed by the shadow thrown by the candle. He is no longer writing now, and the candle is on the parquet, over which he is bending—a position which serves my purpose.

"I hold my breath. I mount the ladder. I am on the uppermost rung of it, and with my left hand seize hold of the window-sill. In this moment of approaching success, I feel my heart beating wildly. I put my revolver between my teeth. A quick spring, and I shall be on the window-ledge. But—the ladder! I had been obliged to press on it heavily, and my foot had scarcely left it, when I felt it swaying beneath me. It grated on the wall and fell. But, already, my knees were touching the window-sill, and, by a movement quick as lightning, I got on to it.

"But the murderer had been even quicker than I had been. He had heard the grating of the ladder on the wall, and I saw the monstrous back of the man raise itself. I saw his head. Did I really see it?—The candle on the parquet lit up his legs only. Above the height of the table the chamber was in darkness. I saw a man with long hair, a full beard, wild-looking eyes, a pale face, framed in large whiskers,—as well as I could distinguish, and, as I think—red in colour. I did not know the face. That was, in brief, the chief sensation I received from that face in the dim half-light in which I saw it. I did not know it—or, at least, I did not recognise it.

"Now for quick action! It was indeed time for that, for as I was about to place my legs through the window, the man had seen me, had bounded to his feet, had sprung—as I foresaw he would—to the door of the ante-chamber, had time to open it, and fled. But I was already behind him, revolver in hand, shouting 'Help!'

"Like an arrow I crossed the room, but noticed a letter on the table as I rushed. I almost came up with the man in the anteroom, for he had lost time in opening the door to the gallery. I flew on wings, and in the gallery was but a few feet behind him. He had taken, as I supposed he would, the gallery on his right,—that is to say, the road he had prepared for his flight. 'Help, Jacques!—help, Larsan!' I cried. He could not escape us! I raised a shout of joy, of savage victory. The man reached the intersection of the two galleries hardly two seconds before me for the meeting which I had prepared—the fatal shock which must inevitably take place at that spot! We all rushed to the crossing-place—Monsieur Stangerson and I coming from one end of the "right" gallery, Daddy Jacques coming from the other end of the same gallery, and Frederic Larsan coming from the 'off-turning' gallery.

"The man was not there!

"We looked at each other stupidly and with eyes terrified. The man had vanished like a ghost. 'Where is he—where is he?' we all asked.

"'It is impossible he can have escaped!' I cried, my terror mastered by my anger.

"'I touched him!' exclaimed Frederic Larsan.

"'I felt his breath on my face!' cried Daddy Jacques.

"'Where is he?—where is he?' we all cried.

"We raced like madmen along the two galleries; we visited doors and windows—they were closed, hermetically closed. They had not been opened. Besides, the opening of a door or window by this man whom we were hunting, without our having perceived it, would have been more inexplicable than his disappearance.

"Where is he?—where is he?—He could not have got away by a door or a window, nor by any other way. He could not have passed through our bodies!

"I confess that, for the moment, I felt 'done for.' For the gallery was perfectly lighted, and there was neither trap, nor secret door in the walls, nor any sort of hiding-place. We moved the chairs and lifted the pictures. Nothing!—nothing! We would have looked into a flower-pot, if there had been one to look into!"

When this mystery, thanks to Rouletabille, was naturally explained, by the help alone of his masterful mind, we were able to realise that the murderer had got away neither by a door, a window, nor the stairs—a fact which the judges would not admit.

# XVII

## THE INEXPLICABLE GALLERY

"Mademoiselle Stangerson appeared at the door of her ante-room," continues Rouletabille's notebook. "We were near her door in the gallery where this incredible phenomenon had taken place. There are moments when one feels as if one's brain were about to burst. A bullet in the head, a fracture of the skull, the seat of reason shattered—with only these can I compare the sensation which exhausted and left me void of sense.

"Happily, Mademoiselle Stangerson appeared on the threshold of her ante-room. I saw her, and that helped to relieve my chaotic state of mind. I breathed her—I inhaled the perfume of the lady in black, whom I should never see again. I would have given ten years of my life—half my life—to see once more the lady in black! Alas! I no more meet her but from time to time,—and yet!—and yet! how the memory of that perfume—felt by me alone—carries me back to the days of my childhood. It was this sharp reminder from my beloved perfume, of the lady in black, which made me go to her—dressed wholly in white and so pale—so pale and so beautiful!—on the threshold of the inexplicable gallery. Her beautiful golden hair, gathered into a knot on the back of her neck, left visible the red star on her temple which had so nearly been the cause of her death.

When I first got on the right track of the mystery of this case I had imagined that, on the night of the tragedy in 'The Yellow Room', Mademoiselle Stangerson had worn her hair in bands. But then, how could I have imagined otherwise when I had not been in 'The Yellow Room'!

"But now, since the occurrence of the inexplicable gallery, I did not reason at all. I stood there, stupid, before the apparition—so pale and so beautiful—of Mademoiselle Stangerson. She was clad in a dressing-gown of dreamy white. One might have taken her to be a ghost—a lovely phantom. Her father took her in his arms and kissed her passionately, as if he had recovered her after being long lost to him. I dared not question her. He drew her into the room and we followed them,—for we had to know!—The door of the boudoir was open. The terrified faces of the two nurses craned towards us. Mademoiselle Stangerson inquired the meaning of all the disturbance. That she was not in her own room was quite easily explained—quite easily. She had a fancy not to sleep that night in her chamber, but in the boudoir with her nurses, locking the door on them. Since the night of the crime she had experienced feelings of terror, and fears came over her that are easily to be comprehended.

"But who could imagine that on that particular night when he was to come, she would, by a mere chance, determine to shut herself in with her women? Who would think that she would act contrary to her father's wish to sleep in the drawing-room? Who could believe that the letter which had so recently been on the table in her room would no longer be there? He who could understand all this, would have to assume that Mademoiselle Stangerson knew that the murderer was coming—she could not prevent his coming again—unknown to her father, unknown to all but to Monsieur Robert Darzac. For he must know it now—perhaps he had known it before! Did he remember that phrase in the Elysee garden: 'Must I commit a crime, then, to win you?' Against whom the crime, if not against the obstacle, against the murderer? 'Ah, I would kill him with my own hand!' And I replied, 'You have not answered my question.' That was the very truth. In truth, in truth, Monsieur Darzac knew the murderer so well that—while wishing to kill him himself—he was afraid I should find him. There could be but two reasons why he had assisted me in my investigation. First, because I forced him to do it; and, second, because she would be the better protected.

"I am in the chamber—her room. I look at her, also at the place where the letter had just now been. She has possessed herself of it; it was evidently intended for her—evidently. How she trembles!—Trembles at the strange story her father is telling her, of the presence of the murderer in her chamber, and of the pursuit. But it is plainly to be seen that she is not wholly satisfied by the assurance given her until she had been told that the murderer, by some incomprehensible means, had been able to elude us.

"Then follows a silence. What a silence! We are all there—looking at her—her father, Larsan, Daddy Jacques and I. What were we all thinking of in the silence? After the events of that night, of the mystery of the inexplicable gallery, of the prodigious fact of the presence of the murderer in her room, it seemed to me that all our thoughts might have been translated into the words which were addressed to her. 'You who know of this mystery, explain it to us, and we shall perhaps be able to save you'. How I longed to save her—for herself, and, from the other!—It brought the tears to my eyes.

"She is there, shedding about her the perfume of the lady in black. At last, I see her, in the silence of her chamber. Since the fatal hour of the mystery of 'The Yellow Room', we have hung about this invisible and silent woman to learn what she knows. Our desires, our wish to know must be a torment to her. Who can tell that, should we learn the secret of her mystery, it would not precipitate a tragedy more terrible than that which had already been enacted here? Who can tell if it might not mean her death? Yet it had brought her close to death,—and we still knew nothing. Or, rather, there are some of us who know nothing. But I—if I knew who, I should know all. Who?—Who?—Not knowing who, I must remain silent, out of pity for her. For there is no doubt that she knows how he escaped from 'The Yellow Room', and yet she keeps the secret. When I know who, I will speak to him—to him!

"She looked at us now—with a faraway look in her eyes—as if we were not in the chamber. Monsieur Stangerson broke the silence. He declared that, henceforth, he would no more absent himself from his daughter's apartments. She tried to oppose him in vain. He adhered firmly to his purpose. He would install himself there this very night, he said. Solely concerned for the health of his daughter, he reproached her for having left her bed. Then he suddenly began talking to her as if she were a little child. He smiled at her and seemed not to know either what he said or what he did. The illustrious professor had lost his head. Mademoiselle Stangerson in a tone of tender distress said: 'Father!—father!' Daddy Jacques blows his nose, and Frederic Larsan himself is obliged to turn away to hide his emotion. For myself, I am able neither to think or feel. I felt an infinite contempt for myself.

"It was the first time that Frederic Larsan, like myself, found himself face to face with Mademoiselle Stangerson since the attack in 'The Yellow Room'. Like me, he had insisted on being allowed to question the unhappy lady; but he had not, any more than had I, been permitted. To him, as to me, the same answer had always been given: Mademoiselle Stangerson was too weak to receive us. The questionings of the examining magistrate had over-fatigued her. It was evidently intended not to give us any assistance in our researches. I was not surprised; but Frederic Larsan had always resented this conduct. It is true that he and I had a totally different theory of the crime.

"I still catch myself repeating from the depths of my heart: 'Save her!—save her without his speaking!' Who is he—the murderer? Take him and shut his mouth. But Monsieur Darzac made it clear that in order to shut his mouth he must be killed. Have I the right to kill Mademoiselle Stangerson's murderer? No, I had not. But let him only give me the chance! Let me find out whether he is really a creature of flesh and blood!—Let me see his dead body, since it cannot be taken alive.

"If I could but make this woman, who does not even look at us, understand! She is absorbed by her fears and by her father's distress of mind. And I can do nothing to save her. Yes, I will go to work once more and accomplish wonders.

"I move towards her. I would speak to her. I would entreat her to have confidence in me. I would, in a word, make her understand—she alone—that I know how the murderer escaped from 'The Yellow Room'—that I have guessed the motives for her secrecy—and that I pity her with all my heart. But by her gestures she begged us to leave her alone, expressing weariness and the need for immediate rest. Monsieur Stangerson asked us to go back to our rooms and thanked us. Frederic Larsan and I bowed to him and, followed by Daddy Jacques, we regained the gallery. I heard Larsan murmur: 'Strange! Strange!' He made a sign to me to go with him into his room. On the threshold he turned towards Daddy Jacques.

"'Did you see him distinctly?' he asked.

"'Who?'

"'The man?'

"'Saw him!—why, he had a big red beard and red hair.'

"'That's how he appeared to me,' I said.

"'And to me,' said Larsan.

"The great Fred and I were alone in his chamber, now, to talk over this thing. We talked for an hour, turning the matter over and viewing it from every side. From the questions put by him, from the explanation which he gives me, it is clear to me that—in spite of all our senses—he is persuaded the man disappeared by some secret passage in the château known to him alone.

"'He knows the château,' he said to me; 'he knows it well.'

"'He is a rather tall man—well-built,' I suggested.

"'He is as tall as he wants to be,' murmured Fred.

"'I understand,' I said; 'but how do you account for his red hair and beard?'

"'Too much beard—too much hair—false,' says Fred.

"'That's easily said. You are always thinking of Robert Darzac. You can't get rid of that idea? I am certain that he is innocent.'

"'So much the better. I hope so; but everything condemns him. Did you notice the marks on the carpet?—Come and look at them.'

"'I have seen them; they are the marks of the neat boots, the same as those we saw on the border of the lake.'

"'Can you deny that they belong to Robert Darzac?'

"'Of course, one may be mistaken.'

"'Have you noticed that those footprints only go in one direction?—that there are no return marks? When the man came from the chamber, pursued by all of us, his footsteps left no traces behind them.'

"'He had, perhaps, been in the chamber for hours. The mud from his boots had dried, and he moved with such rapidity on the points of his toes—We saw him running, but we did not hear his steps.'

"I suddenly put an end to this idle chatter—void of any logic, and made a sign to Larsan to listen.

"'There—below; someone is shutting a door.'

"I rise; Larsan follows me; we descend to the ground-floor of the château. I lead him to the little semi-circular room under the terrace beneath the window of the 'off-turning' gallery. I point to the door, now closed, open a short time before, under which a shaft of light is visible.

"'The forest-keeper!' says Fred.

"'Come on!' I whisper.

"Prepared—I know not why—to believe that the keeper is the guilty man—I go to the door and rap smartly on it. Some might think that we were rather late in thinking of the keeper, since our first business, after having found that the murderer had escaped us in the gallery, ought to have been to search everywhere else,—around the château,—in the park—

"Had this criticism been made at the time, we could only have answered that the assassin had disappeared from the gallery in such a way that we thought he was no longer anywhere! He had eluded us when we all had our hands stretched out ready to seize him—when we were almost touching him. We had no longer any ground for hoping that we could clear up the mystery of that night.

"As soon as I rapped at the door it was opened, and the keeper asked us quietly what we wanted. He was undressed and preparing to go to bed. The bed had not yet been disturbed.

"We entered and I affected surprise.

"'Not gone to bed yet?'

"'No,' he replied roughly. 'I have been making a round of the park and in the woods. I am only just back—and sleepy. Good-night!'

"'Listen,' I said. 'An hour or so ago, there was a ladder close by your window.'

"'What ladder?—I did not see any ladder. Good-night!'

"And he simply put us out of the room. When we were outside I looked at Larsan. His face was impenetrable.

"'Well?' I said.

"'Well?' he repeated.

"'Does that open out any new view to you?'

"There was no mistaking Larsan's bad temper. On re-entering the château, I heard him mutter:

"'It would be strange—very strange—if I had deceived myself on that point!'

"He seemed to be talking to me rather than to himself. He added: 'In any case, we shall soon know what to think. The morning will bring light with it.'"

# XVIII

## ROULETABILLE HAS DRAWN A CIRCLE BETWEEN THE TWO BUMPS ON HIS FOREHEAD

(EXTRACT FROM THE NOTEBOOK OF JOSEPH ROULETABILLE, continued)

"We separated on the thresholds of our rooms, with a melancholy shake of the hands. I was glad to have aroused in him a suspicion of error. His was an original brain, very intelligent but—without method. I did not go to bed. I awaited the coming of daylight and then went down to the front of the château, and made a detour, examining every trace of footsteps coming towards it or going from it. These, however, were so mixed and confusing that I could make nothing of them. Here I may make a remark,—I am not accustomed to attach an exaggerated importance to exterior signs left in the track of a crime.

"The method which traces the criminal by means of the tracks of his footsteps is altogether primitive. So many footprints are identical. However, in the disturbed state of my mind, I did go into the deserted court and did look at all the footprints I could find there, seeking for some indication, as a basis for reasoning.

"If I could but find a right starting-point! In despair I seated myself on a stone. For over an hour I busied myself with the common, ordinary work of a policeman. Like the least intelligent of detectives I went on blindly over the traces of footprints which told me just no more than they could.

"I came to the conclusion that I was a fool, lower in the scale of intelligence than even the police of the modern romancer. Novelists build mountains of stupidity out of a footprint on the sand, or from an impression of a hand on the wall. That's the way innocent men are brought to prison. It might convince an examining magistrate or the head of a detective department, but it's not proof. You writers forget that what the senses furnish is not proof. If I am taking cognisance of what is offered me by my senses I do so but to bring the results within the circle of my reason. That circle may be the most circumscribed, but if it is, it has this advantage—it holds nothing but the truth! Yes, I swear that I have never used the evidence of the senses but as servants to my reason. I have never permitted them to become my master. They have not made of me that monstrous thing,—worse than a blind man,—a man who sees falsely. And that is why I can triumph over your error and your merely animal intelligence, Frederic Larsan.

"Be of good courage, then, friend Rouletabille; it is impossible that the incident of the inexplicable gallery should be outside the circle of your reason. You know that! Then have faith and take thought with yourself and forget not that you took hold of the right end when you drew that circle in your brain within which to unravel this mysterious play of circumstance.

"To it, once again! Go—back to the gallery. Take your stand on your reason and rest there as Frederic Larsan rests on his cane. You will then soon prove that the great Fred is nothing but a fool.

—30th October. Noon.

JOSEPH ROULETABILLE."

*****

"I acted as I planned. With head on fire, I retraced my way to the gallery, and without having found anything more than I had seen on the previous night, the right hold I had taken of my reason drew me to something so important that I was obliged to cling to it to save myself from falling.

"Now for the strength and patience to find sensible traces to fit in with my thinking—and these must come within the circle I have drawn between the two bumps on my forehead!

—30th of October. Midnight."

"JOSEPH ROULETABILLE."

# XIX

## ROULETABILLE INVITES ME TO BREAKFAST AT THE DONJON INN

It was not until later that Rouletabille sent me the notebook in which he had written at length the story of the phenomenon of the inexplicable gallery. On the day I arrived at the Glandier and joined him in his room, he recounted to me, with the greatest detail, all that I have now related, telling me also how he had spent several hours in Paris where he had learned nothing that could be of any help to him.

The event of the inexplicable gallery had occurred on the night between the 29th and 30th of October, that is to say, three days before my return to the château. It was on the 2nd of November, then, that I went back to the Glandier, summoned there by my friend's telegram, and taking the revolvers with me.

I am now in Rouletabille's room and he has finished his recital.

While he had been telling me the story I noticed him continually rubbing the glass of the eyeglasses he had found on the side table. From the evident pleasure he was taking in handling them I felt they must be one of those sensible evidences destined to enter what he had called the circle of the right end of his reason. That strange and unique way of his, to express himself in terms wonderfully adequate for his thoughts, no longer surprised me. It was often necessary to know his thought to understand the terms he used; and it was not easy to penetrate into Rouletabille's thinking.

This lad's brain was one of the most curious things I have ever observed. Rouletabille went on the even tenor of his way without suspecting the astonishment and even bewilderment he roused in others. I am sure he was not himself in the least conscious of the originality of his genius. He was himself and at ease wherever he happened to be.

When he had finished his recital he asked me what I thought of it. I replied that I was much puzzled by his question. Then he begged me to try, in my turn, to take my reason in hand "by the right end."

"Very well," I said. "It seems to me that the point of departure of my reason would be this—there can be no doubt that the murderer you pursued was in the gallery." I paused.

"After making so good a start, you ought not to stop so soon," he exclaimed. "Come, make another effort."

"I'll try. Since he disappeared from the gallery without passing through any door or window, he must have escaped by some other opening."

Rouletabille looked at me pityingly, smiled carelessly, and remarked that I was reasoning like a postman, or—like Frederic Larsan.

Rouletabille had alternate fits of admiration and disdain for the great Fred. It all depended as to whether Larsan's discoveries tallied with Rouletabille's reasoning or not. When they did he would exclaim: "He is really great!" When they did not he would grunt and mutter, "What an ass!" It was a petty side of the noble character of this strange youth.

We had risen, and he led me into the park. When we reached the court and were making towards the gate, the sound of blinds thrown back against the wall made us turn our heads, and we saw, at a window on the first floor of the château, the ruddy and clean shaven face of a person I did not recognise.

"Hullo!" muttered Rouletabille. "Arthur Rance!"—He lowered his head, quickened his pace, and I heard him ask himself between his teeth: "Was he in the château that night? What is he doing here?"

We had gone some distance from the château when I asked him who this Arthur Rance was, and how he had come to know him. He referred to his story of that morning and I remembered that Mr. Arthur W. Rance was the American from Philadelphia with whom he had had so many drinks at the Elysee reception.

"But was he not to have left France almost immediately?" I asked.

"No doubt; that's why I am surprised to find him here still, and not only in France, but above all, at the Glandier. He did not arrive this morning; and he did not get here last night. He must have got here before dinner, then. Why didn't the concierges tell me?"

I reminded my friend, apropos of the concierges, that he had not yet told me what had led him to get them set at liberty.

We were close to their lodge. Monsieur and Madame Bernier saw us coming. A frank smile lit up their happy faces. They seemed to harbour no ill-feeling because of their detention. My young friend asked them at what hour Mr. Arthur Rance had arrived. They answered that they did not know he was at the château. He must have come during the evening of the previous night, but they had not had to open the gate for him, because, being a great walker, and not wishing that a carriage should be sent to meet him, he was accustomed to get off at the little hamlet of Saint-Michel, from which he came to the château by way of the forest. He reached the park by the grotto of Sainte-Genevieve, over the little gate of which, giving on to the park, he climbed.

As the concierges spoke, I saw Rouletabille's face cloud over and exhibit disappointment—a disappointment, no doubt, with himself. Evidently he was a little vexed, after having worked so much on the spot, with so minute a study of the people and events at the Glandier, that he had to learn now that Arthur Rance was accustomed to visit the château.

"You say that Monsieur Arthur Rance is accustomed to come to the château. When did he come here last?"

"We can't tell you exactly," replied Madame Bernier—that was the name of the concierge—"we couldn't know while they were keeping us in prison. Besides, as the gentleman comes to the château without passing through our gate he goes away by the way he comes."

"Do you know when he came the first time?"

"Oh yes, Monsieur!—nine years ago."

"He was in France nine years ago, then," said Rouletabille, "and, since that time, as far as you know, how many times has he been at the Glandier?"

"Three times."

"When did he come the last time, as far as you know?"

"A week before the attempt in 'The Yellow Room'."

Rouletabille put another question—this time addressing himself particularly to the woman:

"In the grove of the parquet?"

"In the grove of the parquet," she replied.

"Thanks!" said Rouletabille. "Be ready for me this evening."

He spoke the last words with a finger on his lips as if to command silence and discretion.

We left the park and took the way to the Donjon Inn.

"Do you often eat here?"

"Sometimes."

"But you also take your meals at the château?"

"Yes, Larsan and I are sometimes served in one of our rooms."

"Hasn't Monsieur Stangerson ever invited you to his own table?"

"Never."

"Does your presence at the château displease him?"

"I don't know; but, in any case, he does not make us feel that we are in his way."

"Doesn't he question you?"

"Never. He is in the same state of mind as he was in at the door of The "Yellow Room" when his daughter was being murdered, and when he broke open the door and did not find the murderer. He is persuaded, since he could discover nothing, that there's no reason why we should be able to discover more than he did. But he has made it his duty, since Larsan expressed his theory, not to oppose us."

Rouletabille buried himself in thought again for some time. He aroused himself later to tell me of how he came to set the two concierges free.

"I went recently to see Monsieur Stangerson, and took with me a piece of paper on which was written: 'I promise, whatever others may say, to keep in my service my two faithful servants, Bernier and his wife.' I explained to him that, by signing that document, he would enable me to compel those two people to speak out; and I declared my own assurance of their innocence of any part in the crime. That was also his opinion. The examining magistrate, after it was signed, presented the document to the Berniers, who then did speak. They said, what I was certain they would say, as soon as they were sure they would not lose their place.

"They confessed to poaching on Monsieur Stangerson's estates, and it was while they were poaching, on the night of the crime, that they were found not far from the pavilion at the moment when the outrage was being committed. Some rabbits they caught in that way were sold by them to the landlord of the Donjon Inn, who served them to his customers, or sent them to Paris. That was the truth, as I had guessed from the first. Do you remember what I said, on entering the Donjon Inn?—'We shall have to eat red meat—now!' I had heard the words on the same morning when we arrived at the park gate. You heard them also, but you did not attach any importance to them. You recollect, when we reached the park gate, that we stopped to look at a man who was running by the side of the wall, looking every minute at his watch. That was Larsan. Well, behind us the landlord of the Donjon Inn, standing on his doorstep, said to someone inside: 'We shall have to eat red meat—now.'

"Why that 'now'? When you are, as I am, in search of some hidden secret, you can't afford to have anything escape you. You've got to know the meaning of everything. We had come into a rather out-of-the-way part of the country which had been turned topsy-turvey by a crime, and my reason led me to suspect every phrase that could bear upon the event of the day. 'Now,' I took to mean, 'since the outrage.' In the course of my inquiry, therefore, I sought to find a relation between that phrase and the tragedy. We went to the Donjon Inn for breakfast; I repeated the phrase and saw, by the surprise and trouble on Daddy Mathieu's face, that I had not exaggerated its importance, so far as he was concerned.

"I had just learned that the concierges had been arrested. Daddy Mathieu spoke of them as of dear friends—people for whom one is sorry. That was a reckless conjunction of ideas, I said to myself. 'Now,' that the concierges are arrested, 'we shall have to eat red meat.' No more concierges, no more game! The hatred expressed by Daddy Mathieu for Monsieur Stangerson's forest-keeper—a hatred he pretended was shared by the concierges led me easily to think of poaching. Now as all the evidence showed the concierges had not been in bed at the time of the tragedy, why were they abroad that night? As participants in the crime? I was not disposed to think so. I had already arrived at the conclusion, by steps of which I will tell you later—that the assassin had had no accomplice, and that the tragedy held a mystery between Mademoiselle Stangerson and the murderer, a mystery with which the concierges had nothing to do.

"With that theory in my mind, I searched for proof in their lodge, which, as you know, I entered. I found there under their bed, some springs and brass wire. 'Ah!' I thought, 'these things explain why they were out in the park at night!' I was not surprised at the dogged silence they maintained before the examining magistrate, even under the accusation so grave as that of being accomplices in the crime. Poaching would save them from the Assize Court, but it would lose them their places; and, as they were perfectly sure of their innocence of the crime they hoped it would soon be established, and then their poaching might go on as usual. They could always confess later. I, however, hastened their confession by means of the document Monsieur Stangerson signed. They gave all the necessary 'proofs,' were set at liberty, and have now a lively gratitude for me. Why did I not get them released sooner? Because I was not sure that nothing more than poaching was against them. I wanted to study the ground. As the days went by, my conviction became more and more certain. The day after the events of the inexplicable gallery I had need of help I could rely on, so I resolved to have them released at once."

That was how Joseph Rouletabille explained himself. Once more I could not but be astonished at the simplicity of the reasoning which had brought him to the truth of the matter. Certainly this was no big thing; but I think, myself, that the young man will, one of these days, explain with the same simplicity, the fearful tragedy in "The Yellow Room" as well as the phenomenon of the inexplicable gallery.

We reached the Donjon Inn and entered it.

This time we did not see the landlord, but were received with a pleasant smile by the hostess. I have already described the room in which we found ourselves, and I have given a glimpse of the charming blonde woman with the gentle eyes who now immediately began to prepare our breakfast.

"How's Daddy Mathieu?" asked Rouletabille.

"Not much better—not much better; he is still confined to his bed."

"His rheumatism still sticks to him, then?"

"Yes. Last night I was again obliged to give him morphine—the only drug that gives him any relief."

She spoke in a soft voice. Everything about her expressed gentleness. She was, indeed, a beautiful woman; somewhat with an air of indolence, with great eyes seemingly black and blue—amorous eyes. Was she happy with her crabbed, rheumatic husband? The scene at which we had once been present did not lead us to believe that she was; yet there was something in her bearing that was not suggestive of despair. She disappeared into the kitchen to prepare our repast, leaving on the table a bottle of excellent cider. Rouletabille filled our earthenware mugs, loaded his pipe, and quietly explained to me his reason for asking me to come to the Glandier with revolvers.

"Yes," he said, contemplatively looking at the clouds of smoke he was puffing out, "yes, my dear boy, I expect the assassin tonight." A brief silence followed, which I took care not to interrupt, and then he went on:

"Last night, just as I was going to bed, Monsieur Robert Darzac knocked at my room. When he came in he confided to me that he was compelled to go to Paris the next day, that is, this morning. The reason which made this journey necessary was at once peremptory and mysterious; it was not possible for him to explain its object to me. 'I go, and yet,' he added, 'I would give my life not to leave Mademoiselle Stangerson at this moment.' He did not try to hide that he believed her to be once more in danger. 'It will not greatly astonish me if something happens tomorrow night,' he avowed, 'and yet I must be absent. I cannot be back at the Glandier before the morning of the day after tomorrow.'

"I asked him to explain himself, and this is all he would tell me. His anticipation of coming danger had come to him solely from the coincidence that Mademoiselle Stangerson had been twice attacked, and both times when he had been absent. On the night of the incident of the inexplicable gallery he had been obliged to be away from the Glandier. On the night of the tragedy in 'The Yellow Room' he had also not been able to be at the Glandier, though this was the first time he had declared himself on the matter. Now a man so moved who would still go away must be acting under compulsion—must be obeying a will stronger than his own. That was how I reasoned, and I told him so. He replied 'Perhaps.'—I asked him if Mademoiselle Stangerson was compelling him. He protested that she was not. His determination to go to Paris had been taken without any conference with Mademoiselle Stangerson.

"To cut the story short, he repeated that his belief in the possibility of a fresh attack was founded entirely on the extraordinary coincidence. 'If anything happens to Mademoiselle Stangerson,' he said, 'it would be terrible for both of us. For her, because her life would be in danger; for me because I could neither defend her from the attack nor tell of where I had been. I am perfectly aware of the suspicions cast on me. The examining magistrate and Monsieur Larsan are both on the point of believing in my guilt. Larsan tracked me the last time I went to Paris, and I had all the trouble in the world to get rid of him.'

"'Why do you not tell me the name of the murderer now, if you know it?' I cried.

"Monsieur Darzac appeared extremely troubled by my question, and replied to me in a hesitating tone:

"'I?—I know the name of the murderer? Why, how could I know his name?'

"I at once replied: 'From Mademoiselle Stangerson.'

"He grew so pale that I thought he was about to faint, and I saw that I had hit the nail right on the head. Mademoiselle and he knew the name of the murderer! When he recovered himself, he said to me: 'I am going to leave you. Since you have been here I have appreciated your exceptional intelligence and your unequalled ingenuity. But I ask this service of you. Perhaps I am wrong to fear an attack during the coming night; but, as I must act with foresight, I count on you to frustrate any attempt that may be made. Take every step needful to protect Mademoiselle Stangerson. Keep a most careful watch of her room. Don't go to sleep, nor allow yourself one moment of repose. The man we dread is remarkably cunning—with a cunning that has never been equalled. If you keep watch his very cunning may save her; because it's impossible that he should not know that you are watching; and knowing it, he may not venture.'

"'Have you spoken of all this to Monsieur Stangerson?'

"'No. I do not wish him to ask me, as you just now did, for the name of the murderer. I tell you all this, Monsieur Rouletabille, because I have great, very great, confidence in you. I know that you do not suspect me.'

"The poor man spoke in jerks. He was evidently suffering. I pitied him, the more because I felt sure that he would rather allow himself to be killed than tell me who the murderer was. As for Mademoiselle Stangerson, I felt that she would rather allow herself to be murdered than denounce the man of 'The Yellow Room' and of the inexplicable gallery. The man must be dominating her, or both, by some inscrutable power. They were dreading nothing so much as the chance of Monsieur Stangerson knowing that his daughter was 'held' by her assailant. I made Monsieur Darzac understand that he had explained himself sufficiently, and that he might refrain from telling me any more than he had already told me. I promised him to watch through the night. He insisted that I should establish an absolutely impassable barrier around Mademoiselle Stangerson's chamber, around the boudoir where the nurses were sleeping, and around the drawing-room where, since the affair of the inexplicable gallery, Monsieur Stangerson had slept. In short, I was to put a cordon round the whole apartment.

"From his insistence I gathered that Monsieur Darzac intended not only to make it impossible for the expected man to reach the chamber of Mademoiselle Stangerson, but to make that impossibility so visibly clear that, seeing himself expected, he would at once go away. That was how I interpreted his final words when we parted: 'You may mention your suspicions of the expected attack to Monsieur Stangerson, to Daddy Jacques, to Frederic Larsan, and to anybody in the château.'

"The poor fellow left me hardly knowing what he was saying. My silence and my eyes told him that I had guessed a large part of his secret. And, indeed, he must have been at his wits' end, to have come to me at such a time, and to abandon Mademoiselle Stangerson in spite of his fixed idea as to the consequence.

"When he was gone, I began to think that I should have to use even a greater cunning than his so that if the man should come that night, he might not for a moment suspect that his coming had been expected. Certainly! I would allow him to get in far enough, so that, dead or alive, I might see his face clearly! He must be got rid of. Mademoiselle Stangerson must be freed from this continual impending danger.

"Yes, my boy," said Rouletabille, after placing his pipe on the table, and emptying his mug of cider, "I must see his face distinctly, so as to make sure to impress it on that part of my brain where I have drawn my circle of reasoning."

The landlady re-appeared at that moment, bringing in the traditional bacon omelette. Rouletabille chaffed her a little, and she took the chaff with the most charming good humour.

"She is much jollier when Daddy Mathieu is in bed with his rheumatism," Rouletabille said to me.

But I had eyes neither for Rouletabille nor for the landlady's smiles. I was entirely absorbed over the last words of my young friend and in thinking over Monsieur Robert Darzac's strange behaviour.

When he had finished his omelette and we were again alone, Rouletabille continued the tale of his confidences.

"When I sent you my telegram this morning," he said, "I had only the word of Monsieur Darzac, that 'perhaps' the assassin would come tonight. I can now say that he will certainly come. I expect him."

"What has made you feel this certainty?"

"I have been sure since half-past ten o'clock this morning that he would come. I knew that before we saw Arthur Rance at the window in the court."

"Ah!" I said, "But, again—what made you so sure? And why since half-past ten this morning?"

"Because, at half-past ten, I had proof that Mademoiselle Stangerson was making as many efforts to permit of the murderer's entrance as Monsieur Robert Darzac had taken precautions against it."

"Is that possible!" I cried. "Haven't you told me that Mademoiselle Stangerson loves Monsieur Robert Darzac?"

"I told you so because it is the truth."

"Then do you see nothing strange—"

"Everything in this business is strange, my friend; but take my word for it, the strangeness you now feel is nothing to the strangeness that's to come!"

"It must be admitted, then," I said, "that Mademoiselle Stangerson and her murderer are in communication—at any rate in writing?"

"Admit it, my friend, admit it! You don't risk anything! I told you about the letter left on her table, on the night of the inexplicable gallery affair,—the letter that disappeared into the pocket of Mademoiselle Stangerson. Why should it not have been a summons to a meeting? Might he not, as soon as he was sure of Darzac's absence, appoint the meeting for the coming night?"

And my friend laughed silently. There are moments when I ask myself if he is not laughing at me.

The door of the inn opened. Rouletabille was on his feet so suddenly that one might have thought he had received an electric shock.

"Mr. Arthur Rance!" he cried.

Mr. Arthur Rance stood before us calmly bowing.

# XX

## AN ACT OF MADEMOISELLE STANGERSON

"You remember me, Monsieur?" asked Rouletabille.

"Perfectly!" replied Arthur Rance. "I recognise you as the lad at the bar. [The face of Rouletabille crimsoned at being called a "lad."] I want to shake hands with you. You are a bright little fellow."

The American extended his hand and Rouletabille, relaxing his frown, shook it and introduced Mr. Arthur Rance to me. He invited him to share our meal.

"No thanks. I breakfasted with Monsieur Stangerson."

Arthur Rance spoke French perfectly,—almost without an accent.

"I did not expect to have the pleasure of seeing you again, Monsieur. I thought you were to have left France the day after the reception at the Elysee."

Rouletabille and I, outwardly indifferent, listened most intently for every word the American would say.

The man's purplish red face, his heavy eyelids, the nervous twitchings, all spoke of his addiction to drink. How came it that so sorry a specimen of a man should be so intimate with Monsieur Stangerson?

Some days later, I learned from Frederic Larsan—who, like ourselves, was surprised and mystified by his appearance and reception at the château—that Mr. Rance had been an inebriate for only about fifteen years; that is to say, since the professor and his daughter left Philadelphia. During the time the Stangersons lived in America they were very intimate with Arthur Rance, who was one of the most distinguished phrenologists of the new world. Owing to new experiments, he had made enormous strides beyond the science of Gall and Lavater. The friendliness with which he was received at the Glandier may be explained by the fact that he had once rendered Mademoiselle Stangerson a great service by stopping, at the peril of his own life, the runaway horses of her carriage. The immediate result of that could, however, have been no more than a mere friendly association with the Stangersons; certainly, not a love affair.

Frederic Larsan did not tell me where he had picked up this information; but he appeared to be quite sure of what he said.

Had we known these facts at the time Arthur Rance met us at the Donjon Inn, his presence at the château might not have puzzled us, but they could not have failed to increase our interest in the man himself. The American must have been at least forty-five years old. He spoke in a perfectly natural tone in reply to Rouletabille's question.

"I put off my return to America when I heard of the attack on Mademoiselle Stangerson. I wanted to be certain the lady had not been killed, and I shall not go away until she is perfectly recovered."

Arthur Rance then took the lead in talk, paying no heed to some of Rouletabille's questions. He gave us, without our inviting him, his personal views on the subject of the tragedy,—views which, as well as I could make out, were not far from those held by Frederic Larzan. The American also thought that Robert Darzac had something to do with the matter. He did not mention him by name, but there was no room to doubt whom he meant. He told us he was aware of the efforts young Rouletabille was making to unravel the tangled skein of "The Yellow Room" mystery. He explained that Monsieur Stangerson had related to him all that had taken place in the inexplicable gallery. He several times expressed his regret at Monsieur Darzac's absence from the château on all these occasions, and thought that Monsieur Darzac had done cleverly in allying himself with Monsieur Joseph Rouletabille, who could not fail, sooner or later, to discover the murderer. He spoke the last sentence with unconcealed irony. Then he rose, bowed to us, and left the inn.

Rouletabille watched him through the window.

"An odd fish, that!" he said.

"Do you think he'll pass the night at the Glandier?" I asked.

To my amazement the young reporter answered that it was a matter of entire indifference to him whether he did or not.

As to how we spent our time during the afternoon, all I need say is that Rouletabille led me to the grotto of Sainte-Genevieve, and, all the time, talked of every subject but the one in which we were most interested. Towards evening I was surprised to find Rouletabille making none of the preparations I had expected him to make. I spoke to him about it when night had come on, and we were once more in his room. He replied that all his arrangements had already been made, and this time the murderer would not get away from him.

I expressed some doubt on this, reminding him of his disappearance in the gallery, and suggested that the same phenomenon might occur again. He answered that he hoped it would. He desired nothing more. I did not insist, knowing by experience how useless that would have been. He told me that, with the help of the concierges, the château had since early dawn been watched in such a way that nobody could approach it without his knowing it, and that he had no concern for those who might have left it and remained without.

It was then six o'clock by his watch. Rising, he made a sign to me to follow him, and, without in the least trying to conceal his movements or the sound of his footsteps, he led me through the gallery. We reached the 'right' gallery and came to the landing-place which we crossed. We then continued our way in the gallery of the left wing, passing Professor Stangerson's apartment.

At the far end of the gallery, before coming to the donjon, is the room occupied by Arthur Rance. We knew that, because we had seen him at the window looking on to the court. The door of the room opens on to the end of the gallery, exactly facing the east window, at the extremity of the 'right' gallery, where Rouletabille had placed Daddy Jacques, and commands an uninterrupted view of the gallery from end to end of the chateau.

"That 'off-turning' gallery," said Rouletabille, "I reserve for myself; when I tell you you'll come and take your place here."

And he made me enter a little dark, triangular closet built in a bend of the wall, to the left of the door of Arthur Rance's room. From this recess I could see all that occurred in the gallery as well as if I had been standing in front of Arthur Rance's door, and I could watch that door, too. The door of the closet, which was to be my place of observation, was fitted with panels of transparent glass. In the gallery, where all the lamps had been lit, it was quite light. In the closet, however, it was quite dark. It was a splendid place from which to observe and remain unobserved.

I was soon to play the part of a spy—a common policeman. I wonder what my leader at the bar would have said had he known! I was not altogether pleased with my duties, but I could not refuse Rouletabille the assistance he had begged me to give him. I took care not to make him see that I in the least objected, and for several reasons. I wanted to oblige him; I did not wish him to think me a coward; I was filled with curiosity; and it was too late for me to draw back, even had I determined to do so. That I had not had these scruples sooner was because my curiosity had quite got the better of me. I might also urge that I was helping to save the life of a woman, and even a lawyer may do that conscientiously.

We returned along the gallery. On reaching the door of Mademoiselle Stangerson's apartment, it opened from a push given by the steward who was waiting at the dinner-table. (Monsieur Stangerson had, for the last three days, dined with his daughter in the drawing-room on the first floor.) As the door remained open, we distinctly saw Mademoiselle Stangerson, taking advantage of the steward's absence, and while her father was stooping to pick up something he had let fall, pour the contents of a phial into Monsieur Stangerson's glass.

# XXI

## ON THE WATCH

The act, which staggered me, did not appear to affect Rouletabille much. We returned to his room and, without even referring to what we had seen, he gave me his final instructions for the night. First we were to go to dinner; after dinner, I was to take my stand in the dark closet and wait there as long as it was necessary—to look out for what might happen.

"If you see anything before I do," he explained, "you must let me know. If the man gets into the 'right' gallery by any other way than the 'off-turning' gallery, you will see him before I shall, because you have a view along the whole length of the 'right' gallery, while I can only command a view of the 'off-turning' gallery. All you need do to let me know is to undo the cord holding the curtain of the 'right' gallery window, nearest to the dark closet. The curtain will fall of itself and immediately leave a square of shadow where previously there had been a square of light. To do this, you need but stretch your hand out of the closet, I shall understand your signal perfectly."

"And then?"

"Then you will see me coming round the corner of the 'off-turning' gallery."

"What am I to do then?"

"You will immediately come towards me, behind the man; but I shall already be upon him, and shall have seen his face."

I attempted a feeble smile.

"Why do you smile? Well, you may smile while you have the chance, but I swear you'll have no time for that a few hours from now.

"And if the man escapes?"

"So much the better," said Rouletabille, coolly, "I don't want to capture him. He may take himself off any way he can. I will let him go—after I have seen his face. That's all I want. I shall know afterwards what to do so that as far as Mademoiselle Stangerson is concerned he shall be dead to her even though he continues to live. If I took him alive, Mademoiselle Stangerson and Robert Darzac would, perhaps, never forgive me! And I wish to retain their good-will and respect.

"Seeing, as I have just now seen, Mademoiselle Stangerson pour a narcotic into her father's glass, so that he might not be awake to interrupt the conversation she is going to have with her murderer, you can imagine she would not be grateful to me if I brought the man of 'The Yellow Room' and the inexplicable gallery, bound and gagged, to her father. I realise now that if I am to save the unhappy lady, I must silence the man and not capture him. To kill a human being is no small thing. Besides, that's not my business, unless the man himself makes it my business. On the other hand, to render him forever silent without the lady's assent and confidence is to act on one's own initiative and assumes a knowledge of everything with nothing for a basis. Fortunately, my friend, I have guessed, no, I have reasoned it all out. All that I ask of the man who is coming tonight is to bring me his face, so that it may enter—"

"Into the circle?"

"Exactly! And his face won't surprise me!"

"But I thought you saw his face on the night when you sprang into the chamber?"

"Only imperfectly. The candle was on the floor; and, his beard—"

"Will he wear his beard this evening?"

"I think I can say for certain that he will. But the gallery is light and, now, I know—or—at least, my brain knows—and my eyes will see."

"If we are here only to see him and let him escape, why are we armed?"

"Because, if the man of 'The Yellow Room' and the inexplicable gallery knows that I know, he is capable of doing anything! We should then have to defend ourselves."

"And you are sure he will come tonight?"

"As sure as that you are standing there! This morning, at half-past ten o'clock, Mademoiselle Stangerson, in the cleverest way in the world, arranged to have no nurses tonight. She gave them leave of absence for twenty-four hours, under some plausible pretexts, and did not desire anybody to be with her but her father, while they are away. Her father, who is to sleep in the boudoir, has gladly consented to the arrangement. Darzac's departure and what he told me, as well as the extraordinary precautions Mademoiselle Stangerson is taking to be alone tonight leaves me no room for doubt. She has prepared the way for the coming of the man whom Darzac dreads."

"That's awful!"

"It is!"

"And what we saw her do was done to send her father to sleep?"

"Yes."

"Then there are but two of us for tonight's work?"

"Four; the concierge and his wife will watch at all hazards. I don't set much value on them before—but the concierge may be useful after—if there's to be any killing!"

"Then you think there may be?"

"If he wishes it."

"Why haven't you brought in Daddy Jacques?—Have you made no use of him today?"

"No," replied Rouletabille sharply.

I kept silence for awhile, then, anxious to know his thoughts, I asked him point-blank:

"Why not tell Arthur Rance?—He may be of great assistance to us?"

"Oh!" said Rouletabille crossly, "then you want to let everybody into Mademoiselle Stangerson's secrets?—Come, let us go to dinner; it is time. This evening we dine in Frederic Larsan's room,—at least, if he is not on the heels of Darzac. He sticks to him like a leech. But, anyhow, if he is not there now, I am quite sure he will be, tonight! He's the one I am going to knock over!"

At this moment we heard a noise in the room near us.

"It must be he," said Rouletabille.

"I forgot to ask you," I said, "if we are to make any allusion to tonight's business when we are with this policeman. I take it we are not. Is that so?"

"Evidently. We are going to operate alone, on our own personal account."

"So that all the glory will be ours?"

Rouletabille laughed.

We dined with Frederic Larsan in his room. He told us he had just come in and invited us to be seated at table. We ate our dinner in the best of humours, and I had no difficulty in appreciating the feelings of certainty which both Rouletabille and Larsan felt. Rouletabille told the great Fred that I had come on a chance visit, and that he had asked me to stay and help him in the heavy batch of writing he had to get through for the "Epoque." I was going back to Paris, he said, by the eleven o'clock train, taking his "copy," which took a story form, recounting the principal episodes in the mysteries of the Glandier. Larsan smiled at the explanation like a man who was not fooled and politely refrains from making the slightest remark on matters which did not concern him.

With infinite precautions as to the words they used, and even as to the tones of their voices, Larsan and Rouletabille discussed, for a long time, Mr. Arthur Rance's appearance at the château, and his past in America, about which they expressed a desire to know more, at any rate, so far as his relations with the Stangersons. At one time, Larsan, who appeared to me to be unwell, said, with an effort:

"I think, Monsieur Rouletabille, that we've not much more to do at the Glandier, and that we sha'n't sleep here many more nights."

"I think so, too, Monsieur Fred."

"Then you think the conclusion of the matter has been reached?"

"I think, indeed, that we have nothing more to find out," replied Rouletabille.

"Have you found your criminal?" asked Larsan.

"Have you?"

"Yes."

"So have I," said Rouletabille.

"Can it be the same man?"

"I don't know if you have swerved from your original idea," said the young reporter. Then he added, with emphasis: "Monsieur Darzac is an honest man!"

"Are you sure of that?" asked Larsan. "Well, I am sure he is not. So it's a fight then?"

"Yes, it is a fight. But I shall beat you, Monsieur Frederic Larsan."

"Youth never doubts anything," said the great Fred laughingly, and held out his hand to me by way of conclusion.

Rouletabille's answer came like an echo:

"Not anything!"

Suddenly Larsan, who had risen to wish us good-night, pressed both his hands to his chest and staggered. He was obliged to lean on Rouletabille for support, and to save himself from falling.

"Oh! Oh!" he cried. "What is the matter with me?—Have I been poisoned?"

He looked at us with haggard eyes. We questioned him vainly; he did not answer us. He had sunk into an armchair and we could get not a word from him. We were extremely distressed, both on his account and on our own, for we had partaken of all the dishes he had eaten. He seemed to be out of pain; but his heavy head had fallen on his shoulder and his eyelids were tightly closed. Rouletabille bent over him, listening for the beatings of the heart.

My friend's face, however, when he stood up, was as calm as it had been a moment before agitated.

"He is asleep," he said.

He led me to his chamber, after closing Larsan's room.

"The drug?" I asked. "Does Mademoiselle Stangerson wish to put everybody to sleep, to-night?"

"Perhaps," replied Rouletabille; but I could see he was thinking of something else.

"But what about us?" I exclaimed. "How do we know that we have not been drugged?"

"Do you feel indisposed?" Rouletabille asked me coolly.

"Not in the least."

"Do you feel any inclination to go to sleep?"

"None whatever."

"Well, then, my friend, smoke this excellent cigar."

And he handed me a choice Havana, one Monsieur Darzac had given him, while he lit his briarwood—his eternal briarwood.

We remained in his room until about ten o'clock without a word passing between us. Buried in an armchair Rouletabille sat and smoked steadily, his brow in thought and a far-away look in his eyes. On the stroke of ten he took off his boots and signalled to me to do the same. As we stood in our socks he said, in so low a tone that I guessed, rather than heard, the word:

"Revolver."

I drew my revolver from my jacket pocket.

"Cock it!" he said.

I did as he directed.

Then moving towards the door of his room, he opened it with infinite precaution; it made no sound. We were in the "off-turning" gallery.

Rouletabille made another sign to me which I understood to mean that I was to take up my post in the dark closet.

When I was some distance from him, he rejoined me and embraced me; and then I saw him, with the same precaution, return to his room. Astonished by his embrace, and somewhat disquieted by it, I arrived at the "right" gallery without difficulty, crossing the landing-place, and reaching the dark closet.

Before entering it I examined the curtain-cord of the window and found that I had only to release it from its fastening with my fingers for the curtain to fall by its own weight and hide the square of light from Rouletabille—the signal agreed upon. The sound of a footstep made me halt before Arthur Rance's door. He was not yet in bed, then! How was it that, being in the château, he had not dined with Monsieur Stangerson and his daughter? I had not seen him at table with them, at the moment when we looked in.

I retired into the dark closet. I found myself perfectly situated. I could see along the whole length of the gallery. Nothing, absolutely nothing could pass there without my seeing it. But what was going to pass there? Rouletabille's embrace came back to my mind. I argued that people don't part from each other in that way unless on an important or dangerous occasion. Was I then in danger?

My hand closed on the butt of my revolver and I waited. I am not a hero; but neither am I a coward.

I waited about an hour, and during all that time I saw nothing unusual. The rain, which had begun to come down strongly towards nine o'clock, had now ceased.

My friend had told me that, probably, nothing would occur before midnight or one o'clock in the morning. It was not more than half-past eleven, however, when I heard the door of Arthur Rance's room open very slowly. The door remained open for a minute, which seemed to me a long time. As it opened into the gallery, that is to say, outwards, I could not see what was passing in the room behind the door.

At that moment I noticed a strange sound, three times repeated, coming from the park. Ordinarily I should not have attached any more importance to it than I would to the noise of cats on the roof. But the third time, the mew was so sharp and penetrating that I remembered what I had heard about the cry of the Bete du bon Dieu. As the cry had accompanied all the events at the Glandier, I could not refrain from shuddering at the thought.

Directly afterwards I saw a man appear on the outside of the door, and close it after him. At first I could not recognise him, for his back was towards me and he was bending over a rather bulky package. When he had closed the door and picked up the package, he turned towards the dark closet, and then I saw who he was. He was the forest-keeper, the Green Man. He was wearing the same costume that he had worn when I first saw him on the road in front of the Donjon Inn. There was no doubt about his being the keeper. As the cry of the Bete du Bon Dieu came for the third time, he put down the package and went to the second window, counting from the dark closet. I dared not risk making any movement, fearing I might betray my presence.

Arriving at the window, he peered out on to the park. The night was now light, the moon showing at intervals. The Green Man raised his arms twice, making signs which I did not understand; then, leaving the window, he again took up his package and moved along the gallery towards the landing-place.

Rouletabille had instructed me to undo the curtain-cord when I saw anything. Was Rouletabille expecting this? It was not my business to question. All I had to do was obey instructions. I unfastened the window-cord; my heart beating the while as if it would burst. The man reached the landing-place, but, to my utter surprise—I had expected to see him continue to pass along the gallery—I saw him descend the stairs leading to the vestibule.

What was I to do? I looked stupidly at the heavy curtain which had shut the light from the window. The signal had been given, and I did not see Rouletabille appear at the corner of the off-turning gallery. Nobody appeared. I was exceedingly perplexed. Half an hour passed, an age to me. What was I to do now, even if I saw something? The signal once given I could not give it a second time. To venture into the gallery might upset all Rouletabille's plans. After all, I had nothing to reproach myself for, and if something had happened that my friend had not expected he could only blame himself. Unable to be of any further assistance to him by means of a signal, I left the dark closet and, still in my socks, made my way to the "off-turning" gallery.

There was no one there. I went to the door of Rouletabille's room and listened. I could hear nothing. I knocked gently. There was no answer. I turned the door-handle and the door opened. I entered. Rouletabille lay extended at full length on the floor.

# XXII

## THE INCREDIBLE BODY

I bent in great anxiety over the body of the reporter and had the joy to find that he was deeply sleeping, the same unhealthy sleep that I had seen fall upon Frederic Larsan. He had succumbed to the influence of the same drug that had been mixed with our food. How was it then, that I, also, had not been overcome by it? I reflected that the drug must have been put into our wine; because that would explain my condition. I never drink when eating. Naturally inclined to obesity, I am restricted to a dry diet. I shook Rouletabille, but could not succeed in waking him. This, no doubt, was the work of Mademoiselle Stangerson.

She had certainly thought it necessary to guard herself against this young man as well as her father. I recalled that the steward, in serving us, had recommended an excellent Chablis which, no doubt, had come from the professor's table.

More than a quarter of an hour passed. I resolved, under the pressing circumstances, to resort to extreme measures. I threw a pitcher of cold water over Rouletabille's head. He opened his eyes. I beat his face, and raised him up. I felt him stiffen in my arms and heard him murmur: "Go on, go on; but don't make any noise." I pinched him and shook him until he was able to stand up. We were saved!

"They sent me to sleep," he said. "Ah! I passed an awful quarter of an hour before giving way. But it is over now. Don't leave me."

He had no sooner uttered those words than we were thrilled by a frightful cry that rang through the château,—a veritable death cry.

"Malheur!" roared Rouletabille; "We shall be too late!"

He tried to rush to the door, but he was too dazed, and fell against the wall. I was already in the gallery, revolver in hand, rushing like a madman towards Mademoiselle Stangerson's room. The moment I arrived at the intersection of the "off-turning" gallery and the "right" gallery, I saw a figure leaving her apartment, which, in a few strides had reached the landing-place.

I was not master of myself. I fired. The report from the revolver made a deafening noise; but the man continued his flight down the stairs. I ran behind him, shouting: "Stop!—stop! Or I will kill you!" As I rushed after him down the stairs, I came face to face with Arthur Rance coming from the left wing of the château, yelling: "What is it? What is it?" We arrived almost at the same time at the foot of the staircase. The window of the vestibule was open. We distinctly saw the form of a man running away. Instinctively we fired our revolvers in his direction. He was not more than ten paces in front of us; he staggered and we thought he was going to fall. We had sprung out of the window, but the man dashed off with renewed vigour. I was in my socks, and the American was barefooted. There being no hope of overtaking him, we fired our last cartridges at him. But he still kept on running, going along the right side of the court towards the end of the right wing of the château, which had no other outlet than the door of the little chamber occupied by the forest-keeper. The man, though he was evidently wounded by our bullets, was now twenty yards ahead of us. Suddenly, behind us, and above our heads, a window in the gallery opened and we heard the voice of Rouletabille crying out desperately:

"Fire, Bernier!—Fire!"

At that moment the clear moonlight night was further lit by a broad flash. By its light we saw Daddy Bernier with his gun on the threshold of the donjon door.

He had taken good aim. The shadow fell. But as it had reached the end of the right wing of the château, it fell on the other side of the angle of the building; that is to say, we saw it about to fall, but not the actual sinking to the ground. Bernier, Arthur Rance and myself reached the other side twenty seconds later. The shadow was lying dead at our feet.

Aroused from his lethargy by the cries and reports, Larsan opened the window of his chamber and called out to us. Rouletabille, quite awake now, joined us at the same moment, and I cried out to him:

"He is dead!—is dead!"

"So much the better," he said. "Take him into the vestibule of the château." Then as if on second thought, he said: "No!—no! Let us put him in his own room."

Rouletabille knocked at the door. Nobody answered. Naturally, this did not surprise me.

"He is evidently not there, otherwise he would have come out," said the reporter. "Let us carry him to the vestibule then."

Since reaching the dead shadow, a thick cloud had covered the moon and darkened the night, so that we were unable to make out the features. Daddy Jacques, who had now joined us, helped us to carry the body into the vestibule, where we laid it down on the lower step of the stairs. On the way, I had felt my hands wet from the warm blood flowing from the wounds.

Daddy Jacques flew to the kitchen and returned with a lantern. He held it close to the face of the dead shadow, and we recognised the keeper, the man called by the landlord of the Donjon Inn the Green Man, whom, an hour earlier, I had seen come out of

Arthur Rance's chamber carrying a parcel. But what I had seen I could only tell Rouletabille later, when we were alone.

Rouletabille and Frederic Larsan experienced a cruel disappointment at the result of the night's adventure. They could only look in consternation and stupefaction at the body of the Green Man.

Daddy Jacques showed a stupidly sorrowful face and with silly lamentations kept repeating that we were mistaken—the keeper could not be the assailant. We were obliged to compel him to be quiet. He could not have shown greater grief had the body been that of his own son. I noticed, while all the rest of us were more or less undressed and barefooted, that he was fully clothed.

Rouletabille had not left the body. Kneeling on the flagstones by the light of Daddy Jacques's lantern he removed the clothes from the body and laid bare its breast. Then snatching the lantern from Daddy Jacques, he held it over the corpse and saw a gaping wound. Rising suddenly he exclaimed in a voice filled with savage irony:

"The man you believe to have been shot was killed by the stab of a knife in his heart!"

I thought Rouletabille had gone mad; but, bending over the body, I quickly satisfied myself that Rouletabille was right. Not a sign of a bullet anywhere—the wound, evidently made by a sharp blade, had penetrated the heart.

# XXIII

## THE DOUBLE SCENT

I had hardly recovered from the surprise into which this new discovery had plunged me, when Rouletabille touched me on the shoulder and asked me to follow him into his room.

"What are we going to do there?"

"To think the matter over."

I confess I was in no condition for doing much thinking, nor could I understand how Rouletabille could so control himself as to be able calmly to sit down for reflection when he must have known that Mademoiselle Stangerson was at that moment almost on the point of death. But his self-control was more than I could explain. Closing the door of his room, he motioned me to a chair and, seating himself before me, took out his pipe. We sat there for some time in silence and then I fell asleep.

When I awoke it was daylight. It was eight o'clock by my watch. Rouletabille was no longer in the room. I rose to go out when the door opened and my friend re-entered. He had evidently lost no time.

"How about Mademoiselle Stangerson?" I asked him.

"Her condition, though very alarming, is not desperate."

"When did you leave this room?"

"Towards dawn."

"I guess you have been hard at work?"

"Rather!"

"Have you found out anything?"

"Two sets of footprints!"

"Do they explain anything?"

"Yes."

"Have they anything to do with the mystery of the keeper's body?"

"Yes; the mystery is no longer a mystery. This morning, walking round the château, I found two distinct sets of footprints, made at the same time, last night. They were made by two persons walking side by side. I followed them from the court towards the oak grove. Larsan joined me. They were the same kind of footprints as were made at the time of the assault in 'The Yellow Room'—one set was from clumsy boots and the other was made by neat ones, except that the big toe of one of the sets was of a different size from the one measured in 'The Yellow Room' incident. I compared the marks with the paper patterns I had previously made.

"Still following the tracks of the prints, Larsan and I passed out of the oak grove and reached the border of the lake. There they turned off to a little path leading to the high road to Epinay where we lost the traces in the newly macadamised highway.

"We went back to the château and parted at the courtyard. We met again, however, in Daddy Jacques's room to which our separate trains of thinking had led us both. We found the old servant in bed. His clothes on the chair were wet through and his boots very muddy. He certainly did not get into that state in helping us to carry the body of the keeper. It was not raining then. Then his face showed extreme fatigue and he looked at us out of terror-stricken eyes.

"On our first questioning him he told us that he had gone to bed immediately after the doctor had arrived. On pressing him, however, for it was evident to us he was not speaking the truth, he confessed that he had been away from the château.

He explained his absence by saying that he had a headache and went out into the fresh air, but had gone no further than the oak grove. When we then described to him the whole route he had followed, he sat up in bed trembling.

"'And you were not alone!' cried Larsan.

"'Did you see it then?' gasped Daddy Jacques.

"'What?' I asked.

"'The phantom—the black phantom!'

"Then he told us that for several nights he had seen what he kept calling the black phantom. It came into the park at the stroke of midnight and glided stealthily through the trees; it appeared to him to pass through the trunks of the trees. Twice he had seen it from his window, by the light of the moon and had risen and followed the strange apparition. The night before last he had almost overtaken it; but it had vanished at the corner of the donjon. Last night, however, he had not left the château, his mind being disturbed by a presentiment that some new crime would be attempted. Suddenly he saw the black phantom rush out from somewhere in the middle of the court. He followed it to the lake and to the high road to Epinay, where the phantom suddenly disappeared.

"'Did you see his face?' demanded Larsan.

"'No!—I saw nothing but black veils.'

"'Did you go out after what passed on the gallery?'

"'I could not!—I was terrified.'

"'Daddy Jacques,' I said, in a threatening voice, 'you did not follow it; you and the phantom walked to Epinay together—arm in arm!'

"'No!' he cried, turning his eyes away, 'I did not. It came on to pour, and—I turned back. I don't know what became of the black phantom.'

"We left him, and when we were outside I turned to Larsan, looking him full in the face, and put my question suddenly to take him off his guard:

"'An accomplice?'

"'How can I tell?' he replied, shrugging his shoulders. 'You can't be sure of anything in a case like this. Twenty-four hours ago I would have sworn that there was no accomplice!' He left me saying he was off to Epinay."

"Well, what do you make of it?" I asked Rouletabille, after he had ended his recital. "Personally I am utterly in the dark. I can't make anything out of it. What do you gather?"

"Everything! Everything!" he exclaimed. "But," he said abruptly, "let's find out more about Mademoiselle Stangerson."

# XXIV

## ROULETABILLE KNOWS THE TWO HALVES OF THE MURDERER

Mademoiselle Stangerson had been almost murdered for the second time. Unfortunately, she was in too weak a state to bear the severer injuries of this second attack as well as she had those of the first. She had received three wounds in the breast from the murderer's knife, and she lay long between life and death. Her strong physique, however, saved her; but though she recovered physically it was found that her mind had been affected. The slightest allusion to the terrible incident sent her into delirium, and the arrest of Robert Darzac which followed on the day following the tragic death of the keeper seemed to sink her fine intelligence into complete melancholia.

Robert Darzac arrived at the château towards half-past nine. I saw him hurrying through the park, his hair and clothes in disorder and his face a deadly white. Rouletabille and I were looking out of a window in the gallery. He saw us, and gave a despairing cry: "I'm too late!"

Rouletabille answered: "She lives!"

A minute later Darzac had gone into Mademoiselle Stangerson's room and, through the door, we could hear his heart-rending sobs.

"There's a fate about this place!" groaned Rouletabille. "Some infernal gods must be watching over the misfortunes of this family!—If I had not been drugged, I should have saved Mademoiselle Stangerson. I should have silenced him forever. And the keeper would not have been killed!"

Monsieur Darzac came in to speak with us. His distress was terrible. Rouletabille told him everything: his preparations for Mademoiselle Stangerson's safety; his plans for either capturing or for disposing of the assailant forever; and how he would have succeeded had it not been for the drugging.

"If only you had trusted me!" said the young man, in a low tone. "If you had but begged Mademoiselle Stangerson to confide in me!—But, then, everybody here distrusts everybody else, the daughter distrusts her father, and even her lover. While you ask me to protect her she is doing all she can to frustrate me. That was why I came on the scene too late!"

At Monsieur Robert Darzac's request Rouletabille described the whole scene. Leaning on the wall, to prevent himself from falling, he had made his way to Mademoiselle Stangerson's room, while we were running after the supposed murderer. The ante-room door was open and when he entered he found Mademoiselle Stangerson lying partly thrown over the desk. Her dressing-gown was dyed with the blood flowing from her bosom. Still under the influence of the drug, he felt he was walking in a horrible nightmare.

He went back to the gallery automatically, opened a window, shouted his order to fire, and then returned to the room. He crossed the deserted boudoir, entered the drawing-room, and tried to rouse Monsieur Stangerson who was lying on a sofa. Monsieur Stangerson rose stupidly and let himself be drawn by Rouletabille into the room where, on seeing his daughter's body, he uttered a heart-rending cry. Both united their feeble strength and carried her to her bed.

On his way to join us Rouletabille passed by the desk. On the floor, near it, he saw a large packet. He knelt down and, finding the wrapper loose, he examined it, and made out an enormous quantity of papers and photographs. On one of the papers he read: "New differential electroscopic condenser. Fundamental properties of substance intermediary between ponderable matter and imponderable ether." Strange irony of fate that the professor's precious papers should be restored to him at the very time when an attempt was being made to deprive him of his daughter's life! What are papers worth to him now?

The morning following that awful night saw Monsieur de Marquet once more at the château, with his Registrar and gendarmes. Of course we were all questioned. Rouletabille and I had already agreed on what to say. I kept back any information as to my being in the dark closet and said nothing about the drugging. We did not wish to suggest in any way that Mademoiselle Stangerson had been expecting her nocturnal visitor. The poor woman might, perhaps, never recover, and it was none of our business to lift the veil of a secret the preservation of which she had paid for so dearly.

Arthur Rance told everybody, in a manner so natural that it astonished me, that he had last seen the keeper towards eleven o'clock of that fatal night. He had come for his valise, he said, which he was to take for him early next morning to the Saint-Michel station, and had been kept out late running after poachers. Arthur Rance had, indeed, intended to leave the château and, according to his habit, to walk to the station.

Monsieur Stangerson confirmed what Rance had said, adding that he had not asked Rance to dine with him because his friend had taken his final leave of them both earlier in the evening. Monsieur Rance had had tea served him in his room, because he had complained of a slight indisposition.

Bernier testified, instructed by Rouletabille, that the keeper had ordered him to meet at a spot near the oak grove, for the purpose of looking out for poachers. Finding that the keeper did not keep his appointment, he, Bernier, had gone in search of him. He had almost arrived at the donjon, when he saw a figure running swiftly in a direction opposite to him, towards the right wing of the château. He heard revolver shots from behind the figure and saw Rouletabille at one of the gallery windows. He heard Rouletabille call out to him to fire, and he had fired. He believed he had killed the man until he learned, after Rouletabille had uncovered the body, that the man had died from a knife thrust. Who had given it he could not imagine. "Nobody could have been near the spot without my seeing him." When the examining magistrate reminded him that the spot where the body was found was very dark and that he himself had not been able to recognise the keeper before firing, Daddy Bernier replied that neither had they seen the other body; nor had they found it. In the narrow court where five people were standing it would have been strange if the other body, had it been there, could have escaped. The only door that opened into the court was that of the keeper's room, and that door was closed, and the key of it was found in the keeper's pocket.

However that might be, the examining magistrate did not pursue his inquiry further in this direction. He was evidently convinced that we had missed the man we were chasing and we had come upon the keeper's body in our chase. This matter of the keeper was another matter entirely. He wanted to satisfy himself about that without any further delay. Probably it fitted in with the conclusions he had already arrived at as to the keeper and his intrigues with the wife of Mathieu, the landlord of the Donjon Inn. This Mathieu, later in the afternoon, was arrested and taken to Corbeil in spite of his rheumatism. He had been heard to threaten the keeper, and though no evidence against him had been found at his inn, the evidence of carters who had heard the threats was enough to justify his retention.

The examination had proceeded thus far when, to our surprise, Frederic Larsan returned to the château. He was accompanied by one of the employees of the railway. At that moment Rance and I were in the vestibule discussing Mathieu's guilt or innocence, while Rouletabille stood apart buried, apparently, in thought. The examining magistrate and his Registrar were in the little green drawing-room, while Darzac was with the doctor and Stangerson in the lady's chamber. As Frederic Larsan entered the vestibule with the railway employee, Rouletabille and I at once recognised him by the small blond beard. We exchanged meaningful glances. Larsan had himself announced to the examining magistrate by the gendarme and entered with the railway servant as Daddy Jacques came out. Some ten minutes went by during which Rouletabille appeared extremely impatient. The door of the drawing-room was then opened and we heard the magistrate calling to the gendarme who entered. Presently he came out, mounted the stairs and, coming back shortly, went in to the magistrate and said:

"Monsieur,—Monsieur Robert Darzac will not come!"

"What! Not come!" cried Monsieur de Marquet.

"He says he cannot leave Mademoiselle Stangerson in her present state."

"Very well," said Monsieur de Marquet; "then we'll go to him."

Monsieur de Marquet and the gendarme mounted the stairs. He made a sign to Larsan and the railroad employee to follow. Rouletabille and I went along too.

On reaching the door of Mademoiselle Stangerson's chamber, Monsieur de Marquet knocked. A chambermaid appeared. It was Sylvia, with her hair all in disorder and consternation showing on her face.

"Is Monsieur Stangerson within?" asked the magistrate.

"Yes, Monsieur."

"Tell him that I wish to speak with him."

Stangerson came out. His appearance was wretched in the extreme.

"What do you want?" he demanded of the magistrate. "May I not be left in peace, Monsieur?"

"Monsieur," said the magistrate, "it is absolutely necessary that I should see Monsieur Darzac at once. If you cannot induce him to come, I shall be compelled to use the help of the law."

The professor made no reply. He looked at us all like a man being led to execution, and then went back into the room.

Almost immediately after Monsieur Robert Darzac came out. He was very pale. He looked at us and, his eyes falling on the railway servant, his features stiffened and he could hardly repress a groan.

We were all much moved by the appearance of the man. We felt that what was about to happen would decide the fate of Monsieur Robert Darzac. Frederic Larsan's face alone was radiant, showing a joy as of a dog that had at last got its prey.

Pointing to the railway servant, Monsieur de Marquet said to Monsieur Darzac:

"Do you recognise this man, Monsieur?"

"I do," said Monsieur Darzac, in a tone which he vainly tried to make firm. "He is an employee at the station at Epinay-sur-Orge."

"This young man," went on Monsieur de Marquet, "affirms that he saw you get off the train at Epinay-sur-Orge—"

"That night," said Monsieur Darzac, interrupting, "at half-past ten—it is quite true."

An interval of silence followed.

"Monsieur Darzac," the magistrate went on in a tone of deep emotion, "Monsieur Darzac, what were you doing that night, at Epinay-sur-Orge—at that time?"

Monsieur Darzac remained silent, simply closing his eyes.

"Monsieur Darzac," insisted Monsieur de Marquet, "can you tell me how you employed your time, that night?"

Monsieur Darzac opened his eyes. He seemed to have recovered his self-control.

"No, Monsieur."

"Think, Monsieur! For, if you persist in your strange refusal, I shall be under the painful necessity of keeping you at my disposition."

"I refuse."

"Monsieur Darzac!—in the name of the law, I arrest you!"

The magistrate had no sooner pronounced the words than I saw Rouletabille move quickly towards Monsieur Darzac. He would certainly have spoken to him, but Darzac, by a gesture, held him off. As the gendarme approached his prisoner, a despairing cry rang through the room:

"Robert!—Robert!"

We recognised the voice of Mademoiselle Stangerson. We all shuddered. Larsan himself turned pale. Monsieur Darzac, in response to the cry, had flown back into the room.

The magistrate, the gendarme, and Larsan followed closely after. Rouletabille and I remained on the threshold. It was a heartbreaking sight that met our eyes. Mademoiselle Stangerson, with a face of deathly pallor, had risen on her bed, in spite of the restraining efforts of two doctors and her father. She was holding out her trembling arms towards Robert Darzac, on whom Larsan and the gendarme had laid hands. Her distended eyes saw—she understood—her lips seemed to form a word, but nobody made it out; and she fell back insensible.

Monsieur Darzac was hurried out of the room and placed in the vestibule to wait for the vehicle Larsan had gone to fetch. We were all overcome by emotion and even Monsieur de Marquet had tears in his eyes. Rouletabille took advantage of the opportunity to say to Monsieur Darzac:

"Are you going to put in any defense?"

"No!" replied the prisoner.

"Very well, then I will, Monsieur."

"You cannot do it," said the unhappy man with a faint smile.

"I can—and I will."

Rouletabille's voice had in it a strange strength and confidence.

"I can do it, Monsieur Robert Darzac, because I know more than you do!"

"Come! Come!" murmured Darzac, almost angrily.

"Have no fear! I shall know only what will benefit you."

"You must know nothing, young man, if you want me to be grateful."

Rouletabille shook his head, going close up to Darzac.

"Listen to what I am about to say," he said in a low tone, "and let it give you confidence. You do not know the name of the murderer. Mademoiselle Stangerson knows it; but only half of it; but I know his two halves; I know the whole man!"

Robert Darzac opened his eyes, with a look that showed he had not understood a word of what Rouletabille had said to him. At that moment the conveyance arrived, driven by Frederic Larsan. Darzac and the gendarme entered it, Larsan remaining on the driver's seat. The prisoner was taken to Corbeil.

# XXV

## ROULETABILLE GOES ON A JOURNEY

That same evening Rouletabille and I left the Glandier. We were very glad to get away and there was nothing more to keep us there. I declared my intention to give up the whole matter. It had been too much for me. Rouletabille, with a friendly tap on my shoulder, confessed that he had nothing more to learn at the Glandier; he had learned there all it had to tell him. We reached Paris about eight o'clock, dined, and then, tired out, we separated, agreeing to meet the next morning at my rooms.

Rouletabille arrived next day at the hour agreed on. He was dressed in a suit of English tweed, with an ulster on his arm, and a valise in his hand. Evidently he had prepared himself for a journey.

"How long shall you be away?" I asked.

"A month or two," he said. "It all depends."

I asked him no more questions.

"Do you know," he asked, "what the word was that Mademoiselle Stangerson tried to say before she fainted?"

"No—nobody heard it."

"I heard it!" replied Rouletabille. "She said 'Speak!'"

"Do you think Darzac will speak?"

"Never."

I was about to make some further observations, but he wrung my hand warmly and wished me good-bye. I had only time to ask him one question before he left.

"Are you not afraid that other attempts may be made while you're away?"

"No! Not now that Darzac is in prison," he answered.

With this strange remark he left. I was not to see him again until the day of Darzac's trial at the court when he appeared to explain the inexplicable.

# XXVI

## IN WHICH JOSEPH ROULETABILLE IS AWAITED WITH IMPATIENCE

On the 15th of January, that is to say, two months and a half after the tragic events I have narrated, the "Epoque" printed, as the first column of the front page, the following sensational article: "The Seine-et-Oise jury is summoned today to give its verdict on one of the most mysterious affairs in the annals of crime. There never has been a case with so many obscure, incomprehensible, and inexplicable points. And yet the prosecution has not hesitated to put into the prisoner's dock a man who is respected, esteemed, and loved by all who knew him—a young savant, the hope of French science, whose whole life has been devoted to knowledge and truth. When Paris heard of Monsieur Robert Darzac's arrest a unanimous cry of protest arose from all sides. The whole Sorbonne, disgraced by this act of the examining magistrate, asserted its belief in the innocence of Mademoiselle Stangerson's fiance. Monsieur Stangerson was loud in his denunciation of this miscarriage of justice. There is no doubt in the mind of anybody that could the victim speak she would claim from the jurors of Seine-et-Oise the man she wishes to make her husband and whom the prosecution would send to the scaffold. It is to be hoped that Mademoiselle Stangerson will shortly recover her reason, which has been temporarily unhinged by the horrible mystery at the Glandier. The question before the jury is the one we propose to deal with this very day.

"We have decided not to permit twelve worthy men to commit a disgraceful miscarriage of justice. We confess that the remarkable coincidences, the many convicting evidences, and the inexplicable silence on the part of the accused, as well as a total absence of any evidence for an alibi, were enough to warrant the bench of judges in assuming that in this man alone was centered the truth of the affair. The evidences are, in appearance, so overwhelming against Monsieur Robert Darzac that a detective so well informed, so intelligent, and generally so successful, as Monsieur Frederic Larsan, may be excused for having been misled by them. Up to now everything has gone against Monsieur Robert Darzac in the magisterial inquiry. Today, however, we are going to defend him before the jury, and we are going to bring to the witness stand a light that will illumine the whole mystery of the Glandier. For we possess the truth.

"If we have not spoken sooner, it is because the interests of certain parties in the case demand that we should take that course. Our readers may remember the unsigned reports we published relating to the 'Left foot of the Rue Oberkampf,' at the time of the famous robbery of the Credit Universel, and the famous case of the 'Gold Ingots of the Mint.' In both those cases we were able to discover the truth long before even the excellent ingenuity of Frederic Larsan had been able to unravel it. These reports were written by our youngest reporter, Joseph Rouletabille, a youth of eighteen, whose fame tomorrow will be worldwide. When attention was first drawn to the Glandier case, our youthful reporter was on the spot and installed in the château, when every other representative of the press had been denied admission. He worked side by side with Frederic

Larsan. He was amazed and terrified at the grave mistake the celebrated detective was about to make, and tried to divert him from the false scent he was following; but the great Fred refused to receive instructions from this young journalist. We know now where it brought Monsieur Robert Darzac.

"But now, France must know—the whole world must know, that, on the very evening on which Monsieur Darzac was arrested, young Rouletabille entered our editorial office and informed us that he was about to go away on a journey. 'How long I shall be away,' he said, 'I cannot say; perhaps a month—perhaps two—perhaps three—perhaps I may never return. Here is a letter. If I am not back on the day on which Monsieur Darzac is to appear before the Assize Court, have this letter opened and read to the court, after all the witnesses have been heard. Arrange it with Monsieur Darzac's counsel. Monsieur Darzac is innocent. In this letter is written the name of the murderer; and—that is all I have to say. I am leaving to get my proofs—for the irrefutable evidence of the murderer's guilt.' Our reporter departed. For a long time we were without news from him; but, a week ago, a stranger called upon our manager and said: 'Act in accordance with the instructions of Joseph Rouletabille, if it becomes necessary to do so. The letter left by him holds the truth.' The gentleman who brought us this message would not give us his name.

"Today, the 15th of January, is the day of the trial. Joseph Rouletabille has not returned. It may be we shall never see him again. The press also counts its heroes, its martyrs to duty. It may be he is no longer living. We shall know how to avenge him. Our manager will, this afternoon, be at the Court of Assize at Versailles, with the letter—the letter containing the name of the murderer!"

Those Parisians who flocked to the Assize Court at Versailles, to be present at the trial of what was known as the "Mystery of The Yellow Room," will certainly remember the terrible crush at the Saint-Lazare station. The ordinary trains were so full that special trains had to be made up. The article in the "Epoque" had so excited the populace that discussion was rife everywhere even to the verge of blows. Partisans of Rouletabille fought with the supporters of Frederic Larsan. Curiously enough the excitement was due less to the fact that an innocent man was in danger of a wrongful conviction than to the interest taken in their own ideas as to the "Mystery of The Yellow Room". Each had his explanation to which each held fast. Those who explained the crime on Frederic Larsan's theory would not admit that there could be any doubt as to the perspicacity of the popular detective. Others who had arrived at a different solution, naturally insisted that this was Rouletabille's explanation, though they did not as yet know what that was.

With the day's "Epoque" in their hands, the "Larsans" and the "Rouletabilles" fought and shoved each other on the steps of the Palais de Justice, right into the court itself. Those who could not get in remained in the neighbourhood until evening and were, with great difficulty, kept back by the soldiery and the police. They became hungry for news, welcoming the most absurd rumours. At one time the rumour spread that Monsieur Stangerson himself had been arrested in the court and had confessed to being the murderer. This goes to show to what a pitch of madness nervous excitement may carry people. Rouletabille was still expected. Some pretended to know him; and when a young man with a "pass" crossed the open space which separated the crowd from the Court House, a scuffle took place. Cries were raised of "Rouletabille!—there's Rouletabille!" The arrival of the manager of the paper was the signal for a great demonstration. Some applauded, others hissed.

The trial itself was presided over by Monsieur de Rocouz, a judge filled with the prejudice of his class, but a man honest at heart. The witnesses had been called. I was there, of course, as were all who had, in any way, been in touch with the mysteries of the Glandier. Monsieur Stangerson—looking many years older and almost unrecognisable—Larsan, Arthur Rance, with his face ruddy as ever, Daddy Jacques, Daddy Mathieu, who was brought into court handcuffed between two gendarmes, Madame Mathieu, in tears, the two Berniers, the two nurses, the steward, all the domestics of the château, the employee of the Paris Post Office, the railway employee from Epinay, some friends of Monsieur and Mademoiselle Stangerson, and all Monsieur Darzac's witnesses. I was lucky enough to be called early in the trial, so that I was then able to watch and be present at almost the whole of the proceedings.

The court was so crowded that many lawyers were compelled to find seats on the steps. Behind the bench of justices were representatives from other benches. Monsieur Robert Darzac stood in the prisoner's dock between policemen, tall, handsome, and calm. A murmur of admiration rather than of compassion greeted his appearance. He leaned forward towards his counsel, Maitre Henri Robert, who, assisted by his chief secretary, Maitre Andre Hesse, was busily turning over the folios of his brief.

Many expected that Monsieur Stangerson, after giving his evidence, would have gone over to the prisoner and shaken hands with him; but he left the court without another word. It was remarked that the jurors appeared to be deeply interested in a rapid conversation which the manager of the "Epoque" was having with Maitre Henri Robert. The manager, later, sat down in the front row of the public seats. Some were surprised that he was not asked to remain with the other witnesses in the room reserved for them.

The reading of the indictment was got through, as it always is, without any incident. I shall not here report the long examination to which Monsieur Darzac was subjected. He answered all the questions quickly and easily. His silence as to the important matters of which we know was dead against him. It would seem as if this reticence would be fatal for him. He resented the President's reprimands. He was told that his silence might mean death.

"Very well," he said; "I will submit to it; but I am innocent."

With that splendid ability which has made his fame, Maitre Robert took advantage of the incident, and tried to show that it brought out in noble relief his client's character; for only heroic natures could remain silent for moral reasons in face of such a danger. The eminent advocate however, only succeeded in assuring those who were already assured of Darzac's innocence. At the adjournment Rouletabille had not yet arrived. Every time a door opened, all eyes there turned towards it and back to the manager of the "Epoque," who sat impassive in his place. When he once was feeling in his pocket a loud murmur of expectation followed. The letter!

It is not, however, my intention to report in detail the course of the trial. My readers are sufficiently acquainted with the mysteries surrounding the Glandier case to enable me to go on to the really dramatic denouement of this ever-memorable day.

When the trial was resumed, Maitre Henri Robert questioned Daddy Mathieu as to his complicity in the death of the keeper. His wife was also brought in and was confronted by her husband. She burst into tears and confessed that she had been the keeper's mistress, and that her husband had suspected it. She again, however, affirmed that he had had nothing to do with the murder of her lover. Maitre Henri Robert thereupon asked the court to hear Frederic Larsan on this point.

"In a short conversation which I have had with Frederic Larsan, during the adjournment," declared the advocate, "he has made me understand that the death of the keeper may have been brought about otherwise than by the hand of Mathieu. It will be interesting to hear Frederic Larsan's theory."

Frederic Larsan was brought in. His explanation was quite clear.

"I see no necessity," he said, "for bringing Mathieu in this. I have told Monsieur de Marquet that the man's threats had biassed the examining magistrate against him. To me the attempt to murder Mademoiselle and the death of the keeper are the work of one and the same person. Mademoiselle Stangerson's murderer, flying through the court, was fired on; it was thought he was struck, perhaps killed. As a matter of fact, he only stumbled at the moment of his disappearance behind the corner of the right wing of the château. There he encountered the keeper who, no doubt, tried to seize him. The murderer had in his hand the knife with which he had stabbed Mademoiselle Stangerson and with this he killed the keeper."

This very simple explanation appeared at once plausible and satisfying. A murmur of approbation was heard.

"And the murderer? What became of him?" asked the President.

"He was evidently hidden in an obscure corner at the end of the court. After the people had left the court carrying with them the body of the keeper, the murderer quietly made his escape."

The words had scarcely left Larsan's mouth when from the back of the court came a youthful voice:

"I agree with Frederic Larsan as to the death of the keeper; but I do not agree with him as to the way the murderer escaped!"

Everybody turned round, astonished. The clerks of the court sprang towards the speaker, calling out silence, and the President angrily ordered the intruder to be immediately expelled. The same clear voice, however, was again heard:

"It is I, Monsieur President—Joseph Rouletabille!"

# XXVII

## IN WHICH JOSEPH ROULETABILLE APPEARS IN ALL HIS GLORY

The excitement was extreme. Cries from fainting women were to be heard amid the extraordinary bustle and stir. The "majesty of the law" was utterly forgotten. The President tried in vain to make himself heard. Rouletabille made his way forward with difficulty, but by dint of much elbowing reached his manager and greeted him cordially. The letter was passed to him and pocketing it he turned to the witness-box. He was dressed exactly as on the day he left me even to the ulster over his arm. Turning to the President, he said:

"I beg your pardon, Monsieur President, but I have only just arrived from America. The steamer was late. My name is Joseph Rouletabille!"

The silence which followed his stepping into the witness-box was broken by laughter when his words were heard. Everybody seemed relieved and glad to find him there, as if in the expectation of hearing the truth at last.

But the President was extremely incensed:

"So, you are Joseph Rouletabille," he replied; "well, young man, I'll teach you what comes of making a farce of justice.

By virtue of my discretionary power, I hold you at the court's disposition."

"I ask nothing better, Monsieur President. I have come here for that purpose. I humbly beg the court's pardon for the disturbance of which I have been the innocent cause. I beg you to believe that nobody has a greater respect for the court than I have. I came in as I could." He smiled.

"Take him away!" ordered the President.

Maitre Henri Robert intervened. He began by apologising for the young man, who, he said, was moved only by the best intentions. He made the President understand that the evidence of a witness who had slept at the Glandier during the whole of that eventful week could not be omitted, and the present witness, moreover, had come to name the real murderer.

"Are you going to tell us who the murderer was?" asked the President, somewhat convinced though still sceptical.

"I have come for that purpose, Monsieur President!" replied Rouletabille.

An attempt at applause was silenced by the usher.

"Joseph Rouletabille," said Maitre Henri Robert, "has not been regularly subpoenaed as a witness, but I hope, Monsieur President, you will examine him in virtue of your discretionary powers."

"Very well!" said the President, "we will question him. But we must proceed in order."

The Advocate-General rose:

"It would, perhaps, be better," he said, "if the young man were to tell us now whom he suspects."

The President nodded ironically:

"If the Advocate-General attaches importance to the deposition of Monsieur Joseph Rouletabille, I see no reason why this witness should not give us the name of the murderer."

A pin drop could have been heard. Rouletabille stood silent looking sympathetically at Darzac, who, for the first time since the opening of the trial, showed himself agitated.

"Well," cried the President, "we wait for the name of the murderer." Rouletabille, feeling in his waistcoat pocket, drew his watch and, looking at it, said:

"Monsieur President, I cannot name the murderer before half-past six o'clock!"

Loud murmurs of disappointment filled the room. Some of the lawyers were heard to say: "He's making fun of us!"

The President in a stern voice, said:

"This joke has gone far enough. You may retire, Monsieur, into the witnesses' room. I hold you at our disposition."

Rouletabille protested.

"I assure you, Monsieur President," he cried in his sharp, clear voice, "that when I do name the murderer you will understand why I could not speak before half-past six. I assert this on my honour. I can, however, give you now some explanation of the murder of the keeper. Monsieur Frederic Larsan, who has seen me at work at the Glandier, can tell you with what care I studied this case. I found myself compelled to differ with him in arresting Monsieur Robert Darzac, who is innocent. Monsieur Larsan knows of my good faith and knows that some importance may be attached to my discoveries, which have often corroborated his own."

Frederic Larsan said:

"Monsieur President, it will be interesting to hear Monsieur Joseph Rouletabille, especially as he differs from me."

A murmur of approbation greeted the detective's speech. He was a good sportsman and accepted the challenge. The struggle between the two promised to be exciting.

As the President remained silent, Frederic Larsan continued:

"We agree that the murderer of the keeper was the assailant of Mademoiselle Stangerson; but as we are not agreed as to how the murderer escaped, I am curious to hear Monsieur Rouletabille's explanation."

"I have no doubt you are," said my friend.

General laughter followed this remark. The President angrily declared that if it was repeated, he would have the court cleared.

"Now, young man," said the President, "you have heard Monsieur Frederic Larsan; how did the murderer get away from the court?"

Rouletabille looked at Madame Mathieu, who smiled back at him sadly.

"Since Madame Mathieu," he said, "has freely admitted her intimacy with the keeper—"

"Why, it's the boy!" exclaimed Daddy Mathieu.

"Remove that man!" ordered the President.

Mathieu was removed from the court. Rouletabille went on:

"Since she has made this confession, I am free to tell you that she often met the keeper at night on the first floor of the donjon, in the room which was once an oratory. These meetings became more frequent when her husband was laid up by his rheumatism. She gave him morphine to ease his pain and to give herself more time for the meetings. Madame Mathieu came to the château that night, enveloped in a large black shawl which served also as a disguise. This was the phantom that disturbed Daddy Jacques. She knew how to imitate the mewing of Mother Angenoux' cat and she would make the cries to advise the keeper of her presence. The recent repairs of the donjon did not interfere with their meetings in the keeper's old room, in the donjon, since the new room assigned to him at the end of the right wing was separated from the steward's room by a partition only.

"Previous to the tragedy in the courtyard Madame Mathieu and the keeper left the donjon together. I learnt these facts from my examination of the footmarks in the court the next morning. Bernier, the concierge, whom I had stationed behind the donjon—as he will explain himself—could not see what passed in the court. He did not reach the court until he heard the revolver shots, and then he fired. When the woman parted from the man she went towards the open gate of the court, while he returned to his room.

"He had almost reached the door when the revolvers rang out. He had just reached the corner when a shadow bounded by. Meanwhile, Madame Mathieu, surprised by the revolver shots and by the entrance of people into the court, crouched in the darkness. The court is a large one and, being near the gate, she might easily have passed out unseen. But she remained and saw the body being carried away. In great agony of mind she neared the vestibule and saw the dead body of her lover on the stairs lit up by Daddy Jacques' lantern. She then fled; and Daddy Jacques joined her.

"That same night, before the murder, Daddy Jacques had been awakened by the cat's cry, and, looking through his window, had seen the black phantom. Hastily dressing himself he went out and recognised her. He is an old friend of Madame Mathieu, and when she saw him she had to tell him of her relations with the keeper and begged his assistance. Daddy Jacques took pity on her and accompanied her through the oak grove out of the park, past the border of the lake to the road to Epinay. From there it was but a very short distance to her home.

"Daddy Jacques returned to the château, and, seeing how important it was for Madame Mathieu's presence at the château to remain unknown, he did all he could to hide it. I appeal to Monsieur Larsan, who saw me, next morning, examine the two sets of footprints."

Here Rouletabille turning towards Madame Mathieu, with a bow, said:

"The footprints of Madame bear a strange resemblance to the neat footprints of the murderer."

Madame Mathieu trembled and looked at him with wide eyes as if in wonder at what he would say next.

"Madame has a shapely foot, long and rather large for a woman. The imprint, with its pointed toe, is very like that of the murderer's."

A movement in the court was repressed by Rouletabille. He held their attention at once.

"I hasten to add," he went on, "that I attach no importance to this. Outward signs like these are often liable to lead us into error, if we do not reason rightly. Monsieur Robert Darzac's footprints are also like the murderer's, and yet he is not the murderer!"

The President turning to Madame Mathieu asked:

"Is that in accordance with what you know occurred?"

"Yes, Monsieur President," she replied, "it is as if Monsieur Rouletabille had been behind us."

"Did you see the murderer running towards the end of the right wing?"

"Yes, as clearly as I saw them afterwards carrying the keeper's body."

"What became of the murderer?—You were in the courtyard and could easily have seen.

"I saw nothing of him, Monsieur President. It became quite dark just then."

"Then Monsieur Rouletabille," said the President, "must explain how the murderer made his escape."

Rouletabille continued:

"It was impossible for the murderer to escape by the way he had entered the court without our seeing him; or if we couldn't see him we must certainly have felt him, since the court is a very narrow one enclosed in high iron railings."

"Then if the man was hemmed in that narrow square, how is it you did not find him?—I have been asking you that for the last half hour."

"Monsieur President," replied Rouletabille, "I cannot answer that question before half-past six!"

By this time the people in the courtroom were beginning to believe in this new witness. They were amused by his melodramatic action in thus fixing the hour; but they seemed to have confidence in the outcome. As for the President, it looked as if he also had made up his mind to take the young man in the same way. He had certainly been impressed by Rouletabille's explanation of Madame Mathieu's part.

"Well, Monsieur Rouletabille," he said, "as you say; but don't let us see any more of you before half-past six."

Rouletabille bowed to the President, and made his way to the door of the witnesses' room.

I quietly made my way through the crowd and left the court almost at the same time as Rouletabille. He greeted me heartily, and looked happy.

"I'll not ask you, my dear fellow," I said, smiling, "what you've been doing in America; because I've no doubt you'll say you can't tell me until after half-past six."

"No, my dear Sainclair, I'll tell you right now why I went to America. I went in search of the name of the other half of the murderer!"

"The name of the other half?"

"Exactly. When we last left the Glandier I knew there were two halves to the murderer and the name of only one of them. I went to America for the name of the other half."

I was too puzzled to answer. Just then we entered the witnesses' room, and Rouletabille was immediately surrounded. He showed himself very friendly to all except Arthur Rance to whom he exhibited a marked coldness of manner. Frederic Larsan came in also. Rouletabille went up and shook him heartily by the hand. His manner toward the detective showed that he had got the better of the policeman. Larsan smiled and asked him what he had been doing in America, Rouletabille began by telling him some anecdotes of his voyage. They then turned aside together apparently with the object of speaking confidentially. I, therefore, discreetly left them and, being curious to hear the evidence, returned to my seat in the court-room where the public plainly showed its lack of interest in what was going on in their impatience for Rouletabille's return at the appointed time.

On the stroke of half-past six Joseph Rouletabille was again brought in. It is impossible for me to picture the tense excitement which appeared on every face, as he made his way to the bar. Darzac rose to his feet, frightfully pale.

The President, addressing Rouletabille, said gravely:

"I will not ask you to take the oath, because you have not been regularly summoned; but I trust there is no need to urge upon you the gravity of the statement you are about to make."

Rouletabille looked the President quite calmly and steadily in the face, and replied:

"Yes, Monsieur."

"At your last appearance here," said the President, "we had arrived at the point where you were to tell us how the murderer escaped, and also his name. Now, Monsieur Rouletabille, we await your explanation."

"Very well, Monsieur," began my friend amidst a profound silence. "I had explained how it was impossible for the murderer to get away without being seen. And yet he was there with us in the courtyard."

"And you did not see him? At least that is what the prosecution declares."

"No! We all of us saw him, Monsieur le President!" cried Rouletabille.

"Then why was he not arrested?"

"Because no one, besides myself, knew that he was the murderer. It would have spoiled my plans to have had him arrested, and I had then no proof other than my own reasoning. I was convinced we had the murderer before us and that we were actually looking at him. I have now brought what I consider the indisputable proof."

"Speak out, Monsieur! Tell us the murderer's name."

"You will find it on the list of names present in the court on the night of the tragedy," replied Rouletabille.

The people present in the courtroom began showing impatience. Some of them even called for the name, and were silenced by the usher.

"The list includes Daddy Jacques, Bernier the concierge, and Mr. Arthur Rance," said the President. "Do you accuse any of these?"

"No, Monsieur!"

"Then I do not understand what you are driving at. There was no other person at the end of the court."

"Yes, Monsieur, there was, not at the end, but above the court, who was leaning out of the window."

"Do you mean Frederic Larsan!" exclaimed the President.

"Yes! Frederic Larsan!" replied Rouletabille in a ringing tone. "Frederic Larsan is the murderer!"

The courtroom became immediately filled with loud and indignant protests. So astonished was he that the President did not attempt to quiet it. The quick silence which followed was broken by the distinctly whispered words from the lips of Robert Darzac:

"It's impossible! He's mad!"

"You dare to accuse Frederic Larsan, Monsieur?" asked the President. "If you are not mad, what are your proofs?"

"Proofs, Monsieur?—Do you want proofs? Well, here is one," cried Rouletabille shrilly. "Let Frederic Larsan be called!"

"Usher, call Frederic Larsan."

The usher hurried to the side door, opened it, and disappeared. The door remained open, while all eyes turned expectantly towards it. The clerk re-appeared and, stepping forward, said:

"Monsieur President, Frederic Larsan is not here. He left at about four o'clock and has not been seen since."

"That is my proof!" cried Rouletabille, triumphantly.

"Explain yourself?" demanded the President.

"My proof is Larsan's flight," said the young reporter. "He will not come back. You will see no more of Frederic Larsan."

"Unless you are playing with the court, Monsieur, why did you not accuse him when he was present? He would then have answered you."

"He could give no other answer than the one he has now given by his flight."

"We cannot believe that Larsan has fled. There was no reason for his doing so. Did he know you'd make this charge?"

"He did. I told him I would."

"Do you mean to say that knowing Larsan was the murderer you gave him the opportunity to escape?"

"Yes, Monsieur President, I did," replied Rouletabille, proudly. "I am not a policeman, I am a journalist; and my business is not to arrest people. My business is in the service of truth, and is not that of an executioner. If you are just, Monsieur, you will see that I am right. You can now understand why I refrained until this hour to divulge the name. I gave Larsan time to catch the 4:17 train for Paris, where he would know where to hide himself, and leave no traces. You will not find Frederic Larsan," declared Rouletabille, fixing his eyes on Monsieur Robert Darzac. "He is too cunning. He is a man who has always escaped you and whom you have long searched for in vain. If he did not succeed in outwitting me, he can yet easily outwit any police. This man who, four years ago, introduced himself to the Surete, and became celebrated as Frederic Larsan, is notorious under another name—a name well known to crime. Frederic Larsan, Monsieur President, is Ballmeyer!"

"Ballmeyer!" cried the President.

"Ballmeyer!" exclaimed Robert Darzac, springing to his feet. "Ballmeyer!—It was true, then!"

"Ah! Monsieur Darzac; you don't think I am mad, now!" cried Rouletabille.

Ballmeyer! Ballmeyer! No other word could be heard in the courtroom. The President adjourned the hearing.

Those of my readers who may not have heard of Ballmeyer will wonder at the excitement the name caused. And yet the doings of this remarkable criminal form the subject-matter of the most dramatic narratives of the newspapers and criminal records of the past twenty years. It had been reported that he was dead, and thus had eluded the police as he had eluded them throughout the whole of his career.

Ballmeyer was the best specimen of the high-class "gentleman swindler." He was adept at sleight of hand tricks, and no bolder or more ruthless crook ever lived. He was received in the best society, and was a member of some of the most exclusive clubs. On many of his depredatory expeditions he had not hesitated to use the knife and the mutton-bone. No difficulty stopped him and no "operation" was too dangerous. He had been caught, but escaped on the very morning of his trial, by throwing pepper into the eyes of the guards who were conducting him to Court. It was known later that, in spite of the keen hunt after him by the most expert of detectives, he had sat that same evening at a first performance in the Theatre Francais, without the slightest disguise.

He left France, later, to "work" America. The police there succeeded in capturing him once, but the extraordinary man escaped the next day. It would need a volume to recount the adventures of this master-criminal. And yet this was the man Rouletabille had allowed to get away! Knowing all about him and who he was, he afforded the criminal an opportunity for another laugh at the society he had defied! I could not help admiring the bold stroke of the young journalist, because I felt certain his motive had been to protect both Mademoiselle Stangerson and rid Darzac of an enemy at the same time.

The crowd had barely recovered from the effect of the astonishing revelation when the hearing was resumed. The question in everybody's mind was: Admitting that Larsan was the murderer, how did he get out of "The Yellow Room"?

Rouletabille was immediately called to the bar and his examination continued.

"You have told us," said the President, "that it was impossible to escape from the end of the court. Since Larsan was leaning out of his window, he had left the court. How did he do that?"

"He escaped by a most unusual way. He climbed the wall, sprang onto the terrace, and, while we were engaged with the keeper's body, reached the gallery by the window. He then had little else to do than to open the window, get in and call out to us, as if he had just come from his own room. To a man of Ballmeyer's strength all that was mere child's play. And here, Monsieur, is the proof of what I say."

Rouletabille drew from his pocket a small packet, from which he produced a strong iron peg.

"This, Monsieur," he said, "is a spike which perfectly fits a hole still to be seen in the cornice supporting the terrace. Larsan, who thought and prepared for everything in case of any emergency, had fixed this spike into the cornice. All he had to do to make his escape good was to plant one foot on a stone which is placed at the corner of the château, another on this support, one hand on the cornice of the keeper's door and the other on the terrace, and Larsan was clear of the ground. The rest was easy. His acting after dinner as if he had been drugged was make believe. He was not drugged; but he did drug me. Of course he had to make it appear as if he also had been drugged so that no suspicion should fall on him for my condition. Had I not been thus overpowered, Larsan would never have entered Mademoiselle Stangerson's chamber that night, and the attack on her would not have taken place."

A groan came from Darzac, who appeared to be unable to control his suffering.

"You can understand," added Rouletabille, "that Larsan would feel himself hampered from the fact that my room was so close to his, and from a suspicion that I would be on the watch that night. Naturally, he could not for a moment believe that I suspected him! But I might see him leaving his room when he was about to go to Mademoiselle Stangerson. He waited till I was asleep, and my friend Sainclair was busy trying to rouse me. Ten minutes after that Mademoiselle was calling out, "Murder!"

"How did you come to suspect Larsan?" asked the President.

"My pure reason pointed to him. That was why I watched him. But I did not foresee the drugging. He is very cunning. Yes, my pure reason pointed to him; but I required tangible proof so that my eyes could see him as my pure reason saw him."

"What do you mean by your pure reason?"

"That power of one's mind which admits of no disturbing elements to a conclusion. The day following the incident of 'the inexplicable gallery,' I felt myself losing control of it. I had allowed myself to be diverted by fallacious evidence; but I recovered and again took hold of the right end. I satisfied myself that the murderer could not have left the gallery, either naturally or supernaturally. I narrowed the field of consideration to that small circle, so to speak. The murderer could not be outside that circle. Now who was in it? There was, first, the murderer. Then there were Daddy Jacques, Monsieur Stangerson, Frederic Larsan, and myself. Five persons in all, counting in the murderer. And yet, in the gallery, there were but four. Now since it had been demonstrated to me that the fifth could not have escaped, it was evident that one of the four present in the gallery must be a double—he must be himself and the murderer also. Why had I not seen this before? Simply because the phenomenon of the double personality had not occurred before in this inquiry.

"Now who of the four persons in the gallery was both that person and the assassin? I went over in my mind what I had seen. I had seen at one and the same time, Monsieur Stangerson and the murderer, Daddy Jacques and the murderer, myself and the murderer; so that the murderer, then, could not be either Monsieur Stangerson, Daddy Jacques, or myself. Had I seen Frederic Larsan and the murderer at the same time?—No!—Two seconds had passed, during which I lost sight of the murderer; for, as I have noted in my papers, he arrived two seconds before Monsieur Stangerson, Daddy Jacques, and myself at the meeting-point of the two galleries. That would have given Larsan time to go through the 'off-turning' gallery, snatch off his false beard, return, and hurry with us as if, like us, in pursuit of the murderer. I was sure now I had got hold of the right end in my reasoning. With Frederic Larsan was now always associated, in my mind, the personality of the unknown of whom I was in pursuit—the murderer, in other words.

"That revelation staggered me. I tried to regain my balance by going over the evidences previously traced, but which had diverted my mind and led me away from Frederic Larsan. What were these evidences?

"1st. I had seen the unknown in Mademoiselle Stangerson's chamber. On going to Frederic Larsan's room, I had found Larsan sound asleep.

"2nd. The ladder.

"3rd. I had placed Frederic Larsan at the end of the 'off-turning' gallery and had told him that I would rush into Mademoiselle Stangerson's room to try to capture the murderer. Then I returned to Mademoiselle Stangerson's chamber where I had seen the unknown.

"The first evidence did not disturb me much. It is likely that, when I descended from my ladder, after having seen the unknown in Mademoiselle Stangerson's chamber, Larsan had already finished what he was doing there. Then, while I was re-entering the château, Larsan went back to his own room and, undressing himself, went to sleep.

"Nor did the second evidence trouble me. If Larsan were the murderer, he could have no use for a ladder; but the ladder might have been placed there to give an appearance to the murderer's entrance from without the château; especially as Larsan had accused Darzac and Darzac was not in the château that night. Further, the ladder might have been placed there to facilitate Larsan's flight in case of absolute necessity.

"But the third evidence puzzled me altogether. Having placed Larsan at the end of the 'off-turning gallery,' I could not explain how he had taken advantage of the moment when I had gone to the left wing of the château to find Monsieur Stangerson and Daddy Jacques, to return to Mademoiselle Stangerson's room. It was a very dangerous thing to do. He risked being captured,—and he knew it. And he was very nearly captured. He had not had time to regain his post, as he had certainly hoped to do. He had then a very strong reason for returning to his room. As for myself, when I sent Daddy Jacques to the end of the "right" gallery, I naturally thought that Larsan was still at his post. Daddy Jacques, in going to his post, had not looked, when he passed, to see whether Larsan was at his post or not.

"What, then, was the urgent reason which had compelled Larsan to go to the room a second time? I guessed it to be some evidence of his presence there. He had left something very important in that room. What was it? And had he recovered it? I begged Madame Bernier who was accustomed to clean the room to look, and she found a pair of eyeglasses—this pair, Monsieur President!"

And Rouletabille drew the eyeglasses, of which we know, from his pocket.

"When I saw these eyeglasses," he continued, "I was utterly nonplussed. I had never seen Larsan wear eyeglasses. What did they mean? Suddenly I exclaimed to myself: 'I wonder if he is long-sighted?' I had never seen Larsan write. He might, then, be long-sighted. They would certainly know at the Surete, and also know if the glasses were his. Such evidence would be damning. That explained Larsan's return. I know now that Larsan, or Ballmeyer, is long-sighted and that these glasses belonged to him.

"I now made one mistake. I was not satisfied with the evidence I had obtained. I wished to see the man's face. Had I refrained from this, the second terrible attack would not have occurred."

"But," asked the President, "why should Larsan go to Mademoiselle Stangerson's room, at all? Why should he twice attempt to murder her?"

"Because he loves her, Monsieur President."

"That is certainly a reason, but—"

"It is the only reason. He was madly in love, and because of that, and—other things, he was capable of committing any crime."

"Did Mademoiselle Stangerson know this?"

"Yes, Monsieur; but she was ignorant of the fact that the man who was pursuing her was Frederic Larsan, otherwise, of course, he would not have been allowed to be at the château. I noticed, when he was in her room after the incident in the gallery, that he kept himself in the shadow, and that he kept his head bent down. He was looking for the lost eyeglasses. Mademoiselle Stangerson knew Larsan under another name."

"Monsieur Darzac," asked the President, "did Mademoiselle Stangerson in any way confide in you on this matter? How is it that she has never spoken about it to anyone? If you are innocent, she would have wished to spare you the pain of being accused."

"Mademoiselle Stangerson told me nothing," replied Monsieur Darzac.

"Does what this young man says appear probable to you?" the President asked.

"Mademoiselle Stangerson has told me nothing," he replied stolidly.

"How do you explain that, on the night of the murder of the keeper," the President asked, turning to Rouletabille, "the murderer brought back the papers stolen from Monsieur Stangerson?—How do you explain how the murderer gained entrance into Mademoiselle Stangerson's locked room?"

"The last question is easily answered. A man like Larsan, or Ballmeyer, could have had made duplicate keys. As to the documents, I think Larsan had not intended to steal them, at first. Closely watching Mademoiselle with the purpose of preventing her marriage with Monsieur Robert Darzac, he one day followed her and Monsieur into the Grands Magasins de la Louvre. There he got possession of the reticule which she lost, or left behind. In that reticule was a key with a brass head. He did not know there was any value attached to the key till the advertisement in the newspapers revealed it. He then wrote to Mademoiselle, as the advertisement requested. No doubt he asked for a meeting, making known to her that he was also the person who had for some time pursued her with his love. He received no answer. He went to the Post Office and ascertained that his letter was no longer there. He had already taken complete stock of Monsieur Darzac, and, having decided to go to any lengths to gain Mademoiselle Stangerson, he had planned that, whatever might happen, Monsieur Darzac, his hated rival, should be the man to be suspected.

"I do not think that Larsan had as yet thought of murdering Mademoiselle Stangerson; but whatever he might do, he made sure that Monsieur Darzac should suffer for it. He was very nearly of the same height as Monsieur Darzac and had almost the same sized feet. It would not be difficult, to take an impression of Monsieur Darzac's footprints, and have similar boots made for himself. Such tricks were mere child's play for Larsan, or Ballmeyer.

"Receiving no reply to his letter, he determined, since Mademoiselle Stangerson would not come to him, that he would go to her. His plan had long been formed. He had made himself master of the plans of the château and the pavilion. So that, one afternoon, while Monsieur and Mademoiselle Stangerson were out for a walk, and while Daddy Jacques was away, he entered the latter by the vestibule window. He was alone, and, being in no hurry, he began examining the furniture. One of the pieces, resembling a safe, had a very small keyhole. That interested him! He had with him the little key with the brass head, and, associating one with the other, he tried the key in the lock. The door opened. He saw nothing but papers. They must be very valuable to have been put away in a safe, and the key to which to be of so much importance. Perhaps a thought of blackmail occurred to him as a useful possibility in helping him in his designs on Mademoiselle Stangerson. He quickly made a parcel of the papers and took it to the lavatory in the vestibule. Between the time of his first examination of the pavilion and the night of the murder of the keeper, Larsan had had time to find out what those papers contained. He could do nothing with them, and they were rather compromising. That night he took them back to the château. Perhaps he hoped that, by returning the papers he might obtain some gratitude from Mademoiselle Stangerson. But whatever may have been his reasons, he took the papers back and so rid himself of an encumbrance."

Rouletabille coughed. It was evident to me that he was embarrassed. He had arrived at a point where he had to keep back his knowledge of Larsan's true motive. The explanation he had given had evidently been unsatisfactory. Rouletabille was quick enough to note the bad impression he had made, for, turning to the President, he said: "And now we come to the explanation of the 'Mystery of The Yellow Room'!"

A movement of chairs in the court with a rustling of dresses and an energetic whispering of "Hush!" showed the curiosity that had been aroused.

"It seems to me," said the President, "that the 'Mystery of The Yellow Room', Monsieur Rouletabille, is wholly explained by your hypothesis. Frederic Larsan is the explanation. We have merely to substitute him for Monsieur Robert Darzac. Evidently the door of 'The Yellow Room' was open at the time Monsieur Stangerson was alone, and that he allowed the man who was coming out of his daughter's chamber to pass without arresting him—perhaps at her entreaty to avoid all scandal."

"No, Monsieur President," protested the young man. "You forget that, stunned by the attack made on her, Mademoiselle Stangerson was not in a condition to have made such an appeal. Nor could she have locked and bolted herself in her room. You must also remember that Monsieur Stangerson has sworn that the door was not open."

"That, however, is the only way in which it can be explained. 'The Yellow Room' was as closely shut as an iron safe. To use your own expression, it was impossible for the murderer to make his escape either naturally or supernaturally. When the room was broken into he was not there! He must, therefore, have escaped."

"That does not follow."

"What do you mean?"

"There was no need for him to escape—if he was not there!"

"Not there!"

"Evidently, not. He could not have been there, if he were not found there."

"But, what about the evidences of his presence?" asked the President.

"That, Monsieur President, is where we have taken hold of the wrong end. From the time Mademoiselle Stangerson shut herself in the room to the time her door was burst open, it was impossible for the murderer to escape. He was not found because he was not there during that time."

"But the evidences?"

"They have led us astray. In reasoning on this mystery we must not take them to mean what they apparently mean. Why do we conclude the murderer was there?—Because he left his tracks in the room? Good! But may he not have been there before the room was locked. Nay, he must have been there before! Let us look into the matter of these traces and see if they do not point to my conclusion.

"After the publication of the article in the 'Matin' and my conversation with the examining magistrate on the journey from Paris to Epinay-sur-Orge, I was certain that 'The Yellow Room' had been hermetically sealed, so to speak, and that consequently the murderer had escaped before Mademoiselle Stangerson had gone into her chamber at midnight.

"At the time I was much puzzled. Mademoiselle Stangerson could not have been her own murderer, since the evidences pointed to some other person. The assassin, then, had come before. If that were so, how was it that Mademoiselle had been attacked after? Or rather, that she appeared to have been attacked after? It was necessary for me to reconstruct the occurrence and make of it two phases—each separated from the other, in time, by the space of several hours. One phase in which Mademoiselle Stangerson had really been attacked—the other phase in which those who heard her cries thought she was being attacked. I had not then examined 'The Yellow Room'. What were the marks on Mademoiselle Stangerson? There were marks of strangulation and the wound from a hard blow on the temple. The marks of strangulation did not interest me much; they might have been made before, and Mademoiselle Stangerson could have concealed them by a collarette, or any similar article of apparel. I had to suppose this the moment I was compelled to reconstruct the occurrence by two phases. Mademoiselle Stangerson had, no doubt, her own reasons for so doing, since she had told her father nothing of it, and had made it understood to the examining magistrate that the attack had taken place in the night, during the second phase. She was forced to say that, otherwise her father would have questioned her as to her reason for having said nothing about it.

"But I could not explain the blow on the temple. I understood it even less when I learned that the mutton-bone had been found in her room. She could not hide the fact that she had been struck on the head, and yet that wound appeared evidently to have been inflicted during the first phase, since it required the presence of the murderer! I thought Mademoiselle Stangerson had hidden the wound by arranging her hair in bands on her forehead.

"As to the mark of the hand on the wall, that had evidently been made during the first phase—when the murderer was really there. All the traces of his presence had naturally been left during the first phase; the mutton-bone, the black footprints, the Basque cap, the handkerchief, the blood on the wall, on the door, and on the floor. If those traces were still all there, they showed that Mademoiselle Stangerson—who desired that nothing should be known—had not yet had time to clear them away. This led me to the conclusion that the two phases had taken place one shortly after the other. She had not had the opportunity, after leaving her room and going back to the laboratory to her father, to get back again to her room and put it in order. Her father was all the time with her, working. So that after the first phase she did not re-enter her chamber till midnight. Daddy Jacques was there at ten o'clock, as he was every night; but he went in merely to close the blinds and light the night-light. Owing to her disturbed state of mind she had forgotten that Daddy Jacques would go into her room and had begged him not to trouble himself. All this was set forth in the article in the 'Matin.' Daddy Jacques did go, however, and, in the dim light of the room, saw nothing.

"Mademoiselle Stangerson must have lived some anxious moments while Daddy Jacques was absent; but I think she was not aware that so many evidences had been left. After she had been attacked she had only time to hide the traces of the man's fingers on her neck and to hurry to the laboratory. Had she known of the bone, the cap, and the handkerchief, she would have made away with them after she had gone back to her chamber at midnight. She did not see them, and undressed by the uncertain glimmer of the night light. She went to bed, worn-out by anxiety and fear—a fear that had made her remain in the laboratory as late as possible.

"My reasoning had thus brought me to the second phase of the tragedy, when Mademoiselle Stangerson was alone in the room. I had now to explain the revolver shots fired during the second phase. Cries of 'Help!—Murder!' had been heard. How to explain these? As to the cries, I was in no difficulty; since she was alone in her room these could result from nightmare only. My explanation of the struggle and noise that were heard is simply that in her nightmare she was haunted by the terrible experience she had passed through in the afternoon. In her dream she sees the murderer about to spring upon her and she cries, 'Help! Murder!' Her hand wildly seeks the revolver she had placed within her reach on the night table by the side of her bed, but her hand, striking the table, overturns it, and the revolver, falling to the floor, discharges itself, the bullet lodging in the ceiling. I knew from the first that the bullet in the ceiling must have resulted from an accident. Its very position suggested an accident to my mind, and so fell in with my theory of a nightmare. I no longer doubted that the attack had taken place before Mademoiselle had retired for the night. After wakening from her frightful dream and crying aloud for help, she had fainted.

"My theory, based on the evidence of the shots that were heard at midnight, demanded two shots—one which wounded the murderer at the time of his attack, and one fired at the time of the nightmare. The evidence given by the Berniers before the examining magistrate was to the effect that only one shot had been heard. Monsieur Stangerson testified to hearing a dull sound first followed by a sharp ringing sound. The dull sound I explained by the falling of the marble-topped table; the ringing sound was the shot from the revolver. I was now convinced I was right. The shot that had wounded the hand of the murderer and had caused it to bleed so that he left the bloody imprint on the wall was fired by Mademoiselle in self-defence, before the second phase, when she had been really attacked. The shot in the ceiling which the Berniers heard was the accidental shot during the nightmare.

"I had now to explain the wound on the temple. It was not severe enough to have been made by means of the mutton-bone, and Mademoiselle had not attempted to hide it. It must have been made during the second phase. It was to find this out that I went to 'The Yellow Room', and I obtained my answer there."

Rouletabille drew a piece of white folded paper from his pocket, and drew out of it an almost invisible object which he held between his thumb and forefinger.

"This, Monsieur President," he said, "is a hair—a blond hair stained with blood;—it is a hair from the head of Mademoiselle

Stangerson. I found it sticking to one of the corners of the overturned table. The corner of the table was itself stained with blood—a tiny stain—hardly visible; but it told me that, on rising from her bed, Mademoiselle Stangerson had fallen heavily and had struck her head on the corner of its marble top.

"I still had to learn, in addition to the name of the assassin, which I did later, the time of the original attack. I learned this from the examination of Mademoiselle Stangerson and her father, though the answers given by the former were well calculated to deceive the examining magistrate—Mademoiselle Stangerson had stated very minutely how she had spent the whole of her time that day. We established the fact that the murderer had introduced himself into the pavilion between five and six o'clock. At a quarter past six the professor and his daughter had resumed their work. At five the professor had been with his daughter, and since the attack took place in the professor's absence from his daughter, I had to find out just when he left her. The professor had stated that at the time when he and his daughter were about to re-enter the laboratory he was met by the keeper and held in conversation about the cutting of some wood and the poachers. Mademoiselle Stangerson was not with him then since the professor said: 'I left the keeper and rejoined my daughter who was at work in the laboratory.'

"It was during that short interval of time that the tragedy took place. That is certain. In my mind's eye I saw Mademoiselle Stangerson re-enter the pavilion, go to her room to take off her hat, and find herself faced by the murderer. He had been in the pavilion for some time waiting for her. He had arranged to pass the whole night there. He had taken off Daddy Jacques's boots; he had removed the papers from the cabinet; and had then slipped under the bed. Finding the time long, he had risen, gone again into the laboratory, then into the vestibule, looked into the garden, and had seen, coming towards the pavilion,

Mademoiselle Stangerson—alone. He would never have dared to attack her at that hour, if he had not found her alone. His mind was made up. He would be more at ease alone with Mademoiselle Stangerson in the pavilion, than he would have been in the middle of the night, with Daddy Jacques sleeping in the attic. So he shut the vestibule window. That explains why neither Monsieur Stangerson, nor the keeper, who were at some distance from the pavilion, had heard the revolver shot.

"Then he went back to 'The Yellow Room'. Mademoiselle Stangerson came in. What passed must have taken place very quickly. Mademoiselle tried to call for help; but the man had seized her by the throat. Her hand had sought and grasped the revolver which she had been keeping in the drawer of her night-table, since she had come to fear the threats of her pursuer. The murderer was about to strike her on the head with the mutton-bone—a terrible weapon in the hands of a Larsan or Ballmeyer; but she fired in time, and the shot wounded the hand that held the weapon. The bone fell to the floor covered with the blood of the murderer, who staggered, clutched at the wall for support—imprinting on it the red marks—and, fearing another bullet, fled.

"She saw him pass through the laboratory, and listened. He was long at the window. At length he jumped from it. She flew to it and shut it. The danger past, all her thoughts were of her father. Had he either seen or heard? At any cost to herself she must keep this from him. Thus when Monsieur Stangerson returned, he found the door of 'The Yellow Room' closed, and his daughter in the laboratory, bending over her desk, at work!"

Turning towards Monsieur Darzac, Rouletabille cried: "You know the truth! Tell us, then, if that is not how things happened."

"I don't know anything about it," replied Monsieur Darzac.

"I admire you for your silence," said Rouletabille, "but if Mademoiselle Stangerson knew of your danger, she would release you from your oath. She would beg of you to tell all she has confided to you. She would be here to defend you!"

Monsieur Darzac made no movement, nor uttered a word. He looked at Rouletabille sadly.

"However," said the young reporter, "since Mademoiselle is not here, I must do it myself. But, believe me, Monsieur Darzac, the only means to save Mademoiselle Stangerson and restore her to her reason, is to secure your acquittal."

"What is this secret motive that compels Mademoiselle Stangerson to hide her knowledge from her father?" asked the President.

"That, Monsieur, I do not know," said Rouletabille. "It is no business of mine."

The President, turning to Monsieur Darzac, endeavoured to induce him to tell what he knew.

"Do you still refuse, Monsieur, to tell us how you employed your time during the attempts on the life of Mademoiselle Stangerson?"

"I cannot tell you anything, Monsieur."

The President turned to Rouletabille as if appealing for an explanation.

"We must assume, Monsieur President, that Monsieur Robert Darzac's absences are closely connected with Mademoiselle Stangerson's secret, and that Monsieur Darzac feels himself in honour bound to remain silent. It may be that Larsan, who, since his three attempts, has had everything in training to cast suspicion on Monsieur Darzac, had fixed on just those occasions for a meeting with Monsieur Darzac at a spot most compromising. Larsan is cunning enough to have done that."

The President seemed partly convinced, but still curious, he asked:

"But what is this secret of Mademoiselle Stangerson?"

"That I cannot tell you," said Rouletabille. "I think, however, you know enough now to acquit Monsieur Robert Darzac!

Unless Larsan should return, and I don't think he will," he added, with a laugh.

"One question more," said the President. "Admitting your explanation, we know that Larsan wished to turn suspicion on Monsieur Robert Darzac, but why should he throw suspicion on Daddy Jacques also?"

"There came in the professional detective, Monsieur, who proves himself an unraveller of mysteries, by annihilating the very proofs he had accumulated. He's a very cunning man, and a similar trick had often enabled him to turn suspicion from himself. He proved the innocence of one before accusing the other. You can easily believe, Monsieur, that so complicated a scheme as this must have been long and carefully thought out in advance by Larsan. I can tell you that he had long been engaged on its elaboration. If you care to learn how he had gathered information, you will find that he had, on one occasion, disguised himself as the commissionaire between the 'Laboratory of the Surete' and Monsieur Stangerson, of whom 'experiments' were demanded. In this way he had been able before the crime, on two occasions to take stock of the pavilion. He had 'made up' so that Daddy Jacques had not recognised him. And yet Larsan had found the opportunity to rob the old man of a pair of old boots and a cast-off Basque cap, which the servant had tied up in a handkerchief, with the intention of carrying them to a friend, a charcoal-burner on the road to Epinay. When the crime was discovered, Daddy Jacques had immediately recognised these objects as his. They were extremely compromising, which explains his distress at the time when we spoke to him about them. Larsan confessed it all to me. He is an artist at the game. He did a similar thing in the affair of the 'Credit Universel,' and in that of the 'Gold Ingots of the Mint.' Both these cases should be revised. Since Ballmeyer or Larsan has been in the Surete a number of innocent persons have been sent to prison."

# XXVIII

## IN WHICH IT IS PROVED THAT ONE DOES NOT ALWAYS THINK OF EVERYTHING

Great excitement prevailed when Rouletabille had finished. The courtroom became agitated with the murmurings of suppressed applause. Maitre Henri Robert called for an adjournment of the trial and was supported in his motion by the public prosecutor himself. The case was adjourned. The next day Monsieur Robert Darzac was released on bail, while Daddy Jacques received the immediate benefit of a "no cause for action." Search was everywhere made for Frederic Larsan, but in vain. Monsieur Darzac finally escaped the awful calamity which, at one time, had threatened him. After a visit to Mademoiselle Stangerson, he was led to hope that she might, by careful nursing, one day recover her reason.

Rouletabille, naturally, became the "man of the hour." On leaving the Palais de Justice, the crowd bore him aloft in triumph. The press of the whole world published his exploits and his photograph. He, who had interviewed so many illustrious personages, had himself become illustrious and was interviewed in his turn. I am glad to say that the enormous success in no way turned his head.

We left Versailles together, after having dined at "The Dog That Smokes." In the train I put a number of questions to him which, during our meal, had been on the tip of my tongue, but which I had refrained from uttering, knowing he did not like to talk "shop" while eating.

"My friend," I said, "that Larsan case is wonderful. It is worthy of you."

He begged me to say no more, and humorously pretended an anxiety for me should I give way to silly praise of him because of a personal admiration for his ability.

"I'll come to the point, then," I said, not a little nettled. "I am still in the dark as to your reason for going to America. When you left the Glandier you had found out, if I rightly understand, all about Frederic Larsan; you had discovered the exact way he had attempted the murder?"

"Quite so. And you," he said, turning the conversation, "did you suspect nothing?"

"Nothing!"

"It's incredible!"

"I don't see how I could have suspected anything. You took great pains to conceal your thoughts from me. Had you already suspected Larsan when you sent for me to bring the revolvers?"

"Yes! I had come to that conclusion through the incident of the 'inexplicable gallery.' Larsan's return to Mademoiselle Stangerson's room, however, had not then been cleared up by the eyeglasses. My suspicions were the outcome of my reasoning only; and the idea of Larsan being the murderer seemed so extraordinary that I resolved to wait for actual evidence before venturing to act. Nevertheless, the suspicion worried me, and I sometimes spoke to the detective in a way that ought to have opened your eyes. I spoke disparagingly of his methods. But until I found the eyeglasses I could but look upon my suspicion of him in the light of an absurd hypothesis only. You can imagine my elation after I had explained Larsan's movements. I remember well rushing into my room like a mad-man and crying to you: 'I'll get the better of the great Fred. I'll get the better of him in a way that will make a sensation!'

"I was then thinking of Larsan, the murderer. It was that same evening that Darzac begged me to watch over Mademoiselle Stangerson. I made no efforts until after we had dined with Larsan, until ten o'clock. He was right there before me, and I could afford to wait. You ought to have suspected, because when we were talking of the murderer's arrival, I said to you: 'I am quite sure Larsan will be here tonight.'

"But one important point escaped us both. It was one which ought to have opened our eyes to Larsan. Do you remember the bamboo cane? I was surprised to find Larsan had made no use of that evidence against Robert Darzac. Had it not been purchased by a man whose description tallied exactly with that of Darzac? Well, just before I saw him off at the train, after the recess during the trial, I asked him why he hadn't used the cane evidence. He told me he had never had any intention of doing so; that our discovery of it in the little inn at Epinay had much embarrassed him. If you will remember, he told us then that the cane had been given him in London. Why did we not immediately say to ourselves: 'Fred is lying. He could not have had this cane in London. He was not in London. He bought it in Paris'? Then you found out, on inquiry at Cassette's, that the cane had been bought by a person dressed very like Robert Darzac, though, as we learned later, from Darzac himself, it was not he who had made the purchase. Couple this with the fact we already knew, from the letter at the poste restante, that there was actually a man in Paris who was passing as Robert Darzac, why did we not immediately fix on Fred himself?

"Of course, his position at the Surete was against us; but when we saw the evident eagerness on his part to find convicting evidence against Darzac, nay, even the passion he displayed in his pursuit of the man, the lie about the cane should have had a new meaning for us. If you ask why Larsan bought the cane, if he had no intention of manufacturing evidence against Darzac by means of it, the answer is quite simple. He had been wounded in the hand by Mademoiselle Stangerson, so that the cane was useful to enable him to close his hand in carrying it. You remember I noticed that he always carried it?

"All these details came back to my mind when I had once fixed on Larsan as the criminal. But they were too late then to be of any use to me. On the evening when he pretended to be drugged I looked at his hand and saw a thin silk bandage covering the signs of a slight healing wound. Had we taken a quicker initiative at the time Larsan told us that lie about the cane, I am certain he would have gone off, to avoid suspicion. All the same, we worried Larsan or Ballmeyer without our knowing it."

"But," I interrupted, "if Larsan had no intention of using the cane as evidence against Darzac, why had he made himself up to look like the man when he went in to buy it?"

"He had not specially 'made up' as Darzac to buy the cane; he had come straight to Cassette's immediately after he had attacked Mademoiselle Stangerson. His wound was troubling him and, as he was passing along the Avenue de l'Opera, the idea of the cane came to his mind and he acted on it. It was then eight o'clock. And I, who had hit upon the very hour of the occurrence of the tragedy, almost convinced that Darzac was not the criminal, and knowing of the cane, I still never suspected Larsan. There are times..."

"There are times," I said, "when the greatest intellects—..." Rouletabille shut my mouth. I still continued to chide him, but, finding he did not reply, I saw he was no longer paying any attention to what I was saying. I found he was fast asleep.

# XXIX

## THE MYSTERY OF MADEMOISELLE STANGERSON

During the days that followed I had several opportunities to question him as to his reason for his voyage to America, but I obtained no more precise answers than he had given me on the evening of the adjournment of the trial, when we were on the train for Paris. One day, however, on my still pressing him, he said:

"Can't you understand that I had to know Larsan's true personality?"

"No doubt," I said, "but why did you go to America to find that out?"

He sat smoking his pipe, and made no further reply. I began to see that I was touching on the secret that concerned Mademoiselle Stangerson. Rouletabille evidently had found it necessary to go to America to find out what the mysterious tie was that bound her to Larsan by so strange and terrible a bond. In America he had learned who Larsan was and had obtained information which closed his mouth. He had been to Philadelphia.

And now, what was this mystery which held Mademoiselle Stangerson and Monsieur Robert Darzac in so inexplicable a silence? After so many years and the publicity given the case by a curious and shameless press; now that Monsieur Stangerson knows all and has forgiven all, all may be told. In every phase of this remarkable story Mademoiselle Stangerson had always been the sufferer.

The beginning dates from the time when, as a young girl, she was living with her father in Philadelphia. A visitor at the house, a Frenchman, had succeeded by his wit, grace and persistent attention, in gaining her affections. He was said to be rich and had asked her of her father. Monsieur Stangerson, on making inquiries as to Monsieur Jean Roussel, found that the man was a swindler and an adventurer. Jean Roussel was but another of the many names under which the notorious Ballmeyer, a fugitive from France, tried to hide himself. Monsieur Stangerson did not know of his identity with Ballmeyer; he learned that the man was simply undesirable for his daughter. He not only refused to give his consent to the marriage but denied him admission into the house. Mathilde Stangerson, however, had fallen in love. To her Jean Roussel was everything that her love painted him. She was indignant at her father's attitude, and did not conceal her feelings. Her father sent her to stay with an aunt in Cincinnati. There she was joined by Jean Roussel and, in spite of the reverence she felt for her father, ran away with him to get married.

They went to Louisville and lived there for some time. One morning, however, a knock came at the door of the house in which they were and the police entered to arrest Jean Roussel. It was then that Mathilde Stangerson, or Roussel, learned that her husband was no other than the notorious Ballmeyer!

The young woman in her despair tried to commit suicide. She failed in this, and was forced to rejoin her aunt in Cincinnati, The old lady was overjoyed to see her again. She had been anxiously searching for her and had not dared to tell Monsieur Stangerson of her disappearance. Mathilde swore her to secrecy, so that her father should not know she had been away. A month later, Mademoiselle Stangerson returned to her father, repentant, her heart dead within her, hoping only one thing: that she would never again see her husband, the horrible Ballmeyer. A report was spread, a few weeks later, that he was dead, and she now determined to atone for her disobedience by a life of labour and devotion for her father. And she kept her word.

All this she had confessed to Robert Darzac, and, believing Ballmeyer dead, had given herself to the joy of a union with him. But fate had resuscitated Jean Roussel—the Ballmeyer of her youth. He had taken steps to let her know that he would never allow her to marry Darzac—that he still loved her.

Mademoiselle Stangerson never for one moment hesitated to confide in Monsieur Darzac. She showed him the letter in which Jean Roussel asked her to recall the first hours of their union in their beautiful and charming Louisville home. "The presbytery has lost nothing of its charm, nor the garden its brightness," he had written. The scoundrel pretended to be rich and claimed the right of taking her back to Louisville. She had told Darzac that if her father should know of her dishonour, she would kill herself. Monsieur Darzac had sworn to silence her persecutor, even if he had to kill him. He was outwitted and would have succumbed had it not been for the genius of Rouletabille.

Mademoiselle Stangerson was herself helpless in the hands of such a villain. She had tried to kill him when he had first threatened and then attacked her in "The Yellow Room". She had, unfortunately, failed, and felt herself condemned to be forever at the mercy of this unscrupulous wretch who was continually demanding her presence at clandestine interviews. When he sent her the letter through the Post Office, asking her to meet him, she had refused. The result of her refusal was the tragedy of "The Yellow Room". The second time he wrote asking for a meeting, the letter reaching her in her sick chamber, she had avoided him by sleeping with her servants. In that letter the scoundrel had warned her that, since she was too ill to come to him, he would come to her, and that he would be in her chamber at a particular hour on a particular night. Knowing that she had everything to fear from Ballmeyer, she had left her chamber on that night. It was then that the incident of the "inexplicable gallery" occurred.

The third time she had determined to keep the appointment. He asked for it in the letter he had written in her own room, on the night of the incident in the gallery, which he left on her desk. In that letter he threatened to burn her father's papers if she did not meet him. It was to rescue these papers that she made up her mind to see him. She did not for one moment doubt that the wretch would carry out his threat if she persisted in avoiding him, and in that case the labours of her father's lifetime would be forever lost. Since the meeting was thus inevitable, she resolved to see her husband and appeal to his better nature. It was for this interview that she had prepared herself on the night the keeper was killed. They did meet, and what passed between them may be imagined. He insisted that she renounce Darzac. She, on her part, affirmed her love for him. He stabbed her in his anger, determined to convict Darzac of the crime. As Larsan he could do it, and had so managed things that Darzac could never explain how he had employed the time of his absence from the château. Ballmeyer's precautions were most cunningly taken.

Larsan had threatened Darzac as he had threatened Mathilde—with the same weapon, and the same threats. He wrote Darzac urgent letters, declaring himself ready to deliver up the letters that had passed between him and his wife, and to leave them forever, if he would pay him his price. He asked Darzac to meet him for the purpose of arranging the matter, appointing the time when Larsan would be with Mademoiselle

Stangerson. When Darzac went to Epinay, expecting to find Ballmeyer or Larsan there, he was met by an accomplice of Larsan's, and kept waiting until such time as the "coincidence" could be established.

It was all done with Machiavellian cunning; but Ballmeyer had reckoned without Joseph Rouletabille.

Now that the Mystery of "The Yellow Room" has been cleared up, this is not the time to tell of Rouletabille's adventures in America. Knowing the young reporter as we do, we can understand with what acumen he had traced, step by step, the story of Mathilde Stangerson and Jean Roussel. At Philadelphia he had quickly informed himself as to Arthur William Rance. There he learned of Rance's act of devotion and the reward he thought himself entitled to for it. A rumour of his marriage with Mademoiselle Stangerson had once found its way into the drawing-rooms of Philadelphia. He also learned of Rance's continued attentions to her and his importunities for her hand. He had taken to drink, he had said, to drown his grief at his unrequited love. It can now be understood why Rouletabille had shown so marked a coolness of demeanour towards Rance when they met in the witnesses' room, on the day of the trial.

The strange Roussel-Stangerson mystery had now been laid bare. Who was this Jean Roussel? Rouletabille had traced him from Philadelphia to Cincinnati. In Cincinnati he became acquainted with the old aunt, and had found means to open her mouth. The story of Ballmeyer's arrest threw the right light on the whole story. He visited the "presbytery"—a small and pretty dwelling in the old colonial style—which had, indeed, "lost nothing of its charm." Then, abandoning his pursuit of traces of Mademoiselle Stangerson, he took up those of Ballmeyer. He followed them from prison to prison, from crime to crime. Finally, as he was about leaving for Europe, he learned in New York that Ballmeyer had, five years before, embarked for

France with some valuable papers belonging to a merchant of New Orleans whom he had murdered.

And yet the whole of this mystery has not been revealed. Mademoiselle Stangerson had a child, by her husband,—a son. The infant was born in the old aunt's house. No one knew of it, so well had the aunt managed to conceal the event.

What became of that son?—That is another story which, so far, I am not permitted to relate.

About two months after these events, I came upon Rouletabille sitting on a bench in the Palais de Justice, looking very depressed.

"What's the matter, old man?" I asked. "You are looking very downcast. How are your friends getting on?"

"Apart from you," he said, "I have no friends."

"I hope that Monsieur Darzac—"

"No doubt."

"And Mademoiselle Stangerson—How is she?"

"Better—much better."

"Then you ought not to be sad."

"I am sad," he said, "because I am thinking of the perfume of the lady in black—"

"The perfume of the lady in black!—I have heard you often refer to it. Tell me why it troubles you."

"Perhaps—some day; some day," said Rouletabille.

And he heaved a profound sigh.

# The Perfume of the Lady in Black

# CONTENTS

| | | |
|---|---|---|
| I. | Which Begins Where Most Romances End | 253 |
| II. | In Which There is Question of the Changing Rumours of Joseph Rouletabille | 266 |
| III. | The Perfume | 273 |
| IV. | En Route | 285 |
| V. | Panic | 299 |
| VI. | The Fort of Hercules | 319 |
| VII. | Which Tells of Some Precautions Taken By Joseph Rouletabille to Defend the Fort of Hercules Against the Attack of an Enemy | 336 |
| VIII. | Which Contains Some Pages From the History of Jean Roussel-Larsan Ballmeyer | 356 |
| IX. | In Which "Old Bob" Unexpectedly Arrives | 361 |
| X. | The Events of The Twelfth of April | 383 |
| XI. | The Attack of the Square Tower | 425 |
| XII. | The Impossible Body | 435 |
| XIII. | In Which the Fears of Rouletabille Assume Alarming Proportions | 445 |

XIV. The Sack of Potatoes 462
XV. The Sighs of the Night 477
XVI. Discovery of "Australia" 484
XVII. Old Bob's Terrible Adventure 496
XVIII. How Death Stalked Abroad at Noon Day 504
XIX. In Which Rouletabille Orders the Iron Doors to be Closed 516
XX. In Which Rouletabille Gives a Corporeal Demonstration of the Possibility of "The Body of Too Many" 524

EPILOGUE 556

# I

## WHICH BEGINS WHERE MOST ROMANCES END

The marriage of Mr. Robert Darzac and Miss Mathilde Stangerson took place in Paris, at the Church of St. Nicolas du Chardonnet, on April 6, 1895, everything connected with the occasion being conducted in the quietest fashion possible. A little more than two years had rolled by since the events which I have recorded in a previous volume—events so sensational that it is not speaking too strongly to say that an even longer lapse of time would not have sufficed to blot out the memory of the famous "Mystery of the Yellow Room."

There was no doubt in the minds of those concerned that, if the arrangements for the wedding had not been made almost secretly, the little church would have been thronged and surrounded by a curious crowd, eager to gaze upon the principal personages of the drama which had aroused an interest almost worldwide and the circumstances of which were still present in the minds of the sensation-loving public. But in this isolated little corner of the city, in this almost unknown parish, it was easy enough to maintain the upmost privacy. Only a few friends of M. Darzac and the Professor Stangerson, on whose discretion they felt assured that they might rely, had been invited. I had the honour to be one of the number.

I reached the church early, and naturally, my first thought was to look for Joseph Rouletabille there. I had been somewhat surprised at not seeing him, but, having no doubt that he would arrive shortly, I entered the pew already occupied by M. Henri-Robert and M. Andre Hesse, who, in the quiet shades of the little chapel, exchanged in undertones reminiscences of the strange affair at Versailles, which the approaching ceremony brought to their memories. I listened without paying much attention to what they were saying, glancing from time to time carelessly around me.

A dreary place enough is the Church of St. Nicolas du Chardonnet. With its cracked walls, the lizards running from every corner and dirt—not the beautiful dust of ages, but the common, ill-smelling, germ-laden dust of today—everywhere, this church, so dark and forbidding on the outside, is equally dismal within. The sky, which seems rather to be withdrawn from than above the edifice, sheds a miserly light which seems to find the greatest difficulty in penetrating through the dusty panes of unstained glass. Have you read Renan's "Memories of Childhood and Youth?" Push the door of St. Nicolas du Chardonnet and you will understand how the author of the "Life of Jesus" longed to die, when as a lad he was a pupil in the little seminary of the Abbe Duplanloup, close by, and could only leave the school to come to pray in this church. And it is in this funeral darkness, in a scene which seemed to have been painted only for mourning and for all rites consecrated to sorrow, that the marriage of Robert Darzac and Mathilde Stangerson was to be solemnised. I could not cast aside the feeling of foreboding that came over me in these dreary surroundings.

Beside me, M. Henri-Robert and M. Andre Hesse continued to chat, and my wandering attention was arrested by a remark made by the former:

"I never felt quite easy about Robert and Mathilde," he said—"not even after the happy termination of the affair at

Versailles—until I know that the information of the death of Frederic Larsan had been officially confirmed. That man was a pitiless enemy."

It will be remembered, perhaps, by the readers of "The Mystery of the Yellow Room" that a few months after the acquittal of the Professor in Sorbonne, there occurred the terrible catastrophe of La Dordogne, a transatlantic steamer, running between Havre and New York. In the broiling heat of a summer night, upon the coast of the New World, La Dordogne had caught fire from an overheated boiler. Before help could reach her, the steamer was utterly destroyed. Scarcely thirty passengers were able to leap into the life boats, and these were picked up the next day by a merchant vessel, which conveyed them to the nearest port. For days thereafter, the ocean cast up on the beach hundreds of corpses. And among these, they found Larsan.

The papers which were found carefully hidden in the clothing worn by the dead man, proved beyond a doubt his identity. Mathilde Stangerson was at last delivered from this monster of a husband to whom, through the facility of the American laws, she had given her hand in secret, in the unthinking ardour of girlish romance. This wretch, whose real name, according to court records, was Ballmeyer, and who had married her under the name of Jean Rouseel, could no longer rise like a dark shadow between Mathilde and the man whom she had loved so long and so well, without daring to become his bride. In "The Mystery of the Yellow Room," I have related all the details of this remarkable affair, one of the strangest which has ever been known in the annals of the Court of Assizes, and which, without doubt, would have had a most tragic denouncement, had it not been for the extraordinary party played by a boy reporter, scarcely eighteen years old, Joseph Rouletabille, who was the only one to discover that Frederic Larsan, the celebrated Secret Service agent, was none other than Ballmeyer himself. The accidental—one might almost say "providential"—death of this villain, had seemed to assure a happy termination to the extraordinary story, and it must be confessed that it was undoubtedly one of the chief factors in the rapid recovery of Mathilde Stangerson, whose reason had been almost overturned by the mysterious horrors at the Glandier.

"You see, my dear friend," said M. Henri-Robert to M. Andre Hesse, whose eyes were roving restlessly about the church, "you see, in this world, one can always find the bright side. See how beautifully everything has turned out—even the troubles of Mlle. Stangerson. But why are you constantly looking around you? What are you looking for? Do you expect anyone?"

"Yes," replied M. Hesse. "I am waiting for Frederic Larsan!"

M. Henri-Robert laughed—a decorous little laugh, in deference to the sanctity of the surroundings. But I felt no inclination to join in his mirth. I was an hundred leagues from foreseeing the terrible experience which was even then approaching us; but when I recall that moment and seek to blot out of my mind all that has happened since—all those events which I intend to relate in the course of this narrative, letting the circumstances come before the reader as they came before us during their development—I recollect once more the curious unrest which thrilled me at the mention of Larsan's name.

"What's the matter, Sainclair?" whispered M. Henri-Robert, who had noticed something odd in my expression. "You know that Hesse was only joking."

"I don't know anything about it," I answered. And I looked attentively around me, as M. Andre Hesse had done. And, indeed, we had believed Larsan dead so often when he was known as Ballmeyer, that it seemed quite possible that he might be once more brought to life in the guise of Larsan.

"Here comes Rouletabille," remarked M. Henri-Robert. "I'll wager that he isn't worried about anything."

"But how pale he is!" exclaimed M. Andre Hesse in an undertone.

The young reporter joined us and pressed our hands in an absentminded manner.

"Good morning, Sainclair. Good morning, gentlemen. I am not late, I hope?"

It seemed to me that his voice trembled. He left our pew immediately and withdrew to a dark corner, where I beheld him kneel down like a child. He hid his face, which was indeed very pale, in his hands, and prayed. I had never guessed that Rouletabille was of a religious turn of mind, and his fervent devotion astonished me. When he raised his head, his eyes were filled with tears. He did not even try to hide them. He paid no attention to anything or anyone around him. He was lost completely in his prayers, and, one might imagine, his grief.

But what could be the occasion of his sorrow? Was he not happy at the prospect of the union so ardently desired by everyone? Had not the good fortune of Mathilde Stangerson and Robert Darzac been in a great measure brought about by his efforts? After all, it was perhaps from joy, that the lad had wept. He rose from his knees, and was hidden behind a pillar. I made no endeavour to join him, for I could see that he was anxious to be alone.

And the next moment, Mathilde Stangerson made her entrance into the church upon the arm of her father, Robert Darzac walking behind them. Ah, the drama of the Glandier had been a sorrowful one for these three! But, strange as it may seem, Mathilde Strangerson appeared only the more beautiful, for all that she had passed through. True, she was no longer the beautiful statue, the living marble, the ancient goddess, the cold Pagan divinity, who, at the official functions at which her father's position had forced her to appear, had excited a flutter of admiration whenever she was seen. It seemed, on the contrary, that fate, in making her expiate for so many long years and imprudence committed in early youth, had cast her into the depths of madness and despair, only to tear away the mask of stone, which hid from sight the tender, delicate spirit. And it was this spirit which shone forth on her wedding day, in the sweetest and most charming smile, playing on her curved lips, hiding in her eyes, filled with pensive happiness, and leavings its impress on her forehead, polished like ivory, where one might read the love of all that was beautiful and all that was good.

As to her gown, I must acknowledge that I remember nothing at all about it, and am unable even to say of what colour it was. But what I do remember, is the strange expression which came over her visage when she looked through the rows of faces in the pews without seeming to discover the one she sought. In a moment she had regained her composure, and was mistress of herself once more. She had seen Rouletabille behind his pillar. She smiled at him and my companions and I smiled in our turn.

"She has the eyes of a mad woman!"

I turned around quickly to see who had uttered the heartless words. It was a poor fellow whom Robert Darzac, out of the kindness of his heart, had made his assistant in the laboratory at the Sorbonne. The man was named Brignolles, and was a distant cousin of the bridegroom. We knew of no other relative of M. Darzac, whose family came originally from the Midi. Long ago he had lost both father and mother; he had neither brother nor sister, and seemed to have broken off all intercourse with his native province, from which he had brought an eager desire for success, an exceptional ability to work, a strong intellect and natural need for affection, which had satisfied itself in his relations with Professor Stangerson and his daughter. He had also as a legacy from Provence, his native place, a soft voice and slight accent, which had often brought a smile to the lips of his pupils at the Sorbonne, who, nevertheless, loved it as they might have loved a strain of music, which made the necessary dryness of their studies a little less arid.

One beautiful morning, in the preceeding spring, and consequently a year after the occurrences in the yellow room, Robert Darzac had presented Brignolles to his pupils. The new assistant had come direct from Aix, where he had been a tutor in the natural sciences, and where he had committed some fault of discipline which had caused his dismissal. But he had remembered that he was related to M. Darzac, the famous chemist, had taken the train to Paris, and had told such a piteous tale to the fiance of Mlle. Stangerson that Darzac, out of pity, had found the means to associate his cousin with him in his work. At this time, the health of Robert Darzac had been far from flourishing. He was suffering from the reaction following the strong emotions which had nearly weighed him down at the Glandier and at the Court of Assizes; but one might have thought that the recovery, now assured, of Mathilde, and the prospect of their marriage would have had a happy influence both upon the mental and physical condition of the professor. We, however, remarked on the contrary, that from the day that Brignolles came to him—Brignolles, whose friendship should have been a precious solace, the weakness of M. Darzac seemed to increase. However, we are obliged to acknowledge that Brignolles was not to blame for that, for two unfortunate and unforeseen accidents had occurred in the course of some experiments, which would have seemed, on the face of them, not at all dangerous. The first resulted from the unexpected explosion of a Gessler tube, which might have severely injured M. Darzac, but which only injured Brignolles, whose hands were badly scarred. The second, which might have been extremely grave, happened through the explosion of a tiny lamp against which M. Darzac was leaning. Happily, he was not hurt, but his eyebrows were scorched, and for some time after his sight was slightly impaired, and he was unable to stand much sunlight.

Since the Glandier mysteries, I had been in such a state of mind that I often found myself attaching importance to the most simple happenings. At the time of the second accident I was present, having come to seek M. Darzac at the Sorbonne. I myself led our friend to a druggist and then to a doctor, and I (rather dryly, I own) begged Brignolles, when he wished to accompany us, to remain at his post. On the way, M. Darzac asked me why I had wounded the poor fellow's feelings. I had told him that I did not care for Brignolles's society, for the abstract reason that I did not care for his manners, and for that concrete reason, on this special occasion, that I believed him to be responsible for the accident. M. Darzac demanded why I thought so, and I did not know how to answer, and he began to laugh—a laugh that was quickly silenced, however, when the doctor told him that he might easily have been made entirely blind, and that he might consider himself very lucky in having gotten off so well.

My suspicions of Brignolles were, doubtless, ridiculous, and no more accidents happened. All the same, I was so strongly prejudiced against the ridiculous, and the accidents never happened again. All of the same, I was so strongly prejudiced against the young man that, at the bottom of my heart, I blamed him for the slow improvement in M. Darzac's physical condition. At the beginning of winter, Darzac had such a bad cough that I entreated him to ask for leave of absence and to take a trip to the Midi—a prayer in which all his friends joined. The physicians advised San Remo. He went thither, and a week later he wrote us that he felt much better—that it seemed to him as though a heavy weight had been lifted from his breast. "I can breathe here," he wrote. "When I left Paris, I seemed to be stifling."

This letter from M. Darzac gave me much food for thought, and I no longer hesitated to take Rouletabille into my confidence.

He agreed with me that it was a most peculiar coincidence that M. Darzac was so ill when Brignolles was with him and so much better when he and his young assistant were separated. The impression that this was actually fact was so strong in my mind that I would on no account have permitted myself to lose sight of Brignolles. No, indeed. I verily believe that if he had attempted to leave Paris, I should have followed him. But he made no such attempt. On the contrary, he haunted the footsteps of M. Stangerson. Under the pretext of asking news of M. Darzac, he presented himself at the house of the Professor almost every day. Once he made an effort to see Mlle. Stangerson, but I had painted his portrait to M. Darzac's fiancee in such unflattering terms, that I had succeeded in disgusting her with him completely—a fact on which I congratulated myself in my innermost soul.

M. Darzac remained four months in San Remo and returned home at the end of that time almost completely restored to health. His eyes, however, were still weak, and he was under the necessity of taking the greatest care of them. Rouletabille and myself had resolved to keep a close watch on Brignolles, but we were satisfied that everything would be right when we were informed that the long-deferred marriage was to occur almost immediately and that M. Darzac would take his wife away on a long honeymoon trip far from Paris—from Brignolles.

Upon his return from San Remo, M. Darzac had asked me:

"Well, how are you getting on with poor Brignolles? Have you decided that you were wrong with him?"

"Indeed, I have not," was my response.

And Darzac turned away, laughing at me, and uttering one of the Provencal jests which he affected when circumstances allowed him to be gay, and which found on his lips a new freshness since his visit to the Midi had accustomed him again to the accents of his childhood.

We knew that he was happy. But we had formed no real idea of how happy he was—for between the time of his return and the wedding day we had had few chances to see him—until we beheld him walking up the aisle of the church, his face fairly transformed. His slight erect figure bore itself as proudly as though he were an Emperor. Happiness had made him another being.

"Anyone could guess that he was a bridegroom!" tittered Brignolles.

I left the neighbourhood of the man who was so repulsive to me, and stepped behind poor M. Stangerson, who stood through the entire ceremony with his arms crossed on his breast, seeing nothing and hearing nothing. I was obliged to touch him on the shoulder when all was over to arouse him from his dream.

As they passed into sacristy, M. Andre Hesse heaved a deep sigh.

"I can breathe again," he murmured.

"Why couldn't you breathe before, my friend?" asked M. Henri- Robert.

And M. Andre Hesse confessed that he had feared up to the last moment that the dead man would reappear.

"I can't help it," was the only response he would make when his friend rallied him. "I cannot bring myself to the idea that Frederic Larsan will stay dead for good."

And now we all—a dozen or so persons—were gathered in the sacristy. The witness signed the register, and the rest of us congratulated the newly wedded pair. The sacristy was yet more dismal than the church, and I might have thought that it was on account of the darkness that I could not perceive Joseph Rouletabille, if the room had not been so small. But, assuredly, he was not there. Mathilde had already asked for him twice, and M. Darzac requested me to go and look for him. I did so, but returned to the vestry without him. He had disappeared from the church.

"How strange it is!" examined M. Darzac. "I can't understand it. Are you sure that you looked everywhere? He may be in some corner dreaming."

"I looked everywhere, and I called his name," I told him.

But M. Darzac was still not satisfied. He wanted to look through the church for himself. His search was better rewarded than mine, for he learned from a beggar, who was sitting in the porch with a tambourine, that Rouletabille has left the church a few minutes before and had been driven away in a hack. When the bridegroom brought this news to his wife, she appeared to be both pained and anxious. She called me to her side and said:

"My dear M. Sainclair, you know that we are to take the train in two hours. Will you hunt up our little friend and bring him to me, and tell him that his strange behaviour is grieving me very much?"

"Count upon me," I said.

And I began a wild goose chase after Rouletabille. But I appeared at the station without him. Neither at his home, nor at the office of his paper, nor at the Cafe du Barreau, where the necessities of his work often called him at this hour of the day, could I lay my hand on him. None of his comrades could tell me where I might chance to find him. I leave you to think how unwillingly I turned my steps in the direction of the railroad station. M. Darzac was greatly disturbed, but as he had to look after the comfort of his fellow travellers (for Professor Stangerson, who was on his way to Mentone, was to accompany his daughter and her husband to Dijon, changing cars there, while the Darzacs continued their trips to Culoz and Mt. Cenis,) he asked me to break the bad news to his bride. I performed the commission, adding that Rouletabille would, without doubt, present himself before the train started. At these words, Mathilde began to cry softly, and shook her head:

"No—no!" she whispered. "It is all over. He will never come again."

And she stepped into the railway carriage.

It was at this point that the insufferable Brignolles, seeing the emotion of the newly-made bride, whispered again to M. Andre Hesse, "Look! Look! Hasn't she the eyes of a maniac? Ah, Robert has done wrong. It would have been better for him to wait." M. Hesse gave him a disdainful glance, and bade him to be silent.

I can still see Brignolles as he spoke those words, and can recall as vividly as though it were yesterday the feeling of horror with which he inspired me. There was no longer any doubt in my mind that he was an evil and a jealous man, and that he would never forgive his relative for having placed him in a position which might be considered subordinate. He had a yellow face and long features that looked as if they had been drawn down from forehead to chin. Everything about him seemed to diffuse bitterness and everything about him was long. He had a long figure, long arms, long legs and a long head. However, to this general rule of length, there were exceptions—the feet and the hands. He had extremities small and almost beautiful.

After having been so rudely silenced for his malicious words by the young lawyer, Brignolles immediately took offense and left the station, after having paid his respects to the bride and bridegroom. At least, I believe that he left the station, for I did not see him again.

There were three minutes yet before the departure of the train. We still hoped that Rouletabille would appear, and we looked across the quay, thinking once or twice that we saw the form of our young friend approaching, among the hurrying throng of travellers. How could it be that he would not advance, as we were so used to seeing him, in his quick, boyish fashion, rushing through the crowds, paying no heed to the cries and protestations that his method of pushing his way usually evoked while he seemed to be hurrying faster than anyone else? What could he be doing that detained him?

Already the doors were closed. The bell on the engine began to sound its first slow strokes, and the calls of hack drivers began to arise: "Carriage, Monsieur? Carriage?" And then the quick last word which gave the signal for the departure. But no Rouletabille. We were all so grieved, and moreover, so surprised, that we remained on the platform, looking at Mme. Darzac, without thinking to wish her a pleasant journey. Professor Stangerson's daughter cast a long glance upon the quay, and, at the moment that the speed of the train began to accelerate, certain now that she was not to see her "little friend" again, she threw me an envelope from the car window.

"For him," she said.

And almost as though moved by an irresistible impulse, her face wearing an expression of something that resembled terror, she added in a tone so strange that I could not help recalling the horrible speeches of Brignolles:

"Au revoir, my friends—or adieu."

# II

## IN WHICH THERE IS QUESTION OF THE CHANGING RUMOURS OF JOSEPH ROULETABILLE

In returning alone from the station I could not help feeling some surprise at the singular sensation of sadness which oppressed me, and of the cause of which I had not the least idea. Since the affair at Versailles, with the details of which my existence had become so strangely intermingled, I had enjoyed the closest intimacy with Professor Stangerson, his daughter, and Robert Darzac. I ought to have been completely happy on the day of this wedding, which seemed in every way so satisfactory. I wondered whether the unexplained absence of the young reporter did not account in some measure for my strange depression. Rouletabille had been treated by the Stangersons and by M. Darzac as their deliverer. And especially since Mathilde had left the sanitarium, in which, for several months, her shattered nervous system had needed and received the most assiduous care—since the daughter of the famous professor had been able to understand the eextraordinary part which the boy had played in the drama that, without his help, would inevitably have ended in the bitterest grief for all those whom she loved—since she had read by the light of her restored reason the short-hand reports of the trial, at which Rouletabille appeared at the last moment like some hero of a miracle—she had surrounded the youngster with an affection little less than maternal. She interested herself in everything which concerned him; she begged for his confidence: she wanted to know more about him than I knew, and, perhaps, more even than he knew himself. She had shown an unobtrusive but strong curiosity in regard to the mystery of his birth, of which all of us were ignorant, and on which the young man had kept silence with a sort of savage pride. Although he fully realised the tender friendship which the poor soul felt for him, Rouletabille maintained his reserve and in his dealings with her affected a formal politeness which astonished me, coming from the boy whom I had known so exuberant, so wholehearted, so strong in his likes and dislikes. More than once I had mentioned the matter to him, and he had answered me in an evasive manner, laying great stress, however, upon his sentiments of devotion for "a lady whom he esteemed beyond anyone in the world, and for whom he would have been ready to sacrifice his all, if fate or fortune had given him anything to sacrifice for anyone." He would take strange whims at such times. For instance, after having made, in my presence, a promise to take a holiday and remain all day with the Stangersons, who had rented for the summer (for they did not wish to live at the Glandier again) a pretty little place at Chennevieres, on the borders of the Marne, and after having shown an almost childish joy at the prospect, he suddenly and without any reason refused to accompany me. And I was obliged to set out alone, leaving him in his little room, in the corner of the Boulevard St. Michel and the Rue Monsieur-le-Prince. I wished as I departed that he might experience as much pain as I knew that he would cause Mlle. Stangerson. One Sunday, she, vexed at the lad's behaviour, made up her mind to go with me to his den in the Latin Quarter, and surprise him.

When we reached his lodgings, Rouletabille, who had answered our knock with an energetic "Come in," sat working at a little table. He arose as we entered, and turned so pale that we believed that he was about to fall in a faint.

"Good heavens!" cried Mlle. Stangerson, hastening toward him. But he was quicker than she, and before she reached the table on which he leaned, he had thrown a cover over the papers which were spread over the surface, hiding them entirely.

Mathilde had, of course, noticed the action. She paused in amazement.

"We are disturbing you," she said.

"Oh, not at all," replied Rouletabille. "I have finished my work. I will show it to you sometime. It is a masterpiece—a piece in five acts, for which I am not able to find the denouement."

And he smiled. Soon he was again entirely master of himself, and made us a hundred droll speeches, thanking us for having come to cheer him in his solitude. He insisted on inviting us to dinner, and we three ate our evening meal in a Latin Quarter restaurant—Foyot's. It was a happy evening. Rouletabille telephoned for Robert Darzac, who joined us at dessert. At this time M. Darzac was not ill, and the amazing Brignolles had not yet made his appearance in Paris. We played like children. That summer night was so beautiful in the solitude of the Luxembourg!

Before bidding adieu to Mlle. Stangerson, Rouletabille begged her pardon for the strange humour which he evinced at times, and accused himself of being at bottom a very disagreeable person. Mathilde kissed him and Robert Darzac put his arm affectionately around the lad's shoulders. And Rouletabille was so moved that he never uttered a word while I walked with him to his door; but at the moment of our parting, he pressed my hand more tenderly than he had ever done before. Poor little fellow! Ah, if I had known! How I reproach myself in the light of the present for having judged him with too little patience!

Thus, sad at heart, assailed by premonitions which I tried in vain to drive away, I returned from the railway station at Lyons, pondering over the numerous fantasies, the strange caprices of Rouletabille during the last two years. But nothing that entered my mind could have warned me of what had happened, or still less have explained it to me. Where was Rouletabille? I went to his rooms in the Boulevard St. Michel, telling myself that if I did not find him there, I could, at least, leave Mme. Darzac's letter. What was my astonishment when I entered the building to see my own servant carrying my bag. I asked him to tell me what he was doing and why, and he replied that he did not know—that I must ask M. Rouletabille.

The boy had been, as it turned out, while I had been seeking him everywhere (except, naturally, in my own house), in my apartments in the Rue de Rivoli. He had ordered my servant to take him to my rooms, and had made the man fill a valise with everything necessary for a trip of three or four days. Then he had directed the man to bring the bag in about an hour to the hotel in the "Boul' Mich."

I made one bound up the stairs to my friend's bed chamber, where I found him packing in a tiny hand satchel an assortment of toilet articles, a change of linen and a night shirt. Until this task was ended, I could obtain no satisfaction from Rouletabille, for in regard to the little affairs of everyday life, he was extremely particular, and, despite the modesty of his means, succeeded in living very well, having a horror of everything which could be called bohemian. He finally deigned to announce to me that "we were going to take our Easter vacation," and that, since I had nothing to do, and the *Epoch* had granted him a three days' holiday, we couldn't do better than to go and take a short rest at the seaside. I made no reply, so angry was I at this high-handed method, and all the more because I had not the least desire to contemplate the beauties of the ocean upon one of the abominable days of early spring, which for two or three weeks every year makes us regret the winter. But my silence did not disturb Rouletabille in the least, and taking my valise in one hand, his satchel in the other, he hustled me down the stairs and pushed me into a hack which awaited us before the door of the hotel. Half an hour later, we found ourselves in a first-class carriage of the Northern Railway, which was carrying us toward Trepot by way of Amiens. As we entered the station, he said:

"Why don't you give me the letter that you have for me?"

I gazed at him in amazement. He had guessed that Mme. Darzac would be greatly grieved at not seeing him before her departure, and would write to him. He had been positively malicious. I answered:

"Because you don't deserve it."

And I gave him a good scolding, to which he interposed no defence. He did not even try to excuse himself, and that made me angrier than ever. Finally, I handed him the letter. He took it, looked at it and inhaled its fragrance. As I sat looking at him curiously, he frowned, trying, as I could see, to repress some strong feeling. But he could no longer hide it from me when he turned toward the window, his forehead against the glass, and became absorbed in a deep study of the landscape. His face betrayed the fact that he was suffering profoundly.

"Well?" I said. "Aren't you going to read the letter?"

"No," he replied. "Not here. When we are yonder."

We arrived at Trepot in the blackest night that I remember, after six hours of an interminable trip and in wretched weather. The wind from the sea chilled us to the bone and swept over the deserted quay with weird sounds of lamentation. We met only a watch man, wrapped in his cloak and hood, who paced the banks of the canal. Not a cab, of course. A few gas jets, trembling in their glass globes, reflected their light in the mud puddles formed by the falling rain. We heard in the distance the clicking noise of the little wooden shoes of some Trepot woman who was out late. That we did not fall into a huge watering trough was due to the fact that we were warned by the hoofs of a stray horse, which passed that way to drink. I walked behind Rouletabille, who made his way with difficulty in this damp obscurity. However, he appeared to know the place, for we finally arrived at the door of a queer little inn, which remained open during the early spring for the fishermen. Rouletabille demanded supper and a fire, for we were half starved and half frozen.

"Ah, now, my friend," I said, when we were settled after a fashion. "Will you condescend to explain to me what we have come to look for in this place, aside from rheumatism and pneumonia?"

But Rouletabille, at this moment, coughed and turned toward the fire to warm his hands again.

"Oh, yes," he answered. "I am going to tell you. We have come to look for the perfume of the Lady in Black."

This phrase gave me so much to think about that I scarcely slept at all that night. Besides, the wind howled continuously, sending its wails over the water, then swallowing itself up in the little streets of the town as if it were entering corridors. I heard someone moving about in the room next to mine, which was occupied by my friend: I arose and tried his door. In spite of the cold and the wind, he had opened the window, and I could see him distinctly waving kisses toward the shadows. He was embracing the night.

I closed the door again and went quietly back to bed. Early in the morning I was awakened by a changed Rouletabille. His face was distorted with grief as he handed me a telegram which had come to him at the Bourg, having been forwarded from Paris, in accordance with the orders that he had left.

Here is the dispatch:

"Come immediately without losing a minute. We have given up our trip to the Orient, and will join M. Stangerson at Mentone, at the home of the Rances at Rochers Rouges. Let this message remain a secret between us. It is not necessary to frighten anyone. You may pretend that you are on your vacation, or make any other excuse that you like, but come. Telegraph me general delivery, Mentone. Quickly, quickly, I am waiting for you.

Yours in despair
Darzac

# III

## THE PERFUME

Well!" I cried, leaping out of bed. "It doesn't surprise me!"

"You never believed that *he* was dead?" demanded Rouletabille, in a tone filled with an emotion that I could not explain to myself, for it seemed greater even than was warranted by the situation, admitting that the terms of M. Darzac's telegram were to be taken literally.

"I never felt quite sure of it," I answered. "It was too useful for him to pass for dead to permit him to hesitate at the sacrifice of a few papers, however important those were which were found upon the victim of the Dordogne disaster. But what is the matter with you, my boy? You look as though you were going to faint. Are you ill?"

Rouletabille had let himself sink into a chair. It was in a voice which trembled like that of an old man that he confided to me that, even while the marriage ceremony of our friends was going on, he had become possessed with a strong conviction that Larsan was not dead. But after the ceremony was at an end, he had felt more secure. It seemed to him that Larsan would never have permitted Mathilde Stangerson to speak the vows that gave her to Robert Darzac if he were really alive. Larsan would only have had to show his face to stop the marriage; and, however dangerous to himself such an act might have been, he would not, the young reporter believed, have hesitated to deliver himself up to the danger, knowing as he did the strong religious convictions of Professor Stangerson's daughter, and knowing, too, that she would never have consented to enter into an alliance with another man while her first husband was alive, even had she been freed from the latter by human laws. In vain had everyone who loved her at tempted to persuade her that her first marriage was void, according to French statute. She persisted in declaring that the words pronounced by the priest had made her the wife of the miserable wretch who had victimised her, and that she must remain his wife so long as they both should live.

Wiping the perspiration from his forehead, Rouletabille remarked:—

"Sainclair, can you ever forget Larsan's eyes? Do you remember, 'The Presbytery has not lost its charm or the garden its brightness?' "

I pressed the boy's hand; it was burning hot. I tried to calm him, but he paid no attention to anything I said.

"And it was after the wedding—just a few hours after the wedding, that he chose to appear!" he cried. "There isn't anything else to think, is there, Sainclair? You took M. Darzac's wire just as I did? It could mean nothing else except that that man has come back?"

"I should think not—but M. Darzac may be mistaken."

"Oh, M. Darzac is not a child to be frightened at bogies. But we must hope—we must hope, mustn't we, Sainclair, that he is mistaken? Oh, it isn't possible that such a fearful thing can be true. Oh, Sainclair, it would be too terrible!"

I had never seen Rouletabille so deeply agitated, even at the time of the most terrible events at the Glandier. He arose from his chair and walked up and down the room, casting aside any object which came in his way and repeating over and over: "No, no! It's too terrible—too terrible!"

I told him that it was not sensible to put himself in such a state merely upon the receipt of a telegram which might mean nothing at all, or might be the result of some delusion. And there, too, I added, that it was not at this time, when we needed all our strength and fortitude, that we ought to give way to imaginary fears which were particularly inexcusable in a lad of his practical temperament.

"Inexcusable! I am glad you think so, Sainclair."

"But, my dear boy, you frighten me. What is there you know that you have not told me?"

"I am going to tell you. The situation is horrible. Why didn't that villain die?"

"And, after all, how do you know that he is not dead?"

"Look here, Sainclair—Don't talk—Be quiet, please—You see, if he is alive, I wish to God that I were dead!"

"You are crazy. It is if he is alive that you have all the more reason to live to defend that poor woman."

"Ah, that is true! That is true! Thanks, old fellow! You have said the only thing that makes me want to live. To defend her! I will not think of myself any longer—never again."

And Rouletabille smiled—a smile which almost frightened me. I threw my arm around him and begged him to tell me why he was so terrified, why he spoke of his own death and why he smiled so strangely.

Rouletabille laid his hand on my shoulder, and I went on:

"Tell your friend what it is, Rouletabille. Speak out. Relieve your mind. Tell me the secret that is killing you. I would tell you anything."

Rouletabille looked down and steadily into my eyes.

Then he said:

"You shall know all, Sainclair. You shall know as much as I do, and when you do, you will be as unhappy as I am, for you are kind and you are fond of me."

Then he straightened back his shoulders as though he had already cast off a burden and pointed in the direction of the railway.

"We shall leave here in an hour," he said. "There is no direct train from Eu to Paris in the winter: we shall not reach Paris until 7 o'clock. But that will give us plenty of time to pack our trunks and take the train that leaves the Lyons station at nine o'clock for Marseilles and Mentone."

He did not ask my opinion on the course which he had laid out. He was taking me to Mentone, just as he had brought me to Trepot. He was well aware that in the present crisis I could refuse him nothing. Besides, he was in such a state of mental strain that even if he had wished it, I should scarcely have left him. And it was not hard for me to accompany him, for we were just beginning our long vacations, and my affairs were so arranged that I felt entirely at liberty.

"Then we are going to Eu?" I inquired.

"Yes: we will take the train from there. It will scarcely take half an hour to drive over."

"We shall have spent only a little time in this part of the country," I remarked.

"Enough, I hope—enough for me to find what I am looking for."

I thought of the perfume of the Lady in Black, but I kept silence. Had he not said that he was going to tell me everything? He led me out to the jetty. The wind was still blowing a gale, and we were almost taken off our feet. Rouletabille stood for an instant as if lost in thought, closing his eyes as if in a dream.

"It was here," he said, "that I last saw her."

He looked down at the stone bench beside which we were standing.

"We were sitting there. She held me to her heart. I was a very little fellow, even for nine years old. She told me to stay there—on this bench—and then she went away, and I never saw her again. It was night—a soft summer evening—the evening of the distribution of prizes. She had not assisted at the distribution, but I knew that she would come that night—that night full of stars and so clear that I hoped every moment that I would be able to distinguish her face. But she covered it with her veil and breathed a heavy sigh. And then she went away. And I have never seen her since."

"And you, my friend?"

"I?"

"Yes, what happened to you? Did you sit on the bench for very long?"

"I would have—but the coachman came to look for me and I went in."

"Where?"

"Into the school."

"Is there a boarding school at Trepot?"

"No, but there is one at Eu—I went to the school at Eu."

He motioned me to follow him.

"We will go there," he said. "I can't talk here. There is too much of a storm."

In another half hour we were at Eu. At the foot of the Rue des Marroniers our carriage rolled over the pavements of the big, cold, empty place, as the coachman announced his arrival by cracking his whip, filling the dead town with the noise of the snapping leather.

Soon we heard the sound of a bell—that of the school, Rouletabille told me—and then everything was quiet again. We alighted and the horse and carriage stood motionless upon the street. The driver had gone into a saloon. We entered the cool shades of a high Gothic church which faced upon the square. Rouletabille cast a glance at the castle—a red brick structure, crowned with an immense Louis XIII roof—a mournful facade which seemed to weep over the glory of departed princes. The young reporter gazed sorrowfully at the square battlements of the City Hall, which extended toward us the hostile lance of its soiled and weather-beaten flag: at the Cafe de Paris; at the silent houses; at the shops and the library. Was it there that the boy had bought those first new books for which the Lady in Black had paid?

"Nothing has changed."

An old dog, colourless and shaggy, upon the library steps, stretched himself lazily on his frozen paws.

"Cham! Cham!" called Rouletabille. "Oh, I remember him well. It is Cham—it is my old Cham."

And he called him again, "Cham! Cham!"

The dog got upon his feet, turned toward us, listening to the voice that called him. He took a few steps, wagged his tail, and stretched himself out in the sun again.

"He doesn't remember me," said Rouletabille sadly.

He drew me into a little street which had a steep down grade, and was paved with sharp pebbles. As we went down the hill he took my hand and I could feel the fever in his. We stopped again in front of a tiny temple of the Jesuit style, which raised in front of us its porch, ornamented with semicircles of stone, the "reversed consoles" which are the characteristic features of an architecture which contributed nothing to the glory of the Seventeenth Century. After having pushed open a little low door, Rouletabille bade me enter, and we found ourselves inside a beautiful mortuary chapel, upon the stone floor of which were kneeling, beside their empty tombs, magnificent marble statues of Catherine of Cleves and Guise le Balafre.

"The college chapel," whispered Rouletabille.

There was no person in the chapel. We crossed the room hastily. On the left wall, Rouletabille tapped very gently a kind of drum, which gave out a queer, muffled sound.

"We are in luck!" he said. "Everything is going well. We are inside the college and the concierge has not seen me. He would surely have remembered me."

"What harm would that have done?"

Just at that moment a man with bare head and a bunch of keys at his side passed through the room and Rouletabille drew me into the shadow.

"It is Pere Simon. Ah, how old he has grown! He is almost bald. Listen: this is the hour when he goes to superintend the study hour of the younger boys. Everyone is in the classroom at this time. Oh, we are very lucky! There is only Mere Simon in the lodge—that is, if she is not dead. At any rate, she can't see us from here. But wait—here is Pere Simon back again!"

Why was Rouletabille so anxious to hide himself? Decidedly, I knew very little of the lad whom I believed that I knew so well. Every hour that I had spent with him of late had brought me some new surprise. While we were waiting for Pere Simon to leave us a clear field once more, Rouletabille and I managed to slip out of the chapel without being seen, and hid ourselves in the corner of a tiny garden, laid out in the middle of a stone court, behind the shrubbery of which we could, leaning over, contemplate at our leisure the grounds and buildings of the school. Rouletabille hung on to my arm as though he were afraid of falling. "Good Heavens!" he murmured, in a voice broken with emotion. "How things are changed! They have torn down the old study where I found the knife and the leather hangings where the money was hidden have, doubtless, been destroyed. But the chapel walls are just the same. Look, Sainclair: lean over the hedge. That door that opens in the rear of the chapel is the door of the infant classroom. But never, never did I leave that class room so gladly, even in my happiest play hours, as when Pere Simon came to fetch me to the parlour where the Lady in Black was waiting for me. Ah—suppose that they have destroyed the parlour!"

And he cast a quick look toward the building behind him.

"No—no: it is all right—beside the mortuary. There is the same door at the right through which she came. We shall go there as soon as Pere Simon is out of the way."

And he set his teeth.

"I believe that I am going crazy!" he said with a short laugh. "But I can't help my feelings. They are stronger than I. To think that I am going to see the parlour—where she waited for me! I had been living only in the hope of seeing her, and after she had gone, although I had promised to be good and sensible, I fell into such a despondent state that after each of her visits, they feared for my health. They were only able to save me from utter prostration by telling me that if I fell ill they would not let me see her any more. So from one visit to another, I had her memory and her perfume to comfort me. Never having seen her dear face distinctly, and being so weak that I was ready to swoon with joy every time she pressed me to her heart, I lived less with her image than with the heavenly odour. Often on the days after she had come and gone, I would escape from my comrades during the recreation hours and steal to the parlour, and when I found it empty, I would draw deep breaths of the air which she had breathed and remain there like a little devotee, and leave with a heart filled with the sense of her presence. The perfume which she always used and which was indissolubly associated in my mind with her, was the most delicate, the most subtle, and the sweetest odour I have ever known, and I never breathed it again in all the years which followed until the day I spoke of it to you, Sainclair. You remember—the day we first went to the Glandier?"

"You mean the day that you met Mathilde Stanger son?"

"That is what I mean," responded the lad in a trembling voice.

(Ah, if I had known at that moment that Professor Stangerson's daughter, as the result of her first marriage in America, had had a child, a son, who would have been, if he had lived, the same age as Rouletabille, perhaps I would have at last comprehended his emotion and grief, and the strange reluctance which he showed to pronounce the name of Mathilde Stangerson there at the school, to which, in the past, had come so often the Lady in Black!)

There was a long silence, which I finally broke.

"And you have never known why the Lady in Black did not return?"

"Oh!" cried Rouletabille. "I am sure that she did return. It was I who was not here."

"Who took you away?"

"No one: I ran away."

"Why? To look for her?"

"No—no! To flee from her—to flee from her, I tell you, Sainclair. But she came back—I know that she came back."

"She may have been broken hearted at not finding you."

Rouletabille raised his arms toward the sky and shook his head.

"I don't know—how can I know? Ah, what an unhappy wretch I am! But, hush, Sainclair! Here comes Pere Simon! Now, he's gone again. Quick—to the parlour!"

We were there in three seconds. It was a common place room enough, rather large, with cheap white curtains in front of the shadeless windows. It was furnished with six leather chairs placed against the wall, a mantel mirror, and a clock. The whole appearance of the place was sombre.

As we entered the room, Rouletabille uncovered his head with an appearance of respect and reverence which one rarely assumes except in a sacred place. His face became flushed, he advanced with short steps, rolling his travelling cap in his hands as if he were embarrassed. He turned to me and said in low tones—far lower than he used in the chapel:

"Oh, Sainclair, this is it—the parlour. Feel how my hands burn. My face is flushed, is it not? I was always flushed when

I came here, knowing that I should find her. I used to run. I felt smothered—I do now. I was not able to wait. Oh, my heart beats just as it used when I was a little lad! I would come to the door—right here—and then I would pause, bashful and shamefaced. But I would see her dark shadow in the corner: she would take me in her arms and hold me there in silence, and before we knew it, we were both weeping, as we clung together. How dear those meetings were. She was my mother, Sainclair. Oh, she never told me so: on the contrary, she used to say that my mother was dead, and that she had been her friend. But she told me to call her Mamma—and when she wept as I kissed her, I knew that she really was my mother. See—she always sat there in the dark corner, and she came always at nightfall, when the parlour had not yet been lit up for the evening. And every time she came, she would place on the window sill a big, white package, tied with pink cord. It was a fruit cake. I have loved fruit cake ever since, Sainclair!"

The poor lad could no longer contain himself. He rested his arms on the mantel and wept like a little child. When he was able to control himself a little, he raised his head and looked at me with a sad smile. And then he sank into a chair as though he were tired out. I had not had the heart to say one word to him during his reminiscences. I knew well that he was not talking with me, but with his memories.

I saw him draw from his breast the letter which he had placed there in the train, and tear it open with trembling fingers. He read it slowly. Suddenly his hand fell, and he uttered a groan. His flushed face grew pallid—so pallid that it seemed as though every drop of blood had left his heart. I stepped toward him, but he waved me away and closed his eyes. He looked almost as though he were sleeping. I walked across the room, moving as softly as one does in the chamber of death. I looked up at the wall, where hung a heavy wooden crucifix. How long did I stand gazing on the cross? I have no idea. Nor do I know what we said to someone belonging to the house, who came into the parlour. I was pondering with all my strength of concentration on the strange and mysterious destiny of my friend—on this mysterious woman who might or might not have been his mother. Rouletabille had been so young in those school days. He longed so for a mother, that he might have imagined that he had found one in his visitor. Rouletabille—what other name did we know him by? Joseph Josephin. It was without doubt under that name that he had pursued his early studies here. Joseph Josephin, the queer appellation of which the editor of the *Epoch* had said to him, "It is no name at all!" And now, what was he about to do here? Seek the trace of a perfume? Revive a memory—an illusion? I turned as I heard him stir. He was standing erect and seemed quite calm. His features had taken on the serenity which comes from assurance of victory.

"We must go now, Sainclair. Come, my friend."

And he left the parlour without even looking back. I followed him.

In the deserted street, which we regained without meeting anyone, I stopped him by asking anxiously:

"Well—did you find the perfume of the Lady in Black?"

He must have seen that all my heart was in the question and that I was filled with an ardent desire that this visit to the scenes of his childhood might have brought a little peace to his soul.

"Yes," he said, very gravely. "Yes, Sainclair, I found it."

And he handed me the letter from Professor Stangerson's daughter.

I looked at him, doubting the evidence of my own senses—not understanding, because I knew nothing. Then he took my two hands and looked into my eyes.

"I am going to confide a secret to you, Sainclair—the secret of my life, and perhaps some day the secret of my death. Let what will come, it must die with you and me. Mathilde Stangerson had a child—a son. He is dead—is dead to everyone except to the two of us who stand here."

I recoiled, struck with horror under such a revelation. Rouletabille the son of Mathilde Stangerson! And then suddenly I received a still more violent shock. In that case, Rouletabille must be the son of Larsan.

Oh, I understood now, all the wretchedness of the boy. I understood why he had said this morning: "Why did he not die? If he is living, I wish to God that I were dead!"

Rouletabille must have read my thoughts in my eyes, and he simply made a gesture which seemed to say, "And now you understand, Sainclair." Then he finished his sentence aloud. The word which he spoke was "Silence!"

When we reached Paris we separated, to meet again at the train. There, Rouletabille handed me a new dispatch, which had come from Valence, and which was signed by Professor Stangerson. It said, "M. Darzac tells me that you have a few days' leave. We should all be very glad if you could come and spend them with us. We will wait for you at Arthur Rance's place, Rochers Rouges—he will be delighted to present you to his wife. My daughter will be pleased to see you. She joins me in kindest greetings."

Just as the train was starting, a concierge from Rouletabille's hotel came rushing up and handed us a third dispatch. This one was sent from Mentone, and signed by Mathilde. It contained two words: "Rescue us."

# IV

## EN ROUTE

Now I knew all. As we continued on our journey, Rouletabille related to me the remarkable and adventurous story of his childhood, and I knew, also, why he dreaded nothing so much as that Mme. Darzac should penetrate the mystery which separated them. I dared say nothing more—give my friend no advice. Ah, the poor unfortunate lad! When he read the words "Rescue us," he carried the dispatch to his lips, and then, pressing my hand, he said: "If I arrive too late, I can avenge her, at least." I have never heard anything more filled with resolution than the cold determination of his tone. From time to time a quick movement betrayed the passion of his soul, but for the most part he was calm—terribly calm. What resolution had he taken in the silence of the parlour, when he sat motionless and with closed eyes in the shadow of the corner where he had used to see the Lady in Black?

While we journeyed toward Lyons, and Rouletabille lay dreaming, stretched out fully dressed in his berth, I will tell you how and why the child that he had been ran away from school at Eu, and what had happened to him.

Rouletabille had fled from the school like a thief. There was no need to seek for another expression, because he had been accused of stealing. This was how it happened.

At the age of nine, he had already an extraordinarily precocious intelligence, and could arrive easily at the solution of the most perplexing problems. By logical deductions of an almost amazing kind, he astonished his professor of mathematics by his philosophical method of work. He had never been able to learn his multiplication tables, and always counted upon his fingers. He would usually get the answers to the problems himself, leaving the working out to be done by his fellow pupils, as one will leave an irksome task to a servant. But first, he would show them exactly how the example ought to be done. Although as yet ignorant of the rudiments of algebra, he had invented for his own personal use a system of algebra carried on with queer signs, looking like hieroglyphics, by the aid of which he marked all the steps of his mathematical reasoning, and thus he was able to write down the general formulae so that he alone could interpret them. His professor used proudly to compare him to Pascal, discovering for himself without knowledge of geometry, the first propositions of Euclid. He applied his admirable faculties of reasoning to his daily life, as well as to his studies, using the rules both materially and morally. For example, an act had been committed in the school—I have forgotten whether it was of cheating or talebearing—by one of ten persons whom he knew, and he picked out the right one with a divination which seemed almost supernatural, simply by using the powers of reasoning and deduction, which he had practiced to such an extent. So much for the moral aspect of his strange gift, and as for the material, nothing seemed more simple to him than to find any lost or hidden object—or even a stolen one. It was in the detection of thefts especially that he displayed a wonderful resourcefulness, as if nature, in her wondrous fitting together of the parts that make an equal whole, after having created the father a thief of the worst kind, had caused the son to be born the evil genius of thieves.

This strange aptitude, after having won for the boy a sort of fame in the school, on account of his detection of several attempts at pilfering, was destined one day to be fatal to him. He found in this abnormal fashion a small sum of money which had been stolen from the superintendent, who refused to believe that the discovery was due only to the lad's intelligence and clearness of insight. This hypothesis, indeed, appeared impossible to almost everyone who knew of the matter, and, thanks to an unfortunate coincidence of time and place, the affair finished up by having Rouletabille himself accused of being the thief. They tried to make him acknowledge his fault; he defended himself with such indignation and anger that it drew upon him a severe punishment. The principal held an investigation and a trial, at which Joseph Josephin was accused by some of his youthful comrades in that spirit of falsehood which children sometimes possess. Some of them complained of having had books, pencils, and tablets stolen at different times, and declared that they believed that Joseph had taken them. The fact that the boy seemed to have no relatives, and that no one knew where he came from, made him particularly likely, in that little world, to be suspected of crime. When the boys spoke of him, it was as "that thief." The contempt in which he was held preyed upon him, for he was not a strong child at best, and he was plunged in despair. He almost prayed to die. The principal, who was really the most kind hearted of men, was persuaded that he had a vicious little creature to deal with, because he was unable to produce an impression on the child, and make him comprehend the horror of what he had done. Finally, he told the lad that if he did not confess his guilt, it had been decided not to keep him in the school any longer, and that a letter would be written to the lady who interested herself in him—Mme. Darbel was the name which she had given—to tell her to come after him.

The child made no reply and allowed himself to be taken to his little room, where he had been kept a prisoner. Upon the morrow he had disappeared. He had run away. He had felt that the principal, to whose care he had been entrusted during the earliest years of his childhood (for in all his little life he could remember no other home than the school), and who had always been so kind to him, was no longer his friend, since he believed him guilty of theft. And he could see no reason why the Lady in Black would not believe it, too—that he was a thief. To appear as a thief in the sight of the Lady in Black! He would far rather have died.

And he made his escape from the place by climbing over the wall of the garden at night. He rushed to the canal, sobbing, and, with a prayer, uttered as much to the Lady in Black as to God Himself, threw himself in the water. Happily, in his despair, the poor child had forgotten that he knew how to swim.

If I have reported this passage in the life of Rouletabille at some length, it is because it seems to me that it is all important to the thorough comprehension of his future. At that time, of course, he was ignorant that he was the son of Larsan. Rouletabille, even as a child of nine years, could not without agony harbour the idea that the Lady in Black might believe him to be a thief, and thus, when the time came that he imagined—an imagination too well founded, alas!—that he was bound by ties of blood to Larsan, what infinite misery he experienced! His mother, in hearing of the crime of which he had been accused, must have felt that the criminal instincts of the father were coming to fight in the son, and, perhaps—thought more cruel than death itself—she may have rejoiced in believing him dead.

For everyone believed him dead. They found his footsteps leading to the canal, and they fished out his cap. How had he lived after leaving the school? In a most singular fashion. After swimming to dry land and making up his mind to fly the country, the lad, while they were searching for him everywhere in the canal and out of it, devised a most original plan for travelling to a distance without being disturbed. He had not read that most interesting tale, *The Stolen Letter*. His own invention served him. He reasoned the thing out, as he always did.

He knew—for he had often heard them told by the heroes themselves—many stories of little rascals who had run away from their parents in search of adventures, hiding themselves by day in the fields and the wood, and travelling by night—only to find themselves speedily captured by the gendarmes, or forced to return home because they had no money and no food, and dared not ask for anything to eat along the road which they followed, and which was too well guarded to admit of their escape if they applied for aid. Our little Rouletabille slept at night like everyone else, and travelled in broad daylight, without hiding himself. But, after having dried his garments (the warm weather was coming on, and he did not suffer from cold), he tore them to tatters. He made rags of them, which barely covered him, and begged in the open streets, dirty and unkempt, holding out his hands and declaring to passers-by that if he did not bring home any money his parents would beat him. And everyone took him for some gypsy child, hordes of which constantly roamed through the locality. Soon came the time of wild strawberries. He gathered the fruit and sold it in little baskets of leaves. And he assured me, in telling the story, that if it had not been for the terrible thought that the Lady in Black must believe that he was a thief, that time would have been the happiest of his life. His astuteness and natural courage stood him well in stead through these wanderings, which lasted for several months. Where was he going? To Marseilles. This was his plan:

He had seen in his illustrated geography views of the Midi, and he had never looked at those pictures without breathing a sigh and wishing that he might some day visit that enchanted country. Through his gypsy-like manner of living, he had made the acquaintance of a little caravan load of Romanies, who were following the same route as himself, and who were journeying to Ste. Marie's of the Sea to render homage to a new king of their tribe. The lad had an opportunity to render them some small service, and finding him a pleasant, well-mannered little fellow, these people, not being in the habit of asking everyone whom they met for his history, desired to know nothing more about him. They believed that, on account of ill treatment, the child had run away from some troop of wandering mountebanks, and they invited him to travel with them. Thus he arrived in the Midi.

In the neighbourhood of Arles, he separated himself from his travelling companions, and at last came to Marseilles. There was his paradise! Eternal summer—and the port.

The port was the favourite resort of all the gamins of the locality, and this fact was the greatest safeguard for Rouletabille. He roamed over the docks as he chose, and served himself according to the measure of his needs, which were not great. For example, he made of himself an "orange fisher." It was at the time that he exercised this lucrative calling that, one beautiful morning upon the quay, he made the acquaintance of M. Gaston Leroux, a journalist from Paris, and this acquaintance was destined to have such an influence upon the future of Rouletabille that I do not consider it out of place to transcribe here in full the article in which the editor of *Le Matin* recorded that first memorable interview.

THE LITTLE ORANGE FISHER.

As the sun, piercing through the cloudless heavens, struck with its ardent rays the golden robe of Notre-Dame-de-la-Garde, I descended toward the quay. The scene which met my eyes was one which was worth going far to see. Townfolk, sailors and workmen were moving about, the former idly looking on, while the others tugged at the pulleys and drew up the cables of their vessels. The great merchant vessels glided like huge beasts of burden between the tower of St. Jean and the fort of St. Nicholas, caressing the sparkling waters of the Old Port in their onward motion. Side by side, shoulder to shoulder, the smaller barks seemed to hold out their arms to each other. To throw aside their veils of mist and to dance upon the water. Beside them, tired with the long journey, worn out from ploughing for so many days and nights over unknown seas, the heavy laden East Indiamen rested peacefully, lifting their great, motionless sails in rags toward the skies.

My eyes, sweeping swiftly over the scene through the forest of masts and sails paused at the tower which commemorated the fact that it was twenty-five centuries since the children of Ancient Phoenicia first cast anchor upon this happy shore, and that they had come by the waterways of Ionia. Then my attention returned to the border of the quay, and I perceived the little orange fisher.

He was standing erect, clad in the rags of a man's coat which hung down almost to his feet, bareheaded and barefooted, with blonde curly locks and black eyes, and I should think that he was about nine years old. A string passed around his shoulder supported a big sailcloth sack. His left hand rested on his waist and his right hand held a stick three times as tall as himself, which was surmounted by a little wooden hook. The child stood motionless and lost in thought. When I asked him what he was doing there, he told me that he was an orange fisher.

He seemed very proud of being an orange fisher and did not ask me for a penny, as the little vagabonds of the neighbourhood are accustomed to demand toll of every bystander. I spoke to him again, but this time he made no answer, for he was too intent on watching the water. On one side of us was the beautiful steamer Fides, in from Castellmare and on the other a three masted schooner from Genoa. Further off were two ships loaded with fruits which had just arrived from Baleares that morning, and I saw that they were spilling a part of their cargo. Oranges were bobbing up and down upon the water and the light current sent them in our direction. My "fisher" leaped into a little canoe, came quickly to the vessel, and, armed with his stick and hook, waited. Then he began his gathering. The hook on his stick brought him one orange, then a second, a third and a fourth. They disappeared in the sack. The boy gathered a fifth, jumped upon the quay and tore open the golden fruit. He plunged his little teeth in the pulp and devoured it in an instant.

"You have a good appetite," I told him.

"Monsieur," he replied, flushing slightly as he spoke, "I don't care for any food but fruit."

"That is a very good diet," I replied as gravely as he had spoken. "But what do you do when there are no oranges?"

"I pick up coal."

And his little hand, diving into the sack, brought out an enormous piece of coal.

The orange juice had rolled down his chin to his coat. The coat had a pocket. The little fellow took a clean handkerchief from this pocket and carefully wiped both chin and coat. Then he proudly put the handkerchief back.

"What is your father's work?" I asked.

"He is poor."

"Yes, but what does he do?"

The orange fisher shrugged his shoulders.

"He doesn't do anything, he is poor."

My inquiries into his family affairs did not seem to please him. He turned away from the quay and I followed him. We came in a moment to the "shelter," a little square of sea which holds the small pleasure yachts—the neat little boats all polished wood and brass, the neat little sailors in their irreproachable toilettes. My ragamuffin looked at them with the eye of a connoisseur and seemed to find a keen enjoyment in the spectacle. A new yacht had just been launched and her immaculate sail looked like a white veil against the blue sky.

"Isn't it pretty?" exclaimed my little companion.

The next moment he fell over a board covered with fresh tar and when he picked himself up, he looked with dismay at the stain on his coat which seemed to be his proudest possession. What a disaster! He looked as if he could have burst into tears. But quick as thought he drew out his handkerchief and rubbed and rubbed the spot, then he looked at me piteously and said:

"Monsieur, are there any other stains? Did I get anything on my back?"

I assured him that he had not, and with an expression of satisfaction, he put the handkerchief back in his pocket once more.

A few steps further on, upon the walk which stretches in front of the red and yellow, and blue houses, the windows of which are brave with wares of many kinds, we found an oyster stand. Upon the little tables were displayed piles of oysters in their shells, and flasks of vinegar.

When we passed by the oyster stand, as the fish appeared fresh and appetizing, I said to the orange fisher.

"If you cared for anything to eat except fruit, I might ask you to have some oysters with me."

His black eyes glistened and we sat down together to eat our oysters. The merchant opened them for us while we waited. He started to bring us vinegar, but my companion stopped him with an imperious gesture. He opened his bag carefully and triumphantly produced a lemon. The lemon, having been in close contact with the bit of coal, might have passed for black itself. But my guest took out his handkerchief and wiped it off. Then he cut the fruit and offered me half, but I like oysters without other flavour, so I declined with thanks.

After our luncheon we went back to the quay. The orange fisher asked me for a cigarette and lighted it with a match which he had in another pocket of his coat.

Then, the cigarette between his lips, puffing rings toward the sky like a man, the little creature threw himself down on the ground and with his eyes fixed upon the statue of Notre-Dame-de-la-Garde, took the very pose of the boy who is the most beautiful ornament of the Brussels tower. He did not lose a line of the attitude, and seemed very proud of the fact and apparently desired to play the part exactly.

Upon the following day Joseph Josephin met M. Gaston Leroux once more upon the quay, and the man handed him a newspaper which he carried in his hand. The boy read the article pointed out to him, and the journalist gave him a bright new 100-sous piece. Rouletabille made no difficulties about accepting it, and seemed to even find the gift a natural one. "I take your money," he said to Gaston Leroux, "because we are collaborators." With his hundred sous he bought himself a fine new bootblack's box and installed himself in business opposite the Bregaillon. For two years he polished the boots of those who came to eat the traditional bouillabaisse at this hostelry. When he was not at work, he would sit on his box and read. With the feeling of ownership which his box and his business had brought him, ambition had entered his mind. He had received too good an education and had been too well instructed in rudimentary things not to understand that if he did not himself finish what others had begun for him, he would be deprived of the best chance which he had of making for himself a place in the world.

His customers grew interested in the little bootblack, who always had on his box some work of history or mathematics, and a harness maker became so attached to him that he took him into his shop.

Soon Rouletabille was promoted to the dignity of working in leather, and was able to save. At the age of sixteen years, having a little money in his pocket, he took the train for Paris. What did he intend to do there? To look for the Lady in Black.

Not one day had passed without his having thought of the mysterious visitor to the parlour of the boarding school, and, although no one had ever told him that she lived in Paris, he was persuaded that no other city in the world was worthy to contain a lady who wore so sweet a perfume. And then his little schoolmates, who had been able to see her form when she glided out of the parlour, had often said: "See the Parisienne is here again today!" It would have been difficult to exactly define the ideas in Rouletabille's head, and perhaps he himself scarcely knew what they were. His longing was merely to see the Lady in Black—to watch her reverently—at a distance, as a devotee watches the image of a saint. Would he dare to speak to her? The importance of the accusation of theft which had been brought against him had only grown greater in Rouletabille's imagination as time had gone by, and he believed that it would always be a barrier between himself and the Lady in Black, which he had not the right to try to throw down. Perhaps even—but, come what might, he longed to see her. That was the only thing of which he was sure.

As soon as he reached the capital, he looked up M. Gaston Leroux, and recalled himself to the latter's memory, telling him that, although he felt no particular liking for the life, which he considered rather a lazy one for a man who liked to be up and doing, he had decided to become a journalist. And he fairly demanded that his old acquaintance should at once give him a trial as a reporter.

Leroux tried to turn the youth from his project. At last, tired of his persistent requests, the editor said:

"Well, my lad, since you have nothing special to do just now, go and find the left foot of the body in the Rue Oberkampf."

And with these words, M. Leroux turned away, leaving poor Rouletabille standing there with half a dozen young reporters tittering around him. But the boy was not daunted in the least. He searched through the files of the paper and found out that the *Epoch* was offering a large reward to the person who would bring to its office the foot which was missing from the mutilated body of a woman, which had been found in the Rue Oberkampf.

The rest we know. In "The Mystery of the Yellow Room," I have told how Rouletabille succeeded on this occasion, and in what manner there revealed itself to him his own singular calling—that of always beginning to reason a matter out from the point where others had finished.

I have told, too, by what chance he was led one evening to the Elysee, where he inhaled as he passed by the perfume of the Lady in Black. He realised then that it was Mlle. Stangerson who had been his visitor at the school, and for whom he had been seeking so long. What more need I add: Why speak of the sensations which his knowledge as to the wearer of the perfume aroused in the heart of Rouletabille during the events at the Glandier, and, above all, after his trip to America? They may be easily guessed. How simple a thing now to understand his hesitations and his whims! The proofs brought by him from Cincinnati in regard to the child of the woman who had been Jean Roussel's wife had been sufficiently explicit to awaken in his mind a suspicion that he himself might be that child, but not enough so to render him certain of the fact. However, his instinct drew him so strongly to the professor's daughter that he could scarcely resist his longing to throw himself into her arms and press her to his heart and cry out to her: "You are my mother! You are my mother!"

And he fled from her presence just as he had fled from the vestry on the day of her wedding, in order that there should not escape from him any sign of the secret tenderness that had burned in his breast through so many long years. For horrible thoughts dwelt in his mind. Suppose he were to make himself known to her, and she were to repulse him—cast him off—turn from him in horror—from him, the little thief of the boarding school—the son of Roussel—Ballmeyer—the heir of the crimes of Larsan! Suppose she were to order him to get out of her sight, never to come near her again, nor to breathe the same air which brought back to him, whenever he came near her, the perfume of the Lady in Black Ah, how he had fought, on account of these frightful visions, to restrain himself from yielding to the almost overwhelming impulse to ask each time that he came near her, "Is it you? Are you the Lady in Black?" As to her, she had seemed fond of him from the first, but, doubtless, that was because of the Glandier affair. If she were really the Lady in Black, she must believe that the child whom he had been was dead. And if it were not she—if by some fatality which set at naught both his instincts and his powers of reasoning, it were not she! Could he, through any imprudence, risk having her discover that he had fled from the school at Eu under ban as a thief? No, no—not that! She had often said to him:

"Where were you brought up, my boy? What school did you attend when you were a child?" And he had replied: "I was in school at Bordeaux."

He might as well have answered, "At Pekin."

However, this torture could not last always, he told himself. If it were she, he would know how to say things to her that must open her heart. Anything would be better than to be sure that she was not the Lady in Black, but some stranger who had never held him to her heart. But he must be certain—certain beyond any doubt, and he knew how to place himself in the presence of his memories of the Lady in Black, just as a dog is sure of finding its master. The simile which presented itself quite naturally to his imagination was simply that of "following the scent." And this led us, under the circumstances which I have narrated, to Trepot and to Eu. However, it is by no means certain that decisive results would have been gained from this expedition—at least in the eyes of a third person, like myself—had it not been for the influence of the odour—if the letter from Mathilde, which I had handed to Rouletabille in the train, had not suddenly, with its faint, sweet perfume, brought to us directly the evidence which we were seeking. I have never read this letter. It is a document so sacred in the eyes of my friend, that other eyes will never behold it, but I know that the gentle reproaches which it contained for the boy's rudeness and lack of confidence in the writer, had been so tender that Rouletabille could no longer deceive himself, even if the daughter of Professor Stangerson had not concluded the note with a final sentence, through which throbbed the heart of a despairing mother, and which said that "the interest which she felt in him arose less from the services he had rendered her, than because of the memories which she had of a little boy, the son of a friend, whom she had loved very dearly, and who had killed himself 'like a little man with a broken heart' at the age of nine years, and whom Rouletabille greatly resembled."

# V

## PANIC

Dijon—Macon—Lyons—certainly the boy could not be sleeping all this time. I called him softly and he did not reply, but I would have wagered my hand that he was not sleeping. What was he planning? How quiet he was! What could it be that had given him such a strange calmness? I seemed to see him again as he had been in the parlour, suddenly standing erect as he said: "Let us go on!" in that voice so composed and tranquil and resolute. Go on to whom? Toward what was he resolved to go? Toward Her, evidently, who was in danger, and who could be rescued only by him—toward her who was his mother and who did not know it.

"It is a secret which must remain between you and me! That child is dead to the whole world, except to us two!"

That was his decision, taken almost in a single moment, never to reveal himself to her. And the poor child had come to seek the certainty that she was indeed the Lady in Black, only to have the right to speak to her! In the very moment that the assurance which he sought was his, he had determined to forget it; he condemned himself to endless silence. Poor little hero soul, which had understood that the Lady in Black, who had such dire need of his help, would have shrunk from a safety bought by the warfare of a son against his father! Where might not such warfare lead? To what bloody conflict? Everything must be expected, no matter how terrible, and Rouletabille must have his hands free to fight to the death for the Lady in Black.

The boy was so quiet that I could not even hear him breathing. I leaned over him; his eyes were open.

"Do you know what I have been thinking of?" he said. "Of the dispatch that came to us from Bourg and was signed 'Darzac,' and the other dispatch which came from Valence and was signed 'Stangerson.' "

"And the more I think of them, the stranger they seem to me. At Bourg, M. and Mme. Darzac were not with M. Stangerson, who left them at Dijon. Besides, the dispatch says: 'We are going to rejoin M. Stangerson.' But the Stangerson dispatch proves that M. Stangerson, who had continued on his journey toward Marseilles, is again with the Darzacs. The Darzacs might have rejoined M. Stangerson the way to Marseilles; but if that were so, the Professor must have stopped on the road. Why was this? He did not expect to do so. At the train, he said: 'Tomorrow at ten o'clock, I shall be at Mentone.' Look at the hour that the dispatch was sent from Valence, and then we'll look in the timetable and find out the hour at which M. Stangerson would have passed through Valence if he had not stopped upon the journey."

We consulted the timetable. M. Stangerson should have passed through Valence at 12:44 o'clock in the morning, and the dispatch was sent at 12:47 o'clock. It had, therefore, been sent by M. Stangerson while he was continuing on the trip which he had planned. At that moment he must have been with M. and Mme. Darzac. Still poring over the timetable, we endeavoured to solve the mystery of this re-encounter. M. Stangerson had left the Darzacs at Dijon, where the whole party had arrived at twenty-seven minutes after six o'clock in the evening. The Professor had then taken the train which leaves

Dijon at eight minutes past seven, and had arrived at Lyons at four minutes after ten and at Valence at forty-seven minutes after midnight. During the same time the Darzacs, leaving Dijon at seven o'clock, continued on their way to Modane, and, by way of Saint-Amour, reached Bourg at three minutes past nine in the evening, on the train which was scheduled to leave at eight minutes past nine. M. Darzac's dispatch was sent from Bourg, and had left the telegraph office at the station at 9:28. The Darzacs, therefore, must have left their train at Bourg, and remained there. Or, it might have happened that the train was late. In any case, we must seek the reason for M. Darzac's telegram somewhere between Dijon and Bourg, after the departure of M. Stangerson. One might even go further, and say 'between Louhans and Bourg,' for the train stops at Louhans, and if anything had happened before he reached there, at eight o'clock, it is altogether likely that M. Darzac would have sent his message from that station.

Finally, seeking the correspondence between Bourg and Lyons, we reasoned that M. Darzac must have sent his wire from Bourg one minute before leaving for Lyons by the 9:29 train. But this train reached Lyons at 10:23 o'clock, while M. Stangerson's train reached Lyons at 10:24. After changing their plans and leaving the train at Bourg, M. and Mme. Darzac must have rejoined M. Stangerson at Lyons, which they reached one minute before him. Now, what had upset their plans? We could only think of the most terrible hypotheses, every one of which, alas! had as its basis the reappearance of Larsan. The fact which gave the greatest colour to this idea was the desire expressed by each of our friends, *not to frighten anyone*. M. Darzac in his message, Mme. Darzac in hers, had not endeavoured to conceal the gravity of the situation. As to M. Stangerson, we asked ourselves whether he had been made aware of the new developments, whatever they might be.

Having thus approximately settled the question of time and distance, Rouletabille invited me to profit by the luxurious accommodations which the International Sleeping Car company places at the disposal of those who wish to sleep while on a journey, and he himself set me the example by making as careful a night toilet as he would have done in his own room at his hotel. A quarter of an hour later he was snoring, but I believed the snores to be feigned. At any rate, I could not sleep.

At Avignon Rouletabille jumped up from his cot, hastily donned his trousers and coat, and rushed out to the refreshment rooms to get a cup of chocolate. I was not hungry. From Avignon to Marseilles, in our anxiety and suspense, neither of us desired to talk, and the journey was continued almost in silence, but at the sight of the city in which he had led such a chequered existence, Rouletabille, doubtless to keep from showing the emotion which he felt, and to lighten the heaviness of both our hearts as we drew near our journey's end, began to tell funny stories, in the narration of which, however, he did not seem to find the least amusement. I scarcely heard what he was saying. And at last we reached Toulon.

What a trip! And it might have been so beautiful!

Ordinarily, it is always with an almost boyish enthusiasm that I come within sight of this marvellous country, with its azure shores, like a bit of dreamland or a corner of paradise after the horrible departure from Paris in the snow and rain and darkness and dampness and dirt. With what joy that night, had things been otherwise, would I have set my foot upon the quay, sure of finding the glorious friend who would be waiting for me in the morning at the end of those two iron rails—the wonderful southern sun!

When we left Toulon, our impatience became extreme. And at Cannes, we were scarcely surprised at all to see M. Darzac upon the platform of the station, anxiously looking for us. He could scarcely have received the dispatch which Rouletabille had sent him from Dijon, announcing the hour at which we would reach Mentone. Having arrived there with Mme. Darzac and M. Stangerson the day before, at ten o'clock in the morning, he must have left Mentone almost at once and have come to meet us at Cannes, for we could understand from his dispatch that he had something to say to us in confidence. His face looked worn and sad. Somehow, it frightened us only to look at him.

"Trouble?" questioned Rouletabille, briefly.

"No, not yet," was the reply.

"God be praised" exclaimed Rouletabille, having a deep sigh. "We have come in time!"

M. Darzac said simply:

"I thank you for coming."

And he pressed both our hands in silence, following us into our compartment, in which we locked ourselves, taking care to draw the curtains and so isolate ourselves completely. When we were comfortably settled, and the train had begun to move on, our friend spoke again. His voice trembled so that he could scarcely utter the words.

"Well," he said: "he is not dead."

"We suspected it!" interrupted Rouletabille. "But are you sure?"

"I have seen him as surely as I have seen you."

"And has Mme. Darzac seen him?"

"Alas, yes! But it is necessary that we should use every means to make her believe that it was an illusion. I could not bear it if she were to lose her mind again, poor, innocent, wretched girl! Ah, my friends, what a fatality pursues us! What has this man come back to do to us? What does he want now?"

I looked at Rouletabille. His face was even more full of grief than that of M. Darzac. The blow which he feared had fallen. He leaned back against the cushions as though he were going to faint. There was a brief pause, and then M. Darzac spoke again:

"Listen! This man must disappear—he must be gotten rid of! We must go to him and ask what it is that he wants. If it is money, he may take all that I have. If he will not go, I shall kill him. It is very simple—after all, I think that would be the simplest way. Don't you think so, too?"

We could not answer. It was too pitiful. Rouletabille, overcoming his own feelings by a visible effort, engaged M. Darzac in conversation, endeavouring to calm him, and asking him to tell us what had happened since his departure from Paris.

And he told us that the event which had changed the face of his existence had taken place at Bourg, just as we had thought. Two compartments of the sleeping car had been reserved by M. Darzac, and these compartments were joined by a little dressing room. In one had been placed the travelling bag with the toilet articles of Mme. Darzac, and in the other the smaller packages. It was in the latter compartment that the Darzacs and Professor Stangerson had travelled from Paris to Dijon, where the three had left the train, and had dined at the buffet. They had arrived at 6:27 o'clock, exactly on time, and M. Stangerson had left Dijon at eight minutes after seven, and the Darzacs at just seven o'clock.

The Professor had bidden adieu to his daughter and his son-in-law upon the platform of the station after dinner. M. and Mme. Darzac had returned to their compartment—the one in which the small parcels had been deposited—and remained at the window, chatting with the Professor until the train started. As it steamed out of the station, the newly wedded pair looked back and waved their hands to M. Stangerson, who was still standing upon the platform, throwing kisses at them from the distance.

From Dijon to Bourg neither M. nor Mme. Darzac had occasion to enter the adjacent compartment, where Mme. Darzac's night bag had been placed. The door of this compartment, opening upon the vestibule, had been closed at Paris, as soon as the baggage had been brought there. But the door had not been locked, either upon the outside with a key by the porter, nor on the inside with the bolt by the Darzacs. The curtain of the glass door had been drawn over the pane from the inside by M. Darzac in such a way that no one could look into the compartment from the corridor. But the curtain between the two compartments had not been drawn. All of these circumstances were brought out by the questions asked by Rouletabille of M. Darzac, and, although I could not understand his reasons for going into such minute detail, I give the facts in order to make the condition under which the journey of the Darzacs to Bourg and of M. Stangerson to Dijon was accomplished.

When they reached Bourg our travellers learned that, on account of an accident on the line at Culoz, the train would be delayed for an hour and a half. M. and Mme. Darzac alighted and took a stroll on the platform. M. Darzac, while talking with his wife, mentioned the fact that he had forgotten to write some important letters before leaving Paris. Both entered the buffet, and M. Darzac asked for writing materials. Mathilde sat beside him for a few moments and then remarked that she would take a little walk through the station while he finished his letters.

"Very well," replied M. Darzac. "As soon as I have finished, I will join you."

From that point, I will quote M. Darzac's own words:

"I had finished writing," he said. "And I arose to go and look for Mathilde, when I saw her approaching the buffet, pallid and trembling. As soon as she perceived me, she uttered a shriek and threw herself into my arms. 'Oh, my God!' she cried. 'Oh, my God!' It seemed impossible for her to utter any other words.

She was shaking from head to foot. I tried to calm her. I assured her that she had nothing to fear when I was with her, and I strove as gently and patiently as I could to draw from her the cause of her sudden terror. I made her sit down, for her limbs seemed too weak to support her, and I begged her to take some restorative, but she told me that she could not even swallow a drop of water. Her teeth chattered as though she had an ague. At length she was able to speak, and she told me, interrupting herself at almost every other word, and looking about her as though she expected to encounter something which she dreaded, that she had started to walk about the station, as she had said she intended to do, but that she had not dared to go far, lest I should finish my writing and look for her. Then she went through the station and out upon the platform. She decided to come back to the buffet, when she noticed through the lighted windows of the cars, the sleeping car porters, who were making up the bed in a berth near our own. She remembered immediately that her night travelling bag, in which she had put her jewels, was standing unlocked, and she decided to go and lock it up without delay, not because she suspected the honesty of the employees, but through a natural instinct of prudence on a journey. She entered the car, walked down the corridor and came to the glass door of the compartment which had been reserved for her, and which neither of us had entered since leaving Paris. She opened the door and instantly uttered a cry of horror. No one heard her, for there was no one in that part of the car, and a train which passed at that moment drowned the sound of her voice with the clamour of the locomotive. What had happened to alarm her? The most terrible, ghastly, monstrous thing that the imagination could devise.

"Within the compartment, the little door opening upon the dressing cabinet was half drawn toward the interior of the section, cutting off diagonally the view of whoever might enter. This little door was ornamented by a mirror. There, in the glass, Mathilde beheld the face of Larsan! She flung herself backward, shrieking for help, and fled so precipitately that, in leaping down from the platform of the car, she fell on her knees in the train shed. Regaining her feet with difficulty, she dragged herself toward the buffet, which she reached in the condition which I have described.

"When she had told me these things, my first care was to try to convince her that she was labouring under some hideous delusion—partly because I prayed that this might be the case, and that the horrible thing which she believed had not happened, but mainly because I felt that it was my duty, if I wished to prevent Mathilde from going mad, to make her think that she must have been mistaken. Wasn't Larsan dead and buried? As I soothed her thus, I really believed what I said, and I continued to reassure her until there remained no doubt in my mind, at least, that what she had seen was merely a phantom, conjured up by fear and imagination. Naturally, I wished to make an investigation for myself, and I offered to accompany Mathilde at once to the compartment, in order to prove to her that she had been the victim of an hallucination. She was bitterly opposed to the idea, crying out that neither she nor I must ever enter the compartment again, and, not only that, but she refused to continue our journey that night. She said all these things in little halting phrases—she could hardly breathe—and it caused me the most intense pain to look at her and listen to her. The more I told her that such an apparition was an impossibility, the more she insisted that it was a reality. I tried to remind her of how seldom she had seen Larsan while the events at the Glandier were going on—which was true—and to persuade her that she could not be certain that it was his face which she had beheld, and not that of someone who might resemble him. She replied that she remembered Larsan's face perfectly—that it had appeared before her twice under such circumstances as would impress it indelibly upon her memory, even if she were to live for a century—once during the strange scene in the gallery, and again at the moment when they came into her sick room to place me under arrest. And then, now that she knew who Larsan was, it was not only the features of the Secret Service agent that she had recognised, but the dreaded countenance of the man who had not ceased pursuing her for so many years.

"She cried out that she could swear on her life and on mine that she had seen Ballmeyer—that Ballmeyer was alive—alive in the glass, with the smooth face of Larsan and his high, bald forehead. She clung to me, crouching upon the ground like a helpless wild animal, as though she feared a separation yet more terrible than the others. She drew me from the buffet where, fortunately, we had been entirely alone, out upon the platform, and then, suddenly she released my arm, and hiding her face in her hands, rushed into the superintendent's office. The man was as alarmed as myself when he saw the poor soul, and I could only repeat under my breath to myself, 'She is going mad again! She will lose her reason!'

"I explained to the superintendent that my wife had been frightened at something she fancied that she had seen while alone in our compartment, and I begged him to keep her in his office while I went myself to discover what it was that she had seen.

"And then, my friends," continued Robert Darzac, his voice beginning to tremble, "I left the superintendent's office, but I had no sooner gotten out of the room than I went back and slammed the door behind me. My face must have looked strange enough, to judge from the expression of the superintendent's face when I reappeared. But there was reason for it. *I, too, had seen Larsan.* My wife had had no illusion. *Larsan was there*—in the station — upon the platform outside that door!"

Robert Darzac paused for an instant, as though the remembrance overcame him. He passed his hand over his forehead, heaved a sigh and resumed: "He was there, in front of the superintendent's door, standing under a gas jet. Evidently, he expected us and was waiting for us. For, extraordinarily enough, he made no effort to hide himself. On the contrary, anyone would have declared that he had stationed himself there for the express purpose of being seen. The gesture which had made me close the door upon this apparition was purely instinctive. When I opened it again, intending to walk straight up to the miserable wretch, he had disappeared.

"The superintendent must have thought that he had fallen in with two lunatics. Mathilde was staring at me, her great eyes wide open, speechless, as though she were a somnambulist. In a moment, however, she came back to herself sufficiently to ask me whether it were far from Bourg to Lyons, and what was the next train which would take us there. At the same time, she begged me to give orders about our baggage, and asked me to accede to her desire to rejoin her father as soon as possible. I could see no other means of calming her, and, far from making any objection to the new project, I immediately entered into her plans. Besides, now that I had seen Larsan with my own eyes — yes, with my own eyes — I knew well that the long honeymoon trip which we had planned must be given up, and, my dear boy," went on M. Darzac, turning to Rouletabille, "I became possessed with the idea that we were running the risk of some mysterious and fantastic danger, from which you alone could rescue us, if it were not already too late. Mathilde was grateful to me for the readiness with which I fell in with her wish to join her father, and she thanked me fervently, when I told her that in a few minutes we would be on board the 9:29 train, which reaches Lyons at about ten o'clock, and when we consulted the timetable, we discovered that we would overtake M. Stangerson himself at that point. Mathilde showed as much gratitude toward me as though I were personally responsible for this lucky chance. She had regained her composure to a certain extent when the nine o'clock train arrived in the station, but at the moment that we boarded the train, as we rapidly crossed the platform and passed beneath the gas jet where I had seen Larsan, I felt her arm trembling in my own. I looked around, but could not see any sign of our enemy. I asked her whether she had seen anything, and she made no reply. Her agitation seemed to increase, however, and she begged me not to take her into a private car, but to enter a car the berths of which were already two-thirds filled with passengers. Under pretext of making some inquiries about the baggage, I left her for an instant, and went to the telegraph office, where I sent the telegram to you. I said nothing to Mathilde of this dispatch, because I continued to assure her that her eyes must have deceived her, and because on no account did I wish her to believe that I placed any faith in such a resurrection. When my wife opened her travelling bag, she found that no one had touched her jewels.

"The few words which we exchanged concerning the secret were in relation to the necessity for concealing it from M. Stangerson, to whom it might have dealt a mortal blow. I will pass over his amazement when he beheld us upon the platform of the station at Lyons. Mathilde explained to him that on account of a serious accident, which had closed the line at Culoz, we had decided, since a change of plans had to be made, that we would join him, and to spend a few days with him at the home of Arthur Rance and his young wife, as we had before been entreated to do by this faithful friend of ours."

At this time, it might be well for me to interrupt M. Darzac's narrative to recall to the memory of the reader of "The Mystery of the Yellow Room" the fact that M. Arthur William Rance had for many years cherished a hopeless devotion for Mlle. Stangerson, but had at last overcome it, and married a beautiful American girl, who knew nothing of the mysterious adventures of the Professor's daughter.

After the affair at the Glandier, and while Mlle. Stangerson was still a patient in a private asylum near Paris, where the treatment restored her to health and reason, we heard one fine day that M. Arthur William Rance was about to wed the niece of an old professor of geology at the Academy of Science in Philadelphia.

Those who had known of his luckless passion for Mathilde, and had gauged its depths by the excess with which it was displayed (for it had seemed at one time to rob the man of sense and reason and turn him into a maniac)—such persons, I say, believed that Rance was marrying in desperation, and prophesied little happiness for the union. Stories were told that the match—which was a good one for Arthur Rance, for Miss Edith Prescott was rich—had been brought about in a rather singular fashion. But these are stories which I may tell at some future time. You will learn then by what chain of circumstances the Rances had been led to locate at Rochers Rouges in the old castle, on the peninsula of Hercules, of which they had become the owners the preceding autumn.

But at present I must give place to M. Darzac, who continued his story, as follows:

"When we had given these explanations to M. Stangerson, my wife and I saw that he seemed to understand very little of what we had said, and that, instead of being glad to have us with him again, he appeared very mournful. Mathilde tried in vain to seem happy. Her father saw that something had happened since we had left him which we were concealing from him. Mathilde began to talk of the ceremony of the morning, and in that way the conversation came around to you, my young friend"—and again M. Darzac addressed himself to Rouletabille—"and I took the occasion to say to M. Stangerson that since your vacation was just beginning at the time that we were all going to Mentone, you might be pleased with an invitation that would give you the chance of spending your holiday in our society. There was, I said, plenty of room at Rochers Rouges, and I was certain that M. Arthur Rance and his bride would extend to you a cordial welcome. While I was speaking, Mathilde looked gratefully at me and pressed my hand tenderly with an effusion which showed me what gladness she was experiencing at the proposition. Thus it happened that when we reached Valence, I had M. Stangerson write the dispatch which you must have received. All night long we did not sleep. While her father rested in his compartments next to ours, Mathilde opened my travelling bag and took out my revolver. She requested me to put it in my overcoat pocket, saying: 'If *he* should attack us, you must defend yourself.' Ah, what a night we passed! We kept silence, each attempting to deceive the other into the belief that we were resting, our eyes closed, with the light burning full force, for we did not dare to sit in the darkness. The doors of our compartment were locked and bolted, but yet, every moment, we dreaded to see *his* face appear. When we heard a step in the corridor, our hearts beat wildly. We seemed to recognize it. And Mathilde had put a cover over the mirror, for fear of glancing toward it and seeing the reflection of that face again. 'Had he followed us?' 'Could we have been mistaken?' 'Would we escape from him?' 'Had he gone on to Culoz on the train which we had left?' 'Could we hope for any such good fortune?' For my own part, I did not believe that we could. And she—she! Ah, how my heart bled for her, wrapped in a silence like that of death, sitting there in her corner. I knew how she was weighed down by despair and agony—how far more unhappy she was even than myself, because of the misery which it seemed to be her lot to bring upon those whom she loved most dearly. I longed to console her, to comfort her, but I found no words. And when once I attempted to speak, she made a gesture so full of misery and desolation that I realised that I would be far kinder if I kept silence. Then, like her, I closed my eyes."

This was M. Darzac's story, although I have shortened it in a certain degree. We felt, Rouletabille and myself, that the narrative was so important that we both resolved on arriving at Mentone, that we would write it down from memory as faithfully as possible. We did as we agreed, and where our versions did not agree, or halted a little, we submitted them to M. Darzac, who made a few unimportant changes, after which the story read just as I have given it here.

The rest of the journey taken by the Darzacs and M. Stangerson presented no incident worthy of note. At the station of Mentone Garavan, they found M. Arthur Rance, who was astonished at beholding the bride and bridegroom; but when he was told that they intended to spend a few days with him, and to accept the invitation which M. Darzac, under various pretexts, had always declined, he was delighted, and declared that his wife would be as glad as himself. He was pleased, too, to learn that Rouletabille might soon join the party. M. Arthur Rance had not, even after his marriage to Miss Edith Prescott, been able to overcome the extreme reserve with which M. Darzac had always treated him. When, during his last trip to San Remo, the young Professor of the Sorbonne had been urged in passing to make a visit at the Château Hercules, he had made his excuses in the most ceremonious manner. But when he met Rance in the station at Mentone Garavan, M. Darzac greeted him most cordially, and complimented him upon his appearance, saying that the air of the country seemed to agree with him perfectly.

We have seen how the apparition of Larsan in the station at Bourg had overthrown all the plans of M. and Mme. Darzac, and had completely overwhelmed them both with grief and consternation, and had made them turn to the Rances' home as to a refuge, casting them, figuratively speaking, into the arms of these people who were not especially congenial to them, but whom they believed to be honest, loyal and willing to protect them. We know that M. Stangerson, to whom nothing had been told of what had occurred, was beginning to suspect something, and we know that all three of the party had called Rouletabille to their aid. It was a veritable panic. And, so far as M. Darzac was concerned, the terror which he felt was increased by news brought to us by M. Arthur Rance when he met us at Nice. But before this there had occurred a little incident which I cannot pass by in silence. As soon as we reached the Nice station, I had jumped from the train and hurried into the telegraph office to ask whether there was any message for me. A dispatch was handed to me, and, without opening it, I went back to M. Darzac and Rouletabille.

"Read this!" I said to the young reporter.

Rouletabille opened the envelope and read:

"Brignolles has not been away from Paris since April 6th. This is an absolute certainty."

Rouletabille looked at me for a moment and then said:

"Well, what does this amount to, now that you have it? What did you suspect, anyway?"

"It was at Dijon," I rejoined, vexed at the attitude of the lad toward the affair, "that the idea came to me that Brignolles might be in some way concerned in the misfortunes that seem to be crowding upon us, and of which warning was given by the telegrams that you received. I wired one of my friends to make inquiries for me in regard to the movements of the fellow during the last few days. I was anxious to learn whether he had left Paris."

"Well," said Rouletabille. "You have your inquiries answered. Are you willing to admit now that Brignolles is not and has never been Larsan in disguise?"

"I never thought of any such thing as that!" I exclaimed with some vexation, for I suspected that Rouletabille was laughing at me.

The truth was that the idea, absurd as it was, had actually entered my mind.

"Will you never stop thinking ill of poor Brignolles?" asked M. Darzac, with a sad smile at me. "He is quiet and shy, I grant you, but he is a good lad, just the same."

"That's where we differ," I retorted.

And I retired to my own corner of the railway carriage. In general my personal intuitions in regard to things were poor enough guides compared to the wonderful insight of Rouletabille, but in this case, we were to receive proof, only a few days later, that even if the personality of Brignolles were not another of Larsan's disguises, the laboratory assistant was nevertheless a miserable wretch. And this time both M. Darzac and Rouletabille begged my pardon and paid their respects to my despised intuitions. But there is no use of anticipating. If I mention this incident here, it is for the purpose of showing to how great an extent I was haunted by the image of Larsan, hiding under some new form, and lurking unknown among us. Dear Heaven! Larsan had so often proved his talent—I may even say his genius—in this respect, that I felt that he was quite capable of defying us now, and of mingling with us while we thought that he was a stranger—or, perhaps, even a friend.

I was soon to change my ideas, however, and to believe that this time Ballmeyer had altered his usual tactics, and the unexpected arrival of M. Arthur Rance was to go far in leading me to this opinion. Instead of hiding himself, the bandit was showing himself openly—at least, to some of us—with an audacity that staggered belief. After all, what had he to fear in this part of the country? He was well aware that neither M. Darzac nor his wife would be likely to denounce him, nor, consequently, would their friends do so. His bold revelation of his presence seemed to have but one end in view—that of ruining the happiness of the couple who had believed that his death had opened the way for their marriage. But an objection arose to that conjecture. Why should he have chosen such a means of vengeance? Would it not have been a better plan to let himself be seen before the marriage had taken place? He would certainly have prevented it by so doing. Yes, but in that case, he would have found it necessary to appear in his own person in Paris. But when had any thought of danger or risk been able to deter Larsan from an undertaking upon which he had determined? Who dared affirm that he knew of one such case?

But now let me tell you of the news brought by Arthur Rance when he joined the three of us on the train at Nice. Rance, of course, knew nothing of what had happened at Bourg, nothing of the appearing of Larsan to Mme. Darzac on the train and to her husband in the station, but he brought alarming tidings. If we had retained the slightest hope that we had lost Larsan on the road to Culoz, Rance's words obliterated it, for he, too, had seen the man whom we so feared, face to face. And he had come to warn us, before we reached his home, so that we might decide upon some plan of action.

"When we were about to return home after having taken you to the station," said Rance to Darzac.; "after the train had pulled out, your wife, M. Stangerson and myself thought that we would leave the carriage for a little while and take a stroll on the promenade walk. M. Stangerson gave his arm to his daughter. I was at the right of M. Stangerson, who, therefore, was walking between the two of us. Suddenly, as we paused for a moment near a sort of public garden to let a tramcar pass, I brushed against a man who said to me, 'I beg your pardon, sir.' The sound of the voice made me tremble and I knew as well beforehand as I did when I raised my head that it was Larsan. The voice was the voice I had heard at the Court of Assizes. He cast a long, calm look upon the three of us. I do not know how I was able to restrain the exclamation which rose to my lips,—how I kept from crying aloud his miserable name! Happily M. Stangerson and Mme. Darzac had not seen him and I hurried them rapidly away. I made them walk around the garden and listen to the music in the park and then we returned to where the carriage was waiting. Upon the sidewalk in front of the station, there was Larsan again! I do not know—I cannot understand how M. Stangerson and Mme. Darzac could have helped but see him—"

"Are you sure that they did not see him?" interrupted Robert Darzac.

"Absolutely sure. I feigned a sudden attack of illness. We got into the carriage and ordered the coachman to drive as fast as he could. The man was still standing on the sidewalk, staring after us with his cold, cruel eyes when we drove away."

"And are you certain that my wife did not see him?" repeated Darzac, who was growing more and more agitated.

"Certain, I assure you."

"But, Good God, M. Darzac!" interposed Rouletabille. "How long do you think you can deceive your wife as to the fact that Larsan has reappeared and that she actually saw him? If you imagine that you can keep her in ignorance for very long, you are greatly mistaken."

"But," replied Darzac, "while we were ending our journey, the idea that she had been the victim of a delusion seemed to grow in her mind and by the time we reached Garavan, she seemed to be quite calm."

"At the time you reached Garavan," said Rouletabille, quietly, "your wife sent me the telegram I am going to ask you to read."

And the reporter held out to M. Darzac the paper which bore the two words, "Save us."

M. Darzac read it with the blood seeming to die away from his face as we looked at him.

"She will go mad again," was all that he said.

That was what he dreaded—all of us—and, strangely enough, when we arrived at the station of Mentone Garavan and found

M. Stangerson and Mme. Darzac (who were awaiting us in spite of the promise which the Professor had made to Arthur Rance not to leave Rochers Rouges nor allow his daughter to do so until we came, for reasons which their host said he would tell them later, not being able to invent them on the spur of the moment) it was with a phrase which seemed the echo of our terror that Mme. Darzac greeted Rouletabille. As soon as she perceived the young man, she rushed toward him and it seemed to us that she was making a great effort not to throw her arms around him. I saw that her spirit was clinging to him as a shipwrecked sailor grips at the hand which is stretched out to save him from drowning. And I heard the words that she whispered to him:

"I know that I am going mad!"

As to Rouletabille, I may have seen his face as pale before, but I had never seen it look like that of a man stricken with his death blow.

# VI

## THE FORT OF HERCULES

When he alights at the Garavan station, whatever may be the season of the year in which he visits that enchanted country, the traveller might almost fancy himself in the Garden of Hesperides whose golden apples excited the desire of the conqueror of the Nemean lion. I might not perhaps, however, have recalled to mind the son of Jupiter and Alcmene merely because of the numerous lemon and orange trees which in the balmy air let their ripened fruit hang heavily on their boughs if everything about the scene had not spoken of his mythological glories and his fabled promenade upon these fair shores. You remember how the Phoenicians in transporting their penates to the shadow of the rocks which were one day to become the abode of the Grimaldi, gave to the little port in which they anchored and to other natural features all along the shore—a mountain, a cape, and an islet—the name of Hercules whom they looked upon as their god—the name which they have always retained. But I like to fancy that the Phoenicians found the name here already, and indeed, if the divinities, fatigued by the white dust of the roads of Hellas, went to seek for a marvellous spot, warm and perfumed, to rest after their strenuous adventures, they could not have found a more beautiful scene. The gods, to my mind, were the first tourists of the Riviera. The Garden of the Hesperides was nowhere else and Hercules had made the place ready for his Olympian comrades by destroying the evil dragon with an hundred heads who wanted to keep the azure shore for himself, all alone. And I am not at all certain that the bones of the ancient elephant discovered a few years ago in the neighbourhood of Rochers Rouges were not those of the dragon himself!

When, after alighting from the train, we came in silence to the bank of the sea, our eyes were immediately struck by a dazzling silhouette of a castle standing upon the peninsula of Hercules, which the works accomplished on the frontier have, alas, nearly destroyed. The oblique rays of the sun which were falling upon the walls and the old Square Tower made the reflection of the tower glisten in the waters like a breastplate. The tower seemed to stand guard like an old sentinel, over the Bay of Garavan which lay before us like a blue lake of fire. And as we advanced nearer, the tower gleaming in the water seemed to grow longer. The sky behind us leaned toward the crest of the mountains; the promontories to the west were already wrapped in clouds at the approach of night and by the time we crossed the threshold of the actual structure the castle in the water was only a menacing hade.

Upon the lower steps of the stairway which led up to one of the towers, we beheld a slender, charming figure. It was Arthur Rance's wife, who had been the beautiful and brilliant Edith Prescott. Certainly the Bride of Lammermoor was not more pale on the day when the black-eyed stranger from Ravenswood first crossed her path, O Edith! Ah, when one wishes to present a romantic figure in a mediaeval frame, the figure of a princess, lost in dreams, plaintive and melancholy, one should not have such eyes, my lady! And your hair was as black as the raven's wing. Such colouring is not of the kind which one is used to attribute to the angels. Are you an angel, Edith? Is this gentle, plaintive little manner natural or acquired? Is the sweet expression that your face wears today an entirely truthful one? Pardon that I ask you all these questions, Edith; but when I beheld you for the first time, after having been entranced by the delicate harmony of your white figure, standing motionless upon the stone stair, I followed the quick, lowering glance of your dark eyes in the direction of the daughter of Professor Stangerson, and it had a cruel look which accorded ill with the sweet tones of your voice and the bright smile on your lips.

The voice of the young wife was her greatest charm although the grace of her entire being was perfect. At the introductions which were, of course, performed by her husband, she greeted us in the simplest and sweetest fashion imaginable—the fashion of the ideal hostess. Rouletabille and myself made an effort to tell her that we had intended to look for a stopping place in the village instead of trespassing upon her hospitality. She made a delicious little grimace, lifted her shoulders with a gesture that was almost childish, said that our rooms were all ready for us and changed the subject.

"Come, come! You haven't seen the château. You must see it—all of you. Oh, I will show you 'la Louve' another time. It is the only gloomy corner in the place. It is horrible—so cold and dismal. It makes me shiver. But, do you know I love to shiver! Oh, M. Rouletabille, you'll tell me stories that will make me shiver someday, won't you?"

And chattering thus, she glided in front of us in her white gown. She walked like an actress. She made a singularly pretty picture in this garden of the Orient, between the threatening old tower and the carved stone flowers of the ruined chapel. The vast court which we were crossing was so completely covered on every side with grass, shrubs and foliage plants, with cactus and aloes, mountain laurel, wild roses and marguerites that one might have sworn that an eternal spring had found its habitation in this enclosure, formerly the drilling ground of the château when the soldiers assembled in time of war. This court, through the help of the winds of heaven and the neglect of man had naturally become a garden, a beautiful wild garden in which one saw that the chatelaine had interfered as little as possible and which she had in no way attempted to restore to the beaten track. Behind all this verdure and this wealth of bloom one could see the most exquisite sight which could be imagined in dead architecture. Figure to yourself the perfect arches of gothic brought up to the doors of the old Roman chapel; the pillars twined with climbing plants, rose geranium and vervain uniting their sweet perfume and raising to the azure heavens their broken arch, which nothing seems to support. There is no longer a roof on the chapel. And there are no more walls. There remains of it only the bit of lace work in stone, which a miracle of equilibrium keeps suspended in the air.

And at our left is the immense tower of the Twelfth Century, which, Mme. Edith tells us, the natives call "la Louve" and which nothing—neither time, nor man, nor peace, nor war, nor cannon, nor tempest has ever been able to destroy. It is just as it appeared in 1107, when the Saracens, who sowed devastation in their wake, were able to make no headway in their attacks upon the château of Hercules,—just as it was seen by Salageri and his corsairs of Genoa, when, after they had seized the fort and the Square Tower and even the castle itself, it resisted attack and its defenders held it until the arrival of the troops of the Princes of Provence, who delivered them. It was there that Mme. Edith had chosen to have her own rooms.

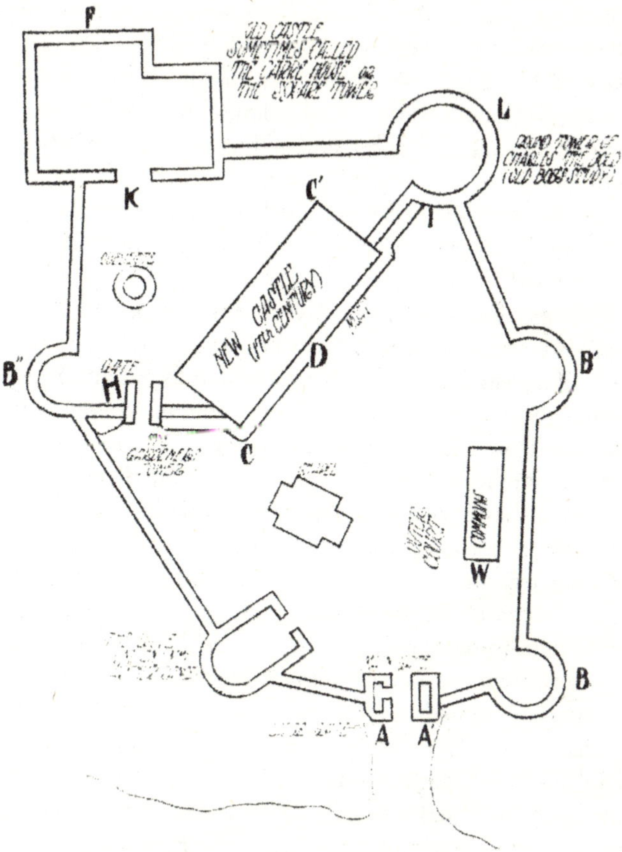


*The Plan of the Fort of Hercules*

But while she spoke to us in her sweet, clear voice, I stopped looking at the objects around us to look at the people. Arthur Rance was gazing at Mme. Darzac, when my eyes fell upon them, and Rouletabille seemed to be lost in thought, and far, far away from us all. M. Darzac and M. Stangerson were talking in low tones. The same thought was filling the minds of each one of these people—both those who kept silence and those who, if they spoke, were careful to say nothing which could give a clue to the thoughts. We reached the postern. "This is what we call the Gardener's Tower," said Edith, childishly. "From this gate one may see all the fort, and all the castle, both north and south. See!"

And she stretched her arms wide to emphasize her words.

"Every stone has its history. I'll tell them to you some day, if you are good."

"How gay Edith is!" murmured her husband. I thought to myself that she was the only one who was gay in the party.

We had passed through the postern and found ourselves in another court. Opposite us was the old donjon. Its appearance was more than impressive. It was high and square, and it was on account of its shape that it was known as the Square Tower. And, as this tower occupies the most important corner of the fortification, it was also known as the Corner Tower. It was the most extraordinary and the most important part of this agglomeration of defensive works. The walls were heavier and higher than those anywhere else, and half way up they were still sealed with the Roman cement with which Caesar's own columns had welded together the stones.

"That tower yonder, in the opposite corner," went on Edith, "is the Tower of Charles the Bold, so called because he was the Duke who furnished the plans when it became necessary to transform the defences of the château, so as to make them resist the attacks of the artillery. Don't you think I am very learned? Old Bob has made this tower his study. It is too bad, for we might have a magnificent dining hall there. But I have never been able to refuse old Bob anything he wanted. Old Bob," she added, with a charming smile, "is my uncle—that is the name he taught me to call him by when I was a little thing. He is not here just now. He went to Paris on the five o'clock train, but he will be back tomorrow. He is going to compare some of the anatomical specimens which he found at Rochers Rouges with those in the Museum of Natural History in Paris. Ah—here is an oubliette!"

And she showed us in the centre part of the second court a small shaft, which she called, romantically, an oubliette, and above which a eucalyptus tree, with its white blossoms and its leafless limbs, leaned like a woman over a fountain.

Since we had entered the second court, we understood better—or at least I did, for Rouletabille, every moment more deeply lost in his own thoughts, seemed neither to see nor to hear—the topographical plan of the Fort of Hercules. As this plan is of the greatest importance in the proper understanding of the incredible events which were to occur so soon after our arrival at Rochers Rouges, I shall place at once before the eyes of the reader the general scheme of the buildings as it was traced later by Rouletabille and myself.

The castle had been built in 1140 by the Seigneurs of Mortola. In order to isolate it completely from the land, they had not hesitated to make an island of the peninsula by cutting away the narrow isthmus which connected it with the mainland. Upon the mainland itself, they had built a barricade in the form of a semicircular fortification, designed to protect the approaches to the drawbridge and the two entrance towers. Not a trace of this fortification was left. And the isthmus, in the course of the centuries, had again resumed its old form, the drawbridge had been thrown down and the trenches had filled up. The walls of the Château of Hercules followed the outline of the peninsula, which was that of an irregular hexagon. The walls were built upon the rocks, and the latter, in some places, extended over the waters in such a manner that a little ship might have taken shelter beneath them, fearing no enemy, while it was protected by this natural ceiling. This design of building was marvellously well adapted for defence, and gave the inmates of the fortress little reason to fear an attack, no matter from what quarter it might come.

The fort was entered by way of the north gate, which guarded the two towers, A and A, connected by a passageway. These towers which had suffered greatly during the last sieges of the Genoese, had been repaired to some slight extent some time afterward, and had, shortly before we came to Rochers Rouges, been made habitable by Mrs. Rance, who used them as servants' quarters. The front of the tower A served as the keeper's lodge. A little door opened in the side of the tower upon the passageway, and enabled anyone looking out to observe all those who came or went. A heavy double door of oak, with bands of iron, was no longer in use, its twin portals having stood for uncounted years open against the inner walls of the two towers, on account of the difficulty which had been experienced in managing them; and the entrance to the castle was only closed by a little gate, which anyone might open at will. This entrance was the only one by which it was possible to get into the château. As I have said, in passing through this gate, one found himself in the first court, closed in on all sides by the walls and the towers. These walls were by no means as high as when they were built. The old high courtyards which connected the towers had been razed to the ground and replaced by a sort of circular boulevard, from which one mounted toward the first court by means of a little terrace. The boulevards were still crowned by a parapet. For the changes which I have described took place in the Fifteenth Century, at the time when every lord of the manor was obliged to consider the possibility of being obliged to meet an attack of artillery. As to the towers B, B' and B", which had for a considerable time longer preserved their uniformity and their first height, and the pointed roofs of which had been replaced by a platform designed to support the artillery, they had later been razed to the height of the boulevard parapets, and their shape seemed almost like that of a half moon. These alterations had taken place in the Seventeenth Century, at the time of the construction of a modern castle, still known as the New Castle, although it had been in ruins for years when we first saw it. The New Castle on the plan is at C C'.

Upon the flat platform roofs of these old towers—roofs which were surrounded by a parapet—palm trees had been planted, which had thriven ill, swept as they were by the sea winds and burned by the sun. When one leaned over the circular parapet which surrounded the whole domain, it seemed to him as though the château were still as completely closed in as it was in the days when the courtyards reached to the second storeys of the old towers. "La Louve," as I have said, had not been changed at all, but still reared its dark hulk against the blue waters of the Mediterranean, a strange, weird figure, looking thousands of years old. I have spoken also of the ruins of the chapel. The ancient commons (shown on the map by W), near the parapet between B and B', had been transformed into the stables and the kitchens.

I am describing now all the anterior portion of the Château of Hercules. One could only penetrate into the second enclosure through the postern (indicated by H), which Mrs. Arthur Rance called "the tower of the gardener," and which was actually only a pavilion, formerly defended by the tower B", and by another tower situated at C, and which had entirely disappeared at the time of the erection of the New Castle (shown at C C'). A moat and a wall started from B" to abut on I at the Tower of Charles the Bold, advancing at C in the form of a spur to the midst of the first court, and entirely isolating the court, which they completely closed in. The moat still exists, wide and deep, but the walls had been torn down all the length of the New Castle and replaced by the walls of the castle itself. A central door at D, now condemned, opened upon a bridge, which had been thrown over the moat, and which formerly permitted direct communication with the outer court. But this bridge had been torn down or was swallowed up in the waters, and as the windows of the castle, rising high above the moat, were still guarded by their heavy iron bars, one might readily believe that the inner court still remained as impenetrable as when it was entirely shut in by its enclosing walls at the time when the New Castle did not exist.

The pavement of the inner court—the Court of Charles the Bold, as the old guide books of the country call it still—was a little higher than that of the outer court. The rocks formed there a very high seat, a natural pedestal of that colossal black column, the Old Castle, standing square and erect, as though it had been carved from a single block of stone, stretching its awesome shadow over the blue waters. One could only penetrate into the Old Castle (designated by F) by a little door, K. The old inhabitants of the country never spoke of it except as the Square Tower, to distinguish it from the Round Tower, or the Tower of Charles the Bold, as they sometimes called the latter. A parapet similar to the one which closed in the outer court was built between the towers B", F and L, closing the inner court as firmly as the outer.

We have seen that the Round Tower had been in years past torn down to half its former height, as it had been built by the Mortola, according to plans drawn by Charles the Bold himself, to whom the Seigneur had been of some service in the Helvetian war. This tower had a number of tiny chambers above, and an immense octagon chamber below. One descended into this chamber by a steep and narrow stairway. The ceiling of the octagon room was supported by four great cylindrical pillars, and from its walls opened three enormous embrasures for three enormous cannons. It was of this room that Mme. Edith had wished to make a dining room, for it was in an admirable state of preservation, on account of the thickness of the walls, and the light could still penetrate through the great windows, which had been enlarged and made square, although they, too, were still guarded by barriers of iron. This tower (shown on the map at L) was the spot chosen by Mme. Edith's uncle for a workshop, and the abiding place of his collection. Its roof was a beautiful little garden, to which the mistress of the domain had had transported fertile soil and wonderful plants and flowers. I have marked upon the map in array all the portions of the buildings which Mme. Edith had restored, improved and put in shape for habitation.

Of the château of the Seventeenth Century, known as the New Castle, they had only repaired two bed chambers on the first floor and a little sitting room for guests. It was to these that Rouletabille and myself were assigned, while M. and Mme. Robert Darzac were lodged in the Square Tower, of which I shall have to give a more special description.

Two rooms, the windows of which opened upon the balcony, were reserved in this Square Tower for "Old Bob," who slept there. M. Stangerson was upon the first floor of "la Louve," in the rear of the suite occupied by the Rances.

Mme. Edith herself showed us to our rooms. She made us cross over the sunken ceilings of ruined apartments, over broken railings and tumble-down walls; but here and there some mouldy hangings, a broken statue or a ragged bit of tapestry, bore witness to the ancient splendours of the New Castle, born of the fantasies of some Mortola of the wonderful Seventeenth Century. But when we reached them, our little rooms recalled to us nothing of that magnificent past. They had been swept and garnished with a care that was almost touching. Clean and hygienic, without carpets, hangings or upholstered chairs, furnished in the simplest of modern styles, they pleased us very much. As I have already said, the two sleeping rooms were separated by a little parlour.

As I tied my cravat, after dressing for dinner, I called Rouletabille to ask him if he were ready. There was no answer. I went into his room and discovered with surprise that he had already gone out. I went to the window of his room, which opened like my own upon the court of Charles the Bold. The court was empty, inhabited only by a large eucalyptus, the fragrance of which mounted to my nostrils. Above the parapet of the boulevard I saw the vast stretch of the silent waters. The blue of the sea had grown dark at the fall of evening, and the shades of night were visible on the horizon of the Italian shore, reaching already to the pointe d'Ospedaletti. Not a sound, not a breath on the land or in the heavens! I have never yet noticed such a silence and such a complete repose of nature except at the moment which precedes the most violent storms and the unchaining of the elements. But now I felt that we had nothing of the sort to fear. The whole appearance of the night was of the calmest, most serene beauty—

But what was that dark shadow? From whence had come that spectre which glided over the waters? Standing erect at the prow of a little boat which a fisherman was rowing, keeping rhythmic time with the two oars, I recognised the form of Larsan. Why should I try to deceive myself by saying even for one moment that I was wrong? He was only too easily to be recognised. And if those who beheld him should have had the slightest doubt as to his identity, he seemed to desire to set it entirely at rest by this open display of himself, utterly without disguise as entirely convincing as though he had shouted aloud, "It is I!"

Oh, yes! I was he! It was "the great Fred," as we used to call him when we looked upon him only as the wonderfully resourceful and brilliant Secret Service agent. The boat, silent, with its motionless statue at the prow, rowed completely around the peninsula. It passed beneath the windows of the Square Tower and then directed its course to the shores of the Pointe de Garibaldi. And the man still stood erect, his arms folded, his face turned toward the tower, a diabolical apparition on the threshold of the night, which slowly crept up behind him, enveloped him in its shades and carried him away.

When he had vanished, I lowered my eyes and beheld two figures in the court of Charles the Bold. They were at the corner of the railing near the little door of the Square Tower. One of these forms—the taller—was supporting the other and speaking in tones of entreaty. The smaller attempted to break away—one would have said that it wished to throw itself into the sea. And I heard the voice of Mme. Darzac say:

"Be careful. It is a gage of defiance which he has thrown down. You shall not leave me this evening."

And then came Rouletabille's voice answering:

"He must land upon the bank! Let me hurry to the bank."

"What will you do there?" moaned Mathilde.

"Whatever may be necessary."

And then Mathilde spoke again, and her voice was terrible to hear.

"I forbid you to touch that man!"

And I heard no more.

I descended to the court, where I found Rouletabille alone, seated upon the edge of the oubliette. I spoke to him, but he did not answer. I felt no surprise, for this had often happened of late. I went on into the outer court, and I saw M. Darzac coming toward me, evidently in the greatest excitement. Before I came up to him, he called out:

"Did you see him?"

"Yes, I saw him," I replied.

"And she—my wife—do you know whether she saw him?"

"She saw him, too. She was with Rouletabille when he passed. What bravado the creature showed!"

Robert Darzac was trembling like an aspen leaf from the shock which he had just experienced. He told me that as soon as he had caught sight of the boat and its passenger, he had rushed like a madman to the shore, but that before he had reached the Pointe de Garibaldi the bark had disappeared as if by enchantment. But even before he finished speaking, Darzac left me and hurried away to seek Mathilde, dreading the thought of the state of mind in which he felt that he would find her. But he returned almost immediately, gloomy and grieved. The door of his wife's apartment was locked, and she had said to him that she wished to be alone for awhile.

"And Rouletabille?" I asked.

"I have not seen him."

We remained together upon the rampart gazing at the night which had carried Larsan away. Robert Darzac was infinitely sorrowful. In order to change the direction of his thoughts, I asked him a few questions regarding the Rance household. Here is in substance the information which I succeeded in extracting from him little by little:

After the trial at Versailles, Arthur Rance had returned to Philadelphia, and there, one evening, at a family dinner party, he had found himself seated beside a charming young girl, who had interested him at once by a display of interest in literature and art, the like of which he had not often seen in his beautiful countrywomen. She was not in the least like the quick, independent and audacious type of young women who are often found in America, nor was she of the "Fluffy Ruffles" variety, so much in favour at present. Somewhat haughty in mien, yet gentle and melancholy, she at once recalled to the young man the heroines of Walter Scott, who he soon learned was her favourite author. From the first, she attracted him strongly. How could this delicate little creature so quickly have impressed Arthur Rance, who had been madly in love with the majestic Mathilde? Of such are the mysteries of the heart. Now, fortunately or unfortunately, as you prefer, Arthur Rance had upon that evening so far forgotten himself as to drink considerably more wine than was good for him. He never realised what his offense had been, but he knew that he must have committed some frightful blunder or breach of politeness, when Miss Edith in a low voice and with heightened colour, requested him not to address her again. Upon the morrow, Arthur Rance went to call on the young lady and entreated her pardon, swearing that he would never permit wine to pass his lips again.

Arthur Rance had already known for some time Miss Prescott's uncle, the fine old man who still bore among his friends the nickname of "Old Bob," which had been given him in his college days, and who was as celebrated for his adventures as an explorer as for his discoveries as a geologist. He seemed as gentle as a sheep, but he had hunted many a tiger through the pampas of South America. He had spent half his life south of the Rio Negro among the Patagonians, in seeking for the man of the tertiary period—or, at least, for his fossils, not as the anthropological relic or some other pithecanthropus, approaching in a greater or less extent the race of monkeys, but as the real living man, stronger, more powerful, than those who inhabit this planet in our own day—the man, to speak clearly, who must have been contemporaneous with the immense mammoths and mastodons, which appeared upon the globe before the quarternary epoch. He generally returned from these expeditions with closely filled notebooks and a respectable collection of tibias and femurs, which may or may not have belonged to the aboriginal man, and also with a rich display of skins of wild beasts, which showed that the spectacled old savant knew how to use more modern arms than the stone ax and bow and arrow. As soon as he was back in Philadelphia, he would dispose of his treasures either in his private cabinets or in those of the Museum, and, opening his notebooks, would resume his lectures, amusing himself as he talked by making the splinters from the long pencils, which he was always sharpening but had never been seen to use, fly almost into the eyes of the students on the front benches. All these details were given me later by Arthur Rance himself. He had been one of "Old Bob's" pupils, but had not seen him in many years until he made the acquaintance of Miss Edith. If I have seemed to dwell too minutely on such apparently unimportant things, I have done so because, by quite a natural train of events, we were to make "Old Bob's" acquaintance at Rochers Rouges.

Miss Edith, upon the occasion when Arthur Rance had been presented to her and had forgotten himself on account of overindulgence in wine, had seemed somewhat more melancholy than she usually was, because she had received disquieting news of her uncle. The latter for four years back had been absent on a trip to Patagonia. In his last letter, he had told his niece that he was ill, and that he feared that he should not live to see her again. One might be tempted to wonder why so tender-hearted a niece, under such circumstances, had not refrained from attending a dinner, no matter how quiet, but Miss Edith, during her uncle's many absences from home, had so frequently received such communications from him and had afterward seen him return in such perfect health that she could scarcely be blamed for not having remained at home to mourn that evening. Three months later, however, having received another letter, she suddenly resolved to go all alone to South America and join her uncle. During those three months important events had transpired. Miss Edith had been touched by the remorse of Arthur Rance, and when Miss Prescott departed for Patagonia, no one was astonished to find that "Old Bob's" old pupil was going to accompany her. If the engagement was not officially announced, it was because the pair preferred to wait for the consent of the geologist. Miss Edith and Arthur Rance were met at St. Louis by the young woman's uncle. He was in excellent health and in a charming humour. Rance, who had not seen him in years, declared to him that he had grown younger—the easiest of compliments to pay and the pleasantest to receive. When his niece informed him of her engagement to this fine young fellow, the uncle manifested the greatest delight. The three returned to Philadelphia, where the wedding took place. Miss Edith had never been in France, and Arthur determined that their honeymoon should be spent there. And it was thus that they found, as will be told a little later, a scientific reason for locating in the neighbourhood of Mentone, not exactly in France, but an hundred meters from the frontier, in Italy, at Rochers Rouges.

The gong had sounded for dinner, and Arthur Rance was coming to look for us, so we repaired to "la Louve," in the lower hall of which we were to dine. When we were all assembled (save "Old Bob," who, as has been mentioned, was absent), Mme. Edith asked whether any of us had noticed a little boat which had made the circle of the fortress, and in which a man was standing erect. The man's strange attitude had struck her, she said. No one replied, and she added:

"Oh, I know who it is, for I know the fisherman who rowed the boat. He is a great friend of Old Bob."

"Ah, then you know the fisherman, madame?" asked Rouletabille.

"He comes to the castle sometimes to sell fish. The people around the village have given him an odd name, which I don't know how to say in their impossible patois, but I can translate it. They call him, 'the hangman of the sea.' A pretty name, isn't it?"

# VII

## WHICH TELLS OF SOME PRECAUTIONS TAKEN BY JOSEPH ROULETABILLE TO DEFEND THE FORT OF HERCULES AGAINST THE ATTACK OF AN ENEMY

Rouletabille had not even the politeness to inquire into the explanation of this amazing sobriquet. He appeared to be plunged in the deepest meditation. A strange dinner! A strange castle! Strange guests! All the graces and coquetries of Mme. Edith had no effect in awakening us to any semblance of life. There were two newly married pairs, four lovers, who ought to have been radiant with the joy of life, and to have made the hours pass gayly and happily. But the repast was one of the most gloomy at which I have ever been present. The spectre of Larsan hovered about our festivities, and it seemed almost as though the man whom we knew to be so near was actually among us.

It is as well to say here that Professor Stangerson, since he had learned the cruel, the miserable truth, had not for one moment been able to free himself from the thought of it. I do not think that I am saying too much in declaring that the first victim of the affair at the Glandier, and the most unfortunate of all, was this good old man. He had lost everything—his faith in science, his love of work, and—more bitter than all the rest—his belief in his daughter. His faith in her had been his religion. She had been such an object of joy and pride. He had thought of her for so many years as a vestal virgin, seeking, with him, the unknown in the world of higher things. He had been so marvellously dazzled with the thought of her angelic purity, and had believed that her reason for having remained unmarried was that she was unwilling to resign herself to any life which would withdraw her from science and her father, to both of which she had dedicated her existence. And while he was thinking of her almost with reverence, he discovered that the reason that his daughter refused to marry was because she was already the wife of Ballmeyer. The day in which Mathilde had decided to confess everything to her father, and to tell him the story of the past, which must clear up the present with a tragic light to the eyes of the professor, already warned by the mysteries of the Glandier—the day when, falling at his feet and embracing his knees, she had told him the story of her youth, Professor Stangerson had raised the form of his beloved child from the ground and had pressed her to his heart; he had placed a kiss of pardon on her brow: he had mingled his tears with the sobs of her whose fault had been so bitterly expiated, and he had sworn to her that she had never been more precious than since he had known how she had suffered. And by these words, she was a little comforted. But he, when she left his presence, was another man—a man alone, all alone—. Professor Stangerson had lost his daughter and his goddess.

He had experienced only indifference in regard to her marriage to Robert Darzac, although the latter had been the best beloved of his pupils. In vain Mathilde, with the warmest tenderness, had endeavoured to rekindle the old feeling in the heart of her father. She knew well that he had changed toward her, that his glance never dwelt upon her in the old fond way, and that his weary eyes were looking back into the past at an image which he had only dreamed was her own. And she knew, too, that when those eyes rested upon her—upon her, Mathilde Darzac—it was to see at her side, not the honoured figure of a good man and tender husband, but the shadow, eternally living, eternally infamous, of the other—the man who had stolen his daughter. The Professor could work no longer. The great secret of the dissolution of matter which he had promised to reveal to mankind, had returned to the unknown from which, for a moment, the scientist had drawn it, and men will go on, repeating for centuries to come the imbecile phrase, "From nothing, nothing."

The evening meal was rendered still more doleful by the setting in which it was served—the sombre hall, lighted by a gothic lamp, with old candelabra of wrought iron, and the walls of the fortress adorned with oriental tapestries, against which were ranged the old suits of armour dating back to the first Saracen invasion and the sieges of Dagobert.

I looked at the members of the party, and it seemed to me that I was able to see reason enough for the general sadness. M. and Mme. Darzac were seated beside each other. The mistress of the house had evidently not desired to separate a bridal pair, whose union only dated back to yesterday. Of the two, I must say that the more unhappy looking was, beyond a doubt, our friend, Robert. He never spoke one word. Mme. Darzac joined to some extent in the conversation, exchanging now and then a few commonplaces with Arthur Rance. Is it necessary for me to add that at this time, after the scene between Rouletabille and Mathilde, which I had witnessed from my window, I expected to see her in a most wretched state—almost overcome by the vision of Larsan, which had surged up in front of her eyes? But no: on the contrary, I discovered a remarkable difference between the terrified aspect with which she had approached us at the station, for instance, and the easy, composed manner which was hers, at present. One would have said that she had been relieved by the sight of the apparition, and when I expressed my opinion to Rouletabille later in the evening, I discovered that he shared it, and he explained the reason for Mathilde's change of manner in the simplest possible fashion. The unhappy woman had dreaded nothing so much as the thought that she was going mad, and the certainty that she had not been the victim of a mental delusion, cruel as that certainty was, had served to make her a little more calm. She preferred to fight even against the living Larsan than against a phantom. In the first interview which she had had with Rouletabille in the Square Tower, while I was dressing for dinner, she had, my young friend told me, been completely possessed by the dread that insanity was coming upon her. Rouletabille, in telling me of this interview, acknowledged to me that he had taken altogether different means to calm Mathilde from those which Robert Darzac had employed—that is, he made no effort to conceal from her that her eyes had seen clearly and had seen Frederic Larsan. When she was told that Robert Darzac had only denied the truth to her because he feared for its effect upon her, and that he had been the first to telegraph to Rouletabille to come to their aid, she heaved a sigh so long and so deep that it was almost a sob. She took Rouletabille's hands in her own and covered them with kisses, just as a mother kisses the hands of her little child. Evidently she was instinctively drawn toward the youth by all the mysterious forces of maternal affection, in spite of the fact that she had every reason to believe that her child had died years before. It was just at this point that the two had first noticed through the window of the tower the form of Frederic Larsan, standing erect in the boat. At first, both had remained, stupefied, motionless and mute at the sight. Then a cry of rage escaped from the agonised heart of Rouletabille, and he longed to pursue the man and reckon with him, face to face. I have told how Mathilde held him back, clinging to him upon the parapet. In her mind, apparently, horrible as was this resurrection of Larsan, it was less horrible than the continual and supernatural resurrection of a Larsan who had no existence save in her own diseased brain. She no longer saw Larsan everywhere around her. She saw him in the flesh, as he was.

At one moment trembling with nervousness, the next gentle and composed, now patient and in another instant impatient, Mathilde, even while conversing with Arthur Rance, showed for her husband the most charming and sweetest solicitude imaginable. She was attentive to him at every moment, serving him herself, and smiling gently at him as she did so, watching him carefully, to be sure that he was not overtired and that the light did not strike too near his eyes. Robert thanked her for her cares, but seemed none the less frightfully unhappy. And his demeanour compelled me to recollect the fact that the resuscitation of Larsan would undoubtedly recall to Mme. Darzac that before she was Mme. Darzac, she had been Mme. Jean Roussel Ballmeyer Larsan before God and herself, and even, so far as the transatlantic laws are concerned, before men as well.

If the design of Larsan in showing himself had been to deal a frightful blow to a happiness which had yet scarcely begun, he had completely succeeded. And, perhaps, as the historian of all parts of this strange affair, I ought to mention the fact that Mathilde had given Robert Darzac at once to understand that she did not regard herself as his wife, since the man to whom she had pledged herself in her early girlhood was still living. I have said that Mathilde Stangerson had been brought up in a very religious manner, not by her father, who cared little for such things, but by her female relatives, especially her old aunt in Cincinnati. The scientific studies which she had pursued with her father had in no wise impaired her faith, while the latter had taken care never to speak against religion to his daughter. She had preserved it, even in the deepest researches into the professor's theory of the creation. She said to him that no matter how plausibly he might prove that everything came from nothingness, that is to say, from the atmosphere, and returned to nothingness in the end, it remained to prove that that nothing, originating from nothing, had not been created by God. And, as she was a good Catholic, she believed that the Vicar of Christ on earth was the Pope. I might have perhaps passed over these religious beliefs of Mathilde in silence, if they had not had so strong an influence on the resolution which she had taken in regard to her second husband, when she discovered that her first husband was still alive. It had seemed to her that Larsan's death had been proven beyond the slightest doubt, and she had gone to her new husband as a widow with the approval of her confessor. And now she learned that in the sight of Heaven, she was not a widow, but a bigamist But, at all events, the catastrophe might not be irremediable, and she herself proposed to poor M. Darzac that the case should be propounded to the ecclesiastical courts of Rome for a settlement as quickly as possible. Thus it was that M. and Mme. Robert Darzac, forty-eight hours after their marriage in the Church of St. Nicolas du Chardonnet, were separated by a gulf over which one could not and the other would not pass. The reader will comprehend from this brief explanation the mournful demeanour of Robert and the gentle sweetness displayed toward him by Mathilde.

Without being entirely conversant with all these details on the evening of which I write, I nevertheless suspected most of them. Leaving the Darzacs, my eyes wandered to the neighbour of Mme. Darzac, M. Arthur William Rance, and my thoughts were taking a new turn, when they were suddenly arrested by the butler's coming to say that Bernier, the concierge, requested to speak to M. Rouletabille. My friend arose, excused himself, and left the room.

"What!" I cried. "The Berniers are no longer at the Glandier?"

Readers of "The Mystery of the Yellow Room" will recall that these Berniers—the man and his wife—were the concierges of M. Stangerson at Ste. Genevieve-des Bois. I have told in that work how Rouletabille had had them set at liberty when they were accused of complicity in the attempt made at the pavilion de la Chenaie. Their gratitude to the young reporter on this account had been of the greatest, and Rouletabille had been ever since the object of their devotion. M. Stangerson replied to my exclamation by informing me that all the servants had left the Glandier at the time that he himself had abandoned it. As the Rances had need of concierges for the Fort of Hercules, the Professor had been glad to send them his faithful domestics, of whom he had never had reason to complain except for one slight infraction of the game laws, which had turned out most unfortunately for them. Now they were lodged in one of the towers of the postern, where they kept the gate, and from which they admitted those who entered and dismissed those who wished to go out of the fort.

Rouletabille had not appeared in the least astonished when the butler announced that Bernier wished to say a word to him, and from that fact, I drew the conclusion that he must be already aware of his presence at Rochers Rouges. So I discovered, without being very greatly surprised at it, that Rouletabille had made excellent use of the few minutes during which I believed him to be in his room, and which I had given up to my toilet and to chatting with M. Darzac.

The unexpected exit of Rouletabille sent a chill to my heart and seemed to spread a general sensation of alarm throughout the company. Every one of us who was in the secret asked himself whether this summons had not something to do with some important event connected with the return of Larsan. Mme. Darzac was very restless. And because Mathilde showed herself to be disturbed and nervous, I fancied that M.

Arthur Rance thought that it behooved him to display some little anxiety. And it may be as well to say at this point that M. Arthur Rance and his wife were not aware of the whole of the unfortunate story of Professor Stangerson's daughter. It had seemed useless to inform them of the fact of Mathilde's secret marriage to Jean Roussel, afterward known as Larsan. That was something which concerned only the family. But they were fully aware—Arthur Rance from having been mixed up in the Glandier business, and his wife from what he had told her—of the way in which the Secret Service agent had pursued the young woman who was now Mme. Darzac. The crimes of Larsan were explained in the eyes of Arthur Rance by a mad passion for Mathilde, and this was by no means surprising to the young American who had been for so long in love with her himself, and who perceived in all of Larsan's acts merely the indications of an insane and hopeless love. As to Mme. Edith, I soon found out why the events which had transpired at the Glandier had not seemed so simple to her when they were related to her as they had to her husband. For her to share his opinions on the subject, it would have been necessary for her to have seen Mathilde with eyes as enthusiastic as those of Arthur Rance, and, on the contrary, her thoughts (which I had good opportunities to read without her suspecting it) ran about in this way: "But what on earth is there about this woman which could inspire such an insane passion, lasting for years and years in the heart of any man! Here is a woman for whose sake a detective officer becomes a murderer; for whom a temperate man becomes a drunkard, and for whom an innocent man permits himself to be pronounced guilty of a felony. What is there about her more than there is about myself who owe my husband to the fact that she refused him before he ever saw me? What is the charm about her? She isn't even young. And yet even now my husband forgets all about me while he is looking at her." That is what I read in Edith's eyes as she watched her husband gazing at Mathilde. Ah, those black eyes of the gentle, languid Mme. Edith!

I am congratulating myself upon the explanations which I have made to the reader. It is as well that he should know the sentiments which dwelt in the heart of each one concerned at the moment when all were about to have their own parts to play in the strange and awful drama which was already drawing near in the shadow which enveloped the Fort of Hercules. As yet, I have said nothing of Old Bob nor of Prince Galitch, but, never fear, their turn will come! I have taken as a rule in the narration of this affair to paint things and people as nearly as possible as they appeared to me in the development of events. Thus the reader will pass through all the phases of the tragedy as we ourselves passed through them—anguish and peace, mysteries and their unravelling, misunderstanding and comprehension. If the light breaks upon the mind of the reader before the hour when it broke upon mine, so much the better. As he will be conversant with the same circumstances, neither more nor less, which came under our observation, he will prove to himself if he solves the mystery before it is revealed to him, that he possesses a brain worthy to rank with that of Rouletabille.

We finished our repast without our young friend having reappeared, and we arose from the table without having mentioned to each other any of the thoughts which troubled us. Mathilde immediately asked me where I thought Rouletabille had gone. As she left the dining room, and I walked with her as far as the entrance to the fort; M. Darzac and Mme. Edith followed us. M. Stangerson had bidden us good-night. Arthur Rance, who had disappeared for a moment, joined us while we were at the passageway. The night was clear and the moon shone brightly. Someone had lighted the lanterns in the archway, however, in spite of the fact that their rays were not needed for seeing. As we passed beneath the arch, we heard

Rouletabille speaking, as though he were encouraging those whom he addressed.

"Come on! One more effort!" he cried, and the voice which answered him was husky and panting, like that of a sailor who was working with his fellows to bring his bark into port. Finally, a great tumult filled our ears. It was the two portals of the immense iron doors, which were being closed for the first time in more than an hundred years.

Mme. Edith looked astonished at the act of her guest, and asked what had happened to the gate, which had always served in place of the doors since she had been mistress of the place. But Arthur Rance caught her arm, and she seemed to understand that he was impressing upon her that she must keep silence. But that did not keep her from exclaiming in a not-too-well pleased tone:

"Really! Anyone would think that we expected to undergo a siege!"

But Rouletabille beckoned our group into the garden and announced to us in a jesting tone that if any of us had any desire to make a trip to the village, we must give it up for that evening, for the order had gone forth and no one could leave the château or enter it. Pere Jacques, he added, still pretending to jest, was charged with the carrying out of the command, and everyone knew that it was impossible to bribe the faithful old servitor. It was then that I learned for the first time that Pere Jacques, whom I had known so well at the Glandier, had accompanied Professor Stangerson on his visit and was acting as his valet. That night he was sleeping in a tiny closet in "la Louve," near his master's bedroom, but Rouletabille had changed that, and it was Pere Jacques who took the place of the concierges in the tower marked A.

"But where are the Berniers?" cried Mme. Edith.

"They are installed in the Square Tower, in the room on the left, near the entrance; they are to act as caretakers of the Square Tower," replied Rouletabille.

"But the Square Tower doesn't need any caretakers!" exclaimed Edith, whose vexation was plainly visible.

"That, Madame," returned the young reporter, "is what we cannot be sure of."

He made no further explanations, but he took M. Arthur Rance to one side and informed him that he ought to tell his wife about the reappearance of Larsan. If there was to be the slightest chance of hiding the truth from M. Stangerson, it could scarcely be accomplished without the aid and intelligence of Mme. Edith. And, then, too, it would be as well, henceforward, for all of those in the Fort of Hercules to be prepared for everything, *and surprised at nothing*!

The next act of Rouletabille was to make us walk across the court and place ourselves at the postern of the gardener. I have said that this postern (H) commanded the entrance to the inner court; but at that point the moat had been filled up a long time ago. Rouletabille, to our amazement, declared that the next day he intended to have the moat dug out and to replace the drawbridge. For the present, he busied himself with ordering the postern to be closed more securely by the servants of the château by means of a sort of fortification built from the boards and bricks which had been used in the repairs of the château, and which had not yet been taken away by the workmen. Thus the château was barricaded and Rouletabille laughed softly to himself, for Mme. Edith, having been apprised by her husband of the facts of the case, made no further objection, but contented herself with smiling a little contemptuously at the timidity of her guests, who were transforming the old stronghold into an absolutely impenetrable spot, because they were afraid of just one man—one man, all alone. But Mme. Edith did not know what manner of man this was. She had not lived through the mysteries of the yellow room.

As to the others—Arthur Rance among them—they found it perfectly natural and reasonable that Rouletabille should fortify the place against that which was unknown and mysterious and invisible, and which plotted in the night they knew not what against the Fort of Hercules.

At the newly fortified postern, Rouletabille had stationed no one, for he reserved that place that night for himself. From there he could obtain a complete view of both the inner and outer courts. It was a strategic point which commanded a view of the whole château. One could reach the apartment of the Darzacs only after passing by Pere Jacques in A; by Rouletabille at H, and by the Berniers, who guarded the Square Tower at the door marked K. The young man had decided that it would be better for those on guard not to retire that night. As we passed by the "oubliette" in the Court of Charles the Bold, I saw by the light of the moon that someone had displaced the circular board which covered it. I saw also on the margin a flask attached to a cord. Rouletabille explained to me that he had wished to know if this old oubliette (which was really nothing but a well) corresponded with the sea, and that he had found that the water was clear and sweet—a proof that it had nothing to do with the Mediterranean.

The young man walked for a few steps with Mme. Darzac, who immediately took leave of us and entered the Square Tower. M. Darzac and Arthur Rance, at the request of Rouletabille, remained with us. Some words of excuse addressed to Mme. Edith made her understand that she was being politely asked to retire, and she bade us good-night with a nonchalant grace, flinging the words, "Good-night, M. le Captain," at Rouletabille over her shoulder as she passed him.

When we were alone, we men, Rouletabille beckoned us toward the postern into the little room of the gardener, a dark, low-ceiled apartment, where we were surprised to find how easily we could see anything that passed near by without being seen ourselves. There, Arthur Rance, Robert Darzac, Rouletabille and myself, without even lighting a lamp, held our first council of war. In truth, I know not what other name to give to this reunion of frightened men, hidden behind the stones of this old fortress.

"We may make our plans here in tranquillity," began Rouletabille. "No one can hear us, and we shall not be surprised by anyone. If any person should attempt to pass the first gate which Jacques is guarding without the old man's seeing him, we shall be immediately warned by the sentinel whom I have stationed in the very middle of the court, hidden in the ruins of the chapel. I have placed your gardener, Mattoni, at that point, M. Rance. I believe from what I have been told that you can depend upon the man. Is not that your opinion?"

I listened to Rouletabille with admiration. Mme. Edith was right. He had indeed constituted himself a captain, and he had not left one impregnable spot without defence, and had neglected nothing in his cogitations. I felt certain that he would never surrender, no matter on what terms, and that he would prefer death to capitulation, either for himself or for any of the rest of us. What a brave little commander he was! And, indeed, it seemed to me that he displayed more bravery in undertaking the defence of the Fort of Hercules against Larsan than the Lords of Mortola had shown in holding the castle against a thousand of the enemy. For they had fought merely against shot and shell and spears. And what had we to fight against? The darkness. Where was our enemy? Everywhere and nowhere. We were able neither to see him, nor to know his whereabouts, nor to guess his designs, nor to take the offensive ourselves, ignorant as we were of where our blows might fall. There remained for us only to be on guard, to shut ourselves in, to watch and to wait.

M. Arthur Rance assured Rouletabille that he could answer for his gardener, Mattoni, and our young man proceeded to explain to us in a general fashion the situation. He lit his pipe, took three or four puffs, and said:

"Well, here we are. Can we hope that Larsan, after having so insolently flaunted himself before us, at our very doors, in order to defy us, will confine himself to such a platonic manifestation? Will he consider that he has accomplished enough in bringing trouble, terror and consternation among the members of the besieged party in the garrison? And content with what he has done, will he go away? I hardly think so. First, because such a thing would be foreign to his character—for he loves a fight, and is never satisfied with a partial success; and, secondly, because no one of us has the power to drive him off. Consider that he can do anything that he will to injure us, but that we can make no move against him save to defend ourselves if he strikes, provided we are able when it may suit him to do so. We have, of course, no hope of any help from outside. And he knows it well; that is what makes him so bold and audacious. Whom can we call to our aid?"

"The authorities," suggested Arthur Rance. He spoke with some hesitation, for he felt that if this plan had not been entertained by Rouletabille, there must be some reason for it.

The young reporter looked at his host with an air of pity, which was not entirely free from reproach. And he said in a chilly tone, which showed plainly to Arthur Rance how little value there was in his proposition:

"You ought to understand, Monsieur, that I did not save Larsan from French justice at Versailles to deliver him over to Italian justice at Rochers Rouges."

M. Arthur Rance, who was, as I have said, ignorant of the first marriage of Professor Stangerson's daughter, could not understand, as did the rest of us, the impossibility of revealing the existence of Larsan without stirring up (especially after the ceremony at St. Nicolas du Chardonnet) the worst of scandals and the most dreadful of catastrophes: but certain inexplicable incidents of the trial at Versailles had impressed him sufficiently to make him realize that we dreaded above all things to bring again to the public mind what someone had called "The Mystery of Mlle. Stangerson."

He comprehended this on the evening of which I speak better than he had ever done before, and knew that Larsan must hold one of those terrible secrets on which life and honour depend, and with which the magistrates of the world can have no concern.

M. Rance bowed to M. Robert Darzac without uttering a word: but the salute signified the declaration that M. Arthur Rance was ready to combat for the cause of Mathilde, whatever it might be, as a noble chevalier, who does not bother himself about the reason of the battle in the moment when he dies for his lady. At least, I thus interpreted his gesture, and I felt certain that, in spite of his recent marriage, the American had by no means forgotten his old love.

M. Darzac said:

"This man must disappear, but in silence, whether we move him by our entreaties, or bribe him or kill him. But the first condition of his disappearance is to keep the fact that he has reappeared at all a secret. Above all—and I am speaking of the heartfelt wish of Mme. Darzac as well as my own—M. Stangerson must never know that we are menaced by the blows of this monster."

"Mme. Darzac's wishes are commands," replied Rouletabille. "M. Stangerson shall know nothing."

We went on to discuss the situation in regard to the servants and to what one might expect from them. Happily, Pere Jacques and the Berniers were already partly in the secret and would be astonished at nothing. Mattoni was devoted enough to render unquestioning obedience to Mme. Edith. The others did not count. Later there would be Walter, the servant of Old Bob, but he had accompanied his master to Paris, and would not return until he did.

Rouletabille arose, exchanged through the window a signal with Bernier, who was standing erect upon the threshold of the Square Tower. Then he came back to us and sat down again.

"Larsan probably is not far off," he said. "During dinner I made a tour of observation around the place. We possess at the North gate a natural means of defence which is really marvellous, and which completely replaces the old fortifications of the château. We have there fifty paces away, at the western shore, the two frontier posts of the French and Italian revenue officers, whose untiring vigilance may be of the greatest assistance to us. Pere Bernier is on the most friendly terms with these worthy people, and I am going with him to talk to them. The Italian customs officer speaks only Italian, but the French officer speaks both languages, as well as the patois of the country, and it is this man, whom Bernier tells me is called Michael, to whom I look to be of the greatest use to us. Through his means we have already learned that the two revenue posts are much interested in the strange manoeuvres of the little boat, which belongs to Tullio, the fisherman, whom they call 'the hangman of the sea.' Old Tullio is one of the former acquaintances of the customs men. He is the most skillful smuggler on the coast. He had with him this evening in his boat an individual whom the revenue officers had never seen. The boat, Tullio and the passenger, all disappeared at the Pointe de Garibaldi. I have been there with Pere Bernier, and we found nothing, any more than M. Darzac, who visited the spot before us. However, Larsan must have landed. I have a presentiment of the fact. In any case, I am sure that Tullio's little boat is anchored near the Pointe de Garabaldi."

"You are sure of that?" cried M. Darzac.

"What reason have you for thinking so?" I demanded.

"Bah!" exclaimed Rouletabille. "It left the marks of the keel in the sand on the bank, and when they anchored, they let fall a little lantern, which I picked up and which the revenue officers recognised as the one used by Tullio when he fishes in the waters on calm nights."

"Larsan certainly landed!" repeated M. Darzac. "He is at Rochers Rouges."

"In any case, if the boat has been left at Rochers Rouges, he has not come back here," exclaimed Rouletabille. "The two revenue posts are situated upon the narrow road which leads from Rochers Rouges to France, and are placed in such a manner that no one can pass by whether by day or by night without being seen. You know besides that the Red Rocks from which the village takes its name from a cul de sac, and that a sentinel is on guard in front of these rocks every hundred meters around the frontier. The sentinel passes between the rocks and the sea. The rocks are steep and form a terrace sixty meters high."

"That is true," said Arthur Rance, who had not recently spoken, and who seemed greatly interested. "It is not easy to scale the rocks."

"He will have hidden himself in the grottoes," said Darzac. "There are some deep pockets in the terrace."

"I thought of that," said Rouletabille. "And I went back alone to Rochers Rouges, after I left Pere Bernier."

"That was very imprudent!" I said.

"It was very prudent," corrected Rouletabille. "I had some things to say to Larsan which I did not wish a third party to hear. Well, I went back to Rochers Rouges and called Larsan's name through all the caves."

"You called him?" cried Arthur Rance.

"Yes, I shouted into the gathering night; I waved my handkerchief as the soldiers wave their flag of truce. But whether it was that he heard me and saw my white flag or not, he did not answer."

"Perhaps he was not there," I suggested.

"Perhaps not: I don't know. I heard a noise in the grotto."

"And you did not enter?" demanded Arthur Rance.

"No," replied Rouletabille, quietly. "But you do not think that it was because I was afraid of him, do you?"

"Let us run!" we all cried in one breath, rising at the same moment. "Let us go and finish up the business immediately."

"I don't think that we shall ever have a better chance of meeting Larsan," said Arthur Rance. "We can do what we like with him at the bottom of Rochers Rouges."

Darzac and Arthur Rance were already starting off; I waited to see what Rouletabille would say. He calmed the two men with a gesture, and begged them to be seated again.

"It is necessary to remember," he said, "that Larsan would have acted exactly as he has done if he had wished to lure us tonight to the grotto of Rochers Rouges. He has shown himself to us; he has landed almost under our eyes at the Point of Garabaldi; he might as well have shouted under our windows, 'You know I am at Rochers Rouges. I'll wait for you there.' He would have been neither more explicit or more eloquent."

"You went to Rochers Rouges," resumed Arthur Rance, who I saw was deeply impressed with the arguments of Rouletabille—"and he did not show himself. He hid himself, meditating on some horrible crime to be committed tonight. We must have him out of that grotto."

"Doubtless," replied Rouletabille, "my promenade to Rochers Rouges produced no result because I was all alone—but if we all go, I can assure you that we shall find some results on our return."

"On our return?" echoed Darzac who did not understand.

"Yes," explained Rouletabille: "on our return to the château, where we have left Mme. Darzac all alone—and where, perhaps, we may not find her. Oh, of course," he added, as a general silence fell upon his companions, "it is only a hypothesis. But at this time we have no other means of reasoning than by hypothesis."

We looked at each other and this hypothesis overwhelmed us. Evidently, without Rouletabille, we should have committed a terrible blunder and perhaps have been responsible for a terrible disaster.

Rouletabille arose and continued, thoughtfully:

"You see, tonight there is nothing that we can do except to barricade ourselves. It is only a temporary barricade, for I want the place put in an absolutely unassailable state tomorrow. I have had the iron doors closed and Pere Jacques is guarding them. I have stationed Mattoni as sentinel at the chapel. I have established a barrier under the postern, the only vulnerable point of the inner court, and I will guard that myself. Pere Bernier will watch all night at the door of the Square Tower, and Mere Bernier, who has a good pair of eyes, and to whom I have given a spyglass, will remain until morning on the platform of the tower. Sainclair will station himself in the little palm leaf pavilion upon the terrace of the Round Tower. From the height of this terrace he will watch as I do all the inner court and the boulevards and parapets. M. Rance and M. Darzac will go into the garden and walk until daylight, the one toward the boulevard on the west, the other toward the boulevard on the east—the two boulevards which are at the edge of the outer court near the sea. The vigil will be hard tonight, because we are not yet organised. Tomorrow we shall draw up a set of rules for our little garrison, and a list of the trustworthy domestics upon whom we may depend with security.

"If there is one on the place who could come under the slightest suspicion, he must be dismissed at once. You will bring here to this cell all the arms which you can gather—rifles and revolvers. We will divide them among those who do guard duty. The sentinel is to draw upon every person who does not reply to 'Who goes there?' and who is not recognised. There is no need of a password, it would be useless. Let the countersign be to utter one's name and to show one's face. Besides, it is only ourselves who have the right to pass. Beginning tomorrow morning I will have raised at the inner entrance of the North gate the grating which until today formed its exterior entrance—the entrance which is closed, henceforth, by the iron doors; and in the daytime the commissaires can come as far as this grating with their provisions. They will place their wares in the little lodge in the tower where I have stationed Pere Jacques. At seven o'clock every night, the iron doors will be closed. Tomorrow morning M. Arthur Rance will send for builders, masons and carpenters. Every person on the place will be counted, and no one allowed, under any pretext, to pass the door of the second court. Before seven o'clock in the evening everyone will be counted again, and the workpeople will be allowed to go out. In this one day the men must completely finish their work, which will consist of making a door for my postern, repairing a small breach in the wall which joins the New Castle to the Tower of Charles the Bold and another little break near the Round Tower (B in the plan), which defends the northeast corner of the outer court. After that, I shall be tranquil, and Mme. Darzac, who is forbidden to leave the château under the new order, having been placed in security, I may attempt a sortie and enter seriously into the search for the camp of Larsan. Come, M. Rance, to arms! Bring me some weapons to pass around this evening. I have loaned my own revolver to Pere Bernier, who is keeping guard before the door of Mme. Darzac's apartments."

Anyone not knowing of the events at the Glandier who had heard the words spoken by Rouletabille would have considered both him who spoke and us who listened to be beside ourselves. But, I repeat, if anyone had lived, like myself, through that terrible and mysterious time, he would have done what I did—loaded his revolver and waited for dawn without uttering a word.

# VIII

## WHICH CONTAINS SOME PAGES FROM THE HISTORY OF JEAN ROUSSEL-LARSAN BALLMEYER

An hour later, we were all at our posts, passing along the parapets in the moonlight, keeping close watch upon the land, the sky and the water, and listening anxiously to the slightest sounds of the night—the sighing of the sea and the voices of the birds which began to sing at about three o'clock in the morning. Mme. Edith, who said that she could not sleep, came out and talked to Rouletabille at his postern. The lad called me, placed me in charge of his postern and of Mrs. Rance, and made his rounds. The fair Edith was in the most charming humour. She looked as fresh as a rose washed in dew, and she seemed to be greatly amused at the wan countenance of her husband, to whom she had brought out a glass of whisky.

"It's the funniest thing I ever heard of," she exclaimed, clapping her tiny hands. "All of you keeping watch out here like this! How I wish I knew your Larsan! I'm sure I should adore him!"

I shuddered involuntarily at the words she uttered so lightly. Beyond a doubt there do exist romantic little creatures who fear nothing, and who in their carelessness jest at fate. Ah! if the unhappy girl had only realised what was to come!

I spent two delightful hours with Mme. Edith, during the greater part of which I related to her some facts regarding the history of Ballmeyer. And since this occasion presents itself, I will at this time relate to the reader, in historical order—if I may use an expression which perfectly interprets my meaning—the characteristics and circumstances in the career of Larsan-Ballmeyer, some of which had been sufficient to make it doubtful whether he still lived at the time that he appeared to play so unexpected a part in "The Mystery of the Yellow Room." As this man's powers will be seen to extend in "The Perfume of the Lady in Black" to heights which some may believe inaccessible, I judge it to be my duty to prepare the mind of the reader to admit in the end that I am only the transcriber of an affair the like of which never has been known before, and that I have invented nothing. And, moreover, Rouletabille, in the event that I might have the hardihood to add to such a wonderful and veracious history any rhetorical ornaments or exaggerations, would certainly contradict me and riddle my story as with bullets. The great interests at stake are such that the slightest exaggeration would assuredly entail the most terrible consequences, so that I shall keep strictly to the exact details of my narrative, even at the risk of making it seem a little dry and methodical. I will refer those who believe in actual records to the stenographic reports of the trial at Versailles. M. Andre-Hesse and M. Henri Robert, who appeared for M. Robert Darzac, made admirable addresses, to which the public may easily obtain access. And it must not be forgotten that before destiny had brought Larsan-Ballmeyer and Joseph Rouletabille into contact, the elegantly mannered bandit had given considerable trouble to the authorities. We have only to open the files of the *Gazette les Tribuneaux* and to read the account of the day when Larsan was condemned by the Court of Assizes to ten years at hard labour, to be assured on this score. Then, one will understand that there is no need of inventing anything about a man concerning whom one can with truth relate such a history: and thus the reader, knowing the sort of man that he is—that is to say, his manner of working and his incredible audacity—will refrain from smiling because Joseph Rouletabille placed a drawbridge between Larsan-Ballmeyer and Mathilde Darzac.

M. Albert Bataille of *le Figaro*, who has published an admirable work on "Criminal and Civil Causes," has devoted some interesting pages to Ballmeyer.

Ballmeyer had a happy childhood and youth. He did not become a criminal as so many others have done because driven to evil doing by the hard blows of poverty and misery. The son of a rich broker in the Rue Molay, he might have chosen any vocation that he desired, but his preferred calling was to lay hands upon the money of other people. At an early age, he decided to become a swindler, just as another lad might have decided to become an engineer. His debut was a stroke of genius, and the history of it is almost incredible. Ballmeyer stole a letter addressed to his father containing a considerable sum of money. Then he took the train for Lyons and from there wrote his parent as follows:

"Monsieur, I am an old soldier, retired and with a medal of honour to show that I have served my country. My son, a post office clerk, has stolen in the mails a letter addressed to you and containing money, to pay a gambling debt. I have called the members of the family together. In a few days we shall be able to raise the sum necessary to repay you. You are a father. Have pity upon a father. Do not bring me down in sorrow and shame to my grave."

M. Ballmeyer willingly granted the petition. He is still waiting for his first remittance—or, rather, he has ceased to expect it, for the law apprised him ten years ago of the identity of the culprit.

Ballmeyer, relates M. Albert Bataille, seems to have received from nature all the gifts which go to make the successful swindler: a wonderful diversity, the talent of persuading new acquaintances to believe in him, the careful attention to the smallest details, the genius for completely disguising himself (he even took the precaution along this line of having his linen marked with different initials every time that he judged it expedient to change his name). But his strongest characteristic of all was his astonishing aptitude for evasion—for coquetting with fraud, for mocking at and defying justice. This was evinced in the malignant pleasure which he took in speaking of himself at Parquet as among those who might have been guilty, knowing how little importance would be attached by the magistrate by the clues which he gave.

This delight in jesting at the judges was apparent in every act of his life.

While he was doing military duty, Ballmeyer stole his companions box and accused the captain.

He committed a theft of forty thousand francs from the Maison Furet, and immediately afterward denounced M. Furet as having stolen it himself.

The Furet affair remained for a long time celebrated among judicial records under the appellation of "the coup of the telephone." Science, applied as an aid to knavery, has never given anything better.

Ballmeyer appropriated a draft for six thousand livres sterling from the messenger of Messrs. Furet, brothers, who were note brokers in the Rue Poissoniere, and who allowed him desk room in their offices.

He went to the Rue Poissoniere, into the house of M. Furet, and, imitating the voice of M. Edouard Furet, asked over the telephone of M. Cohen, a banker, whether he would be willing to discount the draft. M. Cohen replied in the affirmative, and ten minutes later, Ballmeyer, after having cut the telephone wire to prevent further communication and possible explanations, sent for the money by a companion named Rigaud, whom he had known not long before in the African battalion, where their common interests had made them useful to each other.

Ballmeyer kept the lion's share for himself: then he rushed to the court to denounce Rigaud, and, as I have said, M. Furet himself.

A dramatic scene took place when accuser and accused were confronted with each other in the cabinet of M. Espierre, the judge of instruction who had charge of the affair.

"You know, my dear Furet," said Ballmeyer to the amased broker, "I am heartbroken at being obliged to expose you, but you must tell the Justice the truth. It is not an affair from which you need fear serious consequences. Why don't you confess? You needed forty thousand francs to pay a little debt incurred at the race track and you intended to pay back the sum. It was you who telephoned?"

"I! I!" stammered M. Edouard Furet, almost breathless with rage and astonishment.

"You may as well confess," said Ballmeyer. "No one could mistake your voice."

The bold thief was detected within eight days and was caught; and the police furnished such a report upon him that M. Cruppi, then attorney general, now Minister of Commerce, presented to M. Furet the most humble excuses of the Department of Justice. Rigaud was also tried and condemned to twenty years at hard labour.

One might go on relating this kind of stories about Ballmeyer indefinitely. At that time, before he had entered upon the darker and more horrible pages of his career, he played a comedy—and what a comedy! It may be as well to give in detail the history of one of his escapes. Nothing could be more immensely comical than the adventure of the prisoner composing a long memorial during his trial for the sole purpose of hanging over the table of the judge, M. Villars, and of turning over the papers in order to obtain a glimpse of the formula of orders of discharge.

When he was sent back to jail at Mazas, the fellow wrote a letter signed "Villars," in which, according to the prescribed formula, M. Villars requested the superintendent of the prison to set the prisoner, Ballmeyer, at liberty without delay. But he had no paper of the kind used by the Judge for such matters.

However, so small a thing as that scarcely embarrassed Ballmeyer. He went back to the courthouse in the morning, hiding the letter in his sleeve, protested his innocence and feigning great indignation and anger. He picked up the seal that lay on the table and gesticulated with it in expressing his wrath, and he knocked the inkstand over on the blue trousers of his guard. While the poor fellow, surrounded by the inmates of the courtroom, who condoled with him on his ill luck, was sadly sponging off his "Number One," Ballmeyer profited by the general diversion to apply a strong pressure of the stamp upon the order of discharge, and then began loudly excusing himself to the soldier.

The trick succeeded. The thief made his way out amid the confusion, and, negligently tossing the signed and sealed paper to the guards, remarked carelessly:

"What is M. Villars thinking of to order me to carry his papers? Does he take me for his servant?"

Then he went back to his seat. The guards picked up the paper, and one of them carried it to the warden at Mazas, to whom it was addressed. It was the order to set Ballmeyer at liberty without delay. The same night, Ballmeyer was free.

This was his second escape. Arrested for the Furet affair, he had gotten away once by throwing pepper in the eyes of the guard who was taking him to the station, and that same evening he was present in evening dress at a first night at the Comedie Francaise. Prior to this, at the time when he had been sentenced by court martial to five years' imprisonment because he had robbed his companion, he had made his way out of the Cherche Midi by having one of his comrades forge an order of release for him. A variation of the same plan had served him well once more.

But one would never finish if one tried to relate all the amazing adventures of Ballmeyer.

Known at various times as the Count de Maupas, Vicomte Drouet d'erion, Comte de Motteville, Comte de Bonneville, and under many other aliases, as an elegant man about town, setting the fashion, he frequented the summer resorts and watering places—Biarritz, Aix les Bains, Luchon, losing in play at the club as much as ten thousand francs in one evening, surrounded by pretty women, who envied each other his attentions—for this fellow was extremely popular with the fair sex. In his regiment, he had made a conquest—happily platonic—of the Colonel's daughter. Do you know the type now?

Well, it was with this man that Joseph Rouletabille was going to fight.

I thought that morning that I had sufficiently informed Mme. Edith in regard to the personality of the bandit. She listened so silently that my attention was finally drawn to the fact that she had not uttered a remark in some time, and, bending down, I saw that she was fast asleep. This circumstance should not have given me a very good opinion of the little creature. But, as I watched her sleeping face at my leisure, I felt springing up in my soul feelings which I later endeavoured in vain to chase away from my mind.

The night passed without any event. When the day dawned, I saluted it with a deep sigh of relief. Nevertheless, Rouletabille did not permit me to retire until eight o'clock in the morning, after he had settled on how matters should go on through the day. He was already in the midst of the workmen whom he had summoned, and who were labouring actively in repairing the breaches of the tower B. The work was done so expeditiously and so promptly that the strong château of Hercules was soon sealed as hermetically close as it was possible for a building to be. Seated on a big boulder in the bright sunlight, Rouletabille began to draw upon his notebook the plan which I have submitted to the reader, and he said to me while I, worn out with my vigil, was making absurd efforts to keep my eyes open:

"You see, Sainclair, these people believe that I am fortifying the place to defend myself. Well, that is merely a small part of the truth, for I am fortifying the place because reason bids me do so. And, if I close up the breaches, it is less in order that Larsan cannot get in than for the sake of depriving my reason of any chance of accusing me of carelessness. For instance, I can never reason in a forest. How will you reason in a forest? There, reason flies away on every side. But in a closed up château! My friend, it is like a sealed casket. If you are inside and are not insane, your reasoning powers must come back to you."

"Yes, yes," I murmured sleepily, nodding.

"That's it—your reason will come back to you—"

"Well, well, never mind!" answered Rouletabille. "Go to bed, old fellow. You are walking in your sleep now."

# IX

# IN WHICH "OLD BOB" UNEXPECTEDLY ARRIVES

When I heard a knock at my door about eleven o'clock in the morning and the voice of Mere Bernier told me that Rouletabille wanted me to get up, I threw my window wide open and looked out in delight. The bay was of an incomparable beauty, and the sea was so transparent that the rays of the sun pierced through it as they would have done through a mirror without quicksilver, so that one could perceive the rocks, the anemones and the moss in the sea bottom just as if the waters had ceased to cover them and left them bared to the eye. The harmonious curve of the bank on the Mentone side enclosed the sea like a flowery frame. The villas of Garavan, white and rose, looked like fresh flowers which had blossomed overnight. The peninsula of Hercules was a bouquet which floated upon the waters and perfumed the old stones of the château.

Never had nature appeared to me more sweet, more delightful, more exquisite, nor, above all, more worthy of being loved. The serene air, the beautiful shore, the balmy sea, the purple mountains, all this picture to which my Northern senses were so little accustomed, evoked in my mind the thought of some tender, caressing human being. As these thoughts passed through my mind, I noticed a man who was lashing the sea.

Oh! he gave it a box on the ear! I could have wept if I had been a poet! The miserable wretch appeared to be furiously angry. I could not understand what had excited his wrath in this tranquil spot, but he evidently felt that he had some serious cause for vexation, for he never ceased his blows. He was armed with an enormous cudgel, and, standing erect in a tiny boat, into which a timid child might have feared to entrust its weight, he administered to the sea, with the fiercest splashings, such a castigation as provoked the mute indignation of some strangers who were standing on the shore. But as everyone under all circumstances dreads to mix himself in what is none of his affairs, these persons made no protest. What was it that could have so deeply excited the savage? Perhaps it might have been the very calm of the sea which, after having been for a moment disturbed by the insult of the madman, resumed its peaceful tranquillity.

At this point, I was interrupted by the voice of Rouletabille, who told me that breakfast was nearly ready. Rouletabille appeared in the garb of a plasterer, his clothing showing plainly that he had been working in the fresh mortar. In one hand he held a foot rule and in the other a file. I asked him whether he had seen the man who was beating the water, and he told me that it was Tullio who was frightening the fishes to drive them into his nets. It was for this reason, I realised, that Tullio had obtained the nickname of the "hangman of the sea."

Rouletabille went on to tell me that he had asked Tullio that morning about the stranger whom he had rowed about in his boat the night before, and whom he had taken all around the peninsula of Hercules. Tullio had replied that he had no knowledge whatever of whom the man might be; that he was a crazy sort of fellow whom he had taken in as a passenger at Mentone, and who had given him five francs to land him at the point of Rochers Rouges.

I dressed myself quickly and joined Rouletabille, who told me that we were to have a new guest at luncheon, in the person of "Old Bob." We waited for a few moments for him to come to the table, and then, as he did not appear, we began our repast without him in the flowery frame of the round terrace of Charles the Bold.

There was served to us a delicious bouillabaisse, smoking hot, which seemed to have drawn the best of their flavours from fishes of all species, and was tinted by a little *vino del Paese*, and which, in the light and brightness of the daytime, contributed as much as all the precaution of Rouletabille toward making us feel serene and secure. In truth, we felt not the slightest fear of the dreaded Larsan under the beautiful sunshine of the brilliant heavens, whatever we may have felt in the pale gleam of the moon and stars. Ah, how forgetful and easily impressed human nature is! I am ashamed to say it, but we were feeling rather proud (I speak for Arthur Rance and myself, and also for Edith, whose romantic and languid nature was superficial, as such are likely to be) of the fact that we could smile and speak with scorn of our nocturnal vigils and of our armed guard upon the boulevards of the citadel—when Old Bob made his appearance. And—let me say it: let me say it here—it was not this apparition which could have turned our thoughts toward anything dark or gloomy. I have rarely seen anything more droll than Old Bob walking in the blinding sun of the springtime in the Midi, with a tall hat of black beaver; his black trousers, his black spectacles, his white hair and his rosy cheeks. Yes, yes, we sat there and laughed in the tower of Charles the Bold. And Old Bob laughed with us. For Old Bob was as gay as a child.

What was this old savant doing at the Château of Hercules?

Perhaps this is as good a time as any to explain. How could he have made up his mind to quit his collections in America and his work and his drawings and his museum in Philadelphia?

For these reasons: The reader will not have forgotten that M. Arthur Rance was already looked upon in his own country as the anthropologist of the future at the time when his unhappy infatuation for Mlle. Stangerson had weaned him away from his studies and made them almost distasteful to him. After his marriage to Miss Prescott, who was deeply interested in such matters, he felt that he could resume with pleasure his researches in the science of Gall and Lavater. But at the self-same time that they visited the azure shores in the autumn which preceded the events of this history, there was much discussion in regard to the new discoveries which M. Abbo had just made at Rochers Rouges. M.M. Julien, Riviere, Girardin, Delesot had come to the spot to work, and had succeeded in interesting the Institute and the Minister of Public Instruction in their discoveries. These discoveries soon created a profound sensation, for they proved beyond the shadow of a doubt that primeval man had lived in this spot before the glacial epoch. Without doubt, the proof of the existence of the man of the quarternary epoch had been found long before; but this epoch, extending certainly two hundred thousand years into the past, was interesting in that it fixed the quarternary epoch in the proper period. Learned men were always digging at Rochers Rouges, and they came upon surprise after surprise. However, the most beautiful of the grottoes—the Barma Grande, as they called it in the countryside—had remained intact, for it was the private property of M. Abbo, who kept the "Restaurant of the Grotto" not far away on the seashore. M. Abbo was determined to dig in his own grotto himself. But now, public report (for the event had passed the bounds of the scientific world and interested people generally) said that in the Barma Grande there had been found extraordinary human bones, skeletons remarkably preserved by the ferruginous earth, contemporaneous with the mammoths of the beginning of the quarternary epoch, or even of the end of the tertiary epoch.

Arthur Rance and his wife hastened to Mentone, and while the husband passed his days in antiquarian researches, going back two hundred thousand years, digging up with his own hands the humerus of the Barma Grande and measuring the skulls of his ancestors, his young wife seemed to experience an ever renewed pleasure in rambling over the mediaeval ruins of an old fortress which reared its massive silhouette above a little peninsula, united to Rochers Rouges by a few crumbling stones. The most romantic legends were attached to this relic of the old Genoese wars; and it seemed to Edith, pensively leaning from the highest terrace, in the most beautiful scene in the world, that she was one of those noble demoiselles of ancient times, whose romantic adventures she had so dearly loved to read in the pages of her favourite romances. The castle was for sale and the price was very reasonable. Arthur Rance purchased it, and by doing so made his wife the happiest of women. She sent for masons and furnishers, and within three months she had succeeded in transforming the old fortress into an exquisite nest of love—an ideal abode for a young person who revelled in "The Lady of the Lake," or "The Bride of Lammermoor."

When Arthur Rance had found himself standing beside the last skeleton discovered in the Barma Grande, and knew that the *elephus antiquus* had come out of the same bed of earth, he was beside himself with enthusiasm, and his first impulse had been to telegraph to Old Bob and tell him that it might be that someone had discovered, a few kilometers from Monte Carlo, the relics which the old savant had been seeking for so many years in the mountains of Patagonia. But the telegram never reached its destination, for Old Bob, who had previously promised to join his nephew and niece after they had been married for awhile, had already taken the steamer for Europe. Evidently report had already brought to him the story of the treasures of the Rochers Rouges. A few days after the cable had been dispatched, he landed at Marseilles and arrived at Mentone, where he became the companion of Arthur Rance and his wife in the Château of Hercules, which his very presence seemed to fill with life and gayety.

The gayety of Old Bob appeared to us a little theatrical, but that feeling arose without doubt from the effects of our apprehensions of the evening before. The Old Bob had the soul of a child; he was as much of a coquette as an old woman (that is to say, that his coquetries frequently changed their object), and, having once for all adopted a garb of the most severe—black coat, black waistcoat, black trousers, white hair and rosy cheeks—there was constantly attached to him the idea of complete harmony. It was in this professional uniform that Old Bob had chased the tigers in the pampas and this he wore at the present time while he dug in the grottoes of Rochers Rouges in his search for the missing bone of the *elephus antiquus*.

Mrs. Rance presented him to us, and he uttered a few polite phrases, after which he opened his wide mouth in a great hearty laugh. He was jubilant, and we were soon to learn the reason why. He had brought back from his visit to the Museum of Paris the certainty that the skeleton of the Barma Grande was no more ancient than the one which he had discovered in his last expedition to Terra del Fuego. All the Institute was of this opinion, and took for the basis of its reasonings the fact that the bone of the spine of the *elephus* which Old Bob had carried to Paris, and which the owner of the Barma Grande had loaned him after having declared to him that he had found it in the same bed of earth as the famous skeleton—that this spinal bone belonged, let us say, to an *elephus* of the middle of the quarternary period. Ah, it would have done your heart good to hear the joyous contempt with which Old Bob spoke of the middle of the quarternary period. At the very thought of a spinal bone of the middle of the quarternary period, he laughed as heartily as though someone had told him the finest joke in the world. Could it be that in this day and age, a savant, worthy of being dignified by the name, could find anything to interest him in a skeleton of the middle of the quarternary period! His own skeleton (or, to be more exact, that which he had brought from Terra del Fuego) dated from the commencement of this period, and, in consequence, was older by two thousand years—you hear? *Two thousand years*—! And he was sure, because of this shoulder blade having belonged to the cave bear, the shoulder blade which he had found, he, Old Bob, between the arms of his own skeleton. (He said "my own skeleton" in his enthusiasm, making no distinction between the living skeleton which he was carrying about under his black coat, his black trousers, his white hair and his rosy cheeks, and the prehistoric skeleton of Terra del Fuego.)

"Therefore, my skeleton dates from the cave. But that of Baousse-Raousse! Oh, no, no, my children! At furthest from the epoch of the mammoth, and yet—no—no—from the rhinoceros with the cloven nostrils. Therefore—One has nothing left to discover, ladies and gentlemen, in the period of the rhinoceros with the cleft nostrils.—I swear it, upon the honour of Old Bob. My skeleton comes from the chelleenne epoch, as you say in France. Well, what are you laughing at? I am not even sure that the *elephus* of Rochers Rouges dates from the Mousterian epoch. And why not from the Silurian epoch—or yet—or yet—from the Magdalenian epoch? No, no—that's too much. An *elephus antiquus* from the Magdalenian epoch would be an impossibility. That *elephus* will drive me mad! Ah, I shall die of joy. Poor Baousse-Raousse!"

Mme. Edith had the unkindness to interrupt the jubilations of her uncle by announcing to him that Prince Galitch, who had purchased the Grotto of Romeo and Juliet at Rochers Rouges, must have made some sensational discovery, for she had seen him, the very morning of Old Bob's departure for Paris, passing by the Fort of Hercules, carrying under his arm a little box which he had touched as he went by, calling out to her, "See, Mrs. Rance! I have found a treasure!" She said that she had asked him what the treasure was, but he had walked on laughing, with the remark that he would have a surprise for Old Bob on his return. And later, she had heard that Prince Galitch had declared that he had discovered "the oldest skull in the history of the human race."

Mrs. Rance had scarcely pronounced these last words when every vestige of gayety fled from Old Bob's face and manner. His eyes shot fire and his voice was husky with passion as he exclaimed:

"That is a lie—an infernal lie! The oldest skull in the history of the human race is Old Bob's skull—do you understand me?—it is Old Bob's skull."

And he shouted out:

"Mattoni! Mattoni! Bring my trunk here at once!"

Almost as soon as the words were spoken, we saw Mattoni crossing the Court of Charles the Bold with Old Bob's trunk on his shoulder. He obeyed the professor to the letter, and carried the trunk through the room and up to his master. Old Bob took his bunch of keys, got down on his knees and opened the box. From this receptacle, which contained his clothing and piles of clean linen, neatly folded, he took a hat box, and from the hat box he drew out a skull, which he placed in the middle of the table among our coffee cups.

"The oldest skull in the history of humanity!" he echoed. "Here it is! It is Old Bob's skull! Look at it! Oh, I can tell you, Old Bob never goes anywhere without his skull!"

And he took up the frightful object and began to caress it, his eyes sparkling and his thick lips parting once more in a broad smile. If you will represent to yourself that Old Bob knew French only imperfectly and pronounced it like English or Spanish (he spoke Spanish like a native), you will see and hear the scene. Rouletabille and I were unable longer to control ourselves, and nearly split our sides with laughter—all the more, because Old Bob every few moments would interrupt himself in the midst of a peal of merriment to demand of us what was the object of our mirth. His wrath was almost as funny as his mirth, and even Mme. Darzac could not refrain from laughter, for, in truth, Old Bob, with his "oldest skull of the human race," was a droll sight to see. I must acknowledge, too, that a skull two hundred thousand years old is not such an unpleasant sight as one might expect it to be, especially when, like this one, it has all its teeth.

Suddenly Old Bob grew serious. He lifted the skull in his right hand and placed the forefinger of the left hand upon the forehead of his ancestor.

"When one looks at the skull from above, one notices very clearly a pentagonal formation which is due to the notable development of the parietal bumps and the jutting out of the shell of the occipitals. The great breadth of the face comes from the exaggerated development of the zygomatic proportions. While in the head of the troglodytes of the Baousse-Raousse, what do we find?"

I shall never know what it was that Old Bob found in the head of the troglodytes, for I did not listen to him, *but I looked at him.* And I had no further inclination for laughter. Old Bob seemed to me terrifying, horrible, as false as the Father of Lies, with his counterfeit gayety and his scientific jargon. My eyes remained fixed upon him as if they were fascinated. It seemed to me that I could see his hair move, just as a wig might do. One thought—the thought of Larsan, which never left me completely, seemed to expand until it filled my entire brain. I felt as if I must speak it out, when all at once, I felt an arm locked in mine, and I saw Rouletabille looking at me with an expression which I did not know how to read.

"What is the matter, Sainclair?" whispered the lad, anxiously.

"My friend," I returned in a tone as low as his own. "I dare not tell you; you would make sport of me."

He drew me away from the table and we walked toward the west boulevard. After he had looked closely on every side and made sure that no one was near us, he said:

"No, Sainclair, no: I won't make sport of you, for you are in the right in seeing *him* everywhere around us. If he were not there a little while ago, he is perhaps there now. Ah, he is stronger than the stones! He is stronger than anything else in the world. I fear him less within than without. And I should be very glad if the stones which I have called to my aid in hindering his entrance shall aid me to hold him inside. For, Sainclair, *I feel that he is here*!"

I pressed Rouletabille's hand, for, strange as it may seem, I shared the same impression—I felt that the eyes of Larsan were upon me—I could hear him breathe. When and how this sensation had first come over me, I was unable to say. But it seemed to me that it had come with the appearance of Old Bob.

I said to Rouletabille, scarcely daring to put into words what was in my mind:

"Old Bob?"

He did not answer. At the end of a few moments, he said:

"Hold your left hand in your right for five minutes and then ask yourself: *'Is it you, Larsan?' And when you have replied to yourself, do not feel too sure, for he may, perhaps, have lied to you, and he may be in your own skin without your knowing it.*"

With these words, Rouletabille left me alone in the west boulevard. It was there that Pere Jacques came to look for me. He brought me a telegram. Before reading it, I congratulated him on his appearance, for he showed no trace of the fact that, like all the rest of us, he had passed a sleepless night; but he informed me that the pleasure he experienced in seeing his "dear Mlle. Mathilde" happy had made him ten years younger. Then he tried to obtain from me some information in regard to the motives for the strange vigil of the night before, and the reason for the events which had occurred at the château since Rouletabille's arrival and for the exceptional precautions which had been taken to prevent the entrance of any stranger. He added that if "that monster, Larsan," were not dead, it would seem as if we dreaded his return. I told him that this was not the moment for explanations and reasoning, and that, as he was a worthy man, he ought, like all other soldiers, to observe the rules without seeking to understand them or to discuss them. He saluted me with a military gesture and started off, shaking his head. The old man was evidently puzzled, and it did not displease me at all that, since he had the watch of the North Gate, he had thought of Larsan. He also had narrowly escaped being one of Larsan's victims; he had not forgotten the fact. It would make him a better sentinel.

I was not in much of a hurry to open the dispatch which Pere Jacques had brought me, and in this I was wrong, for as soon as I cast my eyes over the words which it contained, I realised that it was of the deepest importance. My friend at Paris, whom I had requested to keep an eye upon Brignolles, sent me word that the said Brignolles had left Paris the evening before for the Midi. He had taken the 10:35 train. My friend informed me that he had reason to believe that Brignolles had taken a ticket for Nice.

What should Brignolles be doing in Nice? That was the question which I propounded to myself, and which I have since so often regretted that a foolish impulse of self-esteem kept me from putting to Rouletabille. The young reporter had made so much fun of me when I showed him the first dispatch, which stated that Brignolles had not quitted Paris, that I resolved to tell him nothing about the one which announced his departure. Since Brignolles amounted to so little, in his opinion, I would not bother him with Brignolles. And I kept Brignolles to myself, all alone and so well, that when, assuming my most indifferent air, I rejoined Rouletabille in the Court of Charles the Bold, I never mentioned the subject.

Rouletabille was ready to fasten down with bars of iron the heavy circularly cut oak board which closed the opening to the "oubliette," and he showed me that even if the shaft communicated with the sea, it would be impossible for anyone to succeed in an attempt to introduce himself into the château by this means, for the reason that he could not raise the board and would be driven to give up his plan. His brow was dripping with perspiration, his arms were bared, his collar thrown off, a heavy hammer was in his hand. It seemed to me that he was devoting considerable time and energy to a comparatively simple task, and, like a fool who does not see beyond the end of his own nose, I could not refrain from telling him so. How could I have helped guessing that the boy was voluntarily exerting himself beyond necessity, and that he was delivering himself up to all sorts of physical fatigue in order to efface the memory of the grief which filled his poor heart? But no! I was only able to understand that, half an hour later, when I came upon him lying beside the ruins of the chapel, murmuring in his dreams the one word which betrayed the sorrow of his heart—"Mother." Rouletabille was dreaming of the Lady in Black! He dreamed, perhaps, that her arms were around him as in days gone by, when he was a little fellow and came into the school parlour, flushed and breathless with running. I waited beside him for a moment, asking myself nervously if I ought to leave him in there, or whether there was any danger of anyone's else passing by and discovering his secret. But, after having relieved his overcharged heart with that one word, the lad left nothing more to be heard except his heavy breathing. He was completely exhausted. I believe that it was the first time that the boy had really slept since we had come from Paris.

I profited by his slumbers to leave the château without informing anyone of my intention, and soon, my dispatch in my pocket, I took the train for Nice. On the way, I chanced to read this item on the first page of the *Petit Nicois*: "Professor Stangerson has arrived at Garavan, where he will spend a few weeks with M. Arthur Rance, the recent purchaser of the Fort of Hercules, who, aided by the beautiful Mme. Arthur Rance, will dispense the most gracious hospitality to his friends in this fine old medieval stronghold. As we go to press, we learn that Professor Stangerson's daughter, whose marriage to M. Robert Darzac has just taken place in Paris, has also arrived at the Fort of Hercules with her husband, the brilliant young professor of la Sorbonne. These new guests descend upon us from the North at the time when strangers usually leave us. How wise they are! There is no more beautiful springtime in the world than that of the 'azure shore.' "

At Nice, hidden behind the blinds of a buffet, I awaited the arrival of the train from Paris, by which Brignolles was due to arrive. And the next moment I saw him alighting from a car. Ah, how my heart beat, for I knew that there must be some strange reason for this journey of which he had not informed M. Darzac beforehand. And I knew that the trip was a secret one, when I saw that Brignolles was trying to avoid observation, was bending his hand as he hurried along, gliding rapidly as a pickpocket among the passengers, so that he was soon lost to sight. But I was behind him. He jumped into a closed hack and I hastily got into another closed just as tightly. At the Place Massena he left his carriage and turned toward the Jetee Promenade, where he took another cab. I still followed him. These manoeuvers seemed to me more and more ambiguous. Finally, Brignolles' carriage came out upon the road de la Corniche, and I directed my coachman to take the same way. The numerous windings of this road, its accentuated curves, permitted me to see without being seen. I had promised my coachman a large tip if he helped me to keep in sight of my quarry, and he did his very best. Finally, we reached the Beaulieu railway station, where I was astonished to see Brignolles' carriage stop and the man himself get out, pay the driver and enter the waiting room. He was going to take the train. For what purpose? If I should attempt to get into the same car as he, would he not be certain to see me in this little station or on the almost deserted platform? But I decided to try it anyway. If he were to see me, I could get out of the difficulty by feigning surprise at his presence, and by sticking to him until I was sure of what he was going to do in this part of the world. But luck was with me and Brignolles did not see me. He got into a passenger coach which was bound for the Italian frontier. I realised that all his movements were bringing him nearer to the Fort of Hercules. I got in the car behind his and watched from my window all the travellers who got out at every station.

Brignolles did not get off until we reached Mentone. He certainly had some reason for reaching there by a different train than the one from Paris, and at an hour when there was little chance of his seeing any acquaintances at the station. I saw him alight: he had turned up the collar of his overcoat and pulled his hat down over his eyes. He cast a stealthy glance around the quay, and then, as if reassured, mingled with the other passengers. Once outside the train shed, he got into a shabby old stage coach which was standing by the sidewalk. I watched him from the corner of the waiting room. What was he doing here? And where was he going in that rackety old vehicle? I inquired of an employee, who told me that that carriage was the stage to Sospel.

Sospel is a picturesque little city lost between the last counterfores of the Alps, two hours and a half from Mentone by coach. No railroad passes through there. It is one of the most retired and quietest corners of France, the most dreaded by revenue officers and by the Alpine hunters. But the road which leads to it is one of the most beautiful in the world, for, in order to reach Sospel, it is necessary to wind through I do not know how many mountain passes, to climb countless precipices, and to follow, until one reaches Castillon, the deep and narrow valley of Carei, as wild as a field in Judaea, but covered with luxuriant herbage, bright with beautiful flowers, fertile and beautiful with the shimmering gold of its forests of olive trees, which descend from the heights to the clear bed of the stream by the terraces of a giant staircase formed by nature. I had been at Sospel a few years previously with a party of English tourists in an immense carriage, drawn by eight horses, and I had brought from the trip a remembrance of vertigo which came over my mind in the future every time the name was mentioned. Why was Brignolles going to Sospel? I must find out. The diligence was crowded and had already started on its way with a loud noise of creaking springs and of shaking window panes. I hired a carriage from the station and in a few moments I, too, was climbing over the rocks to the valley of Carei. How I regretted not having spoken of my telegram to Rouletabille! The strange behaviour of Brignolles would have given him ideas, useful and reasonable, while, for my part, I had not the slightest idea of how to reason. I only knew how to follow this Brignolles as a dog follows his master or a policeman follows his quarry by the clues which he finds. And yet, had I followed them well, these clues? It was at the moment that I felt certain that nothing in the world in regard to this man's movements could be small enough to escape me that I made a formidable discovery. I had let the diligence keep a little way in advance, a precaution which I deemed necessary, and I reached Castillon ten minutes later than Brignolles. Castillon is at the highest point of the road between Mentone and Sospel. My driver asked my permission to let his horse rest for a moment, and while he watered the beast, I descended from the carriage, and, at the entrance of a tunnel through which it was necessary to pass to reach the opposite turn of the mountain, I beheld Brignolles and Frederic Larsan!

I stood staring at them, my feet as helpless as though they had taken root in the soil. I could not utter a sound nor make a gesture. Upon my honour, I was completely stupefied by the revelation. Then I recovered my wits, and at the same time felt myself overwhelmed by a feeling of horror for Brignolles, and by a feeling of admiration for my own intuition in regard to him. Ah, I had known from the start! I had been the only one to guess that the companionship of this devil of a Brignolles had been of the gravest danger to Robert Darzac. If they would have listened to me, the Professor of la Sarbonne would have gotten rid of the creature's presence long ago. Brignolles, the tool of Larsan—the accomplice of Larsan—what a discovery! Why, I had known all along that those accidents in the laboratory had not happened by chance! They would believe me now! I had seen with my own eyes Larsan and Brignolles, talking and consulting together at the entrance of the Castillon tunnel. I *had* seen them—but where were they gone now? For I saw them no longer. They must be in the tunnel. I hastened my steps, leaving my coachman behind me, and reached the tunnel in a few moments, drawing my revolver from my pocket. My state of mind was beyond description. What would Rouletabille say when I told him all about my adventure? It was I—I—who had discovered Brignolles and Larsan.

But where were they? I walked through the dark tunnel—no Larsan, no Brignolles! I looked down the road which descends toward Sospel. Not a living creature! But upon my left, toward ancient Castillon, it seemed to me that I could perceive two forms that hastened. They disappeared. I ran after them. I arrived at the ruins. I stopped. Who could say that those two figures were not lying in wait for me behind a wall?

The old Castillon was no longer inhabited, and for a good reason. It had been entirely ruined—destroyed by the earthquake of 1887. Nothing of it remained but a few piles of stone and a few mural windows, gently covered with dust by time; some headless statues, a few isolated pillars which remained standing upright, spired by the shock, and leaning sorrowfully toward the earth, melancholy at having nothing to support. What a silence there was all around me! With a thousand precautions I searched through the ruins, contemplating with horror the depth of the crevices which the earthquake of 1887 had opened in the rocks. One of these in particular seemed to be a shaft without a bottom, and as I leaned above it, hanging on to an olive tree to keep from falling in, I was almost swept into the abyss by a gust of wind. I felt the draught on my face and recoiled with a cry. An eagle darted out of the abyss, quick as a flash. He rose straight to the sun, and then I saw him descend toward me, and describe some menacing circles above my head, uttering savage shrieks, as though he reproached me for having come to trouble him in his realm of solitude and of death which the elements had given him.

Had I been the victim of an illusion? I could no longer see my two shadows. Was I also the plaything of my imagination, when I stooped and picked up from the road a bit of letter paper which looked to me singularly like that which M. Robert Darzac used at la Sarbonne?

Upon this bit of paper I deciphered two syllables which I believed Brignolles had written. These syllables seemed to be the end of a word the beginning of which was missing. All that it was possible to make out was "bonnet."

Two hours later I reentered the Fort of Hercules and told my story to Rouletabille, who placed the bit of paper in his portfolio and entreated me to be as silent as the grave in regard to my expedition.

Astonished at having produced so different an effect from the one which I had anticipated at a discovery which I believed so important, I stared at Rouletabille. He turned his head away, but not quickly enough to hide from me that his eyes were filled with tears.

"Rouletabille!" I exclaimed.

But again, he motioned me not to speak.

"Silence, Sainclair!"

I took his hand; it was burning with fever. And I thought that this agitation could not come entirely from his apprehensions in regard to Larsan. I reproached him with concealing from me what had passed between him and the Lady in Black, but, as often happened, he made me no answer, and turned away, heaving a deep sigh.

They had waited dinner for me. It was late. The dinner was a dismal affair, in spite of the gayety of Old Bob. We scarcely attempted to hide the deep anxiety which froze our hearts. One would have said that each one of us was resigned to the blow which was threatening and that we had lost hope that it might be averted. M. and Mme. Darzac ate nothing. Mme. Edith kept looking at me with a strange expression. At ten o'clock I went to take up my station at the tower of the gardener, almost with relief. While I was in the little room where we had consulted together the night before, the Lady in Black and Rouletabille passed beneath the arch. The glimmer of the lantern fell on their faces. Mme. Darzac appeared to me to be in a state of the greatest excitement. She was urging Rouletabille to something which I could not hear. The conversation between them looked like an argument and I caught only one word of Rouletabille, "Thief!" The two entered the Court of the Bold. The Lady in Black stretched her arm toward the young man, but he did not see it, for he left her immediately and went toward his own room. She remained standing alone for a moment in the court, leaning against the trunk of the eucalyptus tree in an attitude of unutterable sadness, then, with slow steps, she entered the Square Tower.

It was now the tenth of April. The attack of the Square Tower occurred on the night between the eleventh and twelfth.

# X

## THE EVENTS OF THE TWELFTH OF APRIL

This attack took place under circumstances so mysterious and so inexplicable, to all appearances, under any reasonable hypothesis, that the reader will permit me, in order to make him comprehend the issue more fully, to dwell upon certain details in regard to the manner in which we spent our time on the eleventh day of April, 1895.

(1) *The Morning.*

The day, almost from the rising of the sun, was intolerably hot and the hours on guard were almost overpowering. The sun was as torrid as in the heart of Africa and it would have blinded us to keep watch over the waters which burned like a sheet of steel, brought to a white heat, if we had not been furnished with eyeglasses of smoked glass, without whioh it is difficult to pass the a son of departing winter in this part of the country.

At nine o'clock, I came down fiom my room and went to the postern and entered the room which we had styled "the hall of counsel" to relieve Rouletabille of his guard. I had no time to say a single word to him before M. Darzac appeared, following almost upon my heels, and announcing that he had something very important to communicate to us. We inquired anxiously the cause of his agitation and he replied that he intended to quit the Fort of Hercules at once, taking his wife with him. This declaration left Rouletabille and myself dumb with surprise. I was the first to speak and endeavoured to dissuade M. Darzac from even thinking of such an imprudence. Rouletabille frigidly inquired the reason for our friend's sudden resolution and the latter replied by informing us of a scene which had occurred during the previous evening at the château and which revealed to us in how difficult a position the Darzacs were placed by remaining at the Fort of Hercules. The story may be summed up in a few words: Mme. Edith had had a nervous attack. We understood the reason at once for there was no doubt in the mind of either Rouletabille or myself that Mrs. Rance's jealousy of Mme. Darzac was increasing every hour and that each act of courtesy performed by the husband toward the former object of his admiration was positively insupportable to his wife. The sounds of the fit of hysterics to which she had treated M. Rance and the words which she had spoken the night before had penetrated even through the heavy walls of "la Louve," and M. Darzac, who was doing sentinel duty in the outer court, had been unable to help hearing some of the echoes of the young woman's anger.

Rouletabille implored M. Darzac to endure the situation with fortitude, unpleasant as were the circumstances. He assured him that he agreed with his feeling that the stay of himself and Mme. Darzac at the Fort of Hercules must be made as brief as possible: but he also assured him that the security of both depended in great measure on their remaining in their present quarters for the time being. A new struggle had been begun between them on the one side and Larsan on the other. If they were to go away Larsan would know on the moment how to overtake them and in a time and place that they expected him the least. Here, they were forewarned, they were upon their guard, for they *knew*. Elsewhere, they would be at the mercy of everything and every person that surrounded them, for they would not have the ramparts of the Fort of Hercules to defend them. Certainly, this situation could not endure very long, but Rouletabille asked M. Darzac to wait eight days longer—not a single one more. "Eight days," said Columbus long ago, "and I will give you a new world." "Give me eight days and I will deliver Larsan into your hands," was not what Rouletabille said, but it was what we knew that he was thinking.

M. Darzac left us, shaking his head, doubtfully. He was angrier than we had ever seen him. Rouletabille remarked:

"Mme. Darzac will not leave us and M. Darzac will stay if she does."

And he started off on his rounds.

A few moments later, I caught sight of Mme. Edith. She was charmingly dressed, with a simplicity which suited her marvellously. She smiled at me coquettishly, but her gayety seemed a little forced as she jested at my "new trade." I answered her, perhaps a little too quickly, that she was uncharitable in her jests, because she knew quite well that all the trouble which we were taking and the careful watch which we were maintaining might be the means, at any moment, of saving the sweetest of women from untold misery and danger.

She looked at me mockingly and cried with a sharp little laugh:

"Oh, surely. 'The Lady in Black!' She has you all under her spell."

What a ringing laugh she had! At another time, rest assured, I would not have allowed anyone to speak so lightly of "the Lady in Black," but this morning I had not the strength of mind to assert myself. On the contrary, I laughed, too.

"Perhaps, there is a little truth in that speech," I returned.

"My husband is crazy about her! I never would have believed that he could be so romantic. But, then," she went on, with a droll little sigh, "I am romantic, too!"

And she turned upon me that same curious look which had disturbed me before.

"Ah?" That was all that I could find to answer.

"And, therefore," she continued, "I take very great pleasure in the conversation of Prince Galitch, who is more romantic than all the rest of you put together."

Whereupon I asked her who was this Prince Galitch of whom I had heard so much but had not yet seen. She told me that he was coming to luncheon—that she had invited him on our accounts; and she gave me a few particulars in regard to him from which I learned that Prince Galitch was one of the richest landholders in his own part of Russia—that portion called the "Black Lands," fertile above all others, and situated between the forests of the North and the steppes of the Midi.

Fallen heir, at the age of twenty, to one of the greatest of Muscovite estates, he had increased his patrimony by economical and intelligent management of which no one would have believed a man so young to be capable—especially one who had heretofore had his hounds and his books as his principal objects in life. He was called a hermit, a miser and a poet. He had inherited from his father a high position at court. He was a chamberlain to His Majesty and, on account of the immense services rendered by the parent, the Emperor was supposed to regard the son with a great deal of affection. He was at once as gentle as a woman and as strong as a Turk—in brief, a thorough Russian gentleman.

I cannot tell why, but I felt a singular antipathy for the Prince without ever having set eyes on him.

His relations with the Rances were those of friendly neighbourliness. Having purchased two years before the magnificent property whose hanging gardens, flowery terraces, and beautiful balconies had made it known at Garavan as "the Garden of Babylon," he had had the opportunity to be of assistance to Edith when she had begun to make the outer court of the Château of Hercules into an exotic garden. He had presented her with certain plants which had revived, in some corners of the Fort of Hercules, a tropical vegetation hitherto scarcely known except on the banks of the Tigris and the Euphrates. M. Rance sometimes invited the Prince to dinner, and always after one of these functions the Prince would send to his hostess a wonderful palm tree from Nineveh or a cactus, fabled to have belonged to Semiramis. He declared that they cost him nothing. He had too many; he was tired of them and he did not want them among his roses. Edith said that she was interested in the young Russian because he dedicated such beautiful verses to her. After he had repeated them in Russian, he would translate them into English and he had even composed them in English for her and for her alone. Verses—the verses of a real poet, dedicated to Mme. Edith! This had so flattered her that she had requested the poet to compose English verses for her and translate them into Russian. This "literary game" greatly amused Mme. Edith, but Arthur Rance cared for it not at all. Tie young anthropologist did not attempt to conceal that his feelings toward Prince Galitch were not of the most friendly, and I felt assured that the traits which the husband disliked most heartily were those which the wife found most attractive in the Russian, for M. Rance had no use for "verse writing fellows," nor did he care for those who were quite so prudent in their expenditures. He could not understand how a poet could be something very like a miser. The Prince kept no carriage nor motor car. He used the street cars and often did his own marketing, attended by his servant, Ivan, who carried a basket for the provisions. And—so said Mrs. Edith, who had heard these details from the cook—he haggled over prices with the fishwife when there was only two sous between what she asked and what he offered. Strangely enough, this avariciousness did not seem in the least distasteful to Mme. Edith, who appeared to consider it a mark of originality. And, she finished by saying, "No one has ever set foot within his doors. He has never even invited us to come and see his gardens."

"Isn't it beautifully fascinating?" demanded the young woman when she had completed her description.

"Too beautifully fascinating!" I replied.

"You will see!"

I do not know why this answer should have displeased my hostess, but I could see that it did so. Mme. Edith turned away and left me and I finished my guard duty which was an hour and a half long.

The first stroke of the luncheon bell sounded: I hurried to my room to bathe my hands and face and make a hasty toilet and I mounted the steps of "la Louve" rapidly fearing that I should be late; but I paused in the vestibule, amazed to hear the sound of music. Who, under the present circumstances, cared or dared to play a piano in the Fort of Hercules? And, hark someone was singing. It was a voice at once soft and sonorous singing a strange song which sounded now plaintive, now threatening! I know the song now by heart; I have often heard it since. Ah, reader, you, too, know it well, perhaps, if you have ever passed the frontiers of chill Lithuania, if you have ever entered the vast empires of the North. It is the song of the virgins who surround the traveller as he sails and destroy him without pity; it is the song that Sienkiewicz, one immortal day, made for Michel Vereszezaka. Listen.

> "If you approach the Swiss lakes at the hour of nightfall, the face turned toward the lake, the stars above your head, the stars beneath your feet, and two moons shining before your eyes—you shall see this plant that caresses the bank—the wives and daughters of the Swiss whom God has changed into flowers. They balance their forms above the abyss, their heads white like the

moths; their leaves are green as the needle of the maize tipped with gold.

"Images of innocence during life, they have kept their virginal robe after death; they live in the shadow and no blemish comes near them; mortal hands dare not touch them,

"The Tsar and his guard one day made the attempt when, after having gathered the beautiful flowers, they wished to wreath their brows and adorn their swords with them.

"All those who had gathered the blossoms were smitten with great ill or struck with sudden death.

"When time would have effaced these things from the memory of the people, the memory of the punishment is preserved, and in perpetuating it, the flowers are still called the doom of the Tsars.

"Thus saying the lady of the lake departed slowly; the lake opened for her the most profound of its depths; but the eye seeks in vain for the fair unknown whose face was born out of the mist and whose voice the traveller never heard again."

These were the words, translated into our language, of the song which was sung by the soft yet resonant voice while the piano played a weird accompaniment. I opened the door and found myself face to face with a young man who was standing. I heard the footsteps of Mme. Rance behind me and the next moment she was introducing me to Prince Galitch.

The Prince was of the type that one reads of in romances, "handsome, pensive young man"; his clear cut and rather stern profile might have given a somewhat severe expression to his face if his eyes, as mild and clear as those of a child, and with an expression of perfect candour, had not told an altogether different story. They were framed in long black lashes so black that they almost looked as though they had been touched with a pencil; and when one had noticed this peculiarity, one realised why it was that his countenance looked so strange. His skin was fresh and rosy, almost like that of a young girl. Such was my first impression of him but I felt the prejudice which I had experienced before I saw him rise up in my heart again. But it seemed to me, in spite of this, that he was too young to be of any special importance.

I could find nothing to say to this beautiful youth who chanted foreign poems. Mme. Edith smiled at my embarassment, took my arm (which gave me great satisfaction) and led me away to walk in the perfumed gardens of the outer court while we waited for the second bell for luncheon which was to be served to us in the cabin of palm trees on the platform of the Tower of the Bold.

### (2) *The Luncheon and What Followed—A Contagious Terror Spreads Through Our Midst.*

At noon we seated ourselves at the table on the terrace of Charles the Bold, the view from which was incomparable. The palm leaves covered us with their grateful shade, for the heat of the earth and the heavens was so intense that our eyes would not have been able to endure the glare if we had not taken the precaution to put on the smoked spectacles of which I have spoken before.

Those of us at the table were M. Stangerson, Mathilde, Old Bob, M. Darzac, M. Arthur Rance, Edith, Rouletabille, Prince Galitch and myself. Rouletabille, turning his back to the sea, concerned himself very little with his companions and had placed himself in such a position that he could observe everything which transpired along the entire length of the fort. The servants were at their posts. Pere Jacques was at the entrance gate, Mattoni at the postern of the gardener, and the

Berniers in the Square Tower before the door of the apartments occupied by M. and Mme. Darzac.

The first part of the meal was rather silent. I looked at the others. We were rather a solemn sight to contemplate around a table spread for good cheer—mute, and turning upon each other our dark smoked glasses behind which it was as impossible to see our eyes as to read our thoughts.

Prince Galitch was the first to make a remark. He spoke politely to Rouletabille mentioning the fame which the young reporter had won. This appeared to embarrass the lad a little and he made a confused and rather ungracious reply. The Prince did not seem to feel rebuffed, but went on to explain that he was particularly interested in the exploits of my friend for the reason that, as a subject of the Tsar, he knew that Rouletabille would shortly be sent to Russia. But the reporter replied that nothing had yet been decided and that he would prefer to say nothing on the subject until he had received his directions from his paper; whereupon, the Prince astonished us by drawing a newspaper from his pocket. It was a journal of his own country from which he translated to us a few lines announcing the fact that Rouletabille was soon to be in St. Petersburg. There was occurring in that city, the Prince went on to read to us, a series of events so strange and inexplicable in high governmental circles that, upon the advice of the Chief of the Secret Service at Paris, the Superintendent of Police had decided to ask the Epoch to lend him the young reporter. Prince Galitch had presented the affair so vividly that Rouletabille blushed to the roots of his hair as he replied dryly that he had never in the course of his short life done detective work and that the Chief of the Secret Service at Paris and the Superintendent of Police at St. Petersburg were two idiots. The Prince showed his fine teeth in a hearty laugh and it seemed to me that his laughter was not pleasant but cruel and savage.

He seemed to be of Rouletabille's opinion in regard to the Government officers, and, as if to prove the fact, he added:

"It sounds good to hear anyone talk like that, for now one expects tasks of journalists which have nothing in the world to do with their profession."

Rouletabille made no reply and the subject was abandoned.

Mme. Edith arose from her chair, speaking ecstatically of the beauty of nature. But, in her opinion, she declared, there was nothing more beautiful anywhere near than the "Gardens of Babylon." She added, mischievously: "They seem so much more beautiful, because one may only see them from a distance!"

The attack was so direct that it seemed as though the Prince must reply to it by an invitation. But he said nothing. Mme. Edith looked vexed and a moment later, said suddenly:

"I'm not going to deceive you any longer, Prince. I have seen your gardens."

"Indeed! And how was that?" inquired Galitch, not losing his presence of mind for an instant.

"Yes, I have been there, and I'll tell you all about it."

And she related while the Prince listened with an air of cold imperturbability the story of her visit to the "Gardens of Babylon."

She had come upon them, inadvertently, from the rear, in climbing over a hillock which separated the gardens from the mountains. She had wandered from enchantment to enchantment, but without being in the least astonished. When she had walked upon the seashore, she had seen enough of the "Gardens of Babylon." to prepare her for the marvels, the secrets of which she had so audaciously stolen. She had finally reached the edge of a little pond, black as ink, upon the bank of which she saw a great water lily and a little old woman with a long, peaked chin. When they saw her the water lily and the little old woman had fled away, the latter so light on her feet in running that she fairly skimmed over the ground. Mme. Edith had laughed and had called after her:

"Madame! Madame!"

But the little old woman had seemed only more terrified and had disappeared with her lily behind the barberry hedge. Mme. Edith had continued her stroll but not quite so carelessly. Suddenly she had heard a rustle in the bushes and the strange cry which is made by wild birds when, surprised by the hunter, they escape from the prison of verdure in which they have hidden themselves. It was another little old woman, still more shrivelled and wrinkled than the first, but heavier of build and who carried her cane like a battle axe. She vanished—that is to say, Edith lost sight of her in a turn of the path. And a third little old woman, leaning on two canes appeared a little further on in the mysterious garden: she escaped behind the trunk of a giant eucalyptus tree and she went so much the faster than she had done before, by running on her hands and knees so rapidly that it was amazing that she did not get all tangled up. Mme. Edith still went on. And at last she came to the marble steps of the villa with their climbing roses overhead, but the three little old women were standing guard on the highest step like three rooks on a branch and they opened their threatening beaks from which escaped threatening sounds. It was then Mme. Edith's turn to flee.

The little woman had related her adventure in a manner so charming and with such grace, borrowed as it was from the fairy tales of childhood, that I was enraptured and began to comprehend how certain women who have nothing natural about them can supplant in the heart of men those whose gifts are only those of nature.

The Prince did not seem in the least embarrassed by the little history. He said without a smile:

"Those are my three fairy godmothers. They have never left me since the hour of my birth. I can neither work nor live without them, I can only leave them when they permit it and they watch over my verse-making with a fierce jealousy."

The Prince had scarcely ceased giving us this fantastic explanation of the presence of the three old women in the "Gardens of Babylon" when Walter, Old Bob's man servant, brought a dispatch to Rouletabille. The latter asked permission to open it and read aloud:

"Return as soon as possible. We are waiting for you very anxiously. A magnificent assignment at St. Petersburg."

This dispatch was signed by the Editor in chief of the Epoch.

"Well, what do you say to that, M. Rouletabille?" demanded the Prince. "Will you admit now that I was pretty well informed?"

The Lady in Black could not repress a sigh. "I shall not go to St. Petersburg!" declared Rouletabille.

"They will regret your decision at the Court," said the Prince. "I am certain of that, and, allow me to say, young man, that you are missing a wonderful opportunity."

The term "young man" seemed extremely displeasing to Rouletabille, who opened his lips as though to answer the Prince, but closed them again, to my great surprise, without uttering a word. Galitch went on:

"You would have found an adventure worthy of your skill. One may hope for everything when one has been strong enough to unmask a Larsan!"

The word fell into the midst of us like a bombshell and, as if by a common impulse, we took refuge behind our smoked glasses. The silence which followed was horrible. We sat as motionless as statues. *Larsan*! Why should this name which we ourselves had so often pronounced within the last forty-eight hours and which represented a danger with which we were commencing to almost feel familiar—why, I say, should that name, spoken at that precise moment, have produced an effect upon us, which, speaking for myself, was like nothing ever felt before? It seemed to me as though I had been struck by a thunderbolt. An indefinable terror glided through my body. I longed to flee but it seemed to me that if I were to stand up my limbs would not be able to support me. The unbroken silence on every hand contributed to increase this indescribable state of hypnosis. Why did no one speak? Where had old Bob's gayety vanished? He had scarcely uttered a word during the meal. And why did all the others sit so silent and so motionless behind their dark glasses? All at once, I turned my head and looked behind me. Then I understood, more by instinct than anything else, that I was the object of a common psychical attraction. Someone was looking at me. Two eyes were fixed upon me—*weighing* upon me. I could not see the eyes and I did not know from where the glance fixed upon me came, but it was there. I knew it—and it was *his* glance. But there was no one behind me, nor at the right, nor the left, nor in front, except the people who were seated at the table, motionless, behind their dark glasses. And then—then I knew that Larsan's eyes were glaring at me from behind a pair of those glasses—ah! the dark glasses— the dark glasses behind which were hidden Larsan's eyes.

And then, all at once, the sensation passed. The eyes, doubtless, were turned away from me. I drew a long breath. Another sigh echoed my own. Was it from the breast of Rouletabille—was it the Lady in Black, who perhaps, had at the same time as myself endured the weight of those piercing eyes?

Old Bob spoke:

"Prince, I do not believe that your last spinal bone goes any further back than the middle of the quaternary period."

And all the black spectacles turned in his direction. Rouletabille arose and made a sign to me. I hastened to the council room where he was waiting for me. As soon as I appeared, he closed the door and whispered:

"Well, did you feel it, too?"

I felt smothered. I could scarcely articulate.

"He was there—at that table—unless we are going mad."

There was a pause and then I resumed, more calmly:

"You know, Rouletabille, that it is quite possible that we are going mad. This phantasm of Larsan will land us all in a madhouse yet! We have been shut up here only two days and see the state we are in!"

Rouletabille interrupted me.

"No, no; I felt him. He is there. I could have touched him! But where—but when? Since I came into that room, I have known that it was not necessary for me to go further. I will not fall into his trap. I will not go and look for him outside the castle even though I have seen him outside with my own eyes—even though you saw him with yours."

All in a moment he seemed to grow perfectly calm, passed his hand across his eyebrows, lighted his pipe and said, as he had so often said before, in happier hours when his reasoning powers, which were yet ignorant of the ties which united him to the Lady in Black, were not disturbed by the tumult of his heart:

"Let us reason it out!"

And he returned on the instant to that argument which had already served us and which he repeated again and again to himself (in order that, he said, he should not be lured away by the outer appearance of things): "Do not look for Larsan in that place where he reveals himself; seek for him everywhere else where he hides himself."

This he followed up with the supplementary argument:

"He never shows himself where he seems to be except to prevent us from seeing him where he really is."

And he resumed:

"Ah! the outer appearance of things! Look here, Sainclair! There are moments when, for the sake of reasoning clearly, I want to get rid of my eyes! Let us get rid of our eyes, Sainclair, for five minutes—just five minutes, and, perhaps, we shall see more clearly."

He seated himself, placed his pipe on the table, buried his face in his hands and said:

"Now, I have no eyes. Tell me, Sainclair—*who is within these walls?*"

"What do I see within these walls?" I echoed stupidly.

"No, no! You have no eyes at all; you see nothing. Enumerate them without seeing. Count them ALL."

"There is, first of all, you and I," I said, understanding, at last, what he wished to reach.

"Very well."

"Neither you nor I," I continued, "is Larsan."

"Why?"

"Why?" I echoed.

"Yes, why. Tell me. You must give a reason why you believe so. I acknowledge that I am not Larsan; I am sure of that, for I am Rouletabille; but, face to face with Rouletabille, tell me why you cannot be Larsan?"

"Because you saw him—"

"Idiot!" exclaimed Rouletabille closing his eyes in with his clasped hands more firmly than before. "I have no eyes. I can't see anything! If Jerry, the croupier at Monte Carlo, had not seen the Comte de Maupas sit down at his table, he would have sworn that the man who picked up the cards was Ballmeyer! If Noblet at the garrison had not found himself face to face one evening at the Troyons, with a man whom he recognised as the Vicomte Drouet d'Eslon, he would have sworn that the man whom he came to arrest and whom he did not arrest because he had *seen* him, was Ballmeyer. If Inspector Giraud, who knew the Comte de Motteville as well as you know me, had not *seen* him one afternoon at the race course at Longchamps, chatting with two of his friends—had not *seen*, I say, the Comte de Motteville, he would have arrested Ballmeyer. Ah, you see,

Sainclair!" exclaimed the lad in a voice shaken with sobs, "My father was born before I was! One will have to be very strong and very shrewd to capture my father!"

The words were uttered so despairingly that the little force of reasoning I possessed vanished completely. I threw out my hands before me, a gesture which Rouletabille did not see, for he saw nothing.

"No—no! It isn't necessary to *see* any of them" he repeated. "Neither you, nor M. Stangerson, nor M. Darzac, nor Arthur Rance, nor Old Bob, nor Prince Galitch. But we must know some good reason why each of these cannot be Larsan. Only when that is accomplished shall I be able to breathe freely behind these stone walls!"

There was no freedom in my breathing. We could hear, under the arch of the postern, the regular steps of Mattoni as he kept guard.

"Well, how about the servants?" I asked, with an effort. "Mattoni and the others?"

"I am absolutely certain that none of them was absent from the Fort of Hercules when Larsan appeared to Mme. Darzac and to M. Darzac at the railway station at Bourg."

"Own up, Rouletabille!" I cried. "That you don't trouble yourself about them because none of their eyes were behind the black spectacles."

Rouletabille tapped the ground impatiently with his foot and said:

"Be quiet, please, Sainclair. You make me more nervous than my mother."

This phrase, uttered in vexation, struck me strangely.

I would have questioned Rouletabille in regard to the state of mind of the Lady in Black, but he resumed, meditatively:

"First, Sainclair is not Larsan, because Sainclair was at Trepot with me while Larsan was at Bourg."

"Second: Professor Stangerson is not Larsan because he was on his way from Dijon to Lyons while Larsan was at Bourg. As a fact, reaching Lyons one minute before him, M. and Mme. Darzac saw him alight from the train."

"But all the others, if it is necessary to prove that they were not at Bourg at that moment, might be Larsan, for all of them might have been at Bourg."

"First M. Darzac was there. Arthur Rance was away from home during the two days which preceded the arrival of the Professor and of M. Darzac. He arrived at Mentone just in time to receive them (Mme. Edith herself informed me in reply to a few careless questions of mine that her husband had been absent those two days on business). Old Bob made his journey to Paris. Prince Galitch was not seen at the grottoes nor outside the Gardens of Babylon.

"First, let us take M. Darzac."

"Rouletabille!" I cried. "That is a sacrilege."

"I know it."

"And it is a piece of the grossest stupidity."

"I know that, too. But why?"

"Because," I exclaimed, almost beside myself, "Larsan is a genius, we are aware; he might be able to deceive a detective, a journalist, a reporter, and even a Rouletabille—he might even deceive a friend, under some circumstances, I admit. But he could never deceive a daughter so far that she would take him for her father. That ought to reassure you as to M. Stangerson. Nor would he deceive a woman to the point of taking him for her betrothed. And, my friend, Mathilde Stangerson knew M. Darzac and threw herself into his arms at the railway station."

"And she knew Larsan, too!" added Rouletabille coldly. "Well, my dear fellow, your reasons are powerful but as I do not know at present what form the genius of my father has assumed as a disguise, I prefer rather to bestow, for the sake of supposition, a personality on M. Robert Darzac which

I have never expected to fasten upon him, in order to base my argument against the possibility a little more solidly: If Robert Darzac were Larsan, Larsan would not have appeared on several occasions to Mathilde Stangerson, for it is the apparition of Larsan that has created a gulf between Mathilde Stangerson and Robert Darzac."

"Pshaw!" I cried. "Of what use are such vain reasonings when one has only to open his eyes—open them, Rouletabille!"

He opened them.

"Upon whom?" he asked with a trace of bitterness in his voice. "Upon Prince Galitch?"

"Why not? Do you like him, this prince from the Black Lands who sings Lithuanian folk songs?"

"No," replied Rouletabille. "But he entertains Mme. Edith."

And he smiled. I pressed his hand. He acted as though he had not felt the touch, but I knew that he did.

"Prince Galitch is a Nihilist and I am not troubled over him in the least degree," he said, tranquilly.

"Are you sure of it? Who told you?"

"Bernier's wife, who knows one of the three old women whom Mrs. Edith told about at luncheon. I have made an investigation. She is the mother of one of the three men hanged at Kazan for the attempted assassination of the Emperor. I have seen the photograph of the poor wretches. The other two old women are the other two mothers. There's nothing interesting about that!"

I could not refrain from a gesture of admiration.

"Ah, you haven't lost any time."

"Neither has *he*!" he muttered.

I folded my arms.

"And Old Bob?" I asked.

"No, dear boy, no!" scoffed Roultubille, almost angrily. "Not he, either. You have noticed that he wears a wig, I suppose.

Well, I assure you that when my father wears a wig, it will fit him."

He spoke so mechanically that I rose to leave him, thinking he had no more to say to me. He stopped me:

"Wait a minute. We have said nothing of Arthur Rance."

"Oh, he has not changed at all since we were at Glandier," I exclaimed. "That is out of the question."

"Always the eyes! Take care of your eyes, Sainclair!"

And he put his hand on my shoulder for a moment as I turned away. Through my clothing I felt that his flesh was burning. He left the room and I remained for a moment where I stood, lost in thought. In thought of what? Of the fact that I had been wrong in saying that Arthur Rance had not changed at all. For one thing, now, he wore a slight moustache, something very rarely seen in an American of his type; next, his hair had grown longer with a lock falling over the forehead. And again, I had not seen him in two years—and everyone changes in two years—and again, Arthur Rance, who had used to drink heavily, now tasted only water. But then, there was Edith—what about Edith? Ah! was I going insane, I, too? Why do I say, "I, too," like—like the Lady in Black; like—like Rouletabille. Did I believe that Rouletabille's brain was becoming slightly turned? Ah, the Lady in Black had us all under her spell. Because the Lady in Black lived in the perpetual fear of her memories, here were we all trembling with the same horror as she. Fear is as contagious as the cholera.

### (3) How I Spent My Afternoon up to Five O'clock.

I profited by the fact that I was not on guard to go to my room for a little rest; but I slept badly and dreamed that Old Bob, M. Rance and Mme. Edith had formed themselves into a band of brigands who had sworn death to Rouletabille and myself. And when I awakened under this pleasant impression and saw the old towers and the old château with their menacing walls rising before me, I came near thinking that my nightmare was real and I said to myself half aloud: "It's a fine place in which we have taken refuge!" I put my head out of the window. Mrs. Edith was walking in the Court of the Bold, chatting carelessly with Rouletabille and twisting the stem of a beautiful rose between her pretty fingers. I went down immediately. But when I reached the court, I found no one there. I followed Rouletabille whom I saw on his way to make his inspection of the Square Tower.

I found him quite calm and entirely master of himself—and also, entirely the master of his eyes, which were not closed now but open wide and keenly on the watch for anything that might turn up. Ah, it was worthwhile to see the manner in which he looked at everything around him! Nothing escaped him. And the Square Tower, the abode of the Lady in Black, was the object of his constant surveillance.

And at this point, it seems to me opportune, a few hours before the moment at which that most mysterious attack occurred, to present to the reader the interior plan of the inhabited story of the Square Tower the story which was on a level with the Court of Charles the Bold.

When one entered the Square Tower by the only door (K) one found himself in a large corridor which had previously formed a part of the guard room. The guard room had formerly taken up all the space at O, O', O" and O'" and was shut in by walls of stone which still existed with their doors opening upon the other rooms of the Old Castle. It was Mrs. Arthur Rance who in this guard room had had wooden partitions raised to make quite a large room which she wished to use for a bathroom. This room, also, was now surrounded by the two passages at right angles to each other. The door of the room which served as the lodge of the Berniers was situated at S. It was necessary to pass in front of this door to reach R, where was the only door affording admission to the apartment of the Darzacs. One or other of the Berniers was always in the lodge. And no one save themselves had a right to enter it. From this lodge one could easily see from a little window at Y, the door V which opened off the suite of Old Bob. When M. and Mme. Darzac were not in their apartment, the only key which opened the door R was in the keeping of the Berniers; and it was a special kind of key made purposely for the room within the last twenty-four hours in a place which no one but Rouletabille knew. The young reporter had let no one into the secret.

Rouletabille would have wished that the watch which he had had placed upon the rooms of the Darzacs might have been kept also upon those of Old Bob, but the latter had opposed such an idea with an earnestness so comical that it was necessary to abandon it. Old Bob swore that he would not be treated like a prisoner and he said that on no account would he give up the privilege of going and coming to his own rooms when he saw fit without asking the keys from the lodge-keepers. His door must remain unlocked so that he might go as many times as he liked to his rooms, whether it might be to his bed chamber or to his sitting room in the Tower of Charles the Bold, without disturbing or worrying himself or anyone else. On account of his insistence, it was necessary to leave the door at K open. He demanded it and Mme. Edith upheld her uncle in so intense a manner and spoke so pertly to Rouletabille that he knew she was seeking to convey the idea that she believed that Rouletabille was treating Old Bob with discourtesy at the instigation of Professor Stangerson's daughter. So he had not insisted on what he believed to be best. Mme. Edith had said with her lips pressed together in a narrow little line: "But, M. Rouletabille, my uncle doesn't think that anyone is coming to carry *him* away!" And Rouletabille had realised that there was nothing for him to do save to laugh with the Old Bob over this absurd idea that one could be trying to steal as they would a pretty woman, the man who had the oldest skull in the world. And so he had laughed—had laughed even louder than Old Bob, but had imposed the condition that the door at K should be locked with a key after 10 o'clock at night and that the key should be left in the keeping of the Berniers, who would come and open it whenever anyone desired. Even this was against the inclination of Old Bob, who sometimes worked very late in the Tower of Charles the Bold. But, nevertheless, he declared, he would submit to it for he did not wish to have the appearance of opposing the worthy M. Rouletabille, who had told him that he was afraid of robbers. For, be it said in exculpation of Old Bob, that, if he lent himself so ungraciously to the defensive plans of our young friend it was because it had not been judged expedient to inform him in regard to the resurrection of Larsan. He had, of course, heard of the extraordinary series of fatalities which had formerly occurred in the history of poor Mlle. Stangerson; but he was a thousand miles from doubting that all her troubles had ceased long before she had become Mme. Darzac. And then, too, Old Bob was an egoist, like nearly all savants. Happy because he possessed the oldest skull in the history of the human race, he could not conceive that the whole world did not revolve around his treasure.

Rouletabille, after having politely inquired after the health of Mere Bernier, who was gathering up potatoes and putting them in a bag at her side, requested Pere Bernier to open the door of the Darzacs' room for us.

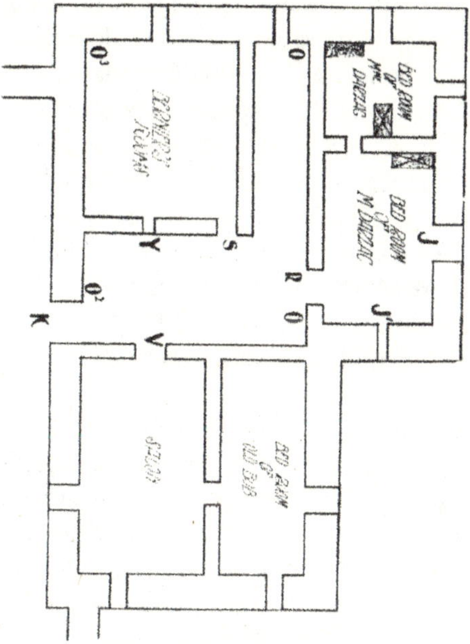

*The Plan of the Inhabitied Floor of the Square Tower*

This was the first time that I had entered the apartment. The atmosphere was almost freezing, and the whole place seemed to me cold and sombre. The room, very large, was furnished with extreme simplicity, containing an oak bed, and a toilet table which was placed at one of the two openings in the wall around which there had formerly been loopholes. So thick was the wall and so large the opening that this embrasure (J) formed a kind of little room beside the big one and of this M. Darzac had made his dressing closet. The second window (J') was smaller. The two windows were fitted with bars of iron between which one could scarcely pass one's arm. The high bedstead had its back to the outer wall and had been drawn up against the partition of stone which separated M. Darzac's apartment from that of his wife. Opposite in the angle of the tower was a panel. In the centre of the room was a reading table on which were some scientific books and writing materials. And there was an easy chair and three straight-backed chairs. That was all. It would have been absolutely impossible for anyone to hide in this chamber, unless, of course, behind the panel. And then, too, Pere and Mere Bernier had received orders to look every time they visited the room both behind the panel and in the closet where M. Darzac hung his clothes, and Rouletabille himself, who, during the absence of the Darzacs often came to cast his eye around this room, never neglected to search it thoroughly.

He did so now, as I stood there. When we at length passed into the sleeping room of Mme. Darzac, we were absolutely certain that we had left nothing behind us of which we did not know. As soon as we entered the room, Bernier, who had followed us, had taken care, as he always did, to draw the bolt which closed from the inside the only door by which the apartment communicated with the corridor.

Mme. Darzacs room was smaller than that of her husband. But it was bright and well lighted from the way that the windows were placed. As soon as we set foot over the threshold, I saw Rouletabille turn pale and he turned to me and said:

"Sainclair, do you perceive the perfume of the Lady in Black?"

I did not. I perceived nothing at all. The window, barred, like all the others which looked out on the sea, was wide open and a light breeze rustled the hangings which had been drawn in front of a set of hooks for gowns which had been placed in one corner. The other corner was occupied by the bed. The hooks were placed so high that the gowns and peignoir which they held were covered by the hangings in front scarcely more than half way down, so that it would have been entirely out of the question for any person to conceal himself there without leaving his legs exposed to view from the knees to the feet. Nor would anyone have been able to hide in the corner where the portmanteaux and trunks were placed, although, nevertheless, Rouletabille examined it with the greatest care. There was no panel in this room. Toilet table, bureau, an easy chair, two other chairs, and the four walls between which there was no one but ourselves, as we could have sworn by all that we held most sacred.

Rouletabille, after having looked under the bed, gave the signal for departure and motioned us from the room. He lingered for a moment, but no longer. Bernier locked the door with the tiny key which he put in his inside pocket and tightly buttoned his coat over it. We made the tour of the corridors and also that of Old Bob's apartment which consisted of a bedroom and sitting room as easy to examine and as incapable of hiding anyone as those of the Darzacs. No one was in the suite, which was furnished rather carelessly, the chief article noticeable being an almost empty bookcase with the doors standing open. When we left the room Mere Bernier brought up her chair and placed it on the threshold where she could see clearly and still go on with her work, which seemed to be always that of paring potatoes.

We entered the rooms occupied by the Berniers and found them like all the others. The other storeys were inhabited and communicated with the ground floor by a little inner stairway which began at the angle O' and ascended to the summit of the tower. A trap door in the ceiling of the Berniers' room closed this stairway. Rouletabille asked for a hammer and nails and nailed up the trap door, thus making the stairway unusable.

One might say, in short and in fact, that nothing escaped Rouletabille and that when we had made the rounds of the Square Tower we had left no one behind us save M. and Mme. Bernier. One would have said, too, that there could have been no human being in the apartment of the Darzacs before

Bernier, a few minutes later, opened the door to M. Darzac himself as I am now about to relate.

It was about five minutes before five o'clock when, leaving Bernier in his corridor in front of the door of the Darzacs' room, Rouletabille and myself found ourselves again in the Court of the Bold.

At that moment we climbed to the platform of the ancient tower at B". We seated ourselves upon the parapet, our eyes looking down to the ground, attracted by the echoes of the Rochers Rouges. At that moment, we noticed upon the edge of the Barma Grande which opened its mysterious mouth in the flaming face of Baousse-Raousse, the disturbed and wrathful countenance of Old Bob. His shadow was the only dark thing about. The red cliffs rose from the waters with such a vivid radiance that one might have readily believed that they were still glowing with the same fires which are found in the interior of the earth. By what a prodigious anachronism it was that this modern scholar with his coat and hat in the height of fashion should be moving about, grotesque and ghoulish, in front of this cavern three hundred thousand years old formed by the ardent lava to serve as the first roof for the first family in the first days of the world! Why this sinister grave-digger in this beautiful corner of the earth? We could see him brandishing his skull as he had done at the table and we could hear him laugh—laugh— laugh! Ah, his laughter made us ill even to think of it! It tore our ears and our hearts.

From Old Bob our attention was drawn to M. Darzac, who was coming through the postern of the gardener and crossing the Court of the Bold. He did not see us. Ah, he was not laughing! Rouletabille felt the deepest pity for him for he saw that he was at the end of his endurance. In the afternoon he had said to my friend, who now repeated the words to me:

"Eight days is too much! I do not believe that I can bear this torment for eight days!"

"And where would you go?" Rouletabille had asked him.

"To Rome," he had replied. Evidently Professor Stangerson's daughter would accompany him nowhere else and Rouletabille believed that it was the idea that the Pope could arrange the affair which was driving him wild with grief that had put the journey to Rome into the mind of poor M. Darzac. Poor, poor M. Darzac! No, in truth, his face wore no smile.

We followed him with our eyes to the door of the Square Tower. We could see from his looks that he could endure no more. His head was moodily bent toward the ground; his hands were in his pockets. He had the air of a man fatigued and disgusted with the whole world. Yes, with his hands buried in his pockets, he looked out of humour with everything. But, patience! He will take his hands out of his pockets and one will not smile at him always. I confess that I smiled. Well, M. Darzac a little after this gave me cause to experience the most frightful thrill of terror which could freeze human bones! And I did not smile then.

M. Darzac went straight to the Square Tower, where, of course, he found Bernier, who opened the door for him. As Bernier had been keeping constant guard before the door of the room, as he had kept the key in his pocket and as we had proven by our investigation that the place was empty when we had left it, we had established the fact that *when M. Darzac entered his room, there could be no one else there*. And this is the truth.

Everything that I have said could have been sworn to "after" by each one of us. If I tell it to you "before," it is that I am haunted by the mystery which lurks in the shadow and makes ready to reveal itself.

At the moment that we saw M. Darzac go to his room, we heard a clock strike five.

### (4) *What Happened from Five O'clock that Night Until the Moment When the Attack on the Square Tower Began.*

Rouletabille and I remained chatting, or, rather, trying to reason things out, upon the platform of the Tower B for another hour. Suddenly, my friend struck me a little tap on the shoulder and exclaimed, "For my part, I think—" and then, without completing the sentence, he started for the Square Tower. I followed him.

I was a thousand miles from guessing what he thought. He thought of Mere Bernier's bag of potatoes which he emptied out on the white floor of the room to the great amazement of the good woman: then, satisfied with this act which evidently corresponded to the state of his mind, he returned with me to the Court of the Bold, while, behind us, we could hear Pere Bernier laughing as he picked up the potatoes.

As we reached the court we saw the face of Mme. Darzac appearing for a moment at the window of the room occupied by her father on the first storey of "la Louve."

The heat had become insupportable. We were threatened with a violent storm and we believed that it would begin to lighten immediately.

Ah, how much the storm would relieve us, we thought. The sea had a thick and heavy quietude as though it had been saturated with oil. The sea was heavy and the air was heavy and our hearts were heavy. No one or nothing on the earth or in the heavens was lighter than Old Bob, whose form had appeared again at the edge of the Barma Grande and who was still moving around agitatedly. One would have said that he was dancing. No, he was making a speech! To whom? We leaned over the railing to see. There was apparently someone upon the strand to whom Old Bob was addressing some long-winded scientific discourse. But the palm leaves hid his auditor from us. Finally, the listener moved and advanced, and approached the "black professor," as Rouletabille called him. And we saw that Old Bob's congregation was composed of two persons. One was Mme. Edith—we could easily recognize her with her languishing graces, clinging like a vine to her husband's arm. To her husband's arm! But this was not her husband? Who, then, was the young man upon whom Mme. Edith was playing off so many pretty airs?

Rouletabille turned around, looking for someone of whom to make inquiries—either Mattoni or Bernier.

We saw Bernier upon the threshold of the door of the Square Tower and Rouletabille beckoned him. Bernier approached and his eye followed the direction indicated by Rouletabille's finger.

"Who is that with Mme. Rance?" asked the young reporter.

"The young man?" responded Bernier without hesitation. "That is Prince Galitch."

Rouletabille and I looked at each other. It is true that we had never seen Prince Galitch walking at a distance, but I would not have imagined that his manner of walking would be like this, and he had not seemed to me to be so tall. Rouletabille understood my thoughts, I knew. He shrugged his shoulders.

"All right," he said to Bernier. "Thanks."

And we continued to gaze at Mme. Edith and her Prince.

"I can only say one thing," said Bernier as he turned to leave us. "And that is that I don't care for this prince at all. He is too soft spoken and too blonde and his eyes are too blue. They say that he is a Russian. That may be, but there are some who leave the country because they have to. But he comes and goes in a strange fashion and takes no leave beforehand. The time before the last that he was invited here to luncheon Madame and Monsieur waited and waited for him and dared not begin without him. Well, after an hour or two they received a wire, begging them to excuse him because he had missed the train. The dispatch was sent from Moscow."

And Bernier, chuckling, returned to his vantage post.

Our eyes remained fixed upon the beach. Mme. Edith and her prince continued their stroll toward the grotto of Romeo and Juliet; Old Bob suddenly ceased to gesticulate, descended from the Barma Grande and came toward the château, entered the gate, crossed the outer court, and we saw, even from the height of the platform of the tower, that he had ceased to smile. Old Bob's face had become sadness itself. He was silent. He passed beneath the arch of the postern. We called him, he did not seem to hear us. He carried before him in the crook of his arm his "oldest skull in the world," and all at once we saw him fly into the fiercest of passions. He addressed the worst of insults to the skull. He descended into the Round Tower and we heard the mutterings of his wrath for moments after he was out of sight. Then heavy blows resounded. One would have said that he was hurling himself against the wall.

At this moment six strokes resounded from the old clock of the New Castle. And at almost the same instant a clap of thunder echoed over the sea. And the line of the horizon grew black.

Then a groom of the stables, Walter, a brave, stupid fellow who was incapable of a single idea, but who had shown for years past the blind devotion of a brute toward his master, Old Bob, passed under the postern of the gardener, entered into the Court of Charles the Bold, and came to us. He held in his hand a letter which he gave to Rouletabille. He handed me another and continued on his way toward the Square Tower.

Rouletabille, calling after him, inquired what errand was taking him to the Square Tower. He answered that he was taking the mail for M. and Mme. Darzac to Pere Bernier. He spoke in English for Walter understood no other language; but we spoke it well enough to understand him and make him understand. Walter was charged with distributing the mail because Pere Jacques had no right to leave his lodge on any account. Rouletabille took the letters from the man's hands and said to him that he would take it in himself.

A few drops of water had begun to fall.

We turned to the door of M. Darzac's room. Bernier was smoking his pipe in the corridor, sitting astride a chair.

"Is M. Darzac still there?" asked Rouletabille.

"He hasn't stirred since he went in," Bernier replied.

We knocked. We heard the heavy bolt drawn from the inside. (These bolts can only be used by the person within the room.)

M. Darzac was writing letters when we entered. He had been seated beside the little reading table facing the door R. Now mark well all our movements. Rouletabille complained that the letter which he held in his hand confirmed the telegram which he had received in the morning and pressed him to return to Paris. His paper insisted upon his proceeding at once to Russia.

M. Darzac read indifferently the two or three letters which we had brought him and put them in his pocket. I held out to Rouletabille the letter which I had received. It was from my friend in Paris who, after having given me some important details regarding the departure of Brignolles, informed me that the laboratory assistant had left his address for mail to be forwarded to Sospel, the Hotel des Alps. This was extremely interesting and M. Darzac and Rouletabille were greatly excited over it. We decided to go to Sospel as soon as it could be arranged and, after talking of the matter for a few minutes, we went out of the room. The door of Mme. Darzac's sleeping room was not closed. Here is what we noticed as we passed out:

I have mentioned that Mme. Darzac was not in her own room. As soon as we made our exit, Pere Bernier immediately—immediately, I say, for I saw him—turned the key in the lock and then took it out and put it in his pocket—in the little inside pocket of his waistcoat. Ah, I can still see him putting the key into his inside pocket—I swear it!—and he buttoned his coat over it!

Then the three of us went out of the Square Tower, leaving Pere Bernier in his corridor like the good watchdog that he never ceased to be until the last day of his life. One may be a poacher and a good watchdog into the bargain, you know. Even watchdogs poach sometimes. And I bear witness here and now, among all the events which followed, Pere Bernier always did his duty and never told lies. And his wife, Mere Bernier, was an excellent servant, faithful, intelligent and not too talkative. Since she has been a widow, I have had her in my service. She will be glad to read here the tribute which I pay to her and to her husband. They both deserved it.

It was about half past six o'clock when, in emerging from the Square Tower, we went to pay a visit to Old Bob in the Round Tower, Rouletabille, M. Darzac and I. As soon as we entered the low basement M. Darzac uttered an exclamation of surprise and indignation at seeing the destruction which had been wrought upon a wash drawing upon which he had been working ever since the evening before in the endeavour to distract his mind, and which represented the plan for a great scaling ladder for the Fort of Hercules of the kind which had existed in the Fifteenth Century and of which Arthur Rance had shown us the pictures. This drawing had been gashed with a knife and paint had been smeared over it. He endeavoured in vain to obtain some explanation from Old Bob, who was kneeling beside a box containing a skeleton and was so wrapped up in a shoulder blade that he did not even answer us.

I desire here, by way of parenthesis, to ask the pardon of the reader for the mathematical precision with which for the last few pages, I have enumerated our every act and movement, but I will assure him, once and for all, that even the smallest circumstances have in reality a considerable importance, for everything which we did at this time was done, though alas, we did not guess it, on the brink of a precipice.

As Old Bob seemed to be in a churlish humour, we left him—that is, Rouletabille and myself did. M. Darzac remained gazing at his spoiled drawing, but thinking, doubtless, of altogether different things.

As we went out of the Round Tower, Rouletabille and I raised our eyes to the sky which was rapidly becoming covered with great, black clouds. The tempest was near at hand. In the meantime, the air seemed to grow more and more stifling.

"I am going to lie down in my room," I said. "I can't stand any more of this. Perhaps it may be cooler there with all the windows open."

Rouletabille followed me into the New Castle. Suddenly, as we reached the first landing of our winding staircase, he stopped me:

"Ah," he said in a low voice; "*she* is there!"

"Who?"

"The Lady in Black. Can't you smell the perfume?"

And he hid himself behind a door, motioning me to continue without waiting for him. I obeyed.

What was my amazement in opening the door of my room to find myself face to face with Mathilde!

She uttered a low cry and disappeared in the shadow, gliding away like a surprised bird. I rushed to the staircase and leaned over the balustrade. She swept down the steps like a ghost. She soon gained the ground floor and I saw below me the face of Rouletabille, who, leaning over the rail of the first landing, looked at her, too.

He mounted the steps to my side.

"Oh, my God!" he cried. "What did I tell you! Poor, poor soul!"

He seemed to be in the greatest agitation.

"I asked M. Darzac for eight days!" he went on. "But this thing must be ended in twenty-four hours or I shall no longer have strength to act."

He entered my room and threw himself into a chair as if exhausted. "I am smothering!" he moaned. "I can't breathe!" He tore his collar away from his throat. "Water!" he entreated. "Water!"

I started to fetch some, but he stopped me.

"No—I want the water from the heavens! I must have it!" and he waved his hands toward the dark skies from which huge drops were slowly beginning to fall.

For ten minutes he remained stretched out in the chair, thinking. What surprised me was that he asked no question or uttered no conjecture as to what the Lady in Black had been seeking in my room. I would not have known how to answer, if he had done so. At length, he rose.

"Where are you going?" I asked.

"To take the guard at the postern."

He would not even come in to dinner and sent word to have some soup brought out to him as though he were a soldier. The dinner was served in la Louve at half past eight. Darzac, who came to the table from Old Bob's workroom, said that the latter refused to dine also. Mme. Edith, fearing that her uncle might be ill, went immediately to the Round Tower. She would not even allow her husband to accompany her—indeed, she seemed to be much out of humour with him.

The Lady in Black came in on the arm of her father. She cast on me a look of sorrowful reproach which disturbed me greatly. Her eyes seemed never to wander from me.

It was a gloomy meal enough. No one ate much. Arthur Rance looked every moment in the direction of the Lady in Black. All the windows were open. The atmosphere was suffocating. A flash of lightning and a heavy clap of thunder came in rapid succession—and then, the deluge! A sigh of relief issued from our overcharged breasts. Mme. Edith reappeared just in time to escape being drenched by the furious rain which beat down like cannon balls upon the peninsula.

The young woman told us in excited tones and with her hands clasped, how she had found Old Bob bending over his desk with his head buried in his hands. He had refused to have anything to say to her. She had spoken to him affectionately and he had treated her like a bear. Then, as he had obstinately held his hands to his ears, she had pricked one of his fingers with a little pin set with rubies which she used to fasten the lace scarf which she wore in the evening over her shoulders. Her uncle, she said, had turned upon her like a mad man, had snatched the little pin from her and thrown it upon the desk. And then he had spoken to her—"brutally, rudely as he had never done before in his life!" she exclaimed. "Get out of here and leave me alone!" was what he had said to her. Mme. Edith had been so much pained that she went out without saying a word, promising herself, however, that she would not soon set foot again in the Round Tower. But she had turned her head for a last look at her old uncle and had been almost struck dumb by what she saw.

The "oldest skull in the history of the human race" was upon the desk, and Old Bob, a handkerchief stained with blood in his hand, was spitting in the skull. He had always treated it with the most severe respect and had insisted that others should do the same. Edith had hurried away, almost frightened.

Robert Darzac reassured her by telling her that what she had taken for blood was only paint and that Old Bob's skull had been spattered by the paints which had been used in the wash drawing.

I left the table to hurry out to Rouletabille and also to escape from Mathilde's glances. What had the Lady in Black been doing in my bedroom? I was not to wait long to know!

When I started out the thunder was pealing loudly and the rain falling with redoubled force. It took me only one bound to reach the postern. No Rouletabille was there! I found him on the terrace B", watching the entrance to the Square Tower and receiving the full strength of the storm at his back.

I entreated him to take shelter under the arch.

"Leave me alone!" he said impatiently. "Leave me alone. This is the deluge. Ah, how good it is! how good—all this anger of the heavens! Have you ever had a desire to roar with the thunder? I have—and I am roaring now. Listen, while I cry out—alas! alas! alas! My voice is stronger than the thunder!"

And he plunged into the darkness making the shadows resound with his savage clamours. I believed this time that he had surely gone mad! But in my heart I knew that the unhappy lad was breathing forth in these indistinct articulations of frightful anguish the misery that burned him, and which he was constantly trying to hinder from burning up the heart and the soul in his body—the misery of being the son of Larsan.

I turned helplessly and as I did so, I felt a hand seize my wrist and a dark form cried out to me above the tempest:

"Where is he?"

It was Mme. Darzac who was also seeking Rouletabille. A new peal of thunder burst and we heard the boy in his mad delirium hurling wild shouts of defiance to the heavens. She heard him. She saw him. We were drenched with water from the rain and the breaking of the sea on the terrace. Mme. Darzac's clothing clung around her like a rag and her skirt dripped as she walked. I took the wretched woman's arm and held her up, for I saw that she was about to fall, and at that moment, in the midst of that terrible unchaining of the elements, in that mad tempest, under this terrible downpour on the breast of the raging sea, I all at once breathed the perfume—the odour so sweet and penetrating and haunting that its fragrance has remained with me ever since—the Perfume of the Lady in Black. Ah, I understood now how Rouletabille had remembered it all these years.

Yes, it was a fragrance full of sadness—something like the perfume of an isolated flower which has been condemned to be seen by no one but to blossom for itself all alone. It was a fragrance which set such ideas as these running through my brain, although I did not analyse them at the time—a sweet, soft and yet insistent perfume which seemed to steal away my senses in the midst of this battle of the elements, as soon as I perceived it. A strange perfume! Surely it was that, for I had seen the Lady in Black hundreds of times without noticing it, and now that I had done so, it was everywhere and above all things and I knew that the memory of it would abide with me while life should last. I understood how when one had—I will not say smelled but seized (for I do not think that everyone would have been able to catch the subtle fragrance of the perfume of the Lady in Black, any more than I myself had done before this night in which my senses seemed to have become sharpened to the keenest point)—yes, when one had seized this adorable and captivating odour, it was for life. And the heart would be perfumed by it, whether it was the heart of a son, like Rouletabille: or the heart of a lover, like M. Darzac.; or the heart of a villain, like Larsan. No, no—the knowledge of it could never pass. And now, by some sudden insight, I seemed to understand Rouletabille and Darzac and Larsan and all the misfortunes which had attended the daughter of Professor Stangerson.

There in the night and the tempest, the Lady in Black called aloud to Rouletabille and he fled from us and rushed further into the night, shrieking aloud, "The perfume of the Lady in Black! The perfume of the Lady in Black!"

The unhappy woman sobbed. She drew me toward the tower. She struck with desperate hands at the door which Bernier opened to us and her weeping would have melted the heart of a stone.

I could only utter the veriest commonplaces, begging her to calm herself, although I would have given everything I had in the world to find words which, without betraying anyone, might perhaps have made her understand my own part in the sorrowful drama which was being played out between the mother and the child.

Suddenly she seemed to recover herself in some degree and she motioned me to enter the little parlour at the right which was just outside the bed chamber of Old Bob. The door stood open but there we were as much alone as we could have been in her own room, for we knew that Old Bob worked late in the Tower of Charles the Bold.

I can assure you that in my memories of that horrible night the thought of the moments which I spent in the company of the Lady in Black are not the least sorrowful. I was put to a proof which I had not expected, and it was like a blow full in the face when, without even taking time to speak of the way in which we had been treated by the elements, Mme. Darzac looked me full in the eyes and demanded: "How long is it, M. Sainclair, that you were at Trepot?"

I was struck dumb—overpowered more completely than I had been by the fury of the storm. And I felt that, at the moment when nature, wearied out, was beginning to grow more quiet, I was to suffer a more dangerous assault than that of thunderbolts or lightning flashes. I must, by my expression, have betrayed the agitation which was aroused in my mind by this unexpected remark, for I could see by her eyes as she looked at me that she was aware how deeply I was moved. At first I made no answer: then I stammered out some disconnected words of which I remember nothing, save that they were ridiculous. It is years now since that night, but as I write I am living over the scene as if I were a spectator instead of the actor which I actually was, and as if it were even now going on in front of my eyes.

There are people who may be drenched to the skin and yet not look in the least ridiculous. The Lady in Black was one of them. Although, like myself, she had experienced the full fury of the storm, she was majestic and beautiful with her dishevelled locks, her bare neck and magnificent shoulders which, through the thin silk which clothed them seemed to have merely a light veil thrown across the flesh. She seemed to be a sublime statue, carved by Phidias from the immortal clay to which his chisel has given form and beauty. I am well aware that, even after all the years which have elapsed, my description sounds too glowing and I will not linger on the subject. But those who have known Professor Stangerson's daughter will understand me, I think, and I desire, here, with Rouletabille near me, to affirm the sentiments of respectful admiration which filled my heart at the sight of this mother, so divinely beautiful, who, in the state of disorder to which the fearful tempest had brought her, and with her whole heart filled with agony, was endeavouring to make me break the oath that I had sworn to the lad who was my friend.

She took both my hands in hers and said in a voice which I shall never forget:

"You are his friend. Tell him, then, that he is not the only one who has suffered." And she added with a sob which shook her whole frame:

"Why will he insist on not telling me the truth!"

I had not a word to say. What could I have answered? This woman had always seemed so cold and formal to the world in general and (as I had thought) to me in particular that it was as if I had not existed for her, and now she was laying bare her heart before me as though I were an old friend. And I had breathed the perfume of the Lady in Black.

Yes, she treated me as an old friend. She told me everything that I already knew in a few sentences as piteous and as simple as a mother's love itself—and she told me other things which Rouletabille had kept a secret from me. Evidently the game of hide and seek could not have lasted long. The relationship between them had been guessed by the one as surely as by the other. Led by a sure instinct Mme. Darzac had resolved to take means to learn who was this Rouletabille who had saved her from death and who was of the age of her own son—and who resembled the lad whom she had mourned as dead. And since her arrival at Mentone, a letter had reached her containing the proof that Rouletabille had lied to her in regard to his early life and had never set foot in any school at Bordeaux. Immediately, she had sought the youth and had asked for an explanation, but he had hurried away without replying. But he had seemed disturbed when she spoke to him of Trepot and of the school at Eu, and the trip which we had made there before coming to Mentone.

"How did you know?" I exclaimed, betraying my secret without realizing that I was doing so. She showed no sign of triumph at my involuntary confession, and in a few words went on to reveal to me her stratagem. That evening when I had taken her by surprise, it was not the first time that she had been in my room. My luggage bore the labels of the hotels at which we had stopped on our recent journey.

"Why did he not throw himself into my arms when I opened them to him?" she moaned. "Ah, my God! If he refuses to be Larsan's son, will he never consent to be mine!"

As she told me her story, it seemed to me that Rouletabille had conducted himself in an atrocious fashion toward this poor woman who had believed him dead, who had mourned for him in despair, and who, in the midst of her terrible dread and mortal anguish, experienced a thrill of the keenest joy in realizing that her son was still alive. Ah, the poor mother! The evening before, he had mocked at her when she had cried out to him with all her soul that she had a son and that that son was he! He had mocked her, even while the tears had streamed down his cheeks. I could never have believed that Rouletabille could have been so cruel or so heartless—or, even, so ill-bred!

Certainly he behaved in an abominable fashion! He had told her with a sardonic smile that "he was nobody's son—not even the son of a thief." It was these words that had sent her flying to her room in the Square Tower and had made her long to die. But she had not found her son only to give him up so easily and she would—she must have him acknowledge her!

I was almost beside myself. I kissed her hands and entreated pardon for Rouletabille. Here was the result of my friend's schemes to save her pain. Under the pretext of saving her from Larsan, he had plunged a knife into her heart. I felt as though I had no wish to know any more of the story. I knew too much already and I longed to run away. I hastened out of the room and called Bernier, who opened the door for me. I went out of the Square Tower, cursing Rouletabille roundly. I went to the Court of the Bold to look for him, but found it deserted.

At the postern gate Mattoni had come to take the ten o'clock watch. I saw a light in Rouletabille's room and I hastened up the rickety stairway of the New Castle and quickly found myself outside his door. I opened it without knocking. Rouletabille looked up.

"What do you want, Sainclair?"

I told him all that I had heard and my opinion of him for his actions which had so deeply wounded Mme. Darzac.

"She didn't tell you everything, my friend," he replied, coldly. "She did not tell you that she forbade me to touch that man."

"That is true!" I cried. "I heard her."

"Well, what have you come here to tell me then?" he went on, roughly. "Do you know what she said to me yesterday? She ordered me to go away. She would rather die than see me take issue *against my father*?

And he laughed—laughed. Such laughter, I hope not to hear again.

"Against my father! She thinks, I suppose, that he is stronger than I!"

His face was not a pleasant sight to see as he uttered the words.

But suddenly it seemed to be transformed and to glow with unearthly beauty.

"She is afraid for me!" he said, softly. "And I—I am afraid for her—only for her. And I do not know my father. And, God help me! I do not know my mother!"

At that moment the sound of a shot rang out on the night, followed by a cry of mortal agony! Ah, it was again the cry that I had heard two years ago in the "inexplicable gallery." My hair rose on my scalp and Rouletabille tottered as though the bullet had struck himself.

And then he bounded toward the open window, filling the fortress with a despairing burst of anguish:

"Mother! Mother! Mother!"

# XI

## THE ATTACK OF THE SQUARE TOWER

I leaped after him and threw my arms around his body, dreading what he might attempt. There was in that cry, "Mother! Mother! Mother!" such a madness of despair, a call, or rather, an assurance of coming aid so beyond the realization of human strength, that I was obliged to fear that the young fellow had forgotten that he was only a man and had not the power to fly straight out of the window of the tower and to traverse, like a bird or a flash of lightning, the black space which separated him from the crime which had been committed and which he filled with his frightful cries. Quickly, he turned on me, threw me off, and precipitated himself wildly, through corridors, apartments, stairways and courts toward the accursed tower from which had come that same death cry that we both had heard—a moment ago, and also two years before when it had resounded through the "inexplicable gallery"

As for me, I had thus far only had the time to gaze out of the window, rooted to my place by the horror of that cry. I was still there when the door of the Square Tower opened, and in its frame of light, there appeared the form of the Lady in Black. She was standing upright, living and unharmed, in spite of that cry of death, but her pale and ghastly visage reflected a terror like that of death itself. She stretched out her arms toward the night and the darkness cast Rouletabille into them, and the arms of the Lady in Black closed around him and I heard no more only sobs and moans and again the two syllables which the night repeated over and over, "Mother! Mother!"

I descended from my tower into the court, my temples throbbing, my heart beating so fast that it almost stifled me. What I had seen on the threshold of the Square Tower had not by any means assured me that nothing terrible had taken place. It was in vain that I attempted to reason with myself and to say: "Nonsense! At the very moment when we believed that all was lost, is not, on the contrary, everything found? Are not the mother and son united?"

But why, then, this cry of death when she was alive and well? Why that scream of agony before she had appeared standing on the threshold of the tower?

Strange to say, I found no one in the Court of the Bold when I crossed it. No one then had heard the pistol shot! No one had heard the cries! Where was M. Darzac? Where was Old Bob? Was he still working in the lower basement of the Round Tower? I might have believed so, for I perceived a light in the window of the tower. But Mattoni—Mattoni—had he heard nothing, either?—Mattoni, who kept watch at the postern of the gardener? And the Berniers? I saw neither of them. And the door of the Square Tower still stood open. Ah, the soft murmur, "Mother! Mother! Mother!" And I heard her voice answer back, tenderly, though choked with sobs, "My boy! My little one!" They had not even taken the precaution to close the door of Old Bob's parlour. It was into that room where I had talked with her a little while before that she had led her child.

And they were there alone, clasped in each other's arms, repeating over and over again, "Mother!" and "My little one!" And then they murmured broken sentences, phrases without end—with the divine foolishness of a mother and her child. "Then, you were not dead!" That was sufficient to make them both fall to sobbing. And then, how they embraced each other, as though to make up for all the years they had lost. I heard him murmur, "You know, mamma, it was not true that I stole!" And one would have thought from the sound of his voice that he was still the little lad of nine years—my poor Rouletabille. "No, my darling—you never stole! My little boy! My little boy!" Ah, it was not my fault that I heard—but my heart was torn in two as I listened.

But where was Bernier? I entered the lodge from the left, for I wished to know the meaning of the cry and of the shot which I had heard.

Mere Bernier was at the back of the room which was lighted only by a tiny taper. She was like a black bundle on a sofa. She must have been in bed when the shot was heard and she had hastily donned some clothing. I picked up the taper and brought it near. Her features were distorted with fear.

"Where is Bernier?" I asked.

"He is there," she replied, trembling.

"There. Where is that?"

But she made no answer.

I took a few steps toward the interior of the lodge and I stumbled. I bent down to know what I had stepped upon and found out that it was Mere Bernier's potatoes. I lowered the light and looked at the floor; it was strewn with potatoes; they had rolled everywhere. Could it be that Mme. Bernier had not gathered them up after Rouletabille had emptied out the bag?

I arose and turned to Mere Bernier.

"Someone fired off a pistol!" I said. "What has happened?"

"I do not know," she responded.

And, at that moment, I heard someone open the door of the tower and Pere Bernier stood on the threshold.

"Ah! it is you, M. Sainclair?"

"Bernier! What has happened?"

"Oh, nothing very serious, M. Sainclair, I am glad to say." (But his voice was too palpably endeavouring to sound strong and brave for me to feel as reassured as he was trying to make me!) "An accident without any importance whatever. M. Darzac, while placing his revolver on the stand beside his bed, accidentally fired it off. Madame, naturally, was frightened, and screamed; and, as the window of their room was open, she thought that you and M. Rouletabille might have heard something and started out to tell you that it was nothing."

"M. Darzac has come in, then?"

"He got here almost as soon as you had left the tower, M. Sainclair. And the shot was fired almost immediately after he entered his bedroom. You can guess that I had a pretty fright! I rushed to the door! M. Darzac opened it, himself. Happily, no one was injured!"

"Did Mme. Darzac go to her own room as soon as I left the tower?"

"At once. She heard M. Darzac when he came in and followed him directly to their apartments. They went in almost at the same moment."

"And M. Darzac? Is he still in his room?"

"Here he is now."

"I turned and saw Robert Darzac; despite the gloom of the place, I saw that his face was ghastly pale. He made me a sign and then said very calmly and quietly:

"Listen, Sinclair! Bernier told you about their little accident. It is not worth mentioning to anyone, unless someone should speak of it to you. The others, perhaps, have not heard the shot. It would be useless to frighten all these good people; don't you think so? Now I have a little favour to ask of you."

"Speak, my friend," I bade him. "Whatever it is, I will do it: you know that without my saying so. Make any use of me that you like."

"Thanks; but it is only to persuade Rouletabille to go to bed: when he is gone, my wife will calm herself and will try to get the rest that she needs. Every one of us has need of rest and calmness, Sainclair. We all need calm and silence."

"Surely, my friend: you may count upon me."

I pressed his hand with a force which attested my sentiments towards him. I was persuaded that both he and Bernier were concealing something from us—something very grave!

Darzac reached his room and I went to find Rouletabille in the sitting room of Old Bob.

But upon the threshold of the apartment, I jostled against the Lady in Black and her son who were passing out. They were both so silent and wore an expression unexpected to me who had overheard their exclamations of love and joy only a few moments before that I stood before them without saying a word or making a movement. The extremity which induced Mme. Darzac to leave Rouletabille so soon under such extraordinary circumstances as those which had attended their reunion, puzzled me so greatly that I could not find words to say what I thought and the submission of Rouletabille in taking leave of her so quickly amazed me. Mathilde pressed a kiss upon the lad's forehead and murmured: "Good-night, my darling," in a voice so soft, so sweet and at the same time so solemn that it seemed to me that it must resemble the leave-taking of one who was about to die. Rouletabille, without answering his mother, took my arm and led me out of the tower. He was trembling like a leaf.

It was the Lady in Black herself who closed the door of the Square Tower. I was sure that something strange was passing within those walls. The account of the pistol shot which had been given me satisfied me not at all: and it is not to be doubted that Rouletabille would have agreed with me if his reasoning powers and his heart had not been giddy from the scene which had taken place between the Lady in Black and himself. And then, after all, how did I know that Rouletabille did not agree with me? We had scarcely gotten outside the Square Tower before I demanded of Rouletabille the meaning of his strange manner. I drew him into that corner of the parapet which joins the Square Tower to the Round Tower in the angle formed by the jutting out of the Square Tower upon the court.

The reporter, who had allowed me as docilely as a little child to lead him wherever I would, spoke to me in a low tone:

"Sainclair, I have sworn to my mother that I will see nothing or hear nothing of that which may pass this night in the Square Tower. It is the first promise that I have made to my mother, Sainclair; but I will break it for her sake just as I would give up my hope of heaven for her. I must see and I must hear!"

We were at that moment not far from a window in which a light was still burning and which opened upon the sitting room of Old Bob and sloped out upon the sea. This window was not closed, and it was this, doubtless, which had permitted us to hear so distinctly in spite of the thickness of the walls of the tower, the pistol shot and the cry of agony that had followed it. From the spot where we were now stationed, we could see nothing through this window, but was it not something to be able to hear? The storm was past, but the waters were not yet appeased and the waves broke on the rocks of the peninsula with a violence that would have rendered the approach of any vessel impossible. The thought of a vessel crossed my mind because I believed for an instant that I could see the shadow of a vessel of some sort appearing or disappearing in the gloom. But what could it be? Evidently a delusion of my mind which beheld hostile shades everywhere—an illusion of a mind which was assuredly more agitated than the waters themselves.

We stood there, motionless, for more than five minutes, before we heard a sigh—ah, how long it was, that mournful sound!—a groan, deep as an expiration, like a moan of agony, a heavy sob, like the last breath of a departing soul—which reached our ears from that window, and brought the sweat of terror to our brows. And then, nothing more—nothing except the intermittent sobbings of the sea.

And suddenly the light in the window went out. The outline of the Square Tower blended with the blackness of the night.

My friend and I grasped each other's hand as if instinctively, commanding each other, by this mute communication, to remain motionless and silent. *Someone was dying, there, in that tower*! Someone whom they had hidden. Why? And who? Someone who was neither M. Darzac nor Mme. Darzac, nor Pere Bernier, nor Mere Bernier, nor—almost beyond the shadow of a doubt, Old Bob; *someone who could not have been in the tower.*

Leaning against the parapet to support ourselves, our necks stretched toward that window through which there had come to us that sigh of agony, we listened. A quarter of an hour passed thus—it might have been a century! Rouletabille pointed out to me the window of his own room in the New Castle which was still illuminated. I understood: it was necessary to extinguish this light and return. I took a thousand precautions. Five minutes later, I was back again with Rouletabille. There was now no other light in the Court of the Bold than the feeble ray which told of the late vigil of Old Bob in the lower basement of the Round Tower and the light at the gardener's postern where Mattoni was standing sentinel. In truth, considering the positions which they occupied, one might easily understand how it was that neither Old Bob nor Mattoni had heard anything that had passed in the Square Tower, nor even, in the heart of the storm, could the clamours of Rouletabille have reached their ears. The walls of the postern were heavy and Old Bob was entombed in a veritable subterranean cavern.

I had scarcely time to steal back to Rouletabille in the corner of the parapet, the post of observation which he had not quitted, before we distinctly heard the door of the Square Tower moving softly upon its hinges. As I attempted to lean further out of my corner, and see further down into the court, Rouletabille pushed me back and allowed only his own head to look over the wall; but as he was leaning far over, I allowed myself to violate his command and looked over his head; and this is was I saw.

First, Pere Bernier, perfectly recognizable, in spite of the darkness, who came out of the tower and directed his steps noiselessly to the gardener's postern. In the middle of the court, he paused, looked up at the side where our windows were, and then returned to the side of the court and made a signal which we interpreted as a sign that all was well. To whom was this signal addressed? Rouletabille leaned further over; but he quickly retreated, pushing me back with him.

When we dared to look out in the court again, no one was there. But in a few moments, we again beheld Pere Bernier (or, rather, we heard him first, for there ensued between him and Mattoni a brief conversation the echoes of which were carried to us.) And then we heard something which climbed under the arch of the gardener's postern and Pere Bernier reappeared with the black and softly rolling form of a carriage beside him. We could see that it was the little English cart drawn by Toby, Arthur Rance's pony. The Court of the Bold was of beaten earth and the little equipage made no more sound than as if it were gliding over a carpet. Toby was so intelligent and so quiet that one would have said that he had received his instructions from Pere Bernier. The latter, reaching, at length, the "oubliette," raised again his face toward our windows, and then, still holding Toby by the bridle, came to the door of the Square Tower. Leaving the little equipage before the door, he entered the tower. A few moments passed by which seemed to us like hours, particularly to Rouletabille, who was seized with a fit of trembling which shook his frame like an aspen leaf. Pere Bernier reappeared. He crossed the court alone and returned to the postern. It was then that we were obliged to lean further out and, certainly, the persons who were now upon the threshold of the Square Tower might have perceived us, if they had looked up at our side, but they were not thinking of us. The night had become clear and a beautiful moon had arisen which threw its rays over the sea and stretched its radiance across the Court of the Bold. The two persons who came out of the tower and approached the carriage appeared so surprised that they almost recoiled at what they saw. But we could hear the Lady in Black repeating again and again in low, firm tones: "Courage, Robert, courage! You must be brave now!"

And Robert Darzac replied in a voice which froze my blood: "It is not courage which I lack!" He was bending over something which he dragged before him and then raised in his arms as though it were a heavy burden and tried to slip under the long seat of the English cart. Rouletabille had taken off his cap. His teeth were chattering. As well as we could distinguish, the thing was in a sack. To move this sack M. Darzac was making the greatest efforts and we heard him breathe a sigh of exhaustion. Leaning against the wall of the tower, the Lady in Black watched him without offering any assistance. And, suddenly, at the moment that M. Darzac had succeeded in loading the sack into the cart, Mathilde pronounced these words in a voice shaken with horror:

"It is *moving?*

"It is the end!" said M. Darzac, wiping his forehead with his pocket handkerchief. Then he took Toby by the bridle and started off, making a sign to the Lady in Black, but she, still leaning against the wall, as though she had been placed there for some punishment, made no signal in reply. M. Darzac seemed to us to be quite calm. His figure straightened up: his step grew firm—one might almost say that his manner was that of an honest man who has done his duty. Still with the greatest precaution, he disappeared with his carriage beneath the postern of the gardener and the Lady in Black went back into the Square Tower.

After this, I wished to emerge from our corner, but Rouletabille restrained me. It was well that he did so, for Bernier came up to the postern and crossed the court, directing his way again toward the Square Tower. When he was not more than two meters from the door, which was closed, Rouletabille glided softly from the corner of the parapet, stepped between the door and the figure of Bernier, who was struck with terror. He put his hands upon the shoulders of the concierge.

"Come with me!" he commanded.

Bernier seemed absolutely powerless. I, too, came out of my hiding place. The old man looked at us both standing there in the moonlight: his face was sorrowful and he murmured sadly:

"This is a great misfortune!"

# XII

## THE IMPOSSIBLE BODY

"It will be a great misfortune if you don't tell the truth," muttered Rouletabille, in smothered tones. "But if you conceal nothing, the trouble may not be so great. Come this way."

And he drew him, clasping him by the fist, toward the New Château, I following. I saw that a great change had come over Rouletabille. He was completely his old self again. Now that he was so happily relieved of the sorrow of separation from his mother which had pressed on his mind ever since his early childhood, now that he had again found the perfume of the Lady in Black, he seemed to have reconquered all the forces of his spirit and was ready to enter eagerly into the strife against the mysteries which surrounded us. And, until the day when all was ended—until the last supreme moment—the most dramatic that I have ever lived through in the whole course of my existence—*the moment in which life and death spoke out and were explained by his lips*—he never again made a sign of hesitation in the forward march: he never spoke another word which could have been taken as an attempt to warn us against the dreadful situation which arose from the siege of the Square Tower by the attack of that night between the twelfth and thirteenth of April.

Bernier resisted him no further. When others tried to do so, he held them in his grasp until they cried for mercy.

Bernier walked in front of us, his head bent, looking like an accused man who is being led on his way to trial. And when we reached Rouletabille's room, the young reporter bade Bernier sit down facing us. I lighted the lamp. Rouletabille sat silent for a moment, looking at Bernier, lighting his pipe the while, and evidently seeking to read in the face of the concierge all the honesty which he could find. Soon his knitted brows relaxed, his eye grew clearer and, after he had blown a few rings of smoke toward the ceiling, he said:

"Well, Bernier, how did they kill him?"

Bernier shook his shaggy head.

"I have sworn to say nothing and I will say nothing, monsieur. And, upon my word of honour, I know nothing."

"All right," went on Rouletabille, unconcernedly. "Tell me what you don't know. For if you do not tell me what you don't know, Bernier, I will be responsible for nothing, no matter what happens."

"And for what could you be responsible in any case, monsieur?"

"For one thing, I won't answer for your safety, Bernier."

"For my safety? I have done nothing."

"For the safety of all of us, then for our lives, even!" replied Rouletabille, arising from his chair and pacing restlessly across the room, in order, doubtless, to give himself an opportunity to perform some necessary mental algebraic operation. Then he paused and went on, "Where was he? In the Square Tower?"

Bernier did not speak but he nodded assent.

"Where? In Old Bob's bedroom?"

"No," Bernier shook his head.

"Hidden in your rooms?"

Bernier shook his head vehemently.

"Well, where was he then? He could certainly not have been in the apartments of M. and Mme. Darzac!"

Bernier bowed his head.

"Miserable hound!" cried Rouletabille and he leaped at Bernier's throat. I rushed to the rescue of the concierge and snatched him from the young man's clutches. As soon as he could breathe, the old servant looked up, piteously.

"Why did you try to strangle me, M. Rouletabille?" he asked.

"How dare you ask, Bernier? How dare you? And you acknowledge that *he* was in the apartment of M. and Mme. Darzac! Who, then, gained him entrance to that apartment? No one but yourself. You, the only person who had the key when the Darzacs were not there!"

Bernier arose to his feet. He was as pale as a ghost, but his look and attitude were full of dignity.

"M. Rouletabille, do you accuse me of being an accomplice of Larsan?"

"I forbid you to pronounce that name!" shouted the reporter. "You know very well that Larsan is dead—and has been dead for months!"

"For months!" echoed Bernier, ironically. "Yes, that is true—I was wrong to forget it. When one devotes oneself to his masters and permits himself to be beaten and abused for them, it is necessary to ignore everything, no matter what they may do to you. I beg your pardon, sir."

"Listen to me, Bernier. I know that you are a brave man and I respect you. It is not your good faith that I am questioning, but I am censuring your negligence."

"My negligence!" Bernier, as pale as his face had been, flushed crimson. "My negligence! I have not budged from my lodge—not even from the corridor. I have always worn the key in my breast pocket and I swear to you that no one entered that room—no one at all—after you were there at five o'clock, except M. and Mme. Darzac, themselves. I do not count, of course, the few moments that you and M. Sainclair were there at about six o'clock."

"What!" exclaimed Rouletabille. "Do you want me to believe that this individual—you have forgotten his name, I think, Bernier—let us call him 'the Man'—that the man was killed in M. Darzac's rooms if he was not there?"

"I do not. And, furthermore, I can swear to you that he *was* there."

"Yes, but how could he have been? That is what I ask you, Bernier. And you are the only one who can answer because you alone had the key in the absence of M. and Mme. Darzac. And M. Darzac never took the key with him when he left the room and no one could have gotten into the room to hide while he was there."

"That is the mystery, monsieur. That is what puzzles M. Darzac more than all the rest. But I have only been able to answer him as I have answered you. There is the mystery."

"When you left the room with M. Darzac, M. Sainclair and myself at about a quarter after six, did you lock the door immediately?"

"Yes, monsieur."

"When did you open it after that?"

"Not at all."

"And where were you in the meantime?"

"In front of the door of my lodge, watching the door of the apartment. My wife and I took our dinner in that same spot at about half after six, on a little table in the corridor, because, on account of the door of the tower being open, it was quite light and was pleasanter. After dinner, I sat in the doorway of the lodge, smoking a cigarette and chatting with my wife. We were so seated that, even if we had wished to do so, we would not have been able to withdraw our eyes from M. Darzac's rooms. It is a mystery!—a mystery more extraordinary than the mystery of the Yellow Room. For, in the former case, we did not know of what had passed *before*. But now, monsieur, one knows all that happened beforehand since you yourself visited the apartment at 5 o'clock and saw that no person was there: one knows all that passed during the interim, for either I had the key in my pocket, or M. Darzac was in his room and must have seen the man who opened his door and entered the room for the purpose of assassinating him. And while I was sitting in the corridor before the door, I must have seen the man pass! And we know what took place *after*. *After*, there was the death of the man and that proved that the man was there. Ah, it is a mystery!"

"And from five o'clock until the moment of the tragedy, you declare that you never quitted the corridor?"

"I swear it."

"You are absolutely certain?" persisted Rouletabille.

"Ah, pardon, monsieur—there was one moment—the moment that you called me."

"That is good, Bernier. I wanted to see if you remembered that."

"But I was not away from my post more than an instant or two, and M. Darzac was in his room then. He did not leave it while I was gone. Ah! what a mystery!"

"How do you know that M. Darzac didn't go out during those moments?"

"Why, because if he had done so, my wife, who was in the lodge, must have seen him! And then all would be explained and we would not be so puzzled, nor Madame either. Ah! must I say it to you over again? No one has entered that room except M. Darzac at five o'clock and you two at six, and no person got in between the time that M. Darzac went out and the time when he came in at night with Mme. Darzac. He was like you—he didn't want to believe me. I swore it to him upon the corpse that lay before us!"

"Where was the corpse?"

"In M. Darzac's bedroom."

"It was really a dead body?"

"Oh, he was breathing still—I heard him."

"Then it was not a corpse, Pere Bernier."

"Oh, M. Rouletabille, where was the difference? He had a bullet in his heart."

At last, Pere Bernier was going to tell us of the body. Had he seen it? Who was it? One would have said that this seemed of secondary importance in the eyes of Rouletabille. The reporter seemed engrossed only with the problem of finding how the body had come to be there. How had that man happened to be killed? But, indeed, Pere Bernier knew only very little. The whole thing had been as sudden as a rifle shot—so it seemed to him—and he was behind the door. He told us that he was going to his lodge and felt so drowsy that he had intended to throw himself down on the bed for a few moments, when he and Mere Bernier heard such a commotion issue from the apartment of M. Darzac that they were seized with terror. It was as if the furniture were being thrown about and blows were rained upon the walls.

"What is the matter?" cried Mere Bernier, and the same instant they heard the voice of Mme. Darzac, shouting, "Help! Help!" This was the cry that we, too, had heard in the New Château. Pere Bernier, leaving his wife almost fainting from horror, rushed to the door of M. Darzac's room and beat against it, crying aloud to him to open, but obtaining no reply. The struggle within was still going on. Bernier heard the laboured breathing of two men and he recognised the voice of Larsan when he heard the words: "With this blow, I shall have your life!" Then he heard M. Darzac, who called his wife to his aid in a voice almost stifled, as though he were gagged, "Mathilde! Mathilde!" Evidently he and Larsan must have been engaged in a life and death struggle when, suddenly, the pistol shot had saved him. This pistol shot had frightened Pere

Bernier less than the cry which had followed it. One would have thought that Mme. Darzac, who had uttered the cry, had been mortally wounded. Bernier was unable to understand Mme. Darzac's attitude in the matter. Why did she not open the door and admit him to help her husband? Why did she not draw the shades? Finally, almost immediately after the pistol shot, the door, upon which Pere Bernier had not stopped knocking all the time, was opened. The room was wrapped in darkness, which did not surprise the concierge, for the light of the chandelier which he had perceived under the door during the fight had been suddenly extinguished and at the same moment he had heard the chandelier itself fall heavily to the floor. It was Mme. Darzac who had opened the door and Bernier could distinguish through the gloom the form of M. Darzac leaning over something which the concierge knew was a dying man. Bernier had called to his wife to bring a light, but Mme. Darzac had cried: "No, no! No light! No light! And, above all, be sure that *he* knows nothing." And immediately she had rushed to the door of the tower, calling out, "He is coming! He is coming! I hear him! Open the door, Pere Bernier! I must go and meet him!" And Pere Bernier had opened the door, the while she kept on moaning, "Hide yourselves! Go in! Don't let him know anything!"

Pere Bernier went on:

"You came like a waterspout, M. Rouletabille. And she drew you into Old Bob's sitting room. You saw nothing. I stayed with M. Darzac. The rattle in the throat of the man on the floor had ceased. M. Darzac still bending over him said to me: "Get a sack, Bernier, a sack and a stone, and we will throw him into the sea and no one will ever hear his voice again!"

"Then," Bernier went on, "I thought of my sack of potatoes; my wife had gathered them up and put them back in the sack after you had emptied them out; I emptied the bag again and brought it to him. We made as little noise as possible. During this time, Madame was, I suppose, telling you the story in Old Bob's sitting room and we heard M. Sainclair questioning my wife in the lodge. Moving very quietly, we had slipped the body, which M. Darzac had tied up, into the sack. But I said to M. Darzac: 'Let me beg of you not to throw it into the water. It is not deep enough to hide it. There are days when the sea is so clear that one may look down to the bottom.' 'What shall we do, then?' whispered M. Darzac. I answered: 'Heaven help us, I don't know, monsieur! All that I could do for you and for Madame and for humanity against a villain like Frederic Larsan, I have done and willingly. But don't ask any more of me and may God protect you!' And I went out of the room and found you in the lodge, M. Sainclair. And then you went for M. Rouletabille at the request of M. Darzac, who had come out of his own apartment. As for my wife, she was almost swooning with terror when she suddenly saw that both M. Darzac and myself were covered with blood. See, messieurs, my hands are red! Pray Heaven, it doesn't bring us misfortune! But we have done our duty. Oh, he was a miserable wretch!—But do you want me to tell you?—well, one could never keep such a history secret—and, in my opinion, it would be better to go immediately with it to the justice. I have promised to keep silence and I did keep silence so long as I was able, but I'm glad enough to relieve myself of such a burden before you gentlemen who are the friends of Monsieur and Madame—and who may, perhaps, be able to make them listen to reason. Why should they hide the facts? Isn't it an honour to have killed Larsan!—Pardon me for having spoken his name—I know well, it was not right—but is it not an honour to have saved the whole world from a scoundrel in saving oneself? Ah! hold! a fortune! Mme. Darzac promised me a fortune, if I would keep silence. What do I care for that? Could one have a better fortune than to be of service to the poor lady who has had so many troubles? Never in the world! But, how she looked! Why should she have feared? I asked her when we thought that you had gone to bed and that we three were all alone in the Square Tower with our corpse. I said to her, 'Tell everyone that you have killed him All the world will praise you!' She answered: 'There has been too much scandal already, Bernier: and as much as it depends on me to do, and as much as is possible, I will hide this new horror forever! It would kill my father!' I had nothing to say to that, but I wanted to speak. It was upon the tip of my tongue to say, 'If the business comes out later, one will believe that you did something wrong and monsieur, your father, will die just as surely.' But it was her idea. She wished that all should be concealed! Well, I promised her. That's all!"

Bernier turned toward the door, showing us his hands.

"I must rid myself of the blood of the accursed pig!" he said, dryly. Rouletabille stopped him.

"And what was M. Darzac saying all this time? What was his opinion?"

"He repeated: 'What Mme. Darzac says is right. She must be obeyed implicitly.' His shirt was torn and he had a slight wound in his throat, but it did not seem to bother him at all, and, indeed, there was only one thing in which he seemed interested, and that was as to how the miserable wretch had gotten into his rooms. I told him what I have told you—that he could not have entered without my seeing him, and I told him just how I had passed every moment of my time. His first words on the subject had been: 'But when I came in a little while ago, there was no one in my room and I shut and bolted the door.'"

"Where did this conversation take place?"

"In the lodge, in the presence of my wife, who was nearly frightened to death, poor thing!"

"And the body? Where was that?"

"It lay in the sleeping room of M. Darzac."

"And how was it decided that it should be disposed of?"

"I can't say as to that for certain, but their resolution was taken, for Mme. Darzac said to me: 'Bernier, I am going to ask of you one last service: go and bring the English cart from the stable and harness Toby to it. Don't waken Walter, if you can help it. If you wake him and he asks for any explanations, say this to him and also to Mattoni, who has the watch at the postern: "It is for M. Darzac, who must be at Castelar at four o'clock in the morning to see the tournament in the Alps." ' Mme. Darzac said also: 'If you meet M. Sainclair, bring him to me, but if you meet M. Rouletabille, say nothing to him and do nothing that may attract his attention.' Ah, Monsieur! Madame did not let me go out until the window of your room was closed and your light extinguished! And, then, we were not entirely certain in regard to the body which we believed to be dead, before it sighed once more—and, my God! what a sigh! The rest, Monsieur, you saw for yourself and now you know as much as I. God help us!"

When Bernier had finished relating this incredible story, Rouletabille put his hand on his arm, thanking him most earnestly for his great devotion to his master and mistress, and begged him to use the utmost discretion. The young reporter entreated the old servant to pardon his roughness and ordered him to say nothing to Mme. Darzac of anything that had passed between them. Bernier extended his hand in token of fidelity, but Rouletabille drew back:

"No—I can't, Bernier! You are covered with blood."

Bernier left us to look for the Lady in Black.

"Well!" I said when we were alone. "Larsan is dead!"

"Yes," answered Rouletabille. "I fear so!"

"You fear so why, in Heaven's name?"

"Because," he answered in a strange tone, which I could scarcely recognize as his. "Because the death of Larsan, who is carried out dead from a place which he never entered dead or alive, terrifies me more than his life itself!"

# XIII

## IN WHICH THE FEARS OF ROULETABILLE ASSUME ALARMING PROPORTIONS

It was literally true that he was frightened. And I was more terrified myself than words could express. I had never seen him in such a state of mental inquietude. He walked up and down the room nervously, occasionally stopping in front of the mirror and passing his hand over his forehead, as if he were asking his own image, "Can it be you, Rouletabille, who have such thoughts? How dare you harbour them?" What thoughts? He seemed rather to be upon the point of thinking than to be actually doing so, and to be using every means of driving thought away. He shook his head savagely and started for the window as though he meant to leap out, leaning forth into the night, listening for the slightest noise on the distant bank of the sea, expecting, perhaps, to hear the wheels of the little carriage and the echo of Toby's shoes. One might have thought him a beast at bay. The surf was quiet; the waves had grown entirely appeased. A white ray appeared suddenly shining over the black waters. It was the dawn. And in a moment the old château seemed to rise out of the night, pale and livid with the same pallor as our own—the pallor of one who has not slept. "Rouletabille," I asked, trembling as I spoke, for I felt that I was intruding upon ground where my feet had no right to tread; "your interview with your mother was very brief and you separated in silence. I want to ask you, my boy, whether she told you the story of the accident with the revolver on the night stand that Bernier told me?"

"No," he answered without turning his face toward me.

"She told you nothing of that kind?"

"No."

"And you did not ask her for any explanation of the pistol shot nor of the death cry—the cry that was the echo of the one which we heard two years ago from her lips in the 'inexplicable gallery'?"

"Sainclair, you are too curious—you are more curious than I. I asked her nothing."

"And you swore to see nothing and to hear nothing without her saying anything to you about the pistol shot and the cry?"

"Truly, Sainclair, it was necessary for me to believe—for my part, I respected the secrets of the Lady in Black. I had nothing to ask of her when she said to me, 'We must leave each other now, my child, but nothing can ever separate us again!"

"Ah, she said that to you—'Nothing can ever separate us again'?"

"Yes, my friend—and there was blood upon her hands."

We looked at each other in silence. I was now at the window and beside the reporter. Suddenly his hand touched mine. Then he pointed to the little taper which was burning at the entrance to the subterranean door which led to Old Bob's study in the Tower of the Bold.

"It is dawn," said Rouletabille. "And Old Bob is still at work. This old fellow is certainly industrious and we will go and have a peep at him at his labours. That will change our current of thought and I shall be able to get away from these horrors that are smothering me and driving me half wild."

And he heaved a long sigh.

"Will Darzac never return!" he murmured, more as though he were speaking to himself than to me.

A few moments later we had crossed the court and had descended into the octagon room of the Tower of Charles the Bold. It was empty. The lamp was burning on the work table, but there was no sign of Old Bob.

"Oh!" cried Rouletabille. He picked up the lamp and carried it from place to place examining everything around him. He tried in turn the lock of every little window which opened from the walls of the basement. Nothing had changed its place, and all was arranged in order and scientific etiquette. While we were looking around at the bones and shells and horns of the prehistoric ages, the "hanging crystals," the rings made out of bone, the buckles formed from teeth, and the other treasures of the savant, we came to the little desk table. There we found the "oldest skull in the history of humanity"; and it was true that it had been spattered with the red paint of the wash drawing which M. Darzac had set to dry upon that part of the desk which faced the window and was exposed to the sun. I went from one window to the other and shook the iron bars in order to assure myself that they had not been touched nor tampered with in any way. Rouletabille saw what I was doing and said:

"What are you about? Before thinking about how he could have gotten out at the windows, wouldn't it be better to find out whether he went by the door?"

He set the lamp upon the parapet and looked for traces of footprints. Then Rouletabille said:

"Go and knock at the door of the Square Tower and ask Bernier whether Old Bob has come in. Ask Mattoni at the postern and Pere Jacques at the iron gate. Go, Sainclair—quick!"

Five minutes after I went out I was back with the information. No one had seen Old Bob in any part of the fortress. He had not passed by anywhere. Rouletabille had his face close to the parapet. He said:

"He left this lamp burning in order to make people believe that he was at work." And then he added, softly: "There is no sign of a struggle of any sort and in the sand I find the traces of the footprints of only M. Arthur Rance and M. Robert Darzac, who came to this room during the storm last night and have brought on their feet a little earth from the court of the Bold and also of the claylike soil of the outer court. There is no footprint which could be Old Bob's. Old Bob reached here before and, perhaps, went out while the tempest was raging, but, in any case, he has not come in since." Rouletabille stood erect. He replaced upon the desk the lamp the rays of which fell directly upon the skull which had been splashed by the red paint in a frightful fashion. Around us there were dozens of skeletons but certainly their presence was less alarming to me than the absence of Old Bob.

Rouletabille stood for a moment staring at the crimson skull, then he took it in his hands and held his eyes close to its empty orbits. Then he raised the skull higher and held it at arms' length, gazing at it with an almost breathless interest; he looked at the profile. Then he placed the hideous object in my hands and told me to raise it to the level of my head, as carefully as thought it were the most precious of burdens while Rouletabille brought the lamp very close to it.

Like a flash an idea pierced through my brain. I let the skull fall on the desk and rushed through the court till I came to the oubliette. I discovered that the iron bars which closed it were still fast. If anyone had fled by that way or had fallen into the shaft or had thrown himself down, the bars would have been opened. I hurried back, more anxious than ever.

"Rouletabille! Rouletabille! There is no way that Old Bob could have gotten out except in the sack!"

I repeated the sentence, but my friend was not listening and I was surprised to see him deeply engrossed in a task of which I found it impossible to guess the meaning. How, at a time as tragic as the present, while we were awaiting only the return of M. Darzac to complete the circle in which the impossible body was found—while in the Square Tower, the Lady in Black, like Lady MacBeth, must be occupied in effacing from her hands the stains of the strangest of crimes, Rouletabille seemed to be amusing himself by making drawings with a foot rule, a square, a measure and a compass. There he was, seated in the old geologist's easy chair with Robert Darzac's drawing board before him and he also was making a plan—quiet and imperturbable as an architect's clerk.

He had pricked the paper with one of the points of his compass while the other point traced the circle which might represent the Tower of the Bold as we could see it in the design of M. Darzac. Then, dipping his brush into a tiny dish half full of the red pain which M. Darzac had been using he carefully spread the paint over the entire space occupied by the circle. In doing this, he was extremely particular, giving the greatest attention to seeing that the paint was of the same thickness at every point, just as a student might have done in preparing a lesson. He bent his head first to the right and then to the left as though to see the effect, moistening his lips with his tongue as though he were meditating earnestly. In a moment he gave a little start and then sat motionless. His eyes were fixed on the drawing as thought they had been glued to it. They did not even move in their sockets. The stillness was horrible, but it was not much better when his lips opened to utter an exclamation of breathless horror. His face looked like that of a maniac. And he turned toward me so quickly that he upset the great easy chair in which he had been seated.

"Sainclair! Sainclair! Look at the red paint! Look at the red paint!"

I leaned over the drawing breathless terrified of the savage exultation of his tone. But I could see a little drawing carefully done. "The red paint! The red paint!" he kept groaning, his eyes staring in his head as though he were witnessing some frightful spectacle.

"But what—what is it?" I stammered.

" '*What is it?*' My god, man, can't you see? Don't you know that that is *blood?*"

No, I did not know it indeed. I was quite sure that it wasn't blood. It was merely red paint. But I took care not to contradict Rouletabille. I feigned to be interested in this idea of blood.

"Whose blood?" I inquired. "Do you think that it can be Larsan's?"

"Oh! Oh! Oh! Larsan's blood? Who knows anything about Larsan's blood? Who has ever seen the colour of it? To see that, it would be necessary to open my own veins, Sainclair. That's the only way!"

I was completely overwhelmed and astonished.

"My father would not let his blood be spilled like that!"

He was speaking again with that strange, desperate pride of his father.

"When my father wears a wig, it will fit! My father would not let his blood be spilled like that!"

"Bernier's hands were covered with it and you yourself saw it upon the hand of the Lady in Black."

"Yes, yes! That is true—that is true! But they could never kill my father like that!"

He seemed to grow more excited every moment and he never ceased gazing on the little wash drawing. At last he spoke, his breast shaken with a great sob.

"O, God! O God! O God, have pity on us! That would be too frightful!"

He ceased for a moment and then spoke again:

"My poor mother did not deserve this! I did not deserve it—nor any one in the world!" A tear ran down his cheek and fell into the little dish of paint.

"Ah!" he cried. "It isn't necessary to fill it any fuller." And he picked up the tiny cup with infinite care and carried it to the cabinet.

Then he took me by the hand and bade me look at him carefully—carefully—and tell him whether he had not really gone suddenly insane.

"Let us go! Let us go!" he said, drearily, at last. "The time is come, Sainclair. No matter what happens, we can never turn back now! The Lady in Black must tell us everything—*everything about the man who is in that sack)*. Ah, if M. Darzac were to return immediately—immediately—it might be less painful—but I dare wait no longer!"

Wait for what? Wait for whom? And why should he be so terrified now? What fear had made his eyes so wild? Why did his teeth chatter?

I could not restrain myself from asking him again: "What are you afraid of: Do you think that Larsan is not dead?"

And he answered, gripping my hand as though he would never release it: "I tell you I fear his death more than I fear his life!"

And he knocked at the door of the Square Tower before which we were standing as he spoke. I asked him whether he did not wish me to leave him alone with his mother. But, to my great surprise, he begged me not to abandon him "for anything in the world—so that the circle should not be closed." And he added mournfully. "Perhaps it may never be!"

The door of the Tower remained closed. He knocked again; then it was opened and we saw Bernier's face appear. He seemed embarrassed at the sight of us. "What do you want? What are you doing here again?" he demanded. "Speak low. Madame is in Old Bob's sitting room. And the old man has not come in yet."

"Let us enter, Bernier" said Rouletabille. And he pushed the door further open.

"But whatever you do, don't let Madame suspect—"

"No, no!" replied Rouletabille, impatiently.

We were in the vestibule of the Tower. The darkness was almost impenetrable.

"What is Madame doing in Old Bob's sitting room?" asked the reporter in a low voice.

"She is waiting—waiting for the return of M. Darzac. She dare not re-enter *the room* until he comes—nor I, either!"

"Well, go back into your lodge, Bernier!" ordered Rouletabille. "And wait until I call you."

The young reporter opened the door of Old Bob's salon, and we saw the form of the Lady in Black, or, rather, her shadow, for the apartment was very dark and the first faint rays of the sun had scarcely penetrated it. The tall, sombre silhouette of Mathilde was standing but it leaned against the corner of the window which looked out upon the court of Charles the Bold. She never moved at our entrance, but her lips opened and a voice that I should never have recognised as hers, murmured:

"Why are you come? I saw you crossing the court. You have been there all night. You know all. What do you want now?"

And she added in a tone of unutterable misery:

"You swore to me that you would seek to know nothing."

Rouletabille went to her side and took her hand reverently.

"Come, Mother, dearest!" he said and the simple words upon his lips sounded like a prayer, tender and imploring. "Come—come!"

And he drew her away. She did not resist in the least. It was as though as soon as he touched her hand, he could bend her to his will. But when he led her to the door of the fatal chamber, her whole frame seemed to recoil. "Not there!" she moaned.

And she reeled against the wall to keep herself from falling. Rouletabille tried the door. It was locked. He called Bernier, who opened the door and then hurried away as though he were bent on escaping from some deadly peril.

Once the door was opened, we looked into the room. What a spectacle we beheld! The chamber was in the most frightful disorder. And the crimson dawn which entered through the vast embrasures rendered the disorder still more sinister. What an illumination for a chamber of horrors! Blood was upon the walls and upon the floor and upon the furniture! The blood of the rising sun and the blood of him whom Toby had carried off in the sack, no one knew whither—in the potato bag! The tables, the chairs, the sofas were all overturned. The curtains of the bed to which the man in his death agony had tried desperately to cling were half torn down and one could distinguish upon one of them the mark of a bloody hand.

It was into this scene that we entered, supporting the Lady in Black, who seemed ready to swoon, while Rouletabille kept murmuring to her in his gentle and pleading tones: "It has to be done, Mother! It has to be done!" And as soon as he had placed her upon a couch which I had turned right side up, he began to question her. She answered in monosyllables, by signs of the head or movements of the hands. And I saw that the further the examination progressed, the more troubled and restless Rouletabille became. He was visibly affected. He endeavoured to regain his composure and to help his mother maintain hers but it was difficult for him to succeed in either effort. He spoke to the unhappy woman as though he were still her little child. He called her "mamma" and tried in every way to show his reverence and love for her. But she had utterly lost courage. He held out his arms and she threw herself into them, the son and mother embraced and that seemed to give her a little more strength and she burst into a fit of weeping which seemed to relieve a little the terrible weight upon her breast. I made a movement as if to retire, but both sought to detain me and I saw that they did not wish to be left alone in this room red with blood.

Mme. Darzac, after her sobs had ceased, murmured:

"We are delivered!"

Rouletabille had fallen upon his knees at her side and, as she uttered the words, he said entreatingly: "Mother, dearest, in order that we may be sure of that—quite sure—you must tell me all that happened—everything that you saw."

Then she told us the story. She looked at the closed door; she looked with what seemed to be new horror at the overturned furniture and the blood-spattered walls and floor and she narrated the details of the frightful scene through which she had passed in a voice so low as to be almost inaudible, and I was obliged to bring my ear close to her to hear at all. In short, halting phrases, she told us that as soon as M. Darzac had entered his room, he had drawn the bolt and had walked straight to the little table which was placed in the centre of the room. The Lady in Black was standing a little nearer the left, ready to pass into her own sleeping room. The apartment was lighted only by a wax candle placed on the night commode, at the left, near Mathilde's door. And this is what happened:

The silence of the room was suddenly broken by a loud crash, like that of a piece of furniture falling to the ground, which made both M. and Mme. Darzac quickly raise their heads while their hearts were struck at the same moment by the same thrill of terror. The crash came from the little panel. And then all was silent. The pair looked at each other without daring to utter a word, perhaps without being able to do so. Darzac made a movement toward the panel which was situated at the back of the room on the right hand side. He was nailed to the spot where he stood by a second crash, louder than the first, and this time it seemed to Mathilde that she could see the panel move. The Lady in Black asked herself whether she were the victim of a hallucination, or if she had really seen the panel move. But Darzac had seen the same thing, for he made a hasty step in that direction. But at that very moment, the panel swung open before them. Pushed by an invisible hand it turned on its hinges. The Lady in Black tried to cry out, but her tongue clove to the roots of her mouth. But she made a gesture of terror and bewilderment which threw the wax candle to the ground at the very moment when a shadowy form issued from the panel. Uttering a cry of rage, Robert Darzac rushed upon the figure.

"And that shadow—that shadow had a face that you could see?" interrupted Rouletabille. "Mamma, why did you not see the face? You have killed the shadow, but how do we know that it was Larsan, if you did not see his face? Perhaps you have not even killed Larsan's shadow."

"Oh, yes," she replied, almost listlessly. "He is dead." And then for a moment, she said no more.

And I looked at Rouletabille, asking myself: Who could have been killed if it were not Larsan? If Mathilde had not seen his face, she had certainly heard his voice. She shuddered yet at the recollection—she heard it yet. And Bernier, too, had heard the voice and recognised it—that terrible voice of Larsan's—the voice of Ballmeyer, who in that fearful conflict in the middle of the night, had promised death to Robert Darzac. "This blow will end your life!" while Darzac could only groan in the tones of a dying man, "Mathilde! Mathilde!" Ah, how he had cried to her!—how he had called with the rattle in his throat, as he lay already vanquished and in the shadow of death! And she—she had only to throw her own shadow, swooning with terror, into the midst of those two other shadows, while the man she loved called upon her for the aid she could not give and which could not come from elsewhere. And then, suddenly, there had come the pistol shot and she had uttered that terrible shriek—as though she had been wounded, herself. "Who was dead? Who was living? Who was speaking? Whose voice would she hear?"

And then it was Robert who spoke.

Rouletabille took the Lady in Black into his arms once more, lifted her up and carried her tenderly to the door of her own room. And there, he said to her: "Mamma, you must leave me now. I have work to do—for you, for M. Darzac and for myself."

"Don't leave me! I beg of you not to leave me until Robert comes back!" she cried in terror. Rouletabille begged her to try and take some rest and promised to remain near her if she would close her door, when someone knocked at the door of the corridor. Rouletabille asked who was there and the voice of Darzac answered.

"At last!" cried Rouletabille, and he threw the door open.

The man who entered looked like a corpse. Never was human face so pallid, so bloodless, so devoid of all semblance of life. So many emotions had ravaged his visage that it expressed not a single one.

"Ah! you were there!" he said. "Well, it is over." And he fell into the chair from which Rouletabille had just raised the Lady in Black. He looked up at her.

"Your wish is realised," he said. "It is where you wished it to be."

"Did you see his face?" questioned Rouletabille excitedly.

"No," answered Darzac, wearily. "I have not seen it. Did you think that I was going to open the sack?"

I thought that Rouletabille would have shown discomfiture at this answer but, on the contrary, he turned to M. Darzac and said:

"Ah, you did not see his face. That's very good, indeed." And he pressed his hand affectionately.

"The important thing now," he went on, "is not that, at all. It is necessary that we should close the circle. And you will help us do that, M. Darzac. Wait a moment."

And almost joyously, he threw himself down on all fours and crawled around among the furniture and under the bed as I had seen him do in the Yellow Room. And from time to time, he raised his head to say:

"Ah, I shall find something—something that will save us."

I answered, looking at M. Darzac: "Aren't we saved already?"

"Which will save our brains," Rouletabille went on.

"The boy is right!" exclaimed M. Darzac. "It is absolutely necessary for us to know how that man got into the room."

Suddenly Rouletabille rose to his feet, holding in his hand a revolver which he had found under the panel.

"Ah! you have found his revolver!" cried M. Darzac.

"Fortunately, he did not have time to use it." As he spoke M. Darzac took from his pocket his own revolver—the revolver which had saved his life—and held it out to the young man.

"This is a good weapon!" he said.

Rouletabille examined it closely and looked into the empty barrel out of which had sped the ball which had dealt death; then he compared the pistol with that which he had found under the panel and which had fallen from the hand of the assassin. The latter was a "bull dog" and bore the mark of a London gunsmith; it seemed to be quite new, every barrel was filled and Rouletabille declared that it had never been fired.

"Larsan only avails himself of firearms in the last extremity," said the young man. "He hates noise of any kind. You may be sure that he intended merely to frighten you with his revolver, otherwise he would have fired it immediately."

And Rouletabille returned M. Darzac's revolver and put Larsan's in his pocket.

"Of what use is it to be armed now?" cried M. Darzac, shaking his head. "I assure you it is quite futile."

"You believe so?" demanded Rouletabille.

"I am certain of it."

Rouletabille made a few steps through the room and said:

"With Larsan, one can never be sure of anything. Where is the body?"

M. Darzac replied.

"Ask my wife. I want to forget all about it. I know nothing more about this horrible thing. When the remembrance of that dreadful journey shall return to me, I shall try to make myself believe that it was a nightmare. And I will drive it away. Never speak to me of it again. No one save Mme. Darzac knows where the body is. She may tell you, if she likes."

"I have forgotten, too!" said Mathilde. "I was obliged to do so."

"Nevertheless," insisted Rouletabille, shaking his head, "you must tell me. You said that he was in his agony. Are you sure that he is dead now?"

"I am perfectly sure," replied M. Darzac, simply.

"Oh, it is finished. Is it not entirely ended?" pleaded Mathilde. She arose and walked to the window. "See! There is the sun! This horrible night is dead—dead, forever! Everything is over!"

Poor Lady in Black! The yearnings of her soul revealed themselves in her words. "It is finished!" And the fact, as she believed it, made her forget all the horror of the scene which had passed in this room. Larsan no more! Larsan buried! Buried in the potato sack!

And we all started up in affright, when the Lady in Black began to laugh—the frantic laugh of a mad woman! She ceased as suddenly as she had begun and a horrible stillness followed. We dared look neither at her nor at each other! She was the first to speak.

"It is all over!" she said. "Forgive me: I won't laugh again."

And then Rouletabille said, speaking in a very low tone:

"It will be over when we know how he got in."

"What good would it do?" replied the Lady in Black.

"It is a question to which he alone knows the answer. He is the only one who could tell us and he is dead."

"He will not be truly dead for us until we know that," responded Rouletabille.

"Evidently," said M. Darzac, "so long as we do not know that, we shall be uneasy and he will be there in our minds. He must be driven away! He must be!"

"Let us try to drive him away then," said Rouletabille.

And he went to the Lady in Black and gently took her hand in his and attempted to draw her into the next room, begging her to lie down and rest. But Mathilde declared that she would not go. She said: "What! You would drive Larsan away and I not here!" And her voice sounded as though she were about to laugh again. I made a sign to Rouletabille not to insist upon her absence.

Rouletabille opened the door leading into the corridor and called Bernier and his wife. They did not wish to enter, but we insisted on their doing so, and a general consultation took place from which we deduced the following facts:

(1) Rouletabille had visited the apartment at five o'clock and searched behind the panel and at that time there was no one in the room.
(2) After five o'clock, the door of the apartment had been twice opened by Pere Bernier, who alone had the right to open it in the absence of M. and Mme. Darzac. The first time was at five o'clock to permit M. Darzac to enter; the next at eleven o'clock to admit M. and Mme. Darzac.
(3) Bernier had locked the door of the apartment when M. Darzac went out with us between a quarter past and half past six.
(4) The door of the apartment had been locked and bolted by M. Darzac as soon as he entered his room, both in the afternoon and in the evening.
(5) Bernier had stood guard before the door of the apartment from five o'clock till eleven o'clock with a brief interruption of not more than two minutes at six o'clock.

When we had discussed and fully established these facts, Rouletabille, who was sitting at M. Darzac's desk taking notes, arose and said:

"So far, it is very simple. We have only one hope. It is in the few moments that Bernier was off guard about six o'clock. At least, at that time, no one was in front of the door. But there was someone behind it. It was you, M. Darzac. Can you reiterate, after having thoroughly searched your memory, that when you went into your room, you instantly closed the door and drew the bolt?"

"I can!" replied M. Darzac, solemnly; and he added:

"And I opened that door only when you and Sainclair knocked upon it. I swear it."

*And in saying this, as later events proved, the man spoke the truth.*

Rouletabille thanked the Berniers and dismissed them to get some rest. Then, his voice trembling, the lad said:

"It is well, M. Darzac, you have closed the circle. The apartment in the Square Tower is now closed as firmly as was the Yellow Room which was like a strong box, or as the 'inexplicable gallery.' "

"One would guess immediately that Larsan was mixed up in the affair!" I exclaimed. "It is the same mode of procedure!"

"Yes," observed Mme. Darzac. "Yes, M. Sainclair, it is the same mode of procedure." And she unfastened her husband's collar to show the wounds hidden beneath it.

"See!" she said. "They are the same nail prints. I know them well."

There was a sorrowful silence.

M. Darzac, caring only to solve this strange problem, reviewed the crime of the Glandier. And he repeated what he had said in the Yellow Room:

"There must be a passage in the floor, in the ceiling or in the walls."

"There is not," replied Rouletabille.

"Then he must have found some way to make one," persisted M. Darzac.

"Why?" asked Rouletabille. "Did he do anything of the sort in the Yellow Room?"

"Oh, this isn't the same thing at all!" I exclaimed. "This apartment is more firmly closed than the Yellow Room since no one could have gotten into it before nor after."

"No, it is not the same thing," pronounced Rouletabille. "It is just the opposite. In the Yellow Room, there was a body missing: in the room in the Round Tower, there is a body too many."

And he tottered out, leaning on my arm so as not to fall. The Lady in Black rushed toward him. He had strength enough left to stop her with a gesture.

"Oh—this is nothing!" he said. "I'm a little tired, that's all!"

# XIV

## THE SACK OF POTATOES

While M. Darzac, with the assistance of Bernier, busied himself, as Rouletabille advised, with obliterating all signs of the tragedy, the Lady in Black, who had hastily changed her dress, hurried to her father's rooms in order not to run the risk of encountering any of the other members of the party. Her last word was to counsel us to prudence and silence. Rouletabille also took leave of us.

It was now about seven o'clock in the morning and things began to stir in and about the château. We could hear the fishermen singing in their boats. I threw myself upon my bed, and in a few moments I was sleeping profoundly, vanquished by the physical weariness which was stronger than my powers of resistance. When I awakened, I lay for a few moments on my couch in a pleasant bewilderment, but as the events of the night dawned on my remembrance, I started up in terror.

"Ah!" I cried out, "A body too many! No, no! It can't be! It's impossible!"

It was this which surged across the dark gulf of my thoughts, above the abyss of my memory; this impossibility of "a body too many." And the horror which I found in my heart at my awakening was not confined to myself—far from it! All those who had mingled, near or far, in this strange drama of the

Square Tower, shared it; and even though the horror of the event itself were appeased—the horror of the body in its last throes of agony thrown into a sack which a man carried off at night to cast it into who knows what far off and profound and mysterious tomb where it might gasp out its last breath of life—even if, I say, this horror should be forgotten and blotted out of the mind, and effaced from the vision, yet still the impossibility of this "body too many" grew and increased and rose up before us higher and higher and more threatening and more dreadful. Certain persons there are—like Mme. Edith, for example—who deny almost from habit, anything which they cannot understand—who deny the presentation of the problem which destiny holds for us (such as we have established in the preceding chapter) even while every event and every circumstance among those which had the Fort of Hercules for their theatre rendered proof of the exactitude of the presentation.

First of all, the attack! How had the attack been made? At what moment? By what means of approach? What mines, trenches, covered paths, breaches—in the domains of the mental fortifications—have served the assailant and delivered the château over into his hands? Yes, under the existing conditions, where was the attack? The answer is—silence. And yet, the facts must be brought to fight. Rouletabille has said so: he ought to know. In a siege as mysterious as this, the attack may be in everything or in nothing. The assailant is as still as the grave itself and the assault is made without clamour and the enemy approaches the walls walking in his stocking feet. The *attack*? It is, perhaps, in the very stillness itself, but again, it may, perhaps, be in the spoken word. It is in a tone, in a sigh, in a breath. It is in a gesture, but if perhaps it may be in all which is hidden, it may be, also, in all that is revealed—in *everything which one sees and which one does not see.*

Eleven o'clock! Where was Rouletabille? His bed had not been disturbed. I dressed myself hurriedly and went to look for my friend, whom I found in the outer court. He took me by the arm and led me into the vast drawing room of "la Louve." There, I was surprised to find, although it was not yet time for luncheon, everybody assembled. M. and Mme. Darzac were there. It seemed to me that M. Rance's manner was rather frigid. When he shook my hand in wishing me good morning, he barely touched my fingers. As soon as we entered the room Mme. Edith, from the dark corner where she was reclining carelessly on a sofa, saluted us with the words:

"Ah, here is M. Rouletabille with his friend, Sainclair. Now we shall know why we have all been summoned here!"

To this remark, Rouletabille responded by first excusing himself for having requested us all to gather at so early an hour; but he had, he went on to say, such a serious and important communication to make to us that he had not wished to delay it one moment longer than was absolutely necessary. His tone was so grave that Edith pretended to shiver and counterfeited an infantile terror. But Rouletabille, without noticing her, continued: "Before you shiver, Madame, wait until you know what you have to be afraid of. I have some news for you which is very far from pleasant."

We all looked at him, and then at each other! What was he about to say? I endeavoured to read in the faces of M. and Mme. Darzac what they thought of the matter. Both showed remarkably little evidence of last night's horrors! But what was it that Rouletabille had to say to us? He entreated those who were standing to be seated and then he began to speak. He addressed himself to Mme. Rance.

"First of all, Madame, permit me to inform you that I have decided to suppress the 'guard' which surrounded the Château of Hercules, like an inner wall, and which I judged necessary for the protection of M. and Mme. Darzac which you kindly allowed me to establish, although it vexed you, showing the most charming of good humour and accommodating spirit."

This direct allusion to the mocking remarks and innuendos of Mme. Edith at the time when we mounted guard made Mr. Rance and his wife both smile. But no smile arose to the lips of M. or Mme. Darzac nor myself, for we had begun to ask ourselves anxiously what the boy was preparing to say.

"Ah, really, are you going to withdraw the guard for the château, M. Rouletabille? Well, I am very glad to hear it, although I assure you that it did not vex me in the least!" exclaimed Mme. Edith with an affectation of gayety. "On the contrary, it had interested me very much, because, you know, I am of a very romantic nature, and if I rejoice at the change, it is because the fact proves to me that M. and Mme. Darzac are no longer in any danger."

"This is true, Madame," replied Rouletabille, "since last night."

Mme. Darzac could not refrain from a hasty movement which no one save myself perceived.

"So much the better!" cried Mme. Edith. "May Heaven be praised! But how is it that my husband and I are the last to hear the news? Interesting things must have been happening last night! The nocturnal trip of M. Darzac to Castelar was one of them, without doubt!" As she spoke, I could see the embarrassment of M. and Mme. Darzac. The former, after a glance at his wife, started to speak, but Rouletabille would not permit him to do so.

"Madame, I do not know where M. Darzac went last night, but it is necessary that you should know one thing: and that is the reason why M. and Mme. Darzac have ceased to run any danger. Your husband, Madame, has told you of the frightful tragedy of the Glandier two years ago and of the villainous part played in it by—"

"Frederic Larsan—yes, monsieur, I know all that."

"You know also, of course, that the reason why we have placed such a strong guard here around M. Darzac and his wife was because we had seen this man again?"

"I do."

"Well, M. and Mme. Darzac are no longer in danger because this man cannot appear again ever."

"What has become of him?"

"He is dead."

"When did he die?"

"Last night."

"And how did he die last night?"

"He was killed, madame."

"And where was he killed?"

"In the Square Tower."

We all sprang to our feet at this declaration in the greatest agitation. M. and Mme. Rance seemed completely stupefied by the words which they had heard and M. and Mme. Darzac and myself were plunged into the most profound agitation by the fact that Rouletabille had not hesitated to reveal the secret.

"In the Square Tower?" cried Mme. Edith. "And who, then, has killed him?"

"M. Robert Darzac," replied Rouletabille. "And he entreats everyone to sit down."

It was astonishing how we seated ourselves with one accord, as though, at such a moment, we had nothing to do except to obey this youngster. But almost immediately Mme. Edith arose and seizing M. Darzac by the hand, she exclaimed with an emphasis which made me decide that I had judged her wrongly when I called her affected:

"Bravo, Monsieur Robert! All right! You are a gentleman!" Then she paid some exaggerated compliments—for after all, it was her nature to exaggerate things—to Mme. Darzac. She swore eternal friendship for her; she declared that she and her husband were ready, under all circumstances, to stand by the Darzacs and that the latter might count upon their zeal and their devotion and that they would swear whatever one liked before all the judges in the tribunal.

"Gently, dear Madame," interrupted Rouletabille. "There is no question of judges and we hope that there may not be. There's no need of it. Larsan was a dead man in the eyes of the whole world long before he was killed last night—he will continue to be dead, that is all! We have decided that it would be useless to reopen a scandal of which M. and Mme. Darzac have already been made the innocent victims and we have counted upon your assistance. The affair has happened in so mysterious a fashion that even you, if we had not informed you in regard to it, would never have suspected. But M. and Mme. Darzac are endowed with sentiments too noble to permit them to forget what they owe to their hosts. The most simple rules of hospitality ordered them to tell you that they killed a man in your house last night. How foolish it would be to lay bare this unfortunate story to some Italian police officer and subject you to the inconvenience of having your names coupled with the miserable business, and, it might easily be, to have a search made of your house and hired servants of the law under your roof! M. and Mme. Darzac, for your sakes alone, are anxious that you should not run the risk of being the object of idle gossip, or, perhaps, of having the police descend upon your home."

M. Arthur Rance, who up to this time had remained speechless, arose and said, his face as pallid as though he had seen a ghost:

"Frederic Larsan is dead. Well, so far so good, and no one is more rejoiced than myself to know it. And if he has received the punishment due to his crimes from the hand of M. Darzac, no one is more to be congratulated than M. Darzac. But I consider that it would be wrong for M. Darzac to make any attempt to conceal an act which is an honour to himself. It would be better to inform the authorities and without delay. If they should come to learn of this affair from others, rather than by our means, think of what the situation would be! If we give out the information ourselves, we shall show that an act of justice has been committed. If we conceal anything, we shall place ourselves in the category of malefactors. People might even suppose—"

To listen to M. Rance's stammering speech and to observe his demeanour, one might almost have imagined that he was the slayer of Frederic Larsan—he who was in danger of being accused of murder and dragged to prison.

"It is necessary to think of everything, gentlemen," he concluded. And Edith added: "I believe that my husband is right. But before we come to a decision, we ought to know just what has happened."

And she addressed herself directly to M. and Mme. Darzac. But both of the latter were still under the spell of surprise which Rouletabille had caused them by his remarks—Rouletabille who that very morning, in my presence, had promised to be silent and had sworn us all to silence. Neither the one nor the other had a word to say. M. Rance repeated, nervously: "Why should we conceal anything? Why should we? We must tell everything."

All at once, the reporter seemed to take a sudden resolution. I understood by the expressions which chased themselves over his face in rapid succession that something of considerable moment was passing through his mind. He leaned toward Arthur Rance, whose right hand was resting on a cane, the head of which was carved in ivory, beautifully cut by a famous carver at Dieppe. Rouletabille took the cane in his hand.

"May I look at it?" he asked. "I am an amateur ivory carver myself and my friend, Sainclair, here, has told me about this beautiful cane. I had not noticed it before. It is really very beautiful. It is a figure by Lambesse and there is no better workman on the Norman shore."

The young man seemed to be entirely engrossed in studying the cane. As he touched the carving, the stick fell from his hand and rolled toward M. Darzac. I picked it up and returned it immediately to M. Rance. Rouletabille cast a withering look at me, and I read in that glance that, somehow or other, I had shown myself an idiot.

Mme. Edith rose to her feet, tapping her little foot impatiently and seemingly very nervous at the tension of the situation—by the carelessness of Rouletabille and the silence of M. and Mme. Darzac.

"Dearest," she said to Mme. Darzac, in the sweetest tones. "You are completely tired out. The experiences of this horrible night have overpowered you. Let me take you into my own room so that you may rest a little."

"Pardon me for asking you to wait a few moments, Madame," interrupted Rouletabille. "What I have yet to say may be of special interest to you."

"Very well, monsieur, but speak out, please. Don't drag the recital along so."

She was perfectly justified in her remarks. Did Rouletabille realize it? At all events, he certainly made up for his previous deliberation by the rapidity and clearness with which he retraced the events of the night. In no other words could the problem of the "body too many" have been presented before us with such mysterious horror. Mme. Edith shivered—and if her shudder was counterfeit, I never saw a real one! As for Arthur Rance, he sat with his chin resting on the head of his cane, murmuring with a truly American coolness, but in accents of the strongest conviction: "What a devilish history! The story of the body which could not have gotten into the room is a page from the notebook of Satan himself!"

While he was speaking, he was gazing at the tip of Mme. Darzac's shoe which peeped out from the hem of her gown. In the moment which followed the closing of Rouletabille's narration, conversation became a little more general; but it was less a conversation than such a confused mixture of exclamations and interruptions, of interjections and indignation and demands for explanations on one point or another that the confusion seemed more increased than ever before. They spoke also of the horrible departure of "the body too many" in the potato sack, and at this point, Mme. Edith took occasion to once more express her admiration for M. Robert Darzac as a hero and a gentleman. Rouletabille never opened his lips during this torrent of words. It was plain to be seen that he despised this verbal manifestation of perturbation of spirits, but he endured it with the air of a professor who permits a few moments relaxation to pupils who have been well behaved in school. This was a mannerism of his which often vexed me and with which I sometimes reproached him, but without having any effect on him, for Rouletabille was likely to give himself whatever airs he chose.

At length—probably when it appeared to him that the recreation had lasted long enough, he asked abruptly of Mrs. Rance:

"Well, Madame, do you think we ought to inform the authorities?"

"I think so more than ever," she replied. "That which we are powerless to discover, they would certainly find out." (This allusion to the intellectual incapacity of my friend left him profoundly indifferent). "And I warn you of one thing, M. Rouletabille, and that is that we may already be too late in seeking out the officers of justice. If we had told them of our fears at the very beginning, you would have been spared some long hours of watching and sleepless nights which have profited you nothing, since, as now appears, they did not prevent what you dreaded from coming to pass."

Rouletabille seated himself, evidently conquering some strong emotion which made him tremble as though he were chilled to the bone. Then with a wave of the hand which he strove to render careless, he motioned Mme. Edith to a chair and again picked up the cane which M. Rance had laid down upon a sofa. I said to myself: "What is he trying to do with that stick? This time, I won't touch it, I'm certain. I must keep a lookout."

Playing with the cane, Rouletabille replied to Mme. Edith with an attack almost as sharp as her own.

"Madame, you are wrong in asserting that all the precautions which I had taken for the safety of M. and Mme. Darzac have been useless. If I am obliged to acknowledge the unexplainable presence of one body too many, I am also compelled to refer to the absence—perhaps less inexplicable—of one member of our own party."

We stared at each other, some of us seeking to understand, the others dreading to do so.

"What is that?" inquired Mme. Edith, with a mocking little smile. "In such a case, I fail to see how you find any mystery at all." And she added with a flippant imitation of the reporter's words and manner: "A body too many on the one side; an unexplained absence on the other! Everything is for the best."

"Perhaps," rejoined Rouletabille. "But the most frightful thing of all is that the unexplained disappearance comes just at the right time to make known to us, apparently, the identity of the 'body too many.' Madame, I deeply regret to tell you that the person for whose whereabouts we are unable to account, is none other than your uncle, Monsieur Bob."

"Old Bob!" screamed the young woman. "Old Bob has disappeared!"

And we all cried out with her:

"Old Bob has disappeared?"

"Unfortunately, it is true!" said Rouletabille.

And he let the cane drop to the ground.

But the news of the sudden disappearance of Old Bob had so seized the Rances and the Darzacs that no one paid any attention to the cane as it fell.

"My dear Sainclair, will you be kind enough to pick up that cane?" asked Rouletabille.

I did as I was ordered and quickly, too, but Rouletabille did not even deign to thank me. Mme. Edith turned like a lioness upon Robert Darzac, who recoiled from her almost in fear as she shrieked:

"You have killed my uncle!"

Her husband and myself, with difficulty, prevented her from flying at him. We entreated her to be calm and to remember that because her uncle had absented himself from the peninsula did not necessarily mean that he had disappeared in the potato sack and we reproached Rouletabille with his brutality in blurting out an idea which could only be, at the present time, at all events, an hypothesis of his uneasy mind. And we added, imploring Mme. Edith to listen to us, that this hypothesis could under no circumstances be looked upon by her either as an injury or an insult, even admitting that it might be the true one, as it would only show the superhuman cunning of Larsan, who must, in that case, have taken the place of her respected uncle. But the young woman ordered her husband to be quiet, and said, turning scornfully to me:

"M. Sainclair, I sincerely hope that my uncle's absence from here will only be of short duration; for if it should turn out otherwise, I should accuse you of being an accomplice in the most cowardly of murders. As to you, monsieur," and she turned to Rouletabille, "the mere idea that you have ever dared to compare a man like Larsan with my uncle, the gentlest, kindliest soul and the greatest scholar of his time, forbids me to ever again consider you in the light of a friend, and I hope that you will have the courtesy to relieve me of your presence as soon as possible."

"Madame," replied Rouletabille, bowing very low, "I was just about to ask your permission to take leave of you. I have a short journey of twenty-four hours to take. At the expiration of that time, I shall return, ready to be of any possible assistance to you in whatever difficulties may arise in accounting for the disappearance of your uncle."

"If my uncle has not returned within twenty-four hours, I shall lodge a complaint in the hands of the police, monsieur."

"It is a good plan, Madame; but before having recourse to it, I advise you to question all the servants in whom you have confidence—particularly Mattoni. You trust Mattoni, do you not?"

"Yes, monsieur, I trust Mattoni."

"Well, then, Madame, question him—question him. Ah—before I take my departure, allow me to leave with you this excellent and historical book." And Rouletabille drew a small volume from his pocket.

"What foolery is this?" demanded Mme. Edith, superbly disdainful.

"This, Madame, is a work of M. Albert Bataille, a copy of his 'Civil and Criminal Cases,' in which I advise you to read the adventures, disguises, travesties and deceptions wrought by an illustrious swindler whose true name was Ballmeyer."

Rouletabille entirely ignored the fact that he had only the day before spent two hours in recounting to Mme. Edith the exploits of Ballmeyer.

"After having read this," he went on, "ask yourself carefully whether the cleverness of such an individual would have found very great difficulty in presenting himself before your eyes under the guise of an uncle whom you had not seen in four years—for it was four years, Madame, since you had seen Old Bob, until that time that you started out to the heart of the Pampas to look for him. As to the memory of M. Arthur Rance, who started out with you on that journey, it would be even less distinct than your own and he would be more capable of being deceived than yourself with your intuition of kinship added to your recollections of your relative. I implore you on my knees,

Madame, do not lose patience with us. The situation, Heaven knows, is grave enough for each and every one of us. Let us remain united. You tell me to rid you of my presence. I am going but I shall return; for if it is necessary, taking everything into consideration, to arrive at the intolerable conclusion that Larsan has assumed the name and likeness of Monsieur Bob, it will remain for us only to seek Monsieur Bob himself, in which case, Madame, I shall be at your disposal and your most humble and obedient servant."

Mme. Edith assumed the attitude of an outraged tragedy queen and Rouletabille, turning to Arthur Rance, continued:

"For all that has happened, M. Rance, I make you my humblest excuses and also to your wife. And I count upon you as the loyal gentleman that you are and always have been to persuade her to have patience a little longer. I realize that you feel that you have reason to reproach me with having stated my hypothesis too quickly and too abruptly, but, please remember, it is only a few moments since Madame reproached me with being too slow."

But Arthur Rance seemed to have ceased to listen. He took his wife's arm and both moved toward the door and were about to leave the room when the portals flew open and the stable boy, Walter, Old Bob's faithful servant, rushed into our midst. His clothing was torn, muddy and covered with burs and thistles. Perspiration was streaming down his forehead and cheeks, his hair was in disorder and his face wore an expression of rage mingled with terror which made us fear some new misfortune. He carried in his hand a dirty rag which he threw upon the table. This repulsive object, stained with great blotches of reddish brown was (as we divined immediately, recoiling from it in horror) nothing other than the sack which had served to carry off the mysterious body.

With a harsh voice and savage gestures, Walter howled forth a thousand incomprehensible things in his broken jumble of

French and English and all of us with the exception of Arthur Rance and Mme. Edith, asked each other, "What is he saying? What is he saying?"

Arthur Rance interrupted him from time to time, while Walter shook his fists menacingly at the rest of us and cast fiery glances at Robert Darzac. Once, for a moment, it seemed as though he intended to seize Darzac by the throat, but a gesture from Mme. Edith restrained him. When he finished speaking, Arthur Rance translated his words for us.

"He says that this morning he noticed blood stains on the English cart and saw that Toby seemed very greatly fatigued. This puzzled him so much that he decided to speak of it at once to Old Bob, but he sought his master in vain. Then, seized by a dark foreboding, he followed the prints of the horse's feet and the wheels of the vehicle which he could easily do because the road was muddy and the wheels had sunk deep. Finally he reached the old Castillon and noticed that the wheels led up to a deep chasm into which he descended, believing that he should find the body of his master; but he saw merely this empty sack which may have contained the corpse of Old Bob, and now, having caught a ride in a peasant's wagon, he has returned to ask for his master, to learn whether anyone has seen him, and, if he is not found, to accuse Robert Darzac of having caused his death."

We stood confounded. But, to our great astonishment, Mme. Edith was the first to recover her self-possession. She spoke a few words to Walter which appeared to quiet him, promising him that she would soon bring him face to face with Old Bob, who was perfectly safe and well. And she said to Rouletabille:

"You have twenty-four hours, Monsieur; make the best use of it."

"Thanks, Madame," said Rouletabille. "But if your uncle should not return in that time, it will be because my idea was correct."

"But where can he be!" she cried.

"I cannot tell you, Madame. He is not in the sack now, at all events."

Mme. Edith cast a withering glance at him and left the room, followed by her husband. The sight of the sack seemed to have stricken Robert Darzac speechless. He had thrown the bag into an abyss and it was brought back empty. After a moment's pause, Rouletabille spoke:

"Larsan is not dead, be sure of that! Never has the situation been so frightful as it is today and I must hurry away at once. I have not a minute to lose. Twenty-four hours—in twenty-four hours, I shall be back. But promise me—swear to me, both of you, that you will not quit the château. Swear to me, M. Darzac, that you will watch over your wife—that you will prevent her from leaving these walls, even by force, if it is necessary. Ah—and again—it is no longer necessary that you should sleep in the Square Tower. No, you ought not to do so. In the same wing where M. Stangerson is lodged, there are two empty rooms. You must occupy them. It is absolutely necessary that you should. Sainclair, you will see that this change is made. After my departure, see that neither the one nor the other of them shall set foot in the Square Tower. Adieu! Ah, wait!—let me embrace you—all three."

He pressed us to his heart: M. Darzac first, then myself, and then, falling into the arms of the Lady in Black, he burst into a passion of sobs. This show of weakness and of grief on the part of Rouletabille, in spite of the gravity of the circumstances of his departure, appeared to me very strange. Alas! how easy it was for me to understand it afterward!

# XV

## THE SIGHS OF THE NIGHT

Two o'clock in the morning! Every person and everything in the castle seemed wrapped in slumber. Silence brooded over the heavens and the earth. While I stood at my window, my forehead burning and my heart frozen, the sea yielded its last sigh and in a moment the moon appeared riding like a queen in the cloudless sky. Shadows no longer veiled the stars of the night. There, in that vast, motionless slumber which seemed to envelope all the world, I heard the words of the Lithuanian folk song: "But his glance seeks in vain for the beautiful unknown who has covered her head with a veil and whose voice he has never heard." The words were carried to my ear, clear and distinct, in the still air of the night. Who had pronounced them? Was the voice that of a man or a woman? Or was the song only an hallucination evoked by my memories? What should the Prince from the Black lands be doing on the Azure shore with his Lithuanian melodies? And why should his image and his songs pursue me thus?

Why was Mme. Edith attracted toward him? He was ridiculous with his melancholy eyes and his long lashes and his Lithuanian songs! And I—I was ridiculous, too. Had I the heart of a college boy? I think not. I would rather believe that the emotion which was excited in me by the personality of Prince

Galitch rose less from my knowledge of the interest which Mme. Edith felt in him than from the thought of *that other*. Yes, it was surely that. In my mind the thought of the Prince and that of Larsan somehow went together. And the Prince had not returned to the château since the famous luncheon at which he was presented to us—that is to say since the day before yesterday.

The afternoon following Rouletabille's departure had brought us nothing new. We received no news from him nor from Old Bob. Mme. Edith had locked herself up in her own apartments, after having questioned the domestics and visiting her uncle's rooms and the Round Tower. She made no effort to penetrate into the apartments of the Darzacs in the Square Tower. "That is an affair for the police," she had said. Arthur Rance had walked for an hour on the western boulevard, his manner restless and impatient. No one had spoken a word to me. Neither M. nor Mme. Darzac had stirred out of "la Louve." All of us had dined in our own rooms. No one had seen Professor Stangerson.

And now, so far as the eye could see, everyone in the château seemed to be lost in dreams. But a shadow appeared on the bosom of the starry night—the shadow of a canoe which slowly detached itself from the shadow of the fort and glided out upon the silvery water. Whose is this silhouette, which arises proudly in the front of the boat while another shade bends over a silent oar? It is yours, Feodor Feodorowitch! Ah, here is a mystery which might be easier to solve than that of the Square Tower, O Rouletabille! And I who believed that Mme. Edith had too good a brain and too fine a mind to lend herself to a vulgar intrigue!

What a hypocrite is the night! Everything seems to sleep and all the while slumber is far from all eyes! Who was there that might be sleeping among those in the château of Hercules?

Was Mme. Edith sleeping, perhaps? Or M. or Mme. Darzac" And how could M. Stangerson, who seemed to have been slumbering all day, be dreaming away the night also?—he whose couch, ever since the revelation of the Glandier, had not ceased to be haunted by the pale ghost of insomnia? And I—could I sleep?

I left my bedchamber and went down into the court of the Bold and my feet bore me rapidly over to the boulevard of the Round Tower—so rapidly that I arrived there in time to see the bark of Prince Galitch landing on the strand in front of the "Gardens of Babylon." He leaped out of the boat and his man, having picked up the oars, followed. I recognised the master and servant. It was Feodor Feodorowitch and his serf, Jean. A few seconds later, they disappeared in the protecting shade of the century plants and the giant eucalypti.

I turned and walked around the boulevard of the court. And then my heart beating wildly, I directed my steps toward the outer court. The stone slabs of the walks resounded under my tread and I seemed to see a form arise in a listening attitude from beneath the arch of the ruined chapel. I paused in the thick darkness of the shadow cast by the gardener's tower and drew my revolver from my pocket. The form did not move. Was it really a human creature who stood there listening? I glided behind a hedge of vervain which bordered the path that led directly to "la Louve" through bushes and thickets, heavy with the perfume of the flowers of the spring. I had made no noise, and the shadow, doubtless reassured, made a slight movement. It was the Lady in Black. The moon, under the half ruined arch, showed me that she was as pale as death. And suddenly her figure vanished as if by enchantment. I approached the chapel and as I diminished the space which lay between me and the ruins, I heard a soft murmur of words mingled with such bitter sobs that my own eyes grew moist as I listened. The Lady in Black was weeping there behind that pillar. Was she alone? Had she not chosen in this night of anguish to come to this altar decked with flowers there to pour out her prayers in solitude to the balmy air?

Suddenly I perceived a shadow beside the Lady in Black and I recognised Robert Darzac. From the corner where I was I could now hear all that they were saying. I knew that my behaviour in listening was degraded and shameless, but, curiously enough, it was borne upon me that it was my duty to listen. Now I thought no longer of Edith and her Prince Galitch. I thought only of Larsan. Why? Why was it on account of Larsan that I bent my ears so anxiously to hear all that went on between those two? I learned from their words that Mathilde had descended stealthily from la Louve to be alone in the garden with her agony and that her husband had followed her. The Lady in Black was weeping. And she took Robert Darzac's hands and said to him:

"I know, dear—I know all your grief. You need not speak of it to me when I see you so changed—so wretched! I accuse myself of being the cause of your sorrow. But do not tell me that I no longer love you. Oh, I will love you dearly, Robert—just as I have always done. I promise you."

And she seemed to sink into a deep fit of thought, while he, almost as though incredulous, still stood as though he were listening to her. In a moment, she looked up again and repeated in a tone of firm conviction: "Yes—I promise you."

She pressed his hand and turned away, casting upon him a smile so sweet and yet so sorrowful that I wondered how this woman could speak to a man of future happiness. She brushed past me without seeing me. She passed with her perfume and I no longer smelled the laurel bushes behind which I was hidden.

M. Darzac remained standing in the same spot, looking after her. Suddenly he said aloud with a violence which startled me:

"Yes, happiness must come! It must!"

Assuredly, he was at the end of his patience. And before withdrawing in his turn, he made a gesture of protest—against fate, it seemed to me—a gesture of defiance to destiny—a gesture which snatched the Lady in Black through the space which divided them and caught her to his breast and held her there.

He had scarcely made this gesture when my thought took form—my thought which had been wandering about Larsan stopped at Darzac. Oh, how well I remember that instant! The fancy was gone in a moment, but as I beheld gesture of defiance and rapture, I dared to say to myself, "If HE should be Larsan!"

And in looking back to the depths of my memory, I realize now that my thought was even stronger than that. To the gesture of this man, my mind answered with the cry, "This is Larsan!"

I was white with terror and when I saw Robert Darzac coming in my direction, I could not refrain from a movement which revealed my presence while I was trying to conceal it. He saw me and recognised me, and, grasping me by the arm, he exclaimed:

"You were there, Sainclair: you were watching. We are all watching, my friend. And you heard what she said. Sainclair, her grief is too great. I can bear no more. We would have been so happy. She began to believe that misfortune had forgotten her when that man reappeared. Then all was finished; she had no longer strength to desire love or to feel it. She is bowed down by destiny. She imagines that she is to be pursued by eternal punishment. It was necessary for the frightful tragedy of last night to prove to me that this woman did love me—once. Yes, for one moment, all her fears were for me—and I, alas, have blood on my hands only because of her. Now she has returned to her old indifference. She cares no longer—her only desire is that the old man shall be kept in ignorance."

He sighed so sorrowfully and so sincerely that the abominable idea which it had harboured fled from my mind. I thought only of what he was saying to me—of the sorrow of this man who seemed to have lost completely the woman whom he loved in the moment when the woman had found a son of whose existence the husband continued to be ignorant. In fact, he had in no way been able to understand the attitude of the Lady in Black as regards the facility with which she had detached herself from him—and he found no explanation for this cruel metamorphosis other than the love heightened by remorse of Professor Stangerson's daughter for her father.

"What good did it do me to kill him?" groaned M. Darzac. "Why did I fire the shot? Why did she impose upon me such a criminal, horrible silence if she did not intend to recompense me for it by her love? Did she fear arrest for me? Ah, no! Not even that, Sainclair, not even that! She fears only the agony of her father and the danger that he will succumb entirely under this new disgrace. Her father! Always her father! I do not exist for her. I have loved her for twenty years and when I believe at last that I have won her, the thought of her father takes my place."

And I said to myself: "The thought of her father—and of her child."

He seated himself on an old moss grown boulder by the chapel and said again, as if speaking to himself: "But I will snatch her away from this place—I cannot see her roaming about on the arm of her father—as if I were not in the world."

And, while he said this, I looked up and I fancied that I beheld the shadow of the father and the daughter passing and repassing in the dawn, beneath the sombre height of the Tower of the North, and I likened them in my mind to the old Oedipus and his daughter, Antigone, walking under the walls of Colone, dragging with them the weight of a grief beyond human endurance.

And then suddenly, without my being able to recall myself to reason, perhaps because Darzac made again the gesture which had startled me before, the same frightful fancy assailed me, and I demanded:

"How did it happen that the sack was empty?"

He was not in the least confused or taken aback.

He replied simply:

"Rouletabille must tell us that." Then he pressed my hand and wandered away through the undergrowth of the garden. I looked after him and said to myself:

"I have gone mad!"

# XVI

## DISCOVERY OF "AUSTRALIA"

The moon was shining full on his face. He believed himself to be alone in the night and certainly it was one of the moments in which he would cast aside the mask of the day. First the black glasses had ceased to shade his eyes. And if his figure, during the hours of disguise, was more bent than nature had made it, if his shoulders were rounded by pretence instead of study, this was the moment when the magnificent body of Larsan, away from all observers, must relax itself. Would it relax now? I hid in the ditch behind the barberry hedge. Not one of his movements escaped me.

Now he was standing erect upon the western boulevard which looked like a pedestal beneath his feet; the rays of the moon enveloped him with a cold and mournful light. Is it you, Darzac? Or your spectre? Or the ghost of Larsan, come back from the house of the dead?

I felt that I had gone mad. What a piteous state was ours—all of us madmen! We saw Larsan everywhere, and, perhaps, Darzac himself might more than once have gazed at me, Sainclair, saying to himself: "Suppose that he were Larsan!" More than—once! I speak as though it were years since we had been locked up in the château and it was now just four days. We came here on the eighth of April in the evening.

It is true that my heart had never beaten so wildly when I had asked myself the same terrible question about the others; perhaps, because it was less terrible when there was question of any of the others. And then, how strange that such a thought should have come to me! Instead of my spirit recoiling in affright before the black abyss of such an incredible hypothesis, it was, on the contrary, attracted, enchained, horribly bewitched by it. It was as though struck with vertigo which it could do nothing to evade. It glued my eyes to that figure standing upon the western boulevard, making me find the attitudes, the gestures, a strong resemblance from the rear—and then, the profile—and even the face. Yes, all—all. He did look like Larsan. Yes, but just as strongly did the face and figure resemble Darzac.

How was it that this idea had come to me that night for the first time? Now that I thought of it—it should have been our first hypothesis of all. Was it not true that, at the time of "The Mystery of the Yellow Room," the silhouette of Larsan had been confounded at the moment of the crime with that of Darzac? Was it not true that the man who was believed to be Darzac, who had come to inquire for Mlle. Stangerson's answer at Post Office Box No. 40, had really been Larsan himself? Was it not true that this emperor of disguises had already undertaken with success to appear to be Darzac?—and to such good purpose that Mlle. Stangerson's fiance had been accused of being the perpetrator of the crimes committed by the other?

It was true—all true—and yet when I ordered my restless heart to be quiet and listen to reason, I knew that my hypothesis was absurd. Absurd? Why? Look at him there, the ghost of Larsan which strides along with long paces like those of the monster! Yes, but the shoulders are those of Darzac.

I must admit that my suspicions are absurd. I say absurd because anyone who was not Darzac might have passed for him in the shade and the mystery that surrounded the drama of the Glandier. But here we have lived with the man. We have talked with him—touched him.

We have lived with him? No!

To begin with, he was rarely there among us. Always locked in his own room or bending over that useless work in the Tower of the Bold. A fine pretext, that of drawing, to prevent anyone's seeing your face and to make it appear natural to answer questions without turning the head!

But he was not drawing all the time! Yes, but at other times, always, except tonight, he wore his dark glasses. Ah! that accident in the laboratory had been well contrived. That little lamp which exploded knew—I have always thought so, it seems to me—the service which it was going to do for Larsan when Larsan should have taken the place of Darzac. It permitted him to evade always and everywhere the full light of day—because of the weakness of his eyes. How then! Was it not always Mlle. Stangerson or Rouletabille who had managed to find dark corners where M. Darzac's eyes could not be exposed to the sun? But, lately, he himself, more than anyone else now that I reflected upon it, had been careful to keep in the shadow—we have seen him seldom and always in the shadow. That little "hall of counsel" was very dark, "la Louve" was dark, and he had chosen the two rooms in the Square Tower which are plunged in semi-darkness.

But still—still—Rouletabille could not be deceived like that—even for three days. But, as the lad himself said, Larsan was born before Rouletabille and was his father.

And suddenly there recurred to my mind the first act of Darzac when he came to meet us at Cannes and entered our compartment with us. He drew the curtain. The shadow—always the shadow!

The figure on the western boulevard is still standing there. I can look him full in the face. No spectacles now! He was not moving. He stood as if he were posing for a photograph. Do not stir! There! That is he! Yes, it is Robert Darzac—only Robert Darzac!

He began to walk again—I was certain no longer. There is something in his walk which is not Darzac's—something in which I seem to recognize Larsan—but what?

Yes, Rouletabille must have seen! And yet—Rouletabille reasons more often than he looks! And has he ever had a chance to look at him like this?

No! We must not forget that Darzac went to spend three months in the Midi—That is true! Ah, what might not have happened in that time! Three months during which none of us saw him. He went away ill; he returned almost well. There could be nothing astonishing in the fact that a man's appearance should be changed when he went away with the look of a dead man and returned with the look of one living and strong!

And the wedding had taken place immediately after that. How little any of us had seen of him before the ceremony! And, besides, a week had not yet elapsed since the marriage. A Larsan could easily wear his mask for so short a time.

The man—was it Darzac or was it Larsan?—descended from his pedestal and came straight toward me. Had he seen me? I crouched down behind my barberries.

(Three months of absence during which Larsan might have had a chance to study every gesture, every mannerism of Darzac! And then—how easy to put Darzac out of the way and to take his place and his bride! Not a difficult trick—for a Larsan!)

The voice? What more easy than to imitate the voice of a native of the Midi? One has a little more or a little less of accent than the other, that is all. Occasionally I have fancied that *his* accent was a little stronger than before the wedding.

He was almost upon me. He passed by. He had not seen me.

"It is Larsan! I could swear that it was Larsan!" But he paused for a second and gazed sorrowfully upon all nature slumbering around him—him whose suffering was in loneliness and solitude, and a groan escaped his lips, unhappy soul that he was!

"It is Darzac!"

And then he was gone—and I remained there behind my hedge overwhelmed with the horror of the thought which I had dared to harbour.

How long did I remain thus, lying on the ground? One hour? Two? When I arose, I was so stiff that I could scarcely stir and my mind was as worn out as my body—worn out and distracted. In the course of my unthinkable hypotheses, I had even gone so far as to ask myself whether, by chance (by chance!) the Larsan who had been in the potato sack had not succeeded in substituting himself for Darzac who had carried him off in the little English cart with Toby drawing it, meaning to throw him into the gulf of Castillon. I could picture the body of the victim rising up suddenly and ordering M. Darzac to take its place. So far from all reason had my wild supposition driven me, that in order to drive away from my mind this ridiculous idea, I was compelled to recall word by word a private conversation that had occurred between M. Darzac and myself that morning when we went out from the terrible session in the Square Tower at which had been so clearly presented the problem of the "body too many." In this conversation, I had received an absolute proof of the impossibility of my supposition. I had, while we talked, proposed to M. Darzac a few questions in relation to Prince Galitch, whose image would not cease to pursue me, and my friend had answered by making allusion to another conversation, involving certain scientific facts, which had taken place between us the night previous, and which could not possibly have been heard by any other person than our two selves and which had also concerned Prince Galitch. On this account, there could be no real doubt in my mind that the Darzac whom I had talked with in the garden was none other than the same man I had seen the evening before.

As senseless as was the idea of this substitution, it was, nevertheless, in a certain degree, pardonable. Rouletabille was a little to blame for it by his fashion of talking of Larsan as a very god of metamorphosis. And after casting it aside, I returned to the sole possible idea under which Larsan could have taken the place of Darzac—the idea of a substitution before the marriage ceremony at the time when Mlle. Stangerson's fiance returned to Paris after three months absence in the Midi.

The despairing plaint which Robert Darzac, believing himself alone, had allowed to escape his lips only a little while before, in my hearing, could not entirely banish this supposition from my head. I saw him again entering the church of St. Nicolas du Chardonnet, in which parish he had requested that the wedding should take place—perhaps, thought I, because there is no darker nor more gloomy church in all Paris.

Ah, one's fancy plays strange tricks on a moonlight night, when one is lurking behind a barberry hedge, with a mind and brain filled with Larsan!

"I am a veritable imbecile!" I told myself, beginning to wish that I were in the quiet little room in the New Castle, where my undisturbed bed awaited me. "For if Larsan had been masquerading as Darzac, he would have been satisfied with carrying off Mathilde and he would not have reappeared in his own likeness to frighten her and he would not have brought her to the Château of Hercules and he would not have committed the foolhardy act of showing himself again in the bark of Tullio. For at that moment, Mathilde belonged to him and it was from that moment that she had cast him off. The reappearance of Larsan had divided the Lady in Black from Darzac, and, therefore, Darzac could not be Larsan."

Dear Heaven, how my head ached! It was the moonlight above which must have turned my brain—I was moonstruck.

And then, too, had not *he* appeared to Arthur Rance himself in the gardens at Mentone after he had accompanied Darzac to the train which had taken him to Cannes, where he met us. If Arthur Rance had spoken the truth, I might go to my couch in tranquility. And why should he have lied?—Arthur Rance who had been in love with the Lady in Black and who had not ceased to love her. Mme. Edith was not a fool—she knew that Mme. Darzac still held the heart of the young American. Well, it was time for me to go to bed!

I was still beneath the arch of the gardener's postern and I was just about to enter the Court of the Bold when it seemed to me that I heard something moving—it sounded as though a door might have been closed. Then there was a sound as of wood striking on iron. I thrust my head out from under the arch and I believed that I could see the shadow of a person near the door of the New Castle—a shadow which somehow seemed to mingle with that of the castle itself. I snatched my revolver from my pocket and with three steps was at the place where I believed I had seen the shape. But it was there no longer. I could see nothing but darkness. The door of the castle was closed and I was certain that I had left it open. I was disturbed and anxious. I felt that I was not alone—who, then, could be near me? Evidently if that shadow had existed elsewhere than in my imagination, it could have vanished only within the New Castle or must still be in the court.

And the court was deserted.

I listened attentively for more than five minutes without making the slightest sound. Nothing! I must have been mistaken. But, nevertheless, I did not even strike a match, and as silently as I could, I ascended the staircase which led to my chamber. When I reached it, I locked myself in and only then began to breathe freely.

This vision or whatever it had been continued to disturb me more than I was willing to confess to myself, and even after I had gotten into bed I could not sleep. Without my being able to account for it at all this vision and the thought of Darzac-Larsan began to mingle strangely in my restless spirit.

The effect on my mind was so strong that, at last, I said to myself: "I shall never know peace again until I am certain that M. Darzac is not Larsan. And I shall take means to make myself certain, one way or the other, on the first occasion." Yes, but how? Pull his beard off? If my suspicion was baseless, he would take me for a madman, or else he would guess what I was thinking of and such a knowledge would add yet another to the load of misfortunes, already too heavy for him to bear. Only this misery was lacking to him still—to know that he was suspected of being Larsan.

Suddenly I threw off the bedclothes, jumped up and cried almost aloud:

"Australia!"

An episode had returned to my mind of which I have spoken at the beginning of this story. The reader may remember that, at the time of the accident in the laboratory, I had accompanied M. Robert Darzac to a druggist. While his injuries were being attended to, he had been obliged to remove his study coat, and the sleeve of his shirt had fallen back, leaving his arm bare through the entire session with the druggist, and placing in full view just above the right elbow, a large birthmark, the shape of which resembled that of Australia as it appears on the maps in the geographies. Mentally, while the chemist was at work, I had amused myself by trying to locate upon the arm in the positions which they occupied on an actual map, the cities of Melbourne, Sydney, Adelaide, etc.; and directly beneath this large mark, there was another smaller one which was situated like the country known as Tasmania.

And when, by any chance, the thought of that accident had happened to recur to my mind, I had always thought of the half hour at the chemist's and the birthmark shaped like the outlines of Australia.

And in this sleepless night, it was the thought of Australia that came to me.

Seated on the edge of my bed, I had scarcely had time to congratulate myself upon having found a means to prove decisively the identity of Robert Darzac and to try to devise some way of bringing it to an immediate test, when a singular sound made me prick up my ears. The sound was repeated—one would have said that gravel was cracking beneath slow and cautious footsteps.

Breathless, I hurried to my door and, with my ear at the keyhole, I listened. Silence for a moment and then once more the same sound—footsteps, beyond a doubt. Someone was now ascending the staircase—and someone who desired his presence to be unknown. I thought of the shadow which I had believed I saw as I was entering the Court of the Bold—whose could this shadow be and what was it doing on the staircase? Was it coming up or going down?

Silence again! I profited by it to hastily don my trousers and, armed with my revolver, I succeeded in opening my door without letting it creak on its hinges. Holding my breath, I advanced to the head of the stairs and waited. I have told of the state of dilapidation of the New Castle. The pale rays of the moonlight entered obliquely through the high windows which opened at each landing, cutting with exact squares of soft light the black darkness of the stairway which was very wide and high. The ruined condition of the château, thus lighted up in spots, only appeared more complete. The broken balustrade and railings of the staircase, the walls overrun with lizards over which here and there hung floating rags of once priceless tapestry—all these things which I had scarcely noticed in the daylight, struck me strangely in this lonely night and my whirling brain felt quite prepared to find in this gloomy scene the fit setting for the appearance of a phantom. Indeed and in truth, I was afraid. The shadow which I had seen a little while ago had practically slipped between my fingers—for I had been near enough to have touched it. But, surely a phantom might walk in an empty house without making any sound. Though the footsteps were silent now!

All at once, as I was leaning on the broken balustrade, I saw the shadow again—it was lighted up by the moonbeams as though it were a flambeau. And I recognised Robert Darzac.

He had reached the ground floor, and, crossing the vestibule, raised his head and looked in my direction as though he felt the weight of my eyes upon him. Instinctively, I drew back. And then I returned to my post of observation just in time to see him disappear into a corridor which led to another staircase winding up to the battlements. What could this mean? Was Robert Darzac spending the night in the New Castle? Why did he take such precautions not to be seen? A thousand suspicions crossed my mind—or rather all the terrible thoughts that had come to haunt me since we had been in the Fort of Hercules seized me again in their grasp and I felt that I must set my spirit at rest, immediately. I must follow Robert Darzac and discover "Australia."

I had reached the corridor almost as soon as he quitted it and I saw him beginning to climb very quietly the moth-eaten wood of the stairway. I saw him pause at the first landing and push open a door. Then I saw nothing more. He had been swallowed up by the darkness—and, perhaps, by the room of which he had opened the door. I reached this door and finding it locked, I gave three little taps, certain that he was inside. And I waited. My heart was beating wildly. All these rooms were uninhabited—abandoned. What should M. Darzac be doing in one of these haunted chambers!

I waited for a few moments which seemed to me like hours and as no one answered and the door did not open, I knocked again and waited again. Then the door was opened and I heard Darzac's voice saying:

"Is it you, Sainclair? What is it, my friend?"

"I wanted to know what you could be doing here at such an hour?" I replied, and it seem d to me that my voice was that of another man, so great was my terror.

Tranquilly, he struck a match and said:

"You see. I am preparing for bed."

And he lit a candle which was placed on a chair, for there was no night stand in this dilapidated apartment. A bed in one corner—an iron bed which must have been brought there during the day, and a single chair, comprised all the furnishings.

"I thought that you were going to sleep near Mme. Darzac and the Professor on the first floor of 'la Louve'?"

"The rooms are too small. I was afraid of inconveniencing Mme. Darzac," answered the unhappy man, bitterly. "I asked Bernier to fetch me a bed here. And then what difference does it make where I am, since I do not sleep?"

We were both silent for a moment. I was ashamed of myself and of my wretched suspicions. And, frankly, my remorse was so great that I could not refrain from giving it expression. I confessed everything to him; my infamous ideas and how I had even believed when I saw him wandering so mysteriously over the New Castle that it was upon some evil errand; and so had decided to go and look for the "Australia" birthmark. For I did not conceal from him that for a moment, I had placed all my hopes upon the Australia.

He listened to me with such an expression of reproachful sorrow that it wrung my heart; then he quietly rolled up his shirt sleeve and bringing his bare arm close to the light, he showed me the birthmark, which made a sane man of me once more. I did not wish to look at it, but he even insisted upon my touching it and I knew beyond a doubt that it was a natural scar upon which one might place little dots with the names of the cities, "Sydney," "Melbourne," "Adelaide." And beneath it there was another little blotch shaped like Tasmania.

"You may rub it as much as you choose," said Darzac, gently, "It will not come off."

I begged his pardon a thousand times over, with tears in my eyes, but he would not forgive me until he had made me pull at his beard which remained firmly attached to his chin, instead of coming off in my hand.

Then, only, he allowed me to go back to my room, which I did, cursing myself for an idiot.

# XVII

## OLD BOB'S TERRIBLE ADVENTURE

When I awakened my thoughts were still dwelling on Larsan. And, in truth, I did not know what to think either of myself or any other person—of Larsan's death or of his life. Had he been wounded less seriously than we had believed? Or shall I say, "Was he *less dead* than we had thought?" Had he been able to extricate himself from the sack which Darzac had cast in the gulf of Castillon? After all, the thing was not impossible, or, rather, the possibility was not altogether without the bounds of what might be looked for from the superhuman cunning and prowess of a Larsan—particularly since Walter had explained that he had found the sack three meters from the mouth of the abyss upon a natural landing place the existence of which M. Darzac assuredly did not suspect when he believed that he was throwing Larsan's body into the orifice.

My second thoughts turned to Rouletabille. What was he doing now? Why had he gone away? Never had his presence at the Fort of Hercules been so necessary as now. If he delayed his return, this day could scarcely pass without bringing the unfriendly feeling between the Rances and the Darzacs to an open issue.

As I lay there puzzling my brain over the outcome of the affair, I heard someone knocking at my door. It was Pere

Bernier, who brought me a brief note from my friend which had been handed to Pere Jacques by a little lad from the village. Rouletabille wrote: "I shall return early in the morning. Get up as soon as this reaches you and be good enough to go fishing for my breakfast and catch some of the fine trout which are so plentiful among the rocks near the Point of Garibaldi. Do not lose an instant. Thanks and remembrances.—ROULETABILLE."

This communication gave me more food for thought, for I knew by experience that whenever Rouletabille seemed most occupied with trivial matters, his activity was really most thoroughly engaged with important subjects.

I dressed myself in haste, provided myself with some old tackle which was furnished me by Bernier, and set out to obey the request of my young friend. As I went out of the North gate, having encountered nobody at that early hour of the morning (it was about seven o'clock), I was joined by Mme. Edith, to whom I showed what Rouletabille had written. The young woman was greatly dejected over the unexplained absence of her uncle, remarked that the letter was "so queer that it made her nervous," and she informed me that she intended to follow me to the trout streams. On the way, she confided to me the fact that her uncle had not an enemy in the world, so far as she knew, and she said that she had been hoping against hope that he would yet return and that everything would be satisfactorily explained, but now the idea had entered her brain that by some frightful mistake, Old Bob had fallen a victim to the vengeance of Darzac and she was nearly wild with apprehension.

And she added, between her pretty teeth, a few words of contempt and wrath for the Lady in Black. "My patience can hold out until noon, I hope!" she said, and then was silent.

We started to fish for Rouletabille's trout. Mrs. Rance and I both removed our shoes and stockings, but I concerned myself more about the dainty bare feet of my pretty hostess than about my own. The fact is, that Edith's feet, as I discovered in the Bay of Hercules, were as beautifully shaped and pink as flowers and they made me forget the trout of my poor Rouletabille to such an extent that he must certainly have gone without his breakfast if Edith had not shown more energy than I. She clambered into the pools and crept among the rocks with a grace which enchanted me more than I dared express. Suddenly we both desisted from our task and pricked up our cars at the same moment. We heard cries from the shore where the grottoes are. Upon the very threshold of the Grotto of Romeo and Juliet we distinguished a little group, the persons in which were making gestures of appeal. Urged on by the same presentiment, we hastily rushed to the beach and in a few seconds we learned that, attracted by moans, two fishermen had just discovered in a cave in the Grotto of Romeo and Juliet an unfortunate human being who had fallen into the chasm and who must have been there helpless for several hours.

The quick conjecture which rushed into both our minds at once proved to be the right one. It was Old Bob who had been fished out of the cave. When he had been drawn up on the beach in the full light of day, he certainly presented a pitiable spectacle. His beautiful black coat was torn and covered with mud and his white shirt was as black as tar. Mme. Edith burst into tears and nearly went into hysterics when she found that the old man had a torn collarbone and a sprained foot, and was so pale that he looked as if he were about to die.

Happily, the old man's injuries were far less serious than it at first had seemed. He was, according to his own account, on his bed in his room in the Square Tower. Would anyone believe that he absolutely refused to become undressed, even so far as to have his coat on before the arrival of the doctors? And Mrs. Rance, increasingly nervous, installed herself next to his bedside until the physicians came, and Old Bob instructed her not only to leave his room but to go outside of the Square

Tower altogether. And he insisted that the door should be locked after her.

The precaution was a great surprise to us all. We stood assembled in the Court of the Bold, M. and Mme. Darzac, M. Arthur Rance and myself, as well as Bernier who haunted my footsteps, waiting the news. When Mme. Edith quitted the tower after the dismissal of the medical men, she came to us and said:

"Let us hope that his injuries won't be serious. Old Bob is solid as a rock. What did I tell you about him? I made him confess, the old sinner! He was trying to steal Prince Galitch's skull which he believe to be more ancient than his own. Just the jealousy of one savant toward another. We shall all laugh at him when he is cured!"

At that moment the door of the Square Tower opened and Walter, Old Bob's faithful servant, appeared. His face was pale and he seemed very nervous.

"Oh, Miss Edith!" he cried out. "He is covered with blood! He doesn't want anything to be said about it, but he must be saved—"

Edith had already rushed into the Square Tower. As to us we dared not utter a word. Soon the young woman returned.

"Oh!" she sobbed. "It is frightful. His whole breast is torn open!" I started to offer her the support of my arm, for, strangely enough M. Arthur Rance had withdrawn to some distance and was walking upon the boulevard, whistling and with his hands behind his back. I tried to comfort and to soothe Mme. Edith, but neither M. nor Mme. Darzac uttered a word.

Rouletabille reached the castle about an hour after these events.

I watched for his return from the highest part of the western boulevard and as soon as I saw his form appearing in the distance I hurried to meet him. He cut short my demands for an explanation and asked me immediately if I had made a good catch, but I was not at all deceived by the expression of his countenance, and wishing to reply to him in his own style of banter, I replied:

"Oh, yes: a very good catch. I fished up Old Bob."

He started violently. I shrugged my shoulders, for I believed that he was counterfeiting surprise, and I went on :

"Oh, go on! You knew very well what kind of fish I should find when you sent your message!"

He fixed an astonished glance on me.

"You certainly must be unaware of the purport of your words, my dear Sainclair, or else you would have spared me the trouble of protesting against such an accusation."

"What accusation?" I cried.

"That of having left Old Bob in the Grotto of Romeo and Juliet, knowing that he might be dying there."

"Oh, nonsense!" I cried. "Old Bob is far from dying. He has a sprained foot and a broken collar bone, and his story of his misfortune is perfectly plain and straightforward. He declares that he was trying to steal Prince Galitch's skull."

"What a funny idea!" exclaimed Rouletabille, bursting out laughing. He leaned toward me and looked full into my eyes.

"Do you believe that story? And—and that is all? No other injuries?"

"Yes," I replied. "There is another injury, but the doctors declare that it is not at all serious. He has a wound in the breast."

"A wound in the breast!" repeated Rouletabille, touching my hand, nervously. "And how was this wound made?"

"We do not know. None of us have seen it. Old Bob is strangely modest. He would not even permit his coat to be taken off in our presence; and the coat hid the wound so well that we should never have suspected it was there if Walter had not come to tell us, frightened at the sight of the blood."

As soon as we came to the château, we encountered Mme. Edith, who appeared to have been watching for us.

"My uncle won't have me near him," she said, regarding Rouletabille with an air of anxiety different from anything I had ever noticed in her before. "It's incomprehensible!"

"Ah, Madame," replied the reporter, making a low bow to his hostess. "I assure you that nothing in the world is incomprehensible, when one is willing to take a little trouble to understand it." And he offered her his congratulations upon having had her uncle restored to her at the moment when she was ready to despair of ever seeing him again.

Mme. Edith seemed about to inquire into the purport of the enigmatical words at the beginning of my friend's remarks when we were joined by Prince Galitch. He had come to ask for news of his old friend, Bob, of whose misfortune he had learned. Mme. Edith reassured him as to her uncle's condition and entreated the Prince to pardon her relative for his too excessive devotion to the "oldest skulls in the history of humanity." The Prince smiled graciously and with the utmost kindliness when he was told that Old Bob had been attempting to steal his skull.

"You will find your skull," Mrs. Rance told him, "in the bottom of the cave in the grotto where it rolled down with him. Your collection will be unimpaired, Prince."

The Prince asked for the details. He seemed very curious about the affair. And Mme. Edith told how her uncle had acknowledged to her that he had quitted the Fort of Hercules by way of the air shaft which communicated with the sea. As soon as she said this, I recalled the experience of Rouletabille with the flask of water and also the close iron bars, and the falsehoods which Old Bob had uttered assumed gigantic proportions in my mind, and I was sure that the rest of the party must hold the same opinion as myself. Mme. Edith told us that Tullio had been waiting with his boat at the opening of the gallery abutting on the shaft, to row the old savant to the bank in front of the Grotto of Romeo and Juliet.

"Why so many twists and turnings when it was so simple to go out by the gate?" I could not restrain myself from exclaiming.

Mme. Edith looked at me reproachfully and I regretted having even seemed to have taken part against her in any way.

"And this is stranger yet!" said the Prince. "Day before yesterday, the 'hangman of the sea' came to bid me adieu, saying that he was going to leave the country, and I am sure that he took the train for Venice, his native city, at five o'clock in the afternoon. How then could he have conveyed your uncle in his boat late that night? In the first place, he was not in this part of the world; in the second, he had sold his boat. He told me so, adding that he would never return to this country."

There was a dead silence and Prince Galitch continued:

"All this is of little importance—provided that your uncle, Madame, recovers speedily from his injuries and, again," he added with another smile, more charming than those which had preceded it—"if you will aid me in regaining a poor piece of flint which has disappeared from the grotto and of which I will give you the description. It is a sharp piece of flint, twenty-five centimeters long and shaped at one end to the form of a dagger—in brief, the oldest dagger of the human race. I value it greatly and, perhaps you may be able to learn, Madame, through your uncle, Bob, what has become of it."

Mme. Edith at once gave her promise to the Prince, with a certain air of haughtiness which pleased me greatly, that she would do everything possible to obtain for him news of so precious an object. The Prince bowed low and left us. When we had finished returning his parting salutes, we saw M. Arthur Rance before us. He must have heard the conversation for he seemed very thoughtful. He had his ivory-headed cane in his hand, and was whistling, according to his habit. And he looked at Mme. Edith with an expression so strange that she appeared somewhat exasperated.

"I know exactly what you are thinking, sir!" she said. "It does not astonish me in the least. And you may keep on thinking so, if it amuses you, for aught I care."

And she stepped nearer Rouletabille, smiling nervously.

"At all events," she exclaimed. "You can never explain to me how, when *he* was outside the Square Tower, *he* could have hidden behind that panel."

"Madame," said Rouletabille, slowly and impressively, looking at the young woman as though he were trying to hypnotize her, "have patience and have courage. If God is with me, before night I shall explain to you all that you wish to know."

# XVIII

## HOW DEATH STALKED ABROAD AT NOON DAY

A little later, I found myself in the lower parlour of "la Louve," tete-a-tete with Mme. Edith. I attempted to reassure her, seeing how restless and nervous she was; but she buried her pale face in her hands and her trembling lips allowed the confession of her fears to escape them.

"I am frightened!" she murmured. I asked her what frightened her and she looked at me wildly and said, "And aren't you afraid, too?" I kept silence, for I was afraid, myself. She said again. "You know something of what is going on— here or there or all around us! Ah, I am all alone! All alone! And I am so frightened."

She turned toward the door.

"Where are you going?" I asked.

"I am going to look for someone. I won't stay here alone."

"For whom are you going to look?"

"For Prince Galitch."

"Your 'Feodor Feodorowitch,'" I cried. "What do you want with him? Am I not here?"

Her nervousness, unfortunately, seemed to increase in proportion to my efforts to drive it away and I began to realize that a fearful doubt as to the personality of her uncle, Old Bob, had entered her mind.

"Let us go out into the air!" she said, impatiently. "I can't breathe in this place." We left "la Louve" and entered the garden. It was approaching the hour of noontide and the court was a dream of perfumed beauty. As we had not donned our smoked spectacles, we were obliged to put our hands before our eyes in order to shield them from the glaring rays of the sun and the too glowing hues of the flowers. The giant geraniums struck on our eyeballs like bleeding wounds. When we had grown a little more used to the dazzling sight, we advanced over the shining sands, Edith clinging to my hand like a little child. Her hand burned hotter than the sun and seemed like a veritable flame. We looked down at our feet in order to prevent our eyes from falling on the blinding expanse of the waters and also, it may be, in order not to glance toward the buildings in which so many strange things had taken place—perhaps, were taking place even now.

"I am afraid!" murmured Edith once more. And I, too, was afraid—overwhelmed after the mysteries of the night by the vast, desolate silence of the noon.

The broad glare of daylight in which one knows that something strange and terrible is going on is more awful than the deepest and darkest night. Everything sleeps and yet everything wakes. Everything is dead and everything is living. Everything is wrapped in silence and still there are sounds everywhere. Listen to your own ear. It sounds as loud as a conch shell filled with the most mysterious sounds of the sea. Close your lids and look into your own eyes; you will find there a throng of crowding visions more mysterious than the phantoms of the night.

I looked at Mme. Edith. Beads of perspiration stood out on her forehead and her face was pale as death. I was trembling and chilled, for, alas! I could do nothing to help her and destiny was weaving its inexorable web all around us and that nothing which we could say or do would hinder in the slightest degree its slow, undeviating march. Edith led the way toward the postern gate which opens upon the Court of the Bold. The vault of this postern formed a black arch in the light and at the extremity of this tunnel, we perceived, facing us, Rouletabille and M. Darzac, who were standing at the edge of the inner court, like two white statues. Rouletabille was holding in his hand Arthur Rance's ivory-headed cane. Why this latter fact should have disturbed me, I do not know, but so it was. Motioning with the cane, he showed Robert Darzac something on the summit of the vault which we could not see and then he pointed us out in the same way. We could not hear what he said. The two talked together for a few moments with their lips scarcely moving, like two accomplices in some dark secret. Mme. Edith paused, but Rouletabille beckoned to her, repeating the signal with his cane.

"Oh, what does he want with me now?" she cried like a frightened child. "Oh, M. Sainclair, I am so miserable. I am going to tell my uncle everything and we shall see what will happen them."

We went on until we reached the vault and the others watched us without making a movement to meet us. They stood like two statues, and I said aloud in a voice which sounded strangely in my own ears:

"What are you two doing here?"

We had come up close to them by this time, upon the threshold of the Court of the Bold, and they bade us turn around with our backs toward the court so that we could see what they were looking at. There was on top of the arch, an escutcheon, the shield of the Mortola, barred with the mark of the cadet branch. This escutcheon had been carved in a stone now loose, which seemed in imminent danger of falling and crushing the heads of the passersby. Rouletabille had without doubt noticed this danger, and he asked Mme. Edith if she had any objections to its being pulled down until it could be replaced more solidly.

"I am sure that it will fall before long and it might do serious damage," he said, touching it with the end of his cane, and then passing the stick to Mme. Edith.

"You are taller than I," he went on. "See if you can reach it."

But both she and I tried in vain to touch the stone; it was too high for us and I was about to inquire what was the meaning of this singular exercise when all at once, behind my back, *I heard the cry of a dying man in his last agony.*

We turned with one impulse, uttering an exclamation of horror.

Ah, that cry of mortal agony which rang out on the air of the noonday just as it had through the night! Would we never be free from murder? When would that fearful sound which I had heard for the first time that night at the Glandier, never be done with announcing to us that a new victim had been struck down among us? That one of our own number had fallen beneath some fatal blow, as suddenly as though by some frightful pestilence? Surely, the mark of the epidemic itself is less invisible and terrible than that of the hand which kills.

We all stood there, shivering, our eyes wide with horror, questioning the deeps of the sky still vibrating from that cry of death. Who was dead? Who was dying? What expiring breath had emitted that terrible sound? One might have thought that it was the clearness of the day itself which cried out in suffering.

Rouletabille was the most terrified of us all. I have seen him, under the most untoward circumstances, maintain a composure which seemed greater than any human creature could hold; I have seen him, at a like horrible cry of death, rush into the danger of the darkness and cast himself like a heroic rescuer into the sea of shadows. Why should he tremble so today in the full splendour of the noon? He remained fixed to the spot, as weak as a baby, he, who a little while ago, declared that he would prove himself the master of the hour. He had not foreseen this moment then? This moment in which a human life had been snatched away under the noonday sun!

Mattoni, who was passing through the garden, and who had also heard the cry, rushed up. At a gesture from Rouletabille he stood rooted to the spot an immovable sentinel; and now the young man had gained sufficient power to advance toward the cry—or, at least, toward the centre of the cry, for it seemed still to echo everywhere around us and to circle about in the all embracing space. And we hurried behind him, our breath coming fast, our arms stretched out, as one holds them when one is groping in the dark and fears to stumble against something which one does not see.

We approached the place from which the shriek had come and when we had passed the shade of the eucalyptus we found the cause. The cry had come, indeed, from a soul passing into the unknown. It was Bernier—Bernier in whose throat sounded the death rattle, who was trying in vain to rise and who was at the last gasp of his life. It was Bernier from whose breast flowed a stream of blood—Bernier over whom we leaned, and who, with one last, fearful struggle, summoned strength enough to utter the two words: "Frederic Larsan!"

Then his head fell back and he was dead. Frederic Larsan! Frederic Larsan! He who was everywhere and nowhere! He always and forever. Here, yet again, was his mark. A dead body—and no one anywhere near who could have committed the murder, by any possibility of human reason. For the only means of egress from the spot on which the crime had occurred was by this postern where we four had been standing. And we had turned, with one impulse and one movement, at the very instant that the cry rang out—so quickly that we had almost seen the stroke of death given. And when we looked, there had not even been a shadow before our eyes—nothing but the light! We rushed, moved by the same sentiment, it seemed to me, into the Square Tower, the door of which still stood open; we entered in a body the bedroom of Old Bob, passing through the empty sitting room. The injured man was lying quietly on his bed within, and near him a woman was watching—Mere Bernier. Both were as calm and still as the day itself. But when the wife of the dead concierge saw our faces she uttered a cry of affright, as though smitten by the knowledge of some calamity. She had heard nothing. She knew nothing. But she rushed into the air like a streak of lightning and went straight, as though impelled by some hidden force, directly to the place where the body was lying.

And now it was her groans that sounded on the air, under the terrible sun of the Midi, over the bleeding corpse. We tore the shirt from the dead man's breast and found a gaping wound just above the heart. Rouletabille looked up with the same expression which I had seen at the Glandier when he came to examine the wound of the "inexplicable body."

"One would say that it was the same stroke of the knife!" he said. "It is the same measurement. But where is the knife?"

We looked for the weapon everywhere without finding it. The man who had struck the blow had carried the knife away. Where was the man? Who was he? What we did not know, Bernier had known before he died and it was, perhaps, because of that knowledge that his life had been forfeited. "Frederic Larsan!" We repeated the last words of the dying man in fear and trembling.

Suddenly on the threshold of the postern, we saw the Prince Galitch, a newspaper in his hand. He was reading as he came toward us. His air was jovial and his face wore a smile. But Mme. Edith rushed up to him, snatched the paper from his hands, pointed to the corpse and cried out:

"A man has been murdered! Send for the police!"

The Prince stared at the body and then at us without uttering a word and then turned hastily away, saying that he would send for the authorities immediately, Mere Bernier kept up her wild lamentations. Rouletabille seated himself on the edge of the shaft. He seemed to have lost all his strength. He spoke to Mme. Edith in a low tone:

"Let the police come then, Madame, but remember, it is you who have insisted upon it!"

Mrs. Rance gave him a withering glance from her black eyes. And I knew what her thoughts were as well as though she had spoken them out. She felt that she hated Rouletabille, who had for a single moment been able to make her suspect Old Bob. While Bernier had been assassinated, had not Old Bob been quietly in his chamber, watched over by Mere Bernier herself?

Rouletabille was examining the iron bars and heavy lid which closed the shaft, but his manner was distrait and discouraged. After he had finished what seemed to be a very careless inspection he stretched himself out on the ground as if it were a couch in which he was trying to get some rest. Turning once more to his hostess, he said in the same low voice:

"And what will you tell the police when they get here?"

"Everything!"

Mrs. Rance fairly snapped out the word between her teeth, her eyes flashing fire. Rouletabille shook his head sorrowfully and closed his eyes. He seemed utterly exhausted and vanquished. Robert Darzac touched him on his shoulder. M. Darzac wanted to search through the Square Tower, the Tower of the Bold, the New Castle—all the dependencies of the fort from which no one could have made his escape, and where, therefore, the assassin must still be concealed. The reporter shook his head drearily, and said that it would be of no use. Rouletabille and I knew only too well that any search would be in vain. Had we not made a search at the Glandier after the phenomenon of the dissolution of matter, for the man who had disappeared in the inexplicable gallery? No, no! I had learned that there was no use in looking for Larsan with one's eyes.

A man had been murdered just behind our backs. We had heard him cry out when the blow struck him down. We had turned around and had seen nothing except the daylight. To see clearly, it was better to close the eyes as Rouletabille was doing at this moment.

And when he opened them, he was another man! A new energy animated his features. He stood erect as though he had thrown off a weight. He clenched his fist and raised it toward the heavens.

"That is not possible!" he cried. "Or there is no more good in reasoning."

And he threw himself on the ground, creeping on his hands and knees, his nose to the earth, like a hound following the scent, going round the body of poor Bernier and around Mere Bernier, who had blankly refused to leave her husband—around the shaft—around each of us. He moved about like a pig, nosing its nourishment out of the mire, and we all stood still, looking at him curiously and half in alarm. Suddenly he started to his feet, almost white with dust and uttered a shout of triumph as though he had found Larsan himself in the gravel. What new victory did the boy feel that he had achieved over the mystery? What had given this new firmness to his step and steadiness to his glance? What had given back to him the strength of his voice? For when he addressed M. Robert Darzac his tones were full of vigour and resolution.

"It's all right, Monsieur! *Nothing is changed*!"

And, turning to Mme. Edith—

"There is nothing more to do, Madame, except to wait for the police. I hope that they will not be long."

The unhappy woman shuddered. I knew that she was again struck with mortal fear.

"Yes, let them come!" she cried, taking my arm. "And let them attend to everything! Let them think for us! Whatever may happen, let it come as soon as it will."

Attracted by the sound of voices we looked around and saw Pere Jacques approaching, followed by two gendarmes. It was the brigadier of la Mortola, who, summoned by Prince Galitch, had hurried to the scene of the crime.

"The gendarmes! The gendarmes! They say that murder has been done!" exclaimed Pere Jacques, who as yet knew nothing of what had happened.

"Be calm, Pere Jacques!" exhorted Rouletabille, and when the old man, panting and breathless, drew near to the reporter, the latter said to him in low tones:

"*Nothing is changed*, Pere Jacques!"

But Pere Jacques was gazing at Bernier's body.

"Only one more dead man!" he sighed. "This is Larsan's work again!"

"It is the work of destiny!" answered Rouletabille. Larsan and destiny—both were as one. But what did Rouletabille mean by his "Nothing is changed," if not that, despite the incidental murder of Bernier, everything which we dreaded, which made us shudder and which we had no understanding of, continued just as before?

The gendarmes were busy examining the body and chattering over it in their uncomprehensible jargon. The brigadier informed us that they had telephoned to the Garibaldi Tavern, a few steps away, where at this moment the delegato, or special commissioner, stationed at Vintimille, was even now breakfasting. The delegato would have power to begin the investigation, which would be continued when the examining magistrate had been notified.

The delegato arrived. It was easily to be seen that he was enchanted, even though he had not had the time to finish his repast. A crime! Actually a crime! And in the Château of

Hercules. He was fairly radiant; his eyes shone. He was full of business, full of importance. He ordered the brigadier to station one of his men at the gate of the château with directions to permit no person to pass in or out. Then he knelt down beside the body while a gendarme, despite her protestations and tears, led Mere Bernier away to the Square Tower, where her groans sounded louder than ever. The delegato examined the wound and said in very good French:

"That was a magnificent stroke!"

The man was enchanted. If he had had the assassin under arrest, he would assuredly have paid him his compliments. He looked at us. Then he looked at us again. Perhaps he was seeking among us for the criminal to tell him of his admiration. At last he rose from his knees.

"And now how did all this happen?" he asked encouragingly, smacking his lips as though in the anticipation of hearing a story of thrilling interest. "It is terrible!" he added—"Terrible! In the five years that I have been delegato, we have never had a murder, Monsieur the examining magistrate—." Here he checked himself but we knew well what he had been on the point of saying: "Monsieur the examining magistrate will be very much pleased." He brushed away the white dust which covered his knees, wiped the perspiration from his forehead and repeated "It is terrible!" his Southern accent seeming to grow stronger. And at that moment, he noticed in a new arrival who entered the court, a doctor from Mentone who had come to continue his treatment of Old Bob.

"Ah, doctor, I am glad that you are here! Just look at this wound and tell me what you think of such a knife stroke. But be as careful as possible about changing the position of the corpse before the arrival of the examining magistrate."

The doctor sounded the depth of the wound and gave us all the technical details which we could desire. There was no doubt about it at all. It was a truly magnificent stroke of the knife which had penetrated from high to low in the cardiac region and the point of the knife had certainly opened a ventricle. During the colloquy between the delegato and the doctor, Rouletabille never took his eyes off Mme. Edith, who was still clinging to my arm as though she knew that I was her only refuge. Her eyes fell before the eyes of Rouletabille which seemed to hypnotize her and to command her to be silent. But I knew that she was trembling with the desire to speak.

At the request of the delegato, we all entered the Square Tower. We took our places in Old Bob's sitting room, where the inquest was to be held and where each of us in turn recounted what we had seen and heard. Mere Bernier was first questioned, but little or nothing could be gained from her testimony. She declared that she knew nothing about anything. She had been in Old Bob's bedroom, attending to the needs of the injured man, when we had rushed madly into the room. She had been with Old Bob for an hour, having left her husband in the lodge of the Square Tower, ready to work at making a rope.

It was a curious fact, but I was less interested at that moment in what was going on under my eyes than in what I could not see and yet knew *that I expected*.

Would Edith speak? She was looking out of the open window, her lips compressed, her brows drawn. A gendarme was standing near the corpse over the face of which a handkerchief had been laid. Edith, like myself, was paying very little heed to what was going on inside the room. Her eyes were fixed upon Bernier's body.

An exclamation from the delegato struck upon our ears. The further the evidence of the witnesses progressed, the greater became the amazement of the Commissioner, and the more and more inexplicable he found the crime. He was on the point of finding it impossible that it should have been committed at all, when it came Mme. Edith's turn to be interrogated.

They questioned her. Her lips were already opened to answer the first question when Rouletabille's quiet voice was heard:

"Look at the end of the shadow of the eucalyptus."

"What is there at the end of the shadow of the eucalyptus?" demanded the delegato.

"The weapon with which the crime was committed," replied the reporter.

He jumped out of the window to the court and picked up from the bloody stones a sharp, shining piece of flint. He brandished it in our eyes. We all recognised it. It was "the oldest dagger of the human race."

# XIX

## IN WHICH ROULETABILLE ORDERS THE IRON DOORS TO BE CLOSED

The weapon belonged to Prince Galitch, but there was no doubt in the mind of any one of us that it had been stolen by Old Bob, and we could not forget that with his latest breath Bernier had accused Larsan of being his assassin. Never had the image of Old Bob and that of Larsan been so inextricably confounded in our restless spirits as since Rouletabille had found "the oldest dagger known to the human race" dripping with the blood of Bernier. Mme. Edith had at once realised that henceforth the fate of Old Bob lay in the hands of Rouletabille. The latter had only to say a few words to the delegato relative to the singular incidents which had accompanied the fall of Old Bob into the cave in the "Grotto of Romeo and Juliet, enumerating the reasons which had given occasion for fear that Old Bob and Larsan were one and the same, and, finally, repeating the accusation made by the last victim of Larsan, in order to fix the suspicions of the delegato firmly upon the wigged head of the professor of geology. And, therefore, Mme. Edith, who in her filial affection had not ceased to believe that the man who lay on his bed in the Square Tower was really her uncle, had begun to imagine, thanks to the bloody weapon, that the invisible Larsan had woven so strong a web of circumstantial evidence around old Bob that it could scarcely be broken, with the design, doubtless, of making the old man suffer the punishment for the wretch's own crimes and also the dangerous weight of his personality. Mme. Edith trembled for Old Bob and for herself. She trembled with fear, like an insect in the centre of the web in which it has lost itself—this mysterious web woven by Larsan, attached by invisible threads to the old walls of the Château of Hercules. She felt as though if she were to make a sudden movement—to say anything even—both she and her uncle would be lost, and that some horrible beast of prey awaited only this signal to spring upon and devour her. So she who had been so anxious to speak out stood silent and when Rouletabille was called upon, it was her turn to fear. She told me afterward of her state of mind at this time and she acknowledged to me that her terror of Larsan had reached such a pitch as even we, who had known so much of his evil power already, had never experienced. This were wolf whose name she had so often heard spoken in accents of horror which had made her smile, had begun to interest her, when she learned of the events of the Yellow Room, because of the impossibility of the police discovering the manner of his exit. Her interest had increased when she had heard the story of the attack of the Square Tower because of the impossibility of anyone's explaining how Larsan could have entered; but, now—now, in the full glare of the noonday sun, Larsan had killed a man almost under her own eyes, and within a radius in which there was at the time only herself, Robert Darzac, Rouletabille, myself, Old Bob and Mere Bernier, each and every one of them far enough away from the body so that not one could have struck Bernier down. And Bernier had accused Larsan! Where was Larsan? *In whose body?*—according to the reasoning which I had set forth to her myself in telling her the story of the "inexplicable gallery"? She had been under the arch with Darzac and myself, standing between us, with

Rouletabille in front of us, when the death cry had resounded at the end of the shadow of the eucalyptus tree—that is to say, at least, seven meters away. As to Old Bob and Mere Bernier, they had not been separated; the one had watched over the other. If she placed them outside the realms of possibility, there was no one left to kill Bernier. Not alone this time was everyone ignorant how *he* had departed but also of *how he had been present.* Ah, she understood now that when one thought of Larsan there were moments in which one shivered to the marrow of one's bones! Nothing! Nothing anywhere around the corpse but the stone knife which Old Bob had stolen! It was frightful—it was reason enough for us to think of everything—to imagine everything!

She read the certainty of this conviction in the eyes and in the manner of Rouletabille and of Robert Darzac. But she understood as soon as the young man began speaking that he seemed to have no other end in view than to save Old Bob from the suspicions of the authorities.

Rouletabille was given a seat between the delegato and the examining magistrate who had arrived while Mme. Edith had been testifying, and he gave his evidence (or rather, reasoned the matter out) holding the "oldest knife known to the human race" in his hand. It seemed definitely established that the guilty person could have been no other than one of the living men and women who were near the dead man and whom I have enumerated above, when Rouletabille proved with a logical accuracy that overwhelmed the examining magistrate and plunged the delegato into despair that the deed could only have been committed by the dead man himself. The four persons at the postern gate and the two persons in Old Bob's room had each been looking at the others and had not lost sight of each other while *someone* was killing Bernier a few steps away, so it was impossible to believe that the killing could have been done by any other than the victim.

To this the examining magistrate, greatly interested, replied by inquiring whether any of us had reason to suspect any motive for suicide on the part of Bernier, to which Rouletabille answered that the supposition of suicide might easily be laid aside and that of accident substituted for it. "The weapon of the crime," as he called ironically the "oldest knife known to the human race," testified to the truth of this theory by its presence. Rouletabille declared that there would be no chance of an assassin meditating the commission of a murder with an old piece of stone as an instrument. And still less could one believe that Bernier, if he had resolved upon suicide, would not have found another means toward his end than the one which had been used. But if, on the contrary, that stone, which might have attracted his attention by its strange form, had been picked up by Pere Bernier, and if he had happened to slip and fall while holding it in his hand, everything would be explained and very simply. Pere Bernier, undoubtedly, must have thus unfortunately fallen upon this triangular flint which had pierced his heart.

After Rouletabille had stated this hypothesis, the physician was recalled, the wound examined once more and confronted with the fatal object from which the scientific conclusion was reached that the wound was made by the object. From this to the theory of accident, as stated by Rouletabille, there was only a step. The judges spent six hours in clearing up the matter—six hours during which they questioned us without weariness but without result.

As to Mme. Edith and your humble servant, after some futile and useless questions, asked while the doctors were at the bedside of Old Bob, we were allowed to leave the room and we went to sit in the little parlour just outside the bedroom and were there when the magistrates were ready to depart. The door of this parlour which opened upon the corridor of the Square Tower had not been closed. We could hear the sobs and groans of Mere Bernier, who was watching beside the body of her husband which had been carried into the lodge. Between this body and the wounded man, the injury to one as inexplicable as the death of the other, the situation of both Mrs. Rance and myself had become extremely painful, in spite of Rouletabille's efforts, and all the terrors which we had experienced before grew pale and simple before the thought of what might be yet to come. Edith suddenly seized me by the hand and cried out:

"Do not leave me! I beg of you, don't leave me! I have only you left. I do not know where Prince Galitch is—I do not know anything about my husband. That is what makes this so horrible. Arthur sent me a message, saying that he was going in search of Tullio. He does not know even yet that Bernier has been murdered. Has he found the 'hangman of the sea'? It is from this man—from Tullio now that I expect the truth! And not a word has come! It is horrible!"

As she took my hand so confidingly and held it for a moment in her own, I felt that I was for Mme. Edith with all my heart and soul and I assured her that she might rely upon my devotion. We murmured a few words of trust and eternal fidelity to each other in low voices while there in the corridor we could see, passing back and forth, the dark forms of the emissaries of justice, now preceded, now followed by Rouletabille and M. Darzac. Rouletabille never failed to cast a glance in our direction every time he had the opportunity. The window remained open.

"Ah, he is watching us!" exclaimed Mme. Edith. "Why is that, I wonder? Probably we are in his way and M. Darzac's when we remain here. But, whatever may happen, we shall not stir, shall we, M. Sainclair?"

"You ought to be grateful to Rouletabille," I ventured to remind her; "for his intervention and his silence relative to the 'oldest knife known to the human race.' If the officers had learned that this stone dagger belonged to your uncle, Bob, what could have hindered them from placing him under arrest? Or if they knew that Bernier in dying had accused Larsan of his murder, the story of the accident would have found very little credence."

I placed an emphasis upon these last words.

"Oh!" she cried, bitterly. "Your friend has as many good reasons to keep silence as I have! And I dread only one thing, M. Sainclair—I dread only one thing!"

"And what is that?"

She arose, her eyes shining with fever.

"I fear lest he has saved my uncle from the authorities only to ruin him more completely."

"How can you think such a thing for a moment?" I asked her, convinced that her fears were robbing her of her senses.

"I am sure that I could read some such plan in the eyes of your friend a little while ago. If I were sure that I were right, I would rather hand my uncle over to the mercies of the authorities."

I managed to quiet her a little and to make her cast aside such an impossible supposition, and, at length, she said:

"At all events, it is necessary to be ready for anything, and I know how to defend him so long as I draw breath."

And she showed me a tiny revolver which was hidden in her gown.

"Ah!" she cried again. "Why is Prince Galitch not here?"

"Again?" I exclaimed, angrily.

"Is it actual truth that you are ready to defend me?" she demanded, turning her beautiful eyes full upon my own."

"I am ready."

"Against the whole world?"

I hesitated. She repeated the words again:

"Against the whole world?"

"Yes."

"Against your friend even?"

"If it should be necessary," I answered with a sigh, passing my hand across my forehead.

"Very well: I believe you!" she answered. "In that case. I will leave you here for a few minutes. You will guard this door for *me*!"

And she pointed to the door behind which Old Bob was resting. Then she ran out of the room. Where was she going? She confessed to me later. She was going to look for the Prince Galitch! Oh, woman, woman!

She had scarcely disappeared under the arch when Rouletabille and M. Darzac entered the room. They had heard all that had passed. Rouletabille advanced to my side and told me quietly that he was aware that I had betrayed him.

"You are using a large word, Rouletabille!" I exclaimed. "You know that I am not in the habit of betraying anyone! Mme. Edith is really very much to be pitied and you do not pity her enough, my friend."

"Ah, well! You pity her too much!"

I blushed to the roots of my hair. I started to make some reply but Rouletabille cut short my words with a dry gesture.

"I ask you only one thing—only one, you understand. It is that, no matter what may happen—*no matter what may happen*—you shall not address one word to either M. Darzac or to myself."

"That will be a very easy thing to promise!" I replied, foolishly irritated, and I turned my back upon him. It seemed to me that it was with difficulty that he refrained from uttering some angry speech.

But at the same moment, the officers, coming out of the New Castle, called to us. The inquest was at an end. There was no doubt, in their eyes, after the declaration of the doctors, that the affair had been an accident and that was the verdict which they felt obliged to render. M. Darzac and Rouletabille accompanied them to the outer gate. And as I stood leaning on my elbows, at the window which opens upon the Court of the Bold, assailed by a thousand sinister presentiments and awaiting with an increasing anxiety for the return of Mme. Edith, while a few steps away in the lodge, where the candles had been lighted around Bernier's bier, Mere Bernier kept on sobbing and praying beside the corpse of her husband, I suddenly heard a sound which fell upon the evening air like the blow of an immense gong; and I knew that it was Rouletabille who had ordered the iron gates to be closed.

Not a single minute passed after that when I saw Mme. Edith rush into the room and hurry to me as though I were her only refuge.

Then I saw M. Darzac appear—

Then Rouletabille, and leaning on his arm was the Lady in Black.

# XX

## IN WHICH ROULETABILLE GIVES A CORPOREAL DEMONSTRATION OF THE POSSIBILITY OF "THE BODY OF TOO MANY"

Through the window I could see Rouletabille and the Lady in Black entering the Square Tower. Never had the young reporter walked with such solemn stateliness. His demeanour might have made one smile, if instead, at this tragic moment, it had not added to our apprehensions. Never had magistrate or counsellor, wearing the purple or the ermine, entered the court room where the accused waited him with more of threatening yet tranquil majesty. But I fancy, too, that never had a judge looked so pale.

As to the Lady in Black, it could easily be seen that she was making a powerful effort to hide the sentiments of horror which, in spite of all, pierced through her troubled glance, and to hide from us the emotion which made her cling feverishly to the arm of her young companion. Robert Darzac, too, had the sombre and resolute mien of a judge. But that which most of all added to our surprise and affright was the entrance of Pere Jacques, Walter and Mattoni into the Square Tower. All three were armed with muskets, and placed themselves in silence before the door, where they stood with military precision while they received from the lips of Rouletabille the order to let no person *go out* from the Old château. Edith was overwhelmed with terror, and demanded of Mattoni and Walter, both of whom were greatly attached to her, what their presence signified and what their weapons threatened; but, to my great astonishment, they returned no answer. Then the little woman rushed to the door which gave access to Old Bob's room, and, extending her two arms across the threshold, as if to bar the passage, she cried:

"What are you going to do? You do not mean to kill *him*?"

"No, Madame," replied Rouletabille, gravely. "We are going to judge him. And in order to be sure that the judges shall not be executioners we are all going to swear upon the body of Pere Bernier, after having laid down our arms, that each of us will keep guard over himself."

And he led us into the chamber where Mere Bernier continued to groan beside the bier of her spouse whom "the oldest knife known to the human race" had smitten. There we laid aside our revolvers and took the oath which Rouletabille exacted. Mrs. Rance alone made some difficulties about giving up the weapon which Rouletabille was well aware that she had concealed in her clothing. But upon the urging of the reporter who made her understand that the general disarming ought to reassure her, she finally consented.

The oath having been taken, Rouletabille, with the Lady in Black still on his arm, went from the funereal chamber into the corridor, but instead of directing our steps toward the apartment of Old Bob as we expected him to do, he went straight to the door which afforded entrance to the chamber of "the body too many." And, drawing from his pocket the little special key of which I have spoken, he opened the door.

We were all astonished in entering the rooms which had been occupied by M. and Mme. Darzac to see upon M.

Darzac's desk the drawing board, the wash drawing upon which our friend had worked at the side of Old Bob in the latter's workshop in the Court of the Bold, and also the little dish full of red paint and the tiny brush drenched with the paint. And, lastly, in the middle of the desk, there was placed, appearing very much at its ease, upon its bloody jaws, "the oldest skull of humanity."

Rouletabille locked and bolted the door and said to us, himself greatly affected, while we listened with stupefaction:

"Sit down, if you please, ladies and gentlemen."

Some chairs were arranged around the table and in these we seated ourselves, a prey to the most disquieting fancies—I might almost say to an agony of suspense. A secret presentiment warned us that all the familiar appurtenances of drawing which were displayed before us might hide, under their apparent commonplace tranquility, the terrible causes which helped to bring about this most fearful of dramas. And as we looked upon it, the skull seemed to smile like Old Bob.

"You will acknowledge," began Rouletabille, "that there is here, around this table one chair too many, and, in consequence, one person too few—to particularize, M. Arthur Rance, for whom we cannot wait much longer."

"Perhaps at this very moment my husband possesses the proofs of Old Bob's innocence!" observed Mme. Edith, whom all these preparations had disturbed more than anyone else. "I entreat Mme. Darzac to join me in imploring these gentlemen to do nothing until Arthur's return."

The Lady in Black had no opportunity to intervene, for before Mme. Edith finished speaking, we heard a loud noise outside the door of the corridor. A knock came at the door and we heard the voice of Arthur Rance begging us to open immediately.

He cried:

*"I have brought the pin with the ruby head!"*

Rouletabille opened the door.

"Arthur Rance, you are come then at last!" he exclaimed.

Edith's husband seemed plunged in the deepest melancholy.

"What have you to tell me? What has happened? Some new misfortune? Ah, I feared so—feared that I had arrived too late when I saw the iron gate closed and heard the prayers for the dead chanted in the tower. Yes—I knew that you had *executed* Old Bob!"

Rouletabille, who had closed and bolted the door behind Arthur Rance turned to the American and said:

"Old Bob is alive and Pere Bernier is dead. Be seated, Monsieur."

Arthur Rance stared at the speaker in amazement; then looked in consternation at the drawing board, the dish of paint and the bloody skull and demanded:

"Who killed him?"

Then, condescending to notice that his wife was there, he pressed her hand, but his eyes were fixed upon the Lady in Black.

"Before his death, Bernier accused Frederic Larsan," answered M. Darzac.

"Do you mean to say by that that he accused Old Bob?" interrupted M. Rance indignantly, "I will not suffer that. I, too, had some doubts in regard to the personality of our beloved uncle, but I tell you that I have the ruby-headed pin!"

What was he talking about with his "little ruby headed pin"? I remembered that Mme. Edith had told us that Old Bob had snatched one from her hand when she had playfully pricked him with it on the night of the drama of the Square Tower. But what relation could there be between this pin and the adventure of Old Bob? Arthur Rance did not wait for us to ask him, but hurried on to tell us that this little pin had disappeared at the same time as Old Bob and that he had found it in the possession of "the Hangman of the Sea," fastening a sheaf of banknotes which the old uncle had paid him on that fated night for his complicity and his silence in having brought him in the fisher boat to the grotto of Romeo and Juliet. And M. Rance told us moreover that Tullio had withdrawn from the spot at dawn, greatly disquieted at the non appearance of his passenger. Rance concluded, triumphantly:

"A man who gives a ruby pin to another man in a boat cannot be at the same moment tied up in a potato sack in the Square Tower."

Upon which Mrs. Rance inquired:

"What gave you the idea of going to San Remo: Did you know that Tullio was to be found there?"

"I received an anonymous letter informing me of his whereabouts."

"It was I who sent it to you," said Rouletabille, tranquilly. And, then, turning to the rest of us, he said in frigid tones:

"Ladies and gentlemen, I congratulate myself upon the prompt return of M. Arthur Rance. At the present moment there are reunited around this table all the members of the house party of the Château of Hercules for whom my corporeal demonstration of the possibility of the 'body too many' may have some interest. I entreat you to give me your undivided attention."

But Arthur Rance halted him with a quick movement.

"What do you mean by the expression: 'There are united around this table all the members of the party for whom the corporeal demonstration of the possibility of the body too many can have any interest'?"

"I mean," declared Rouletabille, "all those among whom we may hope to find Larsan."

The Lady in Black, who had up to this time not uttered a word, arose trembling to her feet.

"Do you mean," she breathed, her eyes filled with agonised apprehension, "that Larsan is now among us?"

"I am sure of it," Rouletabille replied, gravely.

There was an awful silence during which none of us dared look at each other.

The reporter continued, still in the same frigid tone:

"I am sure of it—and there is no reason why the idea should surprise you, Madame, since it has not for a moment left your own mind. As to the rest of us, is it not true, gentlemen, that the idea has occurred to each one of us at the same moment on the day when we took luncheon on the terrace of the Bold when all our eyes were hidden by the black glasses? If I except Mrs. Rance, who is there among us that did not feel the presence of Larsan at that time?"

"That is a question which ought to be propounded to Professor Stangerson as well as to the rest of us," interposed Arthur Rance, instantly. "For from the moment when we begin any course of reasoning along these lines, I can see no object in not having the Professor, who was at the table at luncheon with us on that day, here at this time also."

"Mr. Rance!" cried the Lady in Black.

"Yes, I must repeat it, if you will pardon me," replied Edith's husband, haughtily. "Monsieur Rouletabille was wrong to generalize when he said, 'All the members of the house party—' "

"Professor Stangerson is so far from us in spirit that I have no need of his presence here," pronounced Rouletabille in a tone so stern and solemn that it fell impressively on the ears of each and every one among us. "Although Professor Stangerson had lived with us in the Château of Hercules, he was not one of us in regard to feeling the presence of Larsan on that day. And Larsan is here among us."

This time we stole stealthy glances at each other as though we suspected each other of stealing, and the idea that Larsan might really be among us appeared to me so mad that I exclaimed, forgetting that I had promised not to address Rouletabille:

"But at that luncheon on the terrace, there was still another person whom I do not see here."

Rouletabille cast an angry look at me as he answered: "Still Prince Galitch! I have already told you, Sainclair, with what task the Prince is occupying himself on this frontier and I swear to you that it is not the trouble of Professor Stangerson's daughter which concerns him. Leave Prince Galitch to his humanitarian labours!"

"All that is not reasonable," I remarked almost mechanically.

"To tell the truth, Sainclair, your nonsense prevents me from reasoning."

But I had launched out, and, forgetting that I had promised Mme. Edith to defend Old Bob, started in to attack him for the pleasure of proving Rouletabille in the wrong—and, besides, I felt, Edith would not bear to rancor against me for very long.

"Old Bob," I began, in the clearest and most assured tones I could command, "was also at the luncheon on the terrace and you take him entirely out of your calculations on account of this little ruby pin. But of what use is this little pin to prove to us that Old Bob was rowed away by Tullio, who waited for him at the orifice of a gallery leading from the shaft to the sea, if we cannot discover how Old Bob could, as he said, have gone by way of the shaft which we found closed from above and on the outside?"

"Which *you* found closed, you mean," returned Rouletabille, fixing his eyes upon me with a strange expression which somehow embarrassed me. "I, on the contrary, found the shaft open. I had sent you after Mattoni and Pere Jacques. When you came back, you found me in the same place in the Court of the Bold, but I had time to run to the shaft and find out that it had been opened."

"And to lose it again!" I cried. "And why did you close it? Whom did you wish to deceive?"

"You, *monsieur*!"

He pronounced these two words with a contempt so crushing that the blood rushed to my face. I arose. Every eye was turned upon me and as I remembered the rudeness with which Rouletabille had treated me a little while before M. Darzac, I had trouble feeling that every eye was suspecting me—accusing me! *Yes! I felt myself entirely wrapped around by the atrocious fancy in the mind of each and all that I might be Larsan!*

I! Larsan!

I looked at each one in turn. Rouletabille did not lower his eyes while my own were seeking to make him feel the fierce protestation of my whole being and my indignation against such a monstrous supposition. Anger ran through my veins like a flame. "Now, it is high time to end this farce!" I cried. "If Old Bob is removed from consideration and Professor Stangerson and Prince Galitch, there remain only ourselves—we who are locked up in this room—and if Larsan is among us, show us to him, Rouletabille!"

I repeated the words furiously, for the eyes of the boy, although they were piercing through me, seemed to be fixed upon something outside of and apart from me.

"Show him to us! Name him! You are as slow here as you were at the Court of Assizes."

"Had I not good reason at the Court of Assizes for being as slow as I was?" he replied, without betraying any emotion.

"You want him to escape this time, too, then?"

"No! I swear *to you* that this time he shall *not* escape."

Why did his voice continue to be so threatening when he addressed me? Could it be really—*really* that he suspected me of being Larsan? My eyes wandered to those of the Lady in Black. She was gazing on me in terror.

"Rouletabille!" I cried madly, feeling my voice almost smothered in my throat. "You do not—you cannot suspect!"

At this moment, a pistol shot sounded outside, very near to the Square Tower. We all leaped to our feet, remembering the order given by the reporter to the three servants to fire upon anyone who should attempt to go out of the Square Tower. Edith uttered a cry and tried to run out of the room, but Rouletabille, who had not made so much as a gesture, calmed her with a word.

"If anyone had drawn upon *him*," he said, "the three men would have fired together. That pistol shot was merely a signal—a direction for me to begin."

Turning to me, he continued:

"M. Sainclair, you ought to know that I never suspect any person or anything without previously having satisfied myself upon the 'ground of pure reason.' That is a solid staff which has never yet failed me on the road and on which I invite you all to lean with me. Larsan is here among us, and the power of pure reason is going to show him to you; so be seated again, if you please, and do not take your eyes from me, for I am going to begin on this paper the corporeal demonstration of the possibility of 'the body too many'!"

First of all, he investigated to make sure that the bolts of the door behind him were closely drawn; then, returning to the table, he took up a compass.

"I have the intention of making my demonstration," he said, "along the same lines on which the 'body too many' has produced itself. It will be, thereby, only the more irrefutable."

And, with his compass, he took, upon M. Darzac's drawing, the measure of the radius of the circle which represented the space occupied by the Tower of the Bold, so that he was immediately afterward able to trace the same circle upon an immaculate piece of white paper which he had fastened with copper-headed nails to another drawing board.

When the circle was traced, Rouletabille, putting down his compass, picked up the tiny dish of red paint and asked M. Darzac whether he recognised it as the colouring matter he had used. M. Darzac, who, from all appearances, understood the significance of the young man's words and actions no better than the rest of us, replied that, to the best of his belief, it was the same paint which he had mixed for his wash drawing.

A good half of the paint had dried up in the bottom of the dish, but, according to the opinion expressed by M. Darzac, the part which remained would, upon paper, give nearly the same tint with which he had "washed" the drawing of the peninsula of Hercules.

"No one has touched it," said Rouletabille very gravely, "and nothing has been added to it, save a single tear. Besides, you will see that a tear more or less in the paint cup would detract nothing from the value of my demonstration."

Thus saying, he dipped the brush in the paint and began carefully to "wash" all the space occupied by the circle which he had previously traced. He did this with the care and exactitude which had already astonished me in the Tower of the Bold when I had been nearly stupefied in seeing him absorbed in a drawing when we knew that someone had been assassinated.

When he had finished he looked at his immense silver watch and said:

"You may see, ladies and gentlemen, that the coating of paint which covers my circle is neither more nor less thick than that which covers the circle of M. Darzac. It is almost the same thing—the same tint."

"Undoubtedly," rejoined M. Darzac. "But what does all this signify?"

"Wait!" replied the reporter. "It is understood, then, that it is you who have made this plan and this painting?"

"I was certainly in enough of an ill humour when I found the state it was in that time I went with you into Old Bob's cabinet when we came out of the Square Tower. Old Bob had ruined my drawing by letting his skull roll over it."

"We are there!" spoke up Rouletabille, quick as a flash. And he lifted from the bureau the "oldest skull of the human race." He turned it over and showed the crimsoned jaws to M. Darzac. Then he inquired:

"Is it your opinion that the red which we see upon that under jaw is no different from the red which would be taken off by any object coming in contact with your plan?"

"I don't see how there could be any doubt of it! The skull was upside down on my drawing when we entered the workshop."

"Let us continue then to remain of the same opinion!" said the reporter.

Then he arose, holding the skull in the crook of his arm, and went into the alcove in the wall, lighted by a large window and crossed by bars, which had been a loophole for cannon in the ancient times, and which M. Darzac had used as a dressing room. There he struck a match and lighted a lamp filled with spirits of wine which stood upon a little table. Upon this lamp he set a little pot which he had previously filled with water. The skull still lay in the crook of his arm.

During this weird cookery, we never took our eyes off him. Never had Rouletabille's behaviour appeared to us so incomprehensible nor so mysterious nor so disturbing. The more he explained matters to us and the more he did, the less we understood. And we were afraid because we felt that someone—*someone among us—one of ourselves*—had reason for fear. Who was this one? Perhaps the most calm of us all!

But the calmest of all was Rouletabille between his skull and his casserole.

But what? Why did we all suddenly recoil with a single movement? Why were the eyes of M. Darzac wide with a new terror—why did the Lady in Black—Arthur Rance—

I, myself—utter the same syllable—a name which expired on our lips: "*Larsan*!"?

Where had we seen him? Where had we discovered him this time, we who were gazing at Rouletabille? Ah, that profile, in the red shadow of the approaching twilight, that brow in the background of the alcove upon which the sunset rays stream as did the dawn on the morning of the crime! Oh, that stern jaw, bespeaking an iron will, which appeared before us, not, as in the light of day, gentle though a little bitter, but evil and threatening. How like Rouletabille was to Larsan! How in that moment the son resembled his father! It was Larsan's very self!

Another transformation. At a moan from his mother Rouletabille came out of his funereal frame and appeared before us as a bandit, and as he hurried toward us, he was Rouletabille once more. Mme. Edith, who had never seen Larsan, could not understand. She whispered to me, "What is going on?"

Rouletabille was there before us with his hot water in the casserole, a napkin and his skull. And he washed the skull.

It was soon done. The paint disappeared. He made us bear witness to the fact. Then, placing himself in front of the bureau, he stood in mute contemplation before his own drawing. This lasted for ten minutes, during which he had, by a sign, ordered us to keep silence—ten minutes which seemed as long as the same number of hours. What was he waiting for? What did he expect? Suddenly, he seized the skull in his right hand, and with the gesture familiar to those who play at bowling, he tossed it about so that it rolled hither and yon over the drawing; then he showed us the skull and bade us notice that it bore no trace of red paint. Rouletabille drew out his watch again.

"The paint has dried upon the plan," he said. "It has taken a quarter of an hour to dry. Upon the 11th of April we saw at five o'clock in the afternoon, M. Darzac entering the Square Tower and coming from out of doors. But M. Darzac, after having entered the Square Tower, and after having fastened behind him the bolts of his door, as he tells us, has not gone out again until we came to fetch him after six o'clock. As to Old Bob, we had seen him enter the Square Tower at six o'clock and there was no paint on this skull then!"

*"How was this paint which has taken only a quarter of an hour to dry upon this plan, fresh enough still—more than an hour after M. Darzac had left it—to stain Old Bob's skull when the savant, with a movement of anger, threw it down on the plan as he entered the Round Tower? There is only one explanation of this, and I defy you to find another—and that is that the Robert Darzac who entered the Square Tower at five o'clock and whom no one has seen going out again, was not the same as the one who came to paint in the Round Tower before the arrival of Old Bob at six o'clock and whom we found in the room in the Square Tower without having seen him enter there and with whom we went out. In one word—he was not the same man as the M. Darzac here present before us. The testimony of pure reason shows that there are two personalities appearing in the guise of Robert Darzac!"*

And Rouletabille turned his eyes full upon the man whose name he had uttered.

Darzac, like all the rest of us, was under the spell of the luminous demonstration of the young reporter. We were all divided between a new horror and a boundless admiration. How clear was every word that Rouletabille had uttered! How clear—and how terrible! Here again we found the mark of his prodigious and logical mathematical intelligence!

M. Darzac cried out:

"It was thus, then, that *he* was able to enter the Square Tower under a disguise which made him, without doubt, my very image! It was thus that he was able to hide behind the panel in such a way that I did not see him myself when I came here to write my letters after quitting the Tower of the Bold, where I left my drawing. But how could Pere Bernier have opened to him?"

"Doubtless," replied Rouletabille, who had taken the hand of the Lady in Black in both his own as though he wished to give her courage, "he must have believed that it was yourself."

"That then explains the fact that when I reached my door I had only to push it open. Pere Bernier believed that I was within."

"Exactly: that is good reasoning!" declared Rouletabille. "And Pere Bernier, who had opened to Darzac No. 1, had not troubled himself about No. 2, since he did not see him any more than yourself. You certainly reached the Square Tower at the moment that Sainclair and myself called Bernier to the parapet to see whether he could help us in understanding the strange gesticulations of Old Bob, talking at the threshold of the Barma Grande to Mrs. Rance and Prince Galitch."

"But Mere Bernier" cried M. Darzac. "She had gone into her lodge. Was she not astonished to see M. Darzac come in a second time when she had not seen him go out?"

"Let us suppose," replied the young reporter with a sad smile; "let us suppose, M. Darzac, that Mere Bernier at that moment—the moment when you passed into your apartments—that is to say, when the second apparition of Darzac passed in—was occupied in picking up the potatoes and putting them back into the sack which I had emptied upon her floor—and we shall suppose the truth."

"Well, then, I can congratulate myself on the fact that I am still upon earth!"

"Congratulate yourself, M. Darzac? Congratulate yourself!"

"When I remember that as soon as I entered my room, I drew the bolts as I have told you that I did, that I began to work and that this wretch was hidden behind my back. Why, he might have killed me without hindrance!"

Rouletabille stepped close to M. Darzac and fixed his eyes upon him with a look that seemed to read his soul.

"Why did he not kill you then?" he asked.

"You know very well that he was waiting for someone else," replied M. Darzac, turning his face sorrowfully toward the Lady in Black.

Rouletabille was now so close to M. Darzac that their shadows on the floor looked like that of one strangely formed being. The lad put his two hands on the older man's shoulders.

"M. Darzac," he said, his voice again clear and strong, "I have a confession to make to you. When I began to understand how the 'body too many' had effected an entrance and when I had discovered that you did nothing to undeceive us in regard to the hour of five o'clock at which we had believed—at which everyone, rather, except myself, believed—that you had entered the Square Tower, I felt that I had the right to suspect that the murderer was not the man who at five o'clock entered the Square Tower under the form of Darzac. I thought, on the contrary, that that Darzac might be the true Darzac and you might be the false one. Ah, my dear M. Darzac, how I have suspected you!"

"That was madness!" cried M. Darzac. "If I did not tell you the exact hour at which I entered the Square Tower it was because the time was somewhat vague in my own mind and I did not attach any importance to it."

"In such a manner, M. Darzac," continued Rouletabille, without paying any attention to the interruptions of his interlocutor, the emotion of the Lady in Black and our attitude, more than over-filled with terror. "In such a manner as that you could have stolen away the true Darzac when he came from outside and, by your own carefulness and the too faithful help of the Lady in Black, could have taken his place and have been perfectly able to defy detection of your audacious enterprise. This was my imagination—only my imagination, M. Darzac;

don't let it disturb you. But in such a manner as this, I had thought that, you being Larsan, the man who was put in the sack was Darzac. Ah! the fancies that I have had! And the useless suspicions!"

"Bah!" responded Mathilde's husband, gloomily. "We are all suspicious here!"

Rouletabille turned his back upon M. Darzac, put his hands in his pocket and said, addressing himself to Mathilde, who seemed ready to swoon before the horror of Rouletabille's imaginings:

"Courage for a little while longer, Madame!"

And he began speaking again, in his "teacher's" voice which I knew so well, and with the air of a professor of mathematics propounding or resolving a theorem:

"You see, M. Darzac, there are two manifestations of Robert Darzac. To know which was the true one and which was the one which formed a disguise for Larsan—my duty, M. Darzac—that which the power of pure reason showed me—was to examine, without fear or reproach, both of these manifestations—*in all impartiality*. Thus, I begin with you—M. Darzac."

M. Darzac replied: "It does not matter since you suspect me no longer. But you must tell me immediately who is Larsan. I insist upon it—I demand it!"

"We all demand it—and at once!" we all cried, turning upon both of them. Mathilde rushed up to her child and placed herself in front of him, as if to protect him. We felt the pathos of her attitude but the scene had endured too long and we were beyond the limits of patience.

"If he knows who is Larsan let him speak out and make an end of this!" exclaimed Arthur Rance.

And suddenly, just as the thought crossed my mind that I had heard the same cries of anger and impatience two years before at the Court of Assizes, another pistol shot sounded outside the door of the Square Tower, and we were all so seized with consternation that our anger fell away in a moment and we found ourselves not threatening Rouletabille but entreating him to put an end as soon as possible to this intolerable situation. At this moment, it actually seemed as though we were each imploring him to speak out, as though we calculated that by doing so, we would prove, not only to the others but to ourselves, that we were not Larsan.

As soon as the second shot was heard, the countenance of Rouletabille changed completely. His face seemed transformed and his whole being appeared to vibrate with a savage energy. Laying aside the half bantering manner which he had used toward M. Darzac and which we had all found extremely disagreeable, he gently released himself from the clasp of the Lady in Black, who still clung to him, walked toward the door, folded his arms and said:

"You see, my friends, in an affair like this, it does not do to neglect any point. There were two manifestations of Robert Darzac which entered the Square Tower. There were two manifestations which came out—and one of these was in the sack! That is where one loses oneself. And *even now,* I do not wish to make any mistakes! Will M. Darzac, here present, permit me to say that I had a hundred excuses for suspecting him?"

Then I thought to myself: "How unlucky that he did not mention his suspicions to me! I would have told him about the map of Australia!"

M. Darzac strode across the room and planted himself in front of the young reporter and said in a tone nearly inaudible from anger:

"What excuses? I ask you, what excuses?"

"You will soon understand, my friend," said the reporter with the utmost calmness. "The first thing that I said to myself while I was examining the conditions surrounding *your* manifestation of Larsan, was this: 'Nonsense! If he were Larsan, would not

Professor Stangerson's daughter have perceived it?' That is self evident—the common sense of that thought—is it not? But when I tried to look into the mind of the lady who has become Mme. Darzac, I discovered beyond a doubt, Monsieur, that all the while she could not free herself from just this fear—the fear that you might be Larsan!"

Mathilde, who had fallen half fainting into a chair, gathered strength enough to start up and to protest against the words with a frightened, despairing gesture.

As for M. Darzac, his face was a picture of hopeless anguish. He sank upon a couch and said in a voice so low that it was scarcely audible and so full of wretchedness that it pierced our hearts:

"And could you have thought that, Mathilde?"

His wife dropped her eyes and spoke not a word. Rouletabille, still merciless, continued:

"When I recall all the acts of Mme. Darzac after your return from San Remo, I can see now in each one of them an expression of the terror which she experienced from her fear that she should allow the secret of her suspicion and her constant agony to escape her. Ah, let me speak, M. Darzac! Everything must be said—everything must be explained here and now if there is to be peace in the future! We are about to clear up the situation. To go on then, there was nothing natural or happy in Mlle. Stangerson's behaviour. The very eagerness with which she assented to your desire to hasten the marriage ceremony proved the longing which she felt to definitely banish the torment of her soul. Her eyes—I remember it now!—used to say at that time—how often and how clearly 'Is it possible that I continue to see Larsan everywhere, even in the face of the man who is at my side, who is going to lead me to the altar and to take me away with him?'

"From the moment of your return from the South until the apparition at the railroad station, monsieur, she lived in the most utter misery. She was already crying for help—for help against herself—against her thoughts—and, perhaps, even against *you*! But she dared not reveal her thought to any person because she dreaded that any confidant might say to her—"

And Rouletabille leaned over and said in M. Darzac's ear, not so low that I could not hear, but so softly that the words did not reach Mathilde: "Are you going mad again?"

Then, lifting his head again, he continued:

"You ought to understand everything better now, my dear M. Darzac—both the strange coldness with which you were treated occasionally and also the fits of remorseful tenderness which, in the doubt which filled her brain, would impel Mme. Darzac to surround you with every evidence of attention and affection. And, furthermore, allow me to tell you that I myself have sometimes found you so gloomy and *distrait* that I have fancied that you must have discovered that whenever Mme. Darzac looked at you, she could not, in spite of herself, chase from her mind the image of Larsan. It came upon her when she spoke to you and when she was silent—when you were beside her and when you were at a distance. And, consequently—let us understand each other completely—it was *not* the belief that Professor Stangerson's daughter would have known it which removed my suspicions, since, in spite of herself, she entertained the fear all the while that you and Larsan were one. No! No! My suspicions were removed by another cause!"

"They might have been removed," exclaimed M. Darzac, at once ironically and despairingly—"they might have been removed, it would seem, by the simple course of reasoning that if I had been Larsan, wedded to Mlle. Stangerson, having her for my wife, I would have had every cause for making her believe in Larsan's death! And I would have never resuscitated myself! Was it not upon the day that Larsan returned to earth that I lost Mathilde?"

"Pardon, monsieur, pardon" replied Rouletabille, whose face had grown as white as a sheet. "You are abandoning now, if I may say so, the directions of pure reason. The facts which you mentioned show us just the contrary of that which you believe we should see. For my part, it seems to me that when one has a wife who believes, or who comes very near to believing, that one is Larsan, one has every interest in showing her that *Larsan exists outside of oneself*!"

As Rouletabille uttered these words, the Lady in Black, supporting herself by groping with her hands against the wall as she walked, came stumblingly to the side of Rouletabille, and devoured with her eyes the face of M. Darzac which had grown frightfully harsh and strained. As to the rest of us, we were so struck by the novelty and the irrefutability of Rouletabille's reasoning, that we experienced no other emotion than an ardent desire to know what was to follow, and we took care not to interrupt, asking ourselves to what such a formidable hypothesis might not lead. The young man, imperturbably, went on:

"And, if you had an interest in showing her that Larsan existed elsewhere than in your body, there arose an exigency in which that interest was transformed into an immediate necessity. Imagine—I say *imagine*, M. Darzac, that you had really brought Larsan to life once—once only—in spite of yourself—in your own rooms—before the eyes of Professor Stangerson's daughter—and you will be, I repeat, under the necessity of bringing him to life again and yet again—outside of yourself, in order to prove to your wife that the Larsan whom she has seen returned to life is not you! Ah, calm yourself, my dear M. Darzac, I entreat you. Have I not told you that my suspicion has been banished—completely banished? But it is as well that we should divert ourselves for a few moments in reasoning the matter out a little, after these long hours of anguish when it seemed as though there would never be any place for reasoning again. See, then, where I am obliged to come in considering this hypothesis as realised (these are the procedures of mathematics which you know better than I—you who are a scholar!)—in considering, as I said, as realised the hypothesis that you are the counterfeit Darzac, the one which hides Larsan. According to my reasoning, then, you are Larsan! And I asked myself what could have happened in the railway station at Bourg to make you appear in the form of Larsan before the eyes of your wife. The fact of such an appearance is undeniable. It exists. And its occurrence at that moment cannot be explained by any desire on your part to have Larsan seen!"

He paused for a moment, but Robert Darzac did not utter a word.

"As you were saying, M. Darzac," Rouletabille went on, "it was because of this apparition of Larsan that your cup of happiness was dashed empty to the ground. Therefore, if this resurrection should not have been voluntary there is only one other way in which it could have happened—through accident. And now just let us consider how this latter supposition clears up the entire situation. Oh, I have spent a lot of thought upon the incident at Bourg—you see, I am still reasoning out the problem! You (the you who is Larsan, be it understood) are at Bourg in the buffet. You believe that your wife is waiting for you somewhere in the station as she told you she would do. After having finished your letters, you wish to go to your compartment in the car in order to attend to some detail of your toilet—or, shall we say to cast a critical eye over your disguise to see if in any point it might be lacking? You think to yourself: A few more hours of this comedy and we shall have passed the frontier, she will be all my own—entirely alone with me, and I will throw aside this mask—for the mask wearies you a little, we may imagine—so much so, indeed, that, once arrived in your compartment, you grant yourself the grace of a few moments of repose. You cast away your assumed character and your disguise. You relieve yourself of the false beard and the spectacles—and at that very moment the door of the section opens. Your wife, thrown into a spasm of terror at the sight of Larsan's smooth, beardless face in the glass, does not wait to make any further investigation and rushes out into the night, her screams drowned by the noise of another train. You comprehend the danger at once. You realize that everything is lost unless you can *immediately* arrange matters so that your wife shall see Darzac somewhere else. You quickly resume the mask; you hurry out of the compartment and reach the buffet by a shorter route than that taken by your wife, who rushes there to look for you. She finds you standing up. You have not even had time enough to seat yourself before she enters. Is everything safe now? Alas, no! Your troubles are only beginning. For the fearful thought that you may be at one and the same time both Darzac and Larsan will not leave her mind. Upon the platform of the station, while passing beneath the gas jet, she casts a frightened glance at you, lets go your hand and runs wildly into the office of the station master. You read her thought as though she had spoken it. The abominable idea must be banished without a moment's delay. You quit the office, leaving the lady in the care of the superintendent, and immediately return, closing the door quickly, seeking to give the impression that you, too, have seen Larsan. In order to ease her mind, and, also, for the purpose of deceiving us all, in case she dared reveal her suspicions to anyone, you are the first to warn me that something unforeseen has happened—to send me a dispatch. See how clear and plain as the day your every act becomes! You cannot refuse to take her to rejoin her father. She would go without you. And, since nothing is yet really lost, you have the hope that everything may be regained. In the course of the journey, your wife continues to have alternating periods of faith in you and of fear of you. She gives you her revolver, in a sort of half delirium, which might sum itself up in some such phrase as this: 'If he is Darzac, let him protect me; if he is Larsan, let him kill me! But in pity, let me know which he is.' At Rochers Rouges, you realised once more how utterly she had withdrawn herself from you and in order to reassure her as to your identity, you showed her Larsan again. See how in accordance with reason such a proceeding would be, my dear M. Darzac! Every fact would fit perfectly into every other under the supposition which I am placing before you. There is not a single point up to your appearance as Larsan at Mentone, during your journey as Darzac to Cannes, at the time when you came to meet us, which cannot be explained in the easiest way imaginable. You had taken the train at Mentone-Garavan before the eyes of your friends, but you alighted from the train at the next station, which is Mentone, and there, after a short stay for the purpose of altering your looks, you appeared in the image of Larsan to the same friends who were promenading in the gardens at Mentone. The following train brought you to Cannes, where you met Sainclair and myself. Only, as you had on this occasion the vexation of hearing from the lips of Arthur Rance when he met us at the station at Nice, the news that Mme. Darzac had not, on this occasion, caught sight of Larsan, you were under the necessity that same evening of showing her Larsan under the very windows of the Square Tower, standing erect in the prow of Tullio's boat. So, you see, my dear M. Darzac, how even those things which appear most complicated would have become entirely simple and logically explicable, if, by chance, my suspicions should have been confirmed."

At these words, I myself, who had seen and touched "the map of Australia," was unable to repress a shudder as I looked pityingly at Robert Darzac, just as one might look at some poor man who is on the point of becoming the victim of some hideous judicial error. And all the others, seated around me, shuddered as well, whether for him or on account of him, for the arguments of Rouletabille were becoming so terribly *possible* that each of us was asking himself how, after having so completely established the possibility of guilt, the young reporter could prove Darzac's innocence. As to Robert Darzac, after having at first evinced the deepest agitation, he had grown quite tranquil and calm, as he listened attentively to every word that escaped the young man's lips. And it seemed to me that his eyes held the same expression of astonishment, amazed and frightened, and yet full of breathless interest, which I had seen in the eyes of accused men at the bar of the Assizes when they had heard the Procurer General deliver one of his wonderful disquisitions which almost convinced the prisoners themselves that they were guilty of a crime which sometimes they had never committed.

"But since you no longer have these suspicions, monsieur!" he exclaimed, his intonation singularly calm, in spite of the fact that his voice was raised, "I should be glad to know, after all this exercise of your talent of reasoning, what could have driven them away?"

"In order to have them driven away, monsieur, one thing was essential—an *absolute certitude*! And I found it—a simple but conclusive proof which showed me in a manner complete and undeniable which of the two manifestations of Darzac was in reality Larsan. That proof, monsieur, was, happily, furnished me by yourself at the very moment when you *closed the circle*—the circle in which there had been found the 'body too many'!—the time when, after having sworn that which was the truth—that you had drawn the bolt of your apartment as soon as you had entered your sleeping room, *you had lied to us in concealing from us that you had entered that room at six o'clock instead of at five o'clock as Pere Bernier said and as we ourselves could have proved. You were then the only person except myself who knew that the Darzac who had entered at five o'clock and of whom we had spoken to you as yourself was in reality another man. But you said nothing. And you need not pretend that you did not attach any importance to that hour of five o'clock. What interest could the real Darzac have in hiding the fact that another Darzac, who might be Larsan, had come and hidden in the Square Tower before you came in? Larsan was the only one who could have a reason for concealing the knowledge that there was another Darzac besides himself. Of the two, false and the real Darzac, the false one was necessarily the one who lied. Thus were my suspicions dispelled by a certainty. You were Larsan, and the man in the wardrobe was Darzac*!"

"You are a liar!" howled the man as he sprang at Rouletabille.

But we got between them, and Rouletabille, who was not in the least disturbed, pointed at the cupboard and said:

"*He is in there now*!"

None of us will ever forget what followed. Just as on the memorable night, an invisible hand opened the door of the cupboard, and the body appeared before us again.

Exclamations of surprise, excitement and fear rang through the Square Tower. The voice of the Lady in Black rose above all the others.

"Robert! Robert! Robert!"

And it was a cry of joy! Two Darzacs before us so exactly similar that every one of us save the Lady in Black might have been deceived. But her heart told her the truth, even admitting that her reason, not withstanding the triumphant conclusion of Rouletabille, might have hesitated. Her arms outstretched, her eyes alight with love and joy, she rushed toward the second manifestation of Darzac—the one which had descended from the panel. Mathilde's face was radiant with new life; her sorrowful eyes which I had so often beheld fixed with sombre gloom upon *that other*, were shining upon this one with a joy as glorious as it was tranquil and assured. It was he! It was he whom she had believed lost—whom she had sought in vain in the visage of the other and had not found there and, therefore, had accused herself, during the weary hours of day and night, of folly which was akin to madness.

As to the man who, up to the last moment I had not believed to be guilty—as to that wretch who, unveiled and tracked to earth, found himself suddenly face to face with the living proof of his crimes, he attempted yet again, one of the daring coups which had so often saved him. Surrounded on every side, he yet endeavoured to flee. Then we understood the audacious drama which in the last few moments, he had played for our benefit. When he could no longer have any doubt as to the issue of the discussion which he was holding with Rouletabille, he had had the incredible self-control to permit nothing of his emotions to appear, and had also been able to prolong the situation, permitting Rouletabille to pursue at leisure the thread of the argument at the end of which he knew that he would find his doom, but during the progress of which he might discover perchance some means of escape. And he had effected his manoeuvers so well that at the moment when we beheld the other Darzac advancing toward us, we could not hinder the imposter from disappearing at one bound within the room which had served as the bedchamber of Mme. Darzac and closing the door violently behind him with a rapidity which was nothing less than marvellous. We only knew that he had vanished when it was too late to stop his flight.

Rouletabille, during the scene which had passed had thought only of guarding the door opening into the corridor and he had not noticed that every movement of the false Darzac, as soon as he realised that he was being convicted of his imposture, had been in the direction of Mme. Darzac's room. The reporter had attached no importance to these movements, knowing as he did that this room did not offer any way by which Larsan might escape. But, however, when the scoundrel was behind the door which afforded his last refuge, our confusion increased beyond all proportions. One might have thought that we had become suddenly bereft of our senses. We knocked on the door. We cried out. We thought of all his strokes of genius—of his marvellous escapes in the past!

"He will escape us! He will get away from us again!"

Arthur Rance was the most enraged of us all. Mme. Edith, who was clinging to my arm, drove her fingernails into my hand in a paroxysm of nervous fear. None of us paid any heed to the Lady in Black and Robert Darzac who, in the midst of this tempest, seemed to have forgotten everything, even the clamour and confusion around them. Neither one had spoken a word but they were looking into each other's eyes as though they had discovered another world—the world which is love. But they had not discovered it; they had merely found it again, thanks to Rouletabille.

The latter had opened the door of the corridor and summoned the three domestics to our assistance. They entered with their rifles. But it was axes that were needed. The door was solid and barricaded with heavy bolts. Pere Jacques went out and fetched a beam which served us as a battering ram. Each of us exerted all his strength and, finally, we saw the door beginning to give way. Our anxiety was at its height. In vain, we told ourselves that we were about to enter a room in which there were only walls and barred windows. We expected anything—or, rather, we expected nothing, for in the mind of each and every one of us was the recollection of the disappearances, the flights, the actual "dissolution of matter" which Larsan had brought about in times past and which at this moment haunted us and drove us nearly mad.

When the door had commenced to yield, Rouletabille directed the servants to take up their guns, with the order, however, that the weapons were to be used only in case it should be impossible to capture Larsan living. Then the young reporter set his shoulder to the door with one last powerful effort and as the boards wrenched from their hinges, fell to the ground, he was the first to enter the room.

We followed him. And behind him, upon the threshold, we all halted, stupefied by the sight which met our eyes. Larsan was there—plainly to be seen by everyone. And this time there was no difficulty in recognizing him. He had removed his false beard; he had put aside his "Darzac mask"; he had resumed once more the pale, clean-shaven face of that Frederic Larsan whom we had known at the Château of Glandier. And his presence seemed to fill the entire room. He was lying back comfortably in an easy chair in the centre of the room and was looking at us with his great, calm eyes. His arm was stretched along the arm of the chair. His head was resting on the cushion at the back. One would have said that he was giving us an audience and was waiting for us to make known our business. It seemed to me that I could even discern an ironical smile on his lips.

Rouletabille advanced toward him.

"Larsan," he said in a voice which was not quite steady, "Larsan, do you give yourself up?"

But Larsan did not reply.

Then Rouletabille touched the man's face and his hand and we saw that Larsan was dead.

Rouletabille pointed to a ring on the middle finger. The collet was open and showed a hollow cup which was empty. It must have contained a deadly poison.

Arthur Rance put his head against the man's chest and assured us that all was over. And Rouletabille entreated us to leave him alone in the Square Tower and to try and forget the terrible events which had passed there.

"I will charge myself with everything," he asserted gravely. "Here is the 'body too many.' No one will inquire into the disposition which may be made of it."

And he gave an order to Walter which Arthur Rance translated into English. "Walter, bring me the sack which you found at the Castillon yesterday."

Then he made a gesture to which we were all obedient—a gesture of dismissal. And we left the son face to face with the corpse of the father.

The next moment we saw that M. Darzac was swooning and we were obliged to carry him into Old Bob's sitting room. But it was only a passing faintness and soon he opened his eyes again and smiled at Mathilde when he saw her beautiful face bending over him with the look of dread in which we read the fear of losing her beloved husband at the very moment in which she had, through a chain of circumstances which still remained wrapped in mystery, found him again. He succeeded in convincing her that his life was not in any danger and he added his entreaties to those of Mme. Edith that she would go away for a little while and try to get some rest. When the two women had left us, Arthur Rance and myself turned our attention to our friend, inquiring of him, first of all, in regard to his curious state of health. For how could a man whom all of us had believed to be dead, and who had been, with the death rattle in his throat, tied up in a sack and carried away, have been able to rise again and step-down living from the fateful panel? But when we had opened his shirt and discovered the bandage which hid the wound that he bore in his breast, we recognised the fact that this injury, by a chance so rare that one would scarcely believe that it could exist, after having brought about an almost immediate state of coma, was not a very serious one. The ball which had struck Darzac in the midst of the savage fight which he had been obliged to make against Larsan, had planted itself in the sternum, causing a bad external hemorrhage and weakening the entire organism, but, fortunately, suspending none of the vital functions.

As we finished the task of dressing the wound Pere Jacques came to close the door of the parlour which had remained open and I wondered what might be the reason which had led the old man to this precaution until I heard steps in the corridor and a strange noise—the sound that one hears when a body is carried away on a stretcher. And I thought of Larsan and of the sack which was holding now for the second time "the body too many."

Leaving Arthur Rance to watch over M. Darzac I hurried to the window. I had not been mistaken. I beheld the sinister funeral cortege in the court outside.

It was nearly nightfall. A gathering gloom surrounded everything. But I could distinguish Walter, who had been stationed as a sentinel under the arch of the gardener's postern. He was looking toward the outer court, ready, evidently, to bar the passage of anyone who might desire to penetrate into the Court of the Bold.

Moving onward in the direction of the oubliette, I saw Rouletabille and Pere Jacques—two dark shadows bending over another shadow—a shadow which I recognised and which, on that other night of horror, I had believed to contain another dead body. The sack seemed heavy. The two men were scarcely able to lift it to the edge of the shaft. And I could see that the little passageway was open—yes, the heavy wooden lid which ordinarily closed it had been removed and was lying on the ground. Rouletabille leaped lightly over the edge of the oubliette and then made a step downward. He showed no hesitation; the way seemed to be familiar to him. In a few moments his figure vanished from sight. Then Pere Jacques pushed the sack into the passageway and leaned over the edge, apparently still holding on to his burden which I could no longer see. Then he stood back, closed up the opening and adjusted the iron bars and in doing so made a sound which

I suddenly remembered—the sound which had puzzled me so much that evening when, before the "discovery of Australia," I had rushed in pursuit of a shadow which had suddenly disappeared and which I had searched for up to the very door of the New Castle.

I felt that I must see—up to the very last moment. I must know all!

Too many strange and inexplicable things were filling my soul with anxiety already. I had learned the most important part of the truth, but I had not all of the truth—or, rather, something which would explain the truth was still lacking.

I left the Square Tower: I went to my own room in the New Castle, I stationed myself at the window and my eyes lost themselves in the depths of the shadows which covered the sea. Thick darkness: jealous shadows. Nothing more. And then I strained my ears to listen, although I knew that there was not the faintest sound of the strokes of the oar.

All at once—far—very far off—it seemed to me that all this was passing so far over the sea that it crossed the horizon—or, rather, approached the horizon—I fancied that I could see in the narrow red band which was all that remained of the setting sun something that seemed more unreal than a vision.

Into that narrow red band an object entered—something dark and very small, but to my eyes, which were fixed upon it in breathless suspense, it seemed the greatest and most formidable sight that I had ever beheld. It was the shadow of a fishing smack which glided over the waters as automatically as though it were propelled by machinery and as its movements became slower, and I saw it emerging from the gloom, I recognised the form of Rouletabille. The oars ceased to move and I saw my friend rise to his feet. I could recognize him and see everything which he did as clearly as if he had not been ten yards away from me. His gestures were outlined against the red background of the sunset with a fantastic precision.

What he had to do did not take long. He leaned over and got up again, lifting in his arms something which seemed to mix with his form and become a part of himself in the darkness. And then the burden glided down into the water and the man's figure reappeared alone, still bending, still leaning over the edge of the boat, remaining thus for an instant motionless, and then once more picking up the oars of the bark which resumed its automatic motion until it had disappeared completely from the dying glare of the ever narrowing band of red. And then the band of red, too, vanished.

Rouletabille had consigned the body of Larsan to the waves of Hercules.

# EPILOGUE

Nice—Cannes—Saint-Raphael—Toulon. I saw without regret all the stages of my return trip passing before my eyes. Upon the very day which had followed all the horrible things I have related, I hastened to quit the Midi, anxious to find myself once more in Paris and to plunge into my business affairs—and anxious also to find myself alone with Rouletabille, who was now only a few feet away from me, locked up in a private compartment with the Lady in Black. Up to the very last moment—that is to say, as far as Marseilles, where they were obliged to separate, I was unwilling to interrupt their tender and sorrowful confidences, their plans for the future, their fond farewells. Despite all the prayers of Mathilde Rouletabille was determined to leave her, to return to Paris and to his paper. The son had the superb heroism of effacing himself for the sake of the husband. The Lady in Black had not been able to resist Rouletabille and the boy had dictated exactly what should be done. He had directed that *M. and Mme. Darzac* must continue their honeymoon trip as if nothing remarkable had happened at Rochers Rouges. It was one Darzac who had begun the journey; it was another Darzac who was to finish it—this trip which had become such a happy one—but in the eyes of all the world Darzac would be the same man without any suspicion that things had ever been otherwise.

M. and Mme. Darzac were married. The civil law united them. As to the religious law, as Rouletabille said, the affair might easily be laid before the Pope while the couple were in Rome and there would, without doubt, be found means of regularizing the situation, if there was found to be need of it or if the conscientious scruples of the couple desired it. And Robert Darzac and his wife were happy—completely happy. They belonged to each other.

At Rochers Rouges—at the "Louve" itself, we had said adieu to Professor Stangerson. Robert Darzac had departed immediately for Bordighera, where Mathilde was to join him. Arthur Rance and Mme. Edith accompanied us to the railroad station. My charming hostess, contrary to my hope, evinced no great amount of concern at my departure. I attributed this indifference to the fact that Prince Galitch had come to the quay to see us off. Mme. Edith was giving him the latest bulletin from Old Bob's bedside (which was excellent, by the way), and paid no further attention to me. I felt a real pang of—was it grief or wounded self love? And here and now, I have a confession to make to the reader. Never would I have allowed myself to betray the sentiments which I had entertained toward her, if, several years later, after the death of Arthur Rance, which was surrounded and followed by a most terrible tragedy of which I may relate the history one day, I had not married the dark eyed, melancholy, romantic Edith!

We were approaching Marseilles. Marseilles!

The farewells were heart rending, although neither Rouletabille nor the Lady in Black uttered a word. And as the train bore us away we saw her standing on the platform in the station, without a movement or gesture, her arms hanging at her side, looking in her sombre draperies like a statue of mourning and of sorrow.

I saw in front of me Rouletabille's shoulders shaken with sobs.

Lyons. We could not sleep. We alighted from the train and walked about the station. Both of us recalled the moment when we had been there before—only a few days past—when we were rushing to the rescue of the most unhappy of women. My thoughts plunged once more into the memories of the tragedy and I knew that Rouletabille's were following the same track. And now Rouletabille spoke—spoke in a voice which he tried to make sound careless and light-hearted and which made me understand that he was endeavouring to efface from his mind the thought of the grief which had made him sob like a little child only a short while ago.

"Old man!" he said, with a smile, throwing his arm across my shoulder. "That Brignolles was really a beast!" and he looked at me with such an air of reproach that he almost succeeded in making me believe for a moment that I had ever taken the creature for an honest man.

And then he told me everything—all the marvellous, horrible story which I am compressing here into a few lines. Larsan had had need of some relative of Darzac in order that he might obtain the necessary signature for the incarceration of the Sorbonne professor in a madhouse. And he discovered Brignolles. He could not have fallen upon a better man for his purpose. Everyone knows how simple it is, even today, to have a human being, no matter who he may be, locked up in a cell. The desire of a relative and the signature of a medical man is sufficient in France, impossible as the thing appears, for the accomplishment of this task which may be performed with the utmost celerity. The matter of a signature never embarrassed Larsan in his life. He forged one—that of an eminent alienist—and Brignolles, richly reimbursed, charged himself with the rest. When Brignolles came to Paris, he was already a party to the combination. Larsan had formed his plan—to take Darzac's place before the wedding. The accident to the young professor's eyes had been, as I had believed from the first, the result of design. Brignolles had been directed to manage in some manner so that Darzac's eyes might be sufficiently injured that Larsan, when he took his place, might have in his trickery the important adjunct of dark spectacles, or, failing spectacles, which one cannot wear always, the right to sit in the shadow without arousing suspicion.

The departure of Darzac for the Midi must have strangely facilitated the plans of the two villains. It was not until the end of his sojourn at San Remo that Darzac had been, by the efforts of Larsan who had never ceased to spy upon him, actually dragged to the lunatic asylum. He had been assisted materially in this affair by that "special police force" which has nothing to do with police officials and which puts itself at the disposal of families in certain disagreeable cases which demand as much discretion as rapidity in their execution.

One day M. Darzac was taking a walk in the mountains. The asylum was not far away—in fact, only a few steps from the Italian frontier—and every preparation for the reception of "the unfortunate man" had been made some time beforehand. Brignolles, before leaving for Paris at all, had made arrangements with the proprietor and had presented to him his proofs of relationship, and his representative—Larsan himself. There are certain directors of such institutions who do not ask for explanations, provided that the provisions of the law are complied with—and that one pays well. And both these conditions were easily carried out. And such things are done everyday!

"But how did you find out all these things?" I demanded of Rouletabille.

"You remember, my friend," the reporter replied, "that little piece of paper which you brought back to the Château of Hercules on the day when, without giving me any warning, you took it upon yours. If to follow the trail of the excellent Brignolles, who had come to make a short stay in the Midi? That bit of paper, which bore the heading of the Sorbonne and the two syllables, *bonnet*, gave me the most important assistance. First of all, the circumstances under which you found it—you recollect that you picked it up after you had seen Larsan and Brignolle?—rendered it precious to me. And then the place where it had been thrown was nearly a revelation for me when I began to take up the search for the real Darzac, after I had gained the conviction that his was 'the body too many' which had been tied up in the sack and carried out in it."

And Rouletabille went on in the simplest manner possible, taking me in his narrative over the different phases necessary for my comprehension of the mysteries which, up to that time, had remained so inexplicable to every one of us. The first step in his reasoning had come from the conclusions which he had drawn from the fact that the paint on the drawing would dry less than fifteen minutes after it had been laid on, and following that, the other formidable fact that a lie must have been told by one of the two manifestations of Darzac. Bernier, under the cross examination to which Rouletabille subjected him before the return of the man who had carried the sack, had reported the lying words of the man whom everyone had believed to be Darzac. That was what had astonished Bernier—that the man who had come in at six o'clock had not told him that the man who had entered at six o'clock *was not he*! He was trying to conceal the fact that there existed a second manifestation of Darzac and he would have had no interest in concealing it, if his own personality had been the true one. That was clear as the light of day! When the horror of the thing dawned upon Rouletabille, he nearly swooned. His limbs refused to support him: his teeth chattered; everything grew black in front of his eyes. But he was not entirely without hope, even yet. Bernier might have been mistaken. Perhaps he had not correctly understood the words which M. Darzac had spoken in his amazement and confusion! Rouletabille decided that he himself would question M. Darzac. Then he would soon see. How he longed for his return! It would be for M. Darzac himself to "close the circle." He waited impatiently—and when Darzac returned how the young reporter's feeble hopes were crushed! "Did you look at the man's face?" he had asked: and when the so-called Darzac replied, "No, I did not look at him!" Rouletabille could hardly hide his joy.

It would have been so easy for Larsan to have answered, "I saw him. The face was that of Larsan!" And the young man had not understood that this was the last piece of malice, the furthest limit of hatred in the mind of the villain, and too, one which fitted so well into his role. The real Darzac would not have acted otherwise. He would have gotten rid of his frightful booty as soon as possible without wishing to look at it. But what could all the articles of a Larsan accomplish against the reasonings of a Rouletabille? The false Darzac, under the questionings of Rouletabille had "closed the circle." He had lied. Now Rouletabille *knew*! And besides his eyes, which always looked *behind* the reason, could see now.

But what was to be done? Could he expose Larsan and in doing so, perhaps, give him a chance to escape? Could he reveal to his mother the fact that she was married to Larsan and had helped him to kill Darzac? He felt the need of reflection of combining circumstances and possibilities. He wished to strike a blow when he was ready to strike at all. He asked for twenty-four hours. He made sure of the safety of the Lady in Black by begging her to take the unoccupied room in Professor Stangerson's suite and he made her take a secret oath that she would not leave the chateu. He deceived Larsan by making him think that he was firmly convinced of the guilt of Old Bob. And when Walter rushed into the chateu with his empty sack the first gleam of hope that Darzac might still be alive dawned upon his mind. At last, he rushed off to find him, dead or living. He had in his possession the revolver belonging to the real Darzac which he had found in the Square Tower—a new revolver of which he had noticed the style in a shop at Mentone. He went to that shop; he showed the clerk the revolver; he learned that the weapon had been purchased a few days before by a man of whom he was given a description—a soft hat, a loose grey overcoat and a heavy beard. From there he lost all trace of the man, but he was not discouraged. He took up another trail, or, rather, he resumed that one which had led Walter to the gulfs of Castillon. When he arrived there, he did what Walter had not done. The latter, as soon as he had found the sack, looked for nothing more but hurried back to the Fort of Hercules. But Rouletabille, on the contrary, continued to follow the scent—and he perceived that this scent (which consisted of the exceptional clearness of the impressions left by the two wheels of the little English cart) instead of going back toward Mentone, after having stopped at the abyss of Castillon, went toward the other side, crossing by the mountain toward Sospel. Sospel! Had not Brignolles been reported as having gone to Sospel? Brignolles! Rouletabille remembered my sudden and interrupted journey. What could Brignolles be doing in these parts? His presence might be closely allied to the solution of the mystery. Certainly, the reappearance and disappearance of the true Darzac suggested the idea that he must have been kept somewhere in confinement. But where? Brignolles, who was undoubtedly in the confidence of Larsan, had not made the journey from Paris for nothing. Perhaps he had come at that critical moment to watch over this place *of confinement*.

Meditating thus and pursuing the logical tenor of his reasoning, Rouletabille had questioned the landlord of the inn near the Castillon tunnel, who had acknowledge to him that he had been very much puzzled the day before by the passage through the tunnel of a man who perfectly answered the description which had been given by the gunsmith. This man had entered the tavern to drink. His manner and appearance were so strange that the landlord had feared that he might have escaped from the sanatorium. Rouletabille felt that he was right on track and asked as indifferently as he could, "You have a sanatorium near here then?" "Oh, yes," replied the landlord; "the Mount Barbonnet sanatorium for mental diseases." It was at this point that the memory of the two syllables "bonnet" flashed in full significance upon the brain of Rouletabille. Henceforth, he had no longer any doubt that the real Darzac had been immolated by the false one as a madman in the sanatorium of Mount Barbonnet. He was resolved to know everything and to venture everything! He was certain that as a reporter of the Epoch he possessed the means of loosening the tongue of proprietors of sanatoriums of the kind which take college professors as patients and ask no questions. He hired a carriage and had himself driven to Sospel, which is at the foot of the mountains. He realised that he was running the change of encountering Brignolles. But, fortunately, nothing of the kind happened and the young man reached Mount Barbonnet and the sanatorium in safety. His mind was filled now with the thought that he was at least definitely to learn what had become of Robert Darzac! For at the moment that the sack had been found without the corpse— from the moment that the tracks of the little carriage descended toward Sospel or elsewhere and lost themselves; from the moment he had discovered that Larsan had not considered it prudent to relieve himself of Darzac by throwing him in the sack into one of the gulfs of Castillon, Rouletabille had believed that Larsan might have been found it to his interest to return the living Darzac to the madhouse at Sospel. And the reasoning powers of Rouletabille showed him that this might well be so. Darzac living might be more useful to Larsan than Darzac dead. What hostage would he have otherwise on the day when Mathilde should discover his imposture?

And Rouletabille had guessed right. At the very door of the asylum, he had encountered Brignolles. Immediately, without warning, he had seized him by the throat and threatened him with his revolver. Brignolles was a coward. He entreated Rouletabille to spare him, vowed that Darzac was living. A quarter of an hour later, Rouletabille knew the whole story. But the revolver had not sufficed, for Brignolles, who feared and hated the thought of death, loved life and everything which renders life desirable, particularly money. Rouletabille had not much trouble to convince him that he was lost if he did not betray Larsan and that he had much to gain if he helped the Darzac family to extricate itself from the present situation without scandal. At the close of the interview, both men entered the institution and were received by the director, who listened to what they had to say with an amazement which soon transformed into terror and later to the greatest affability which showed itself in immediate preparations for the release of Robert Darzac.

Darzac, by the miraculous chance which I have already explained, had sustained only a very slight injury from a wound which might easily have been mortal. Rouletabille, almost wild with joy, took him at once to Mentone. I will pass over the transports of both the rescuer and the rescued. They had disposed of Brignolles by agreeing to meet him in Paris for the settling of the accounts. On the journey, Rouletabille learned from the lips of Darzac that the Sorbonne Professor in his prison had a few days before happened to see the newspaper which spoke of the fact that M. and Mme. Darzac, whose wedding had just taken place in Paris, were guests at the Fort of Hercules. He had no further to look in order to comprehend why all his misfortunes had taken place and it was not difficult to guess who had had the fantastic audacity to take his place at the side of the unfortunate woman whose still wavering mind would have rendered so wild an enterprise not impossible. This discovery seemed to give him strength which he had not guessed that he possessed. After having stolen the overcoat of the director in order to conceal his asylum garb and having found a purse containing an hundred francs in the pocket, he had succeeded, at the risk of his life, in scaling a wall which under any other circumstances he would certainly have found insurmountable, and he had gone to Mentone. He had hastened to the Fort of Hercules. And he had seen Darzac with his own eyes! He had seen his very self. He spent a few hours in making himself so like his double in dress and appearance that the other Darzac himself might have been puzzled to find out which was which. His plan was simple. He would make his way into the Fort of Hercules in his own proper person—would enter the apartment of Mathilde and show himself to the other man in Mathilde's presence, confounding him with the truth. He had questioned the people of the coast and had learned that the Darzacs' suite was located at the back part of the Square Tower. "The Darzacs' suite"! All that he had suffered up to that time seemed like nothing in comparison with what he felt at those words. And this suffering had been without surcease until he had seen with his own eyes, at the time of the corporeal demonstration of the possibility of the "body too many," the Lady in Black. Then he had understood all. Never would she have dared to look at him like that, never would have so joyously flown to the refuge of his arms, if for a single instant, in body or in spirit, she had been the victim of the machinations of that other man and had belonged to him as his wife. Robert Darzac and Mathilde had been separated—but they had never lost each other!

Before putting his project into execution, Darzac had purchased a revolver at Mentone, had disembarrassed himself of his overcoat which he had managed to lose, believing that it would be a means of identification, had procured a suit of clothes which in colour and in cut was the counterpart of that worn by the other Darzac and had waited until five o'clock—the hour at which he had resolved to act. He had hidden himself behind the Villa Lucie, high up on the boulevard at Garavan, at the top of a little hillock from which he could see plainly all that was passing in the château. When he had passed by us and we had both seen him he had had a fierce desire to cry out and tell us who he was, but he had strength of mind enough to contain himself, desiring to be recognised first of all by the Lady in Black. This hope alone sustained his steps. This only was worth the trouble of living and an hour afterward, when he had had the life of Larsan at his disposal while the latter sat in the same room with his back turned to him, writing letters, he had not even been tempted by the idea of vengeance. After so many sorrows, there was no room in Robert Darzac's heart for hatred of Larsan; it was too full of love for the Lady in Black. Poor dear pitiful M. Darzac!

We know the rest of the adventure. That which I did not know was the way in which the true M. Darzac had penetrated a second time into the Fort of Hercules and had obtained entrance a second time into the recess hidden by the panel. And Rouletabille told me how on the same night that he had taken M. Darzac to Mentone, he had learned through the flight of Old Bob that there existed an entrance to the castle through the oubliette and so he had, by the help of a little boat, smuggled M. Darzac into the château by the way which Old Bob had taken in going out. Rouletabille wished to be master of the hour when he came to confound Larsan and strike him down. On that night it was too late to act, but he felt that he could count upon finishing up the affair on the night following. The only thing was how to hide M. Darzac on the peninsula. And with the aid of Bernier, he had found him a quiet, deserted little corner in the New Château.

At this point of the narrative, I could not hinder myself from interrupting Roultabille with a cry which had the effect of sending him into a burst of laughter.

"It was really he then!" I exclaimed.

"It really was!" answered my friend.

"That was how I was able to find the 'map of Australia'! It was the true Darzac with whom I stood face to face that night! And I who understood nothing that was going on! For it was not only the Australia—it was the beard as well. And it did not come off—it was natural! Oh, now, I understand everything!"

"You've taken time enough about it!" replied Rouletabille, tranquilly. "That night, old fellow, you caused us a lot of trouble. When you made your appearance in the Court of the Bold, M. Darzac had come to take me back to my underground passage. I had only time enough to close the wooden lid above my head, while M. Darzac rushed back to the New Castle. But when you had retired, after your experience with the beard, he came back to me and we were bothered enough, I assure you. If, by chance, you should speak of this adventure upon the morrow to the other M. Darzac, believing that he was the same man you had seen in the New Château, there would be a catastrophe. But I dared not yield to the pleadings of M. Darzac, who begged me to go to you and tell you the whole truth. I was afraid that, knowing how matters stood, you would be unable to hide your feelings during the following day. You have a rather impulsive nature, Sainclair, and the sight of a bad man usually arouses in you a praiseworthy irritation which at such a moment might have ruined us. And then, the other Darzac was so cunning and so clever! I resolved to bring about the climax without saying anything to you! I would return to the château the next morning. And from that time on it was necessary to manage things so that you should not speak to Darzac. That was why, as soon as it was daylight, I sent you word to go fishing for brook trout—"

"Oh, I understand!"

"You always finish by understanding, Sainclair! I hope that you have forgiven me for that fault which gave you such a charming hour with Mme. Edith!"

"Apropos of Mme. Edith, why did you take such a mischievous pleasure in putting me into such a fit of anger?" I demanded.

"In order to have the right to abuse you and to forbid you to speak henceforward, one word to me *or to M. Darzac*! I repeat to you that, after your adventure of the night before, it would not have done to let you talk to M. Darzac. Try to understand the position, Sainclair!"

"I'll try, my friend!"

"Much obliged!"

"And still there is one thing that I don't understand!" I exclaimed. "The death of Pere Bernier. Who killed Bernier?"

"It was the cane!" said Rouletabille, gloomily. "It was that damned cane!"

"I thought that it was 'the oldest dagger known to humanity.'"

"It was both of them; the cane and the flint. But it was the cane which decided his death; the stone was only his executioner." I stared at Rouletabille, asking myself whether, this time, I had not come to the end of his intelligence.

"You never understood, Sainclair—among other things—why upon the morrow of the day on which I had come to comprehend everything, I had let fall Arthur Rance's ivory-headed cane in front of M. and Mme. Darzac. It was because I hoped that M. Darzac would pick it up. You remember, Sainclair, the ivory headed cane which Larsan used to carry and the gestures he was in the habit of making with it while we were at the Glandier? He had a fashion of holding his cane which was all his own. I wanted to see whether Darzac would hold an ivory-headed cane as Larsan had used to do. And this fixed idea pursued me until the morrow, even after my visit to the insane asylum. Even after I had seen and felt the true Darzac, I longed to see the imposter make the gestures of Larsan. Ah, to see him suddenly brandish his cane like a bandit—forget the disguise of his figure for one single moment! Throw back his falsely stooped shoulders. 'Knock it, please! Knock at the shield of the Mortolas with heavy blows of the cane, dear, dear M. Darzac!' And he knocked it—and I saw his form—erect—undisguised and another man saw it and he is dead! It was poor Bernier, who was so horrified at the sight that he stumbled and fell so unfortunately on the 'oldest dagger' that the wound killed him. He is dead because he picked up the flint which, doubtless, had fallen out of Old Bob's overcoat and which Bernier had intended to take to the workshop of the Professor in the Round Tower! He is dead, because at the same moment that he picked up the flint he saw Larsan brandishing his cane—saw the scoundrel's figure and his gestures. All battles, Sainclair, have their innocent victims!"

We were both silent for a moment. And I could not keep myself from mentioning the bitterness which I felt at the knowledge that he had had so little confidence in me. I could not pardon him for having deceived me as he had done everyone else in regard to Old Bob.

He smiled.

"That was something that didn't bother me at all. I was certain enough that he was not in the sack! However on the night before he was fished out of the grotto after I had hidden the true Darzac, under the guidance of Bernier, in the New Château, and had left the gallery of the underground passage after having left there my boat in readiness for my projects of the morrow—my boat which had belonged to Paolo, a fisherman, and a friend of 'the Hangman of the Sea,' I regained the bank by my oars. I was undressed and carried my clothing in a package on my head. As I went on, I met Paolo who was amazed to see me taking a bath at such an hour and invited me to go fishing with him. I accepted. And then I learned that the bark which I had used belonged to Tullio. The 'Hangman of the Sea' had suddenly become rich and had announced to everyone that he was about to return to his native country. He said that he had sold some precious shells to the old professor for a very great deal of money and, in fact, for many days past, he had been seen a great deal in the old professor's company. Paolo knew that before going to Venice, Tullio intended to stop at San Remo. When I heard all this, I had a clear insight into Old Bob's behaviour and disappearance. He had needed a boat in quitting the château and this boat was that of the 'Hangman of the Sea.' I asked him for the address of Tullio in San Remo and sent it to Arthur Rance in an anonymous letter. Rance started for San Remo, believing that Tullio could inform him as to the fate of Old Bob. And, in fact, Old Bob had paid Tullio to take him to the grotto and then to disappear. It was out of pity for the old savant that I had decided to warn Arthur Rance; for I feared that some accident might have befallen his relative. As for myself, all that I could ask was that the old dandy would not put in an appearance before I had finished with Larsan, for I wanted the false Darzac to believe that Old Bob was occupying my mind to the exclusion of everything else. And when I learned that he really had returned, I was, at first, only half pleased, but I confess that the news of the wound in his breast (because of the wound in the breast of the man in the sack) did not cause me any pain at all. Thanks to that injury, I might hope to continue my game a few hours longer."

"And why should you not have abandoned it immediately."

"Don't you understand that it would have been impossible for me to have gotten rid of the body of Larsan in the daylight? A whole day was necessary to prepare for the disappearance by night. But what a day we had with the death of Bernier! The arrival of the gendarmes only served to simplify the affair. I waited until I knew that they were gone. The first rifle shot that you heard when we were in the Square Tower was to inform me that the last gendarme had quitted the tavern at Albo, at the Point of Garibaldi: the second told me that the customs officers had gone into their cabins and were at supper and that the *sea was free*!"

"Tell me, Rouletabille," I said, looking into his clear eyes. "When you left Tullio's boat at the end of the gallery of the passageway, for the carrying out of your plans, did you know already *what that boat would carry away on the morrow?*"

Rouletabille bowed his head.

"No," he answered, sadly and slowly. "No—do not think that, Sainclair! I did not expect that it would carry away a corpse. After all—he was my father! *I believed that the boat would carry the 'body too many' to the madhouse*! You understand, Sainclair? I would only have condemned him to prison—forever. But he killed himself. It is God who did it. May God forgive him!"

We never spoke again of that night.

At Laroche I was anxious for a hot supper, but Rouletabille refused to join me. He bought all the Paris papers and buried himself in the events of the day. The journals were filled with news from Russia. A great conspiracy against the Czar had been discovered at St. Petersburg. The facts related were so wonderful that they were almost incredible.

I unfolded the Epoch and I read in great black letters on the first column of the first page:

"DEPARTURE OF JOSEPH ROULETABILLE FOR RUSSIA."

And underneath:

"THE CZAR IMPLORES HIS AID."

I passed the paper to Rouletabille, who shrugged his shoulders and said: "'That's a nice thing! Without even asking my opinion!

What does that fool of an editor think that I am going to do out there? I'm not interested in the Czar. Let him and his Nihilists settle their squabbles for themselves! It is their affair, not mine! To Russia? I shall apply for a vacation—that's what I'll do! I need rest. I'll tell you, Sainclair, you and I will go somewhere together. We'll take a nice, quiet rest—"

"Not if I know it!" I cried hastily. "Thanks very much but I have had enough of your kind of 'nice, quiet rest!' I have a wild desire to work!"

"Just as you like. I won't insist."

As we drew nearer Paris, he bathed his hands and face, combed his hair and turned out his pockets. And in one of them he was surprised to find a red envelope which had come there without anyone knowing how.

"What nonsense is this?" he remarked carelessly, tearing it open.

Then he burst into a peal of laughter. I had found my gay Rouletabille again and I was anxious to know the reason for this hilarity.

"Why, I'm going, old man!" he exclaimed. "I'm going to start immediately! When things begin to come like this, it's a little different. I shall take the train tonight."

"Where to?"

"To St. Petersburg."

He handed me the letter and I read:

"We know, monsieur, that your paper has decided to send you to Russia, on account of the incidents which are at this time disturbing the court of Turkoie-Selo. *We are obliged to warn you that you will not reach St. Petersburg alive?*

(Signed)

THE CENTRAL REVOLUTIONARY COMMITTEE

I looked at Rouletabille, whose eyes were shining with delight. "Prince Galitch was at the station," I remarked. He understood me and shrugging his shoulders indifferently, he repeated:

"Ah, now, old fellow, this begins to be amusing!"

And this was all that I could get out of him, in spite of my protestations. And that night when, at the Northern station, I put my arms around him and begged him not to go, the tears in my eyes as I spoke—he laughed again and repeated:

"This is just beginning to be amusing!"

And that was his farewell.

The following day I took up the work which was waiting for me at the Palace. The first of my colleagues whom I saw were M.M. Henri Robert and Andre Hesse.

"Did you have a pleasant holiday?" they asked me.

"Delightful!" I responded.

But I made such a grimace as I spoke that they both dragged me off to take a drink with them.

THE END

# A NOTE ABOUT THE AUTHOR

Gaston Leroux (1868-1927) was a French journalist and writer of detective fiction. Born in Paris, Leroux attended school in Normandy before returning to his home city to complete a degree in law. After squandering his inheritance, he began working as a court reporter and theatre critic to avoid bankruptcy. As a journalist, Leroux earned a reputation as a leading international correspondent, particularly for his reporting on the 1905 Russian Revolution. In 1907, Leroux switched careers in order to become a professional fiction writer, focusing predominately on novels that could be turned into film scripts. With such novels as *The Mystery of the Yellow Room* (1908), Leroux established himself as a leading figure in detective fiction, eventually earning himself the title of Chevalier in the Legion of Honour, France's highest award for merit. *The Phantom of the Opera* (1910), his most famous work, has been adapted countless times for theatre, television, and film, most notably by Andrew Lloyd Webber in his 1986 musical of the same name.